**Outstanding Praise for Lisa Black and her
Gardiner and Renner Thrillers**

"She is, quite simply, one of the best
storytellers around."
—**Tess Gerritsen**

"Lisa Black writes with immediacy and
unmatched authenticity."
—**Jeff Lindsay**

PERISH
"A solid position in suspense, a solid backbone
of detection."
—*Kirkus Reviews*

"As always with Black, this psychological suspense
is incredible. And her way of describing the financial
world makes you want to run out, take any money
you have invested, cash it in and place it under
your pillow instead."
—*Suspense Magazine*

UNPUNISHED
"Breaking news: this is a terrific mystery. Timely,
tense, and thought provoking, this fast-paced
insider's view of the dangerous intersection
between journalism and murder will keep you
guessing at every turn—and turning pages as
fast as you can."
—**Hank Phillippi Ryan**, Anthony, Agatha and
Mary Higgins Clark award-winning author of
Say No More

"Intriguing forensic details help drive the plot to its satisfying conclusion."
—*Publishers Weekly*

"Black is one of the best writers of the world of forensics, and her latest introduces Maggie Gardiner, who works for the Cleveland Police Department. Her relentless pursuit of answers in a dark world of violence is both inspiring and riveting. Readers who enjoy insight into a world from an expert in the field should look no further than Black. Although Cornwell is better known, Black deserves more attention for her skillful writing – and hopefully this will be her breakout book."
—*RT Book Reviews*, **4 Stars**

"The surprising ending is sure to keep readers coming back for more."
—*Booklist*

"Black, a former forensics investigator, skillfully portrays the stark realities of homicide cases in her latest thriller. In this series launch, she pairs Maggie with Jack Renner, a determined detective with secrets of his own who has no intention of allowing murderers to evade their punishment. A great choice for readers of psychological suspense, forensic investigations, and mystery."
—*Library Journal*

"A crime thriller with a sharp psychological edge running through it. . . .*That Darkness* left me thinking for days about the intricacies of the plot, the beauty of

Lisa Black's writing, and the profound relationship between law and justice. Lisa Black, through her incredible characters and narration, shows the delicate balance between the two and how hard it is to know which side is the right one. With *That Darkness*, Lisa Black has written a book that everyone should read. But if you are a lover of mystery and suspense, this is an absolute must read."
—*Suspense Magazine*

Perish

Also by Lisa Black

Perish

LISA BLACK

KENSINGTON BOOKS
http://www.kensingtonbooks.com

KENSINGTON BOOKS are published by

Kensington Publishing Corp.
119 West 40th Street
New York, NY 10018

All Kensington titles, imprints, and distributed lines are available at special quantity discounts for bulk purchases for sales promotion, premiums, fund-raising, educational, or institutional use. Special book excerpts or customized printings can also be created to fit specific needs. For details, write or phone the office of the Kensington Special Sales Manager: Attn. Special Sales Department. Kensington Publishing Corp., 119 West 40th Street, New York, NY 10018. Phone: 1-800-221-2647.

Kensington and the K logo Reg. U.S. Pat. & TM Off.

ISBN-13: 978-1-4967-1355-1
ISBN-10: 1-4967-1355-9
First Kensington Hardcover Edition: February 2018
First Kensington Mass Market Edition: August 2018

eISBN-13: 978-1-4967-1356-8
eISBN-10: 1-4967-1356-7
First Kensington Electronic Edition: February 2018

10 9 8 7 6 5 4 3 2 1

Printed in the United States of America

To my family:
Every day I realize more how remarkable you are.

May your money perish with you. . . .
—Acts 8:20

Chapter 1

The murder had taken place in the living room, which Maggie found odd. Bedrooms, kitchens, entryways, even garages tended to backlight the scenes of high emotion, not the always slightly generic area where the hottest debates tended to be about the location of the remote. Especially *this* living room, with its original artwork, crystal vases, marble tiles, and leather furniture. The two walls covered in windows let in enough light to blind her, especially when the occasional sunbeam bounced off the lake's waves to reach in and reflect off the white walls. Maggie would bet the sofa alone equaled three months of her paycheck, or at least it had until the owner's blood had left a series of ugly red splotches across its smooth surface.

"Wow," she said.

"Twenty-two rooms," the cop at her side agreed. She recognized his face but not his name—including her, over sixteen hundred people worked at the Cleveland police department. "Five bedrooms, seven baths—five up and two down. Nice to have for parties, I guess.

In my house I've got one . . . and I have three kids. This girl had seven, all for her."

"She lived here alone?"

"Just her. So little activity that the cleaning lady only had to come in twice a week. Unfortunately, for said cleaning lady, this was the day."

Maggie gave the opulence around her one last survey. Summer raged outside but air-conditioning kept the inside temperature right on the edge of chilly. "What was she, some sort of heiress? Genius software designer? Stockbroker?"

The cop shrugged. "All I know is she wasn't a cop. Or she'd have one bathroom and no cleaning lady."

Maggie transferred her attention to the victim, her condition even more attention grabbing than her house—but in a very bad way.

Not exactly a girl, twenty-eight-year-old Joanna Moorehouse had silky chestnut hair and long legs. She appeared trim, though the damage to her torso made it difficult to tell. Sightless eyes stared at the high ceiling as her body cooled against the marble tiles. The blood pool expanded to reach a nearby Persian rug and had dried to near black. It came from the wounds on her neck and upper arms, from a few gaping slashes in her thighs, one puncture just below her eye, and mostly from the opened chest cavity. Crisscrossed slices had peeled back the flesh to reveal the inner organs, letting some of the small intestines slide out to rest beside her, still tethered by various sinew and fibroids.

The Persian rug next to the body had a sofa on one border and a matching love seat on the other, with the remaining two edges open to the edge of the dais and the rest of the house.

Maggie raised her camera, snapped a few pictures, then adjusted the flash to compensate for all the white in the room.

The victim had been wearing a blue T-shirt and a pair of gray dress slacks. From the thighs up the clothes had been cut to literal ribbons by the attack to her torso and flopped at her sides, stiff with dried fluid, along with filmy red panties and a matching bra. Only the lower right leg escaped, while the left pant leg had been sliced open to the ankle, even though there were no injuries below the knee. Whether this had happened before, as a result of, or after her evisceration might be impossible to tell and might be a combination of all three. Joanna Moorehouse had been completely exposed for the world to see, but the grotesque near-disembowelment had robbed the firm and naked body of any salacious quality. Her feet were bare, the nails manicured and shining with clear polish, as were the fingernails.

"Wow," Maggie said again, softly.

"You oughta see the rest of the place," Detective Riley said as he walked into the room, followed by his partner, Jack Renner.

"I meant her," Maggie told him.

The cops stopped inside the interior French doors. Most of the living room, for no apparent reason other than style, existed on a dais, two steps up from the rest of the first floor. It defined her scene nicely and they saw no need to enter it and possibly step on or kick something useful. Even the cop who had accompanied her remained on the lower level.

"Yeah, that's pretty impressive too," Thomas Riley agreed, rubbing his eyes with one meaty hand. Greetings weren't necessary when the city had enough murders to keep the homicide detectives and the forensic technicians perpetually running into each other. Maggie looked at his partner, Jack, and he returned a barely perceptible nod. She could look at him without flinching now, tamping the bad memories down and convincing herself that all would again be well in her world, in her mind, in her self-esteem. They had settled into an uneasy truce, imperfect people in an imperfect world working together for the greater good.

Though in his case the greater good would be if he just stopped killing people, no matter how much they deserved it. She wished he would gather his belongings and move on, as he had promised, even if it was only to become someone else's worry. More than one of the six months they'd agreed upon had elapsed. Maybe then she could finally believe that everything had been a momentary aberration, one bad moment in an otherwise blameless life, one trigger pull that altered her reality. Maybe then she could stop smelling the burnt nitrites. And the blood.

Maggie turned back to the dead Joanna Moorehouse, carefully planting her booty-clad feet to avoid the viscera. She told herself to focus. She had a job to do right here and right now. *Focus*.

Aside from the grievous maceration of the torso, the woman had two small cuts to her right index finger and a deep slash in the fleshy area under the thumb. Blood coated the skin of her left hand but there didn't seem to be any wounds, and both arms were equally covered in the red substance. She had probably been right handed, put up her hand to block the weapon coming at her, failed to stop it, and then clasped the other hand to the resulting wound. Maggie commented as much to the hovering detectives. She doubted it would help their investigation, but one never knew, and it all went toward justifying her take-home pay.

Stud earrings with diamonds the size of healthy peas still twinkled in Joanna Moorehouse's earlobes, making robbery an unlikely motive. She also wore rings with equally impressive stones and an elegant gold watch. If she had been wearing a necklace, it had come off in the attack.

Maggie peeked under the shoulders, tilting her head toward the blood-covered floor.

"Mind your hair," Jack said.

She grabbed a swath to keep it out of the dried stains. She didn't move Joanna's body or even touch it—the Medical Examiner's office would have some choice words for her if she did. The crime scene and everything in it belonged to the cops, but the body itself came under the ME's jurisdiction. Photographing was fine, but no moving, searching, or otherwise molesting until the ME investigator arrived.

"What?" Jack asked.

"I don't see a lot of blood underneath her, and she's only got a few defensive wounds. I'm guessing she went down and stayed down."

"Giving him room to carve her up," Riley said. "Without a drawn-out battle. None of the furniture is even out of place. Course in a room this huge he had plenty of space to work in."

Maggie added, "And carve he did. He had a pretty good time playing in the guts."

Jack asked what that meant.

"When you cut open a body, the contents don't burst out like a spring snake in a can. She's lying on her back and if I'm right about her not moving around after the worst cuts, there's no real reason for the internal organs to be protruding like this."

"So he tried to remove them?"

"Or he was looking for something?" Riley asked.

"No idea. We'll see what the ME thinks." Without getting up she looked around, noting the gleaming marble tile spinning off in every direction. "Have you found any blood anywhere else?"

Jack said, "No, but we haven't done a thorough search yet."

"Hmm."

"What's 'hmm'?" Riley groused. "I hate it when you do that."

"Where did he go?" She looked down at the body, then back at them. "All this blood, all this up close and personal . . . he had to be covered in gore. So how does he tiptoe away without leaving at least a smudge or two of bloody footprint? He should have left tracks all the way out to the driveway."

Both detectives and the patrol officer looked around themselves as if they might have missed a pattern of red outlines leading from the room. They hadn't.

Maggie took another look at the dark patterns surrounding the body. Plenty of swirls and streaks had moved through the liquid before it dried, turning the floor into a large, bizarre finger painting. Fabric imprints told the story of an attacker sitting on the victim's hips as he plunged the knife into her chest again and again, then perhaps moving down to work on the abdomen, only to add a few closing slashes to her thighs before this outpouring of passion and hatred sated him. Maggie looked closely but didn't see any suggestion of a shoeprint in the dried blood patterns. Where and how had he straightened up and moved away?

She could have it reversed, of course. He could have started on the thighs and worked upward, but then Joanna Moorehouse probably would have sat up to fight him, resulting in more defensive wounds and more flopping around. Instead the pool spreading from her shoulders had not been disturbed but allowed to dry to a smooth, even finish. A triangular pattern shadowed each elbow like a pair of still-folded angel wings, as if Joanna had tried to push off her killer, but had not held out long before her arms flopped open, useless. After that, Maggie guessed, Joanna Moorehouse never moved again.

Then there was that singular blow to the face, that odd little coup de grâce marring an otherwise flawless complexion. A straight slit that formed an underline to her right eye, it had probably been made with the same knife that did the rest of the damage but hadn't gone as deep, stopped by the cheekbone. The edges of the wound were already drying to a leathery crust but aside from some traces on those edges, no blood had flowed outward. Joanna Moorehouse had already been dead when her killer stabbed her in the face.

Wow, indeed.

It wasn't that Maggie had never seen such a ferocious attack—in her nearly ten years in crime scene work she had seen plenty—but never in such gorgeous and otherwise undisturbed surroundings. This room should be filled with Ravel playing softly from a home theater system while elegant guests circulated with glasses of champagne, not the tinny smell of dried body fluids and the desultory small talk of officers who had no idea where to start in finding out how that blood had come to flow over the finely marbled tile.

"And she lived here alone?" Maggie asked.

Jack's low voice rumbled out the vitals. "No signs of anyone else. No clothes in the other bedrooms, no male accoutrements in the bathroom—"

"He means razors, shaving cream," Riley translated for the uniformed officer, who said he had figured that out.

"Drawers, closet, jewelry in perfect order, purse on the kitchen counter, cell phone on its charging station, and the laptop closed. All doors locked except the one leading from the garage to the inside, home alarm not set."

So no interest in robbery, and either Joanna Moorehouse had let her killer in or hadn't locked her door behind her when she'd come home. Shoes and socks had been shed, so she hadn't *just* walked in the door from work. "Last seen?"

"Don't know yet. We haven't called the number on her business cards, and the phone and the laptop both have passcodes."

She gave the detectives a look, wishing it to be as steely as it felt. "You tried them?"

"Only the home button," Riley said.

Personal electronics came with so many protections now that putting in the wrong code might cause it to lock up and wipe all of its own data. Gone were the days when detectives would try the victim's birth date and open all their photos and texts there at the scene. The forensic IT people, a group who did not include Maggie, schooled the cops over and over to keep their curious fingers to themselves.

Though if it contained anything to implicate the killer, why would he have left it behind? One who could commit such carnage and yet stay cool enough to enter and then exit the scene without a physical trail would have thought of the phone.

"They both have fingerprint locks," Riley went on. "After the ME moves the body we can open them with her cold, dead finger. Sure was easier when people kept written address books. . . . Now without the electronics we have no way to find next of kin."

"Prior contacts?" Had the police department ever encountered Joanna Moorehouse before—a traffic ticket, a noise complaint, a drunk and disorderly?

"None."

Talk about starting from scratch. She again surveyed the room, her thighs beginning to protest from the prolonged squat. The pools emanating from the lower half of the body were still tacky in the deeper spots, the blood not completely dried, with a series of smears, splotches, and swipes where Joanna's feet had kicked and the killer had shifted his position as he'd straddled her. The edges of this amorphous area were not as smooth as around the upper half of the body, but blotted and feathered as if by footsteps.

"Anybody step in this?" she asked the cops.

They all promised her they hadn't but couldn't make any promises about the EMT staff. They had entered to pronounce the desecrated corpse officially dead.

She eyed their six booty-clad feet. Without being asked each man inspected the bottoms. Riley hesitated, swaying awkwardly on one leg while trying to view the bottom of the other. Finally, he gave up and straightened.

"Anything?" Maggie asked.

"Nope."

His face flushing from either exertion or embarrassment, she didn't quite believe him. It was too easy to take an inadvertent step at a crime scene and go home wearing someone else's blood. She had done it far too often herself.

"How'd your testimony go yesterday?" Riley asked her, possibly as a distraction. They had all been witnesses for the prosecution in the trial of a gang gunman accused of several drive-by shootings, some for the gang's business and some for his own personal reasons. His name was Gerry Graham and his victims had included a grandmother napping inside the house and a four-year-old playing outside on her sidewalk.

"Fine. Defense tried to pick apart the print identification, but he didn't really know what he was talking about. He'd downloaded a few phrases off the Internet. No big deal."

Riley said, "Yeah, me too. He tried to say I planted the gun and bribed the witness with a plea deal. I bit his head off."

Jack said nothing, though he had worked the case with Riley and must have testified as well.

Without moving her feet Maggie photographed the floor in all directions from the body. Sometimes the camera could pick up something the human eye missed.

Another uniformed officer appeared in the French doors, startling them all. "There's a guy at the front door."

"Don't let him in," Jack said.

"Who is it?" Riley asked.

The officer nodded toward Maggie and the corpse. "Says he's her boyfriend."

Riley grinned. "Enter suspect number one." The two detectives left without another word. The first uniformed cop developed a pained look, belying a preference to be where the action was instead of babysitting a quiet, still body.

Maggie had no desire to move, despite her tiring thighs. She sumo-walked along the inner edge of the dais without crossing the area next to the lower half of the body. She inspected each piece of white stone, marbled through with various mineral colors. The sun appeared somewhere outside, turning the windows aglow, and she used the too bright light to her advantage, tilting her head to see any variation in the tile's surface. Aside from one tiny smear about twenty inches from the body she could not see the slightest trace of blood.

So the killer had either murdered Joanna Moorehouse while tilting his feet in the air and then somehow stood up without putting his toes in the muck, or he had—what? Flown? Dangled from the ceiling? Not possible. Balanced on one foot while he removed his shoes, then carefully set down stockinged feet outside the stained perimeter in order to tiptoe off in his socks? Possible.

That eliminated Riley, at least. He'd never have the balance to pull that off.

Nor could she picture Jack having that kind of flexibility. She realized that with a sense of relief that surprised her. She'd only been joking to herself about

Riley, but now saw that suspecting Jack of every murder that took place in Cleveland city limits might be a default position for her.

Focus.

She used her fingerprint kit to brush black powder on the tile floor between the body and bottom of the dais, including the steps. Bits and pieces of smears, but nothing that even suggested a shoe, much less a size or type. All it did was dirty the perfect marble.

This had been a bloodbath. The killer had been up close and personal and had to have gotten a great deal of the red liquid on himself. If he had worn something absorbent he might not have dripped, but anyone who had ever had so much as a minor kitchen accident knows that blood tends to fly into unexpected areas, and wiping with pants or shirt could not get every trace. He'd have to leave a smear on a doorknob or a jamb or a windowsill. Or a floor tile.

So where did he go?

She stepped off the dais and went to find out.

Chapter 2

The uniformed cop remained with the body and Maggie avoided the faint voices she heard from the front of the house. Dealing with grieving and/or suspicious loved ones was *so* not her job, and she might break up a flow or a campaign of pressure if she popped into view and interrupted them. If the guy broke down and confessed, she'd hear about it soon enough.

Instead she passed through each room, subjecting each door and window to a methodical examination for smears of dried red color. But the pewter-colored window latches and the doorknobs that gleamed as if they were real gold (and they might be, Maggie thought) and the chrome faucets and raised porcelain bowls of those two ground-floor bathrooms the patrol officer envied so much did not show the slightest hint of having come into contact with those bloodied fingers.

She photographed each one of these surfaces, because surely a defense attorney would someday ask her if she had really looked at them all.

She used black powder to process every doorknob

and light switch for latent prints left in the usual body oils and sweat, without finding a single useable one. This didn't surprise her—those areas should be obvious places for an intruder to touch, but always proved stubbornly resistant to retaining decent prints. Even those flat, wide types of light switches almost always gave her nothing.

Maggie had moved through all the rooms in the rear half of the house, though she couldn't have given any of them a name—parlor, conservatory, sunroom, library? They lacked furniture or much décor to speak of, remaining generic. A large area connected to the kitchen via a door was probably a dining room, but without a table and chairs, Maggie couldn't tell. Perhaps Joanna Moorehouse had been in the process of moving in. Or moving out. It certainly made the rooms easier to photograph. Maggie went into people's homes nearly every day and had seen the gamut. Homes that were clean but cluttered, ones that were strictly tidy but layered in grime. The most obsessively clean had belonged to illegal immigrants involved in stolen credit card trafficking and one of the filthiest to a sweet little family of four. And overall, when it came to décor there was definitely no accounting for taste.

Perhaps Joanna Moorehouse simply didn't care to entertain and had no interest in furnishing rooms she wouldn't use, because the home office . . . that room she very definitely furnished. Maggie had only seen a quarter of the living space so far but would have bet that this is where the victim spent all her time.

Two walls were built-in floor-to-ceiling bookcases, filled as high as Joanna Moorehouse could have reached with file folders, business textbooks, and heavy refer-

ence tomes on real estate law, mortgage financing regulations, and corporate accounting. One wall had the
gorgeous high windows in keeping with the rest of the
architecture, and next to the door on the fourth wall ran
a wide credenza with cardboard file boxes obscuring
its mahogany finish. In the center sat a massive desk of
glossy dark wood, the surface scattered with legal
pads, pen cups, and a mug of coffee, its milk curdled.
Another laptop sat closed.

The tidiness found in the rest of the house did not
apply here. Papers overlapped each other from haphaz-
ard piles. There were no framed photos, but there was
an empty phone-charging station and a stress relief
squeezie shaped like a house with a logo for Sterling
Financial. The desk blotter showed a calendar, which
Joanna hadn't used for this pedestrian purpose but as a
doodle pad with stars, loops, and stick figures of horses
in black ink. Maggie looked but didn't touch. If this had
been an apparent suicide or a probable heart attack, she
would have opened drawers and closets to look for relevant medications or recent notes and journals. But in
a brutal homicide like this, searching was the detectives' job.

Still, she thought, no truly personal items. No snap-
shots with friends or family. No greeting cards or knickknacks, a souvenir from Aruba, or a plastic tchotchke
from an office party. No book of matches from a local
bar. Again, it appeared that Joanna had been moving in
or moving out. Or she *really* had no social life.

From the papers scattered on the desk it became clear
that Joanna Moorehouse worked at a company called
Sterling Financial, which had something to do with mortgage loans. Copies of online articles referred to the cur-

rent rates of mortgage-backed securities. Stock reports showed the value of Sterling shares. A statement from the Banco Nacional de Panama showed an account in the name of Joanna Moorehouse, her address a PO box in Cleveland, numbers, interest rate, deposits, balance—.

Maggie blinked.

Her brain wasn't accustomed to seeing that many zeros. She mentally added commas where they needed to be and determined that Joanna's personal account held $686,472,791. And 48 cents.

Not pesos. *Dollars*.

That explained the house.

Or rather, it *had* held over $600,000,000. An entry farther down the statement casually noted a disbursement of $350,000,000 and some odd change to Ergo Insurance.

Okay, well, Maggie told herself, surely this was the corporate's account. A large financial firm might easily have that value. Wall Street dealt in billions every day. Just because Joanna worked there didn't mean it had anything to do with her murder. Robbers and corporate raiders didn't usually eviscerate their targets, not when a decent .38 could do the job much more quickly without the need for calisthenics to avoid leaving a blood trail to the front door.

Still, as a motive it ranked third after love and anger. Over half a billion dollars . . .

Maggie snapped a picture of the statement. Maybe nothing. Maybe everything.

* * *

Jack followed Riley and the uniformed officer to the front porch—though *porch* seemed much too plebian a word to describe the sweeping teak decking and tall pillars of the front of Joanna Moorehouse's mansion, with delicate ironwork seating and trellised plant life with blooms drooping in the heat. Veranda, perhaps, or a gallery.

Except that this was Cleveland, and people here didn't have verandas. They had porches. Even in multi-million-dollar estates on the shores of a Great Lake. Porches.

A young man stood on the structure. He seemed completely at home in this setting in a tailored gray suit of material that even at ten feet seemed both soft and rich, a snow white dress shirt with no tie and un-scuffed shoes. Silky black locks had the exact *GQ* tussle and his face had been trimmed to give him a ghost of a five o'clock shadow, just enough to keep him from prettiness. The expression on his face combined equal parts rattled, worried, and impatient.

"What's going on?" he said immediately. "Where the hell is Joanna?"

"Who're you?" Riley asked.

The uniformed officer had filled them in with the basics—Jeremy Mearan, worked with Joanna at Sterling Financial; they would date ("sounds more like friends with benefits," the cop had confided); Joanna hadn't shown up for work this morning and wasn't answering her phone so he had driven from their office downtown to see why not.

But Riley had him go through it again. Nothing changed, and Mearan only grew more anxious to find out what a bunch of cops were doing at his girlfriend's house.

Riley didn't enlighten him yet. "When did you last speak to her?"

The guy thought for a brief moment. "At the office last night. We were working with the regulator. . . . She left about nine-thirty, I think."

"Left the office? You didn't have a date, see her later?"

"No. Why don't you ask her?"

Riley glanced at the complicated furniture. "Let's sit."

Mearan glanced at the filigreed iron seat, exposed to the elements, and doubtless thought of his expensive suit pants. "I'd rather not. Can't we go inside?"

"No." At this point this young man remained the only suspect to appear in the drama thus far, and police everywhere had learned a few things from the Jon-Benét Ramsey case. No one would be entering the crime scene, aka house.

"Then I'd rather stand. What are you *doing* here? Where is Joanna?"

"Nine-thirty—is that normal hours for you both to be working, or was something going on?"

He snorted. "Nothing is normal in this line of work. But yeah, we're working on a merger, and . . . other things. Where—"

"How long have you been dating?"

More cautiously: "Coupla months."

"How long have you known her? Does she have family in the area?"

A year, and no. She never mentioned family. She

had bought this house six months ago. She'd been with Sterling Financial since its inception, five years prior.

"And she isn't 'with' it," Mearan clarified. "She owns it. She founded it. She *is* Sterling Financial."

Jack digested this.

"So you were dating the boss," Riley said.

"Yeah. So? What is going on? Is she even here? Who called you guys?"

Riley said, "I'm sorry to have to tell you this, but Joanna Moorehouse is dead."

Silence. Jeremy Mearan heard this, absorbed it, mulled it over. Then he said, "Well, *that* seems a bit extreme."

As shocked reactions to news of death went, this was a new one for Jack. "Beg pardon?"

Mearan said, as if speaking to himself, "I wouldn't have figured her for the type. To give up so easily. She never gave up *anything* easily. Not in the gym, not in bed, certainly not in the market."

Jack and Riley exchanged a look. Riley said, "Can you tell us what had been going on in her life?"

"I mean, she probably wouldn't have gone to *jail*."

Riley could be the soul of patience when he wanted to, and relaxed his voice into soothing, paternal confessor mode. "Can you tell us about it?"

"We're working on a merger with DJ Bryan, but the regulators are making a fuss and now Bryan might back out and their quant is such a tool. It's"—he shook his head—"it's complicated."

"Try," Riley encouraged.

Jack, meanwhile, observed the guy. He seemed genuinely discombobulated, unless he had missed his calling and should have been picking up Oscars along the red carpet. He also seemed to have a lot to tell them and couldn't figure out where to begin. Or didn't want to.

"Well . . . what do you know about mortgage-backed securities?"

"Squat," Jack said.

Riley would never admit to ignorance. "Give us the short version."

"Okay. Sterling is a mortgage originator. We take those loans that we've made and securitize them into CDOs—collateralized debt obligations—which are sold to investors. That's standard. But everyone is still freaky about the subprime market so the Fed chick is picky about the capital requirements and the Bryan guy is using her to choke a better price out of us—"

Riley interrupted. "I said the short version."

Mearan raised one eyebrow. "That *is* the short version. To get the long version we'd have to go back to SIVs, Glass-Steagall, and the change in securitization."

Riley lost the paternal voice. "Where does jail come in?"

"It doesn't. I mean, it won't. The regulator is rattling our cage to justify her GS-12 salary and the merger will go through. It's all posturing, at this point. That's all it ever is."

"Why would Joanna Moorehouse be concerned about going to jail? What for?"

Mearan was almost visibly squirming now. "Um . . . she wouldn't. Really. At worst we'd get a fine. That's what always happens. I mean even if—she wouldn't. That's why I can't believe . . . she didn't even seem worried about it. But then Joanna never worries. . . ."

His voice trailed off, and Jack and Riley exchanged another glance. Then Riley spoke.

"You seem to think Joanna might have committed suicide."

A pause. "She didn't? Then—but she's dead? What happened? An accident?"

"No. Ms. Moorehouse's death is clearly a homicide."

This flat-out stunned Mearan. So much so that he staggered over and dropped onto the wrought iron chair, expensive pants be damned. And Jack mentally scratched him off the suspect list. Even A-listers couldn't pull this scene off.

Riley slid over a companionable chair, apparently relieved to take a load off without giving a damn about his pants. "You're going to need to tell us everything you possibly can about Ms. Moorehouse. Take your time and think it through."

The man sucked in a deep breath, then coughed on either emotion or spring pollen. "No matter what anyone says," he began, haltingly, "she wasn't a terrible person."

Chapter 3

Maggie had photographed everything she could in the office and gotten tired of waiting for the cops to catch up with her. She moved upstairs and repeated her process, taking overall photos of the mostly empty rooms and examining every window latch and balcony door and bathroom fixture for a telltale smear of red. She didn't find one. Their killer wasn't a second-story man, though the second story wouldn't require an aerialist to reach in some spots with decorative overhangs, balconies, and porticos. The master bedroom had a terrace of sorts, wide enough to hold a breakfast set and a pot with a dead azalea. From that and the stiffness of the door lock, Maggie didn't think the victim had stepped out there for quite some time. The rear of the house looked out on Lake Erie, of course, but from a corner window she could see the distant edge of the lawn of the next mansion, its drapes drawn in each oversized window. Joanna Moorehouse had lived in isolation, hermetically sealed into her own little dollhouse. Had that been by design or accident?

The victim's bedroom didn't appear to hold any more secrets than the first floor had. Plenty of gorgeous clothes, a few diamond rings tossed casually into the jewelry box, but still no personal photos, letters, or knickknacks save for a blue porcelain bunny about six inches high. It sat on a shelf, alone, perfectly centered, between a basket of lip colors and another of nail polish. Finally, Maggie thought, something sentimental. It had a number of chips and one ear had been repaired with glue more than once and a childish hand had rubbed nearly all the pink paint off its little triangle nose—definitely not some historic artwork bought as an investment. Maggie felt almost absurdly pleased at this show of humanity and snapped a picture of it, which would no doubt mystify attorneys at some future date. "Why did you take this photo of the victim's knickknack, Specialist Gardiner?" "Because it serves as a link to Joanna Moorehouse's past, her childhood dreams and goals, and might give us direction as to how those dreams translated into the life that ended in murder. Besides, it was cute."

The bathroom held enough cosmetics to stock a Sephora and little else. No drugs, legal or otherwise, beyond the standard analgesics; feminine necessities; and a box of condoms—plain ones that would get the job done with a minimum of fuss. Maggie began to suspect that Joanna Moorehouse appreciated efficiency.

Maggie returned downstairs, photographed the remaining rooms there, checked on the body and its guard to see if the Medical Examiner's office staff had arrived (they hadn't), and finished in the kitchen, where she found an unexpected occupant.

A middle-aged woman with dark brown skin and a polyester smock decorated with kittens sat at the table, knocking back a slug of what smelled like Jack Daniel's.

"Hello," Maggie said.

The woman didn't look surprised to see Maggie. She had obviously stopped being surprised by anything else that could happen that day. "Pretty perfect."

"I—beg your pardon?"

"Pretty Perfect Cleaning Services. We don't leave until it's perfect. Or in this case until Mr. Po-Po says I can."

Ah. The cleaning lady who had found the body . . . and then apparently helped herself to Ms. Moorehouse's liquor cabinet. Maggie couldn't blame her. Anyone would need a stiff one after that sight. Joanna wouldn't miss it anyway.

Now the woman hefted the glass. "Be a dear and top me off, would you?"

Maggie pulled out a chair at the heavy oak table with her foot, and set her fingerprint kit on the seat. "Sorry. We're not supposed to touch anything—"

"Too late."

"—until we finish processing the scene." Maggie explained herself and her job. Talking to witnesses was not part of her duties and she avoided it, but, on the other hand, perhaps giving the woman an outlet would keep her from drinking herself silly before the detectives had a chance to get her story down.

"Grace," the woman said. "Pleased ta meetcha."

A patrol officer Maggie didn't know appeared in the doorway, saw Maggie, gave the woman's glass a sharp look, and retreated, hovering between the kitchen and the front door. Maggie tried to frown at him. He had a witness sitting in the middle of a crime scene—the victim's phone and laptop were sitting on the counter, for crying out loud—and he should not let her out of his sight for anything other than a bathroom break, instead of trying to eavesdrop on the detectives' interview.

But he had already gone, so she brushed black powder onto the granite countertop where Joanna Moorehouse's cell phone and laptop lay connected to their chargers and tried to think of something to say that didn't have the potential to derail a future trial. She opened her mouth to ask how long Grace had been with Pretty Perfect.

"Quite a sight," Grace said.

"I'm sure it must have been a shock."

"No, walking out of my house last month to find someone had stolen all four tires off my new car, that was a shock. This was—I don't even know what this was. I couldn't even be sure that was her. I only met her the first day I came here. That would have been about four, five months ago. Since then—she ain't never here. I come about nine on Tuesdays and Fridays, she's at work, that's it. She don't have any pictures of herself around. I'd forgotten what she looked like."

"The officers used her driver's license photo to identify her," Maggie said.

"Not bad."

Maggie waited, hoping to sort out what Grace referred to with that comment.

"This job, I mean. Some of the places I go aren't any nicer than where I live. I do a few offices, too, on Wednesday nights. But as huge as this place is, it wasn't too much work. I just clean the two bathrooms she'd use and the kitchen—and she didn't cook, let me tell you, take-out everything, precut veggies, that's all she'd eat—bedroom, that was it. Touch up the floors. Once a month I'd use the floor cleaner on all the marble—*that* was a job, let me tell you. Not hard but took some time."

"Uh-huh," Maggie said.

Grace nodded at the dark powder now coating most of the kitchen counter. "You going to clean that stuff up?"

Maggie apologized sincerely. "Sorry. That's not part of our services. But it wipes up easily with soap and water off a hard surface like this, and besides . . . your agency won't ask you to come back here, will they? The estate will probably have to get a crime scene cleaning company to deal with . . . the biohazards."

The woman considered this and her face relaxed. "Yeah, that's true. 'Cause I'll quit before I'll go back into that room. Funny . . . this was my best assignment. Until now."

Maggie spotted a few decent prints, usually overlapping others, and covered them with wide transparent tape.

"Quiet. No kids running around because their mama thinks while I'm there I might as well provide day-care services at the same time even though she *ain't* paying for that. Hardly ever any kind of mess to clean up. The floors could tire me out because there're so many of them, but other than that . . . only place I couldn't go was the office. She kept that locked. Don't want the help stealing her secrets, I guess. Okay by me. One less thing to do." She drained the Jack Daniel's.

Maggie transferred the transparent tape to a glossy index card and jotted a few notes on its back.

"Gave me a nice bonus at Easter—I thought that was special of her. Lots of people give bonuses at Christmas, but Easter? And she left it in cash in an envelope with my name on it, right here." She patted the tabletop. "That way the agency didn't take a cut."

Maggie examined the sink, photographed, tried a UV light, and saw no signs of blood. She brushed the stainless fixtures with powder and lifted a few prints. "So she paid well?"

Grace shrugged. "The agency pays me the same no matter where I work. I don't have any idea what they gouged out of her every month—they keep that sort of thing to themselves."

"She didn't have any pets?" This seemed a safe topic, and relevant to the work at hand. From the counter Maggie moved on to the door leading to the garage, where Joanna had parked her car for the last time.

"Not even a goldfish." The crystal tumbler thumped back onto the oak. "Emptiest house I ever saw. 'Cept one time. I'd been coming here, I don't know, about three weeks. I walk in, right through that door there, and see a fair-haired boy poking around the refrigerator shelves! I nearly screamed. He looks at me like he knew I'd be around and says, 'She got *anything* to eat in this house?'"

"Who was he?"

"Dunno. Some gigolo, that type you look at and know he never had an honest job in his life, oozing germs out his damn pores. After he left I made sure all the doors were locked. I'd have counted the silver if she had any. And I thought, uh-uh, I am not going to be walking in on your nasty men all the time; I'm going to have to have a word with my bosses. But it never happened again."

She rotated the glass with her fingers, eyeing one of the cabinets thoughtfully. Maggie applied powder to the alarm panel mounted on the wall next to the garage door and kept the conversation going. "The doors were locked when you got here today? Alarm on?"

"Yeah. Yes." Grace appeared to think on this. "I guess so. I have a remote for it, see. I come in through the front, press the *Unlock* button. If it says anything I can't hear it out there, so I guess I don't know whether it was armed or not. I used my key, don't know if the knob was locked or not. Might have been able to tell if I'd been paying attention, but I wasn't. It was just another day, you know?"

Her eyes abruptly filled with tears, whether shock, pity for the victim, or pity for herself, Maggie couldn't tell. Probably all three. "She was a pretty girl—I mean . . . when I met her that one time. She should have been married, having pretty children. What'd she do to get somebody that mad at her?"

The alarm panel, that pesky plastic like the light switches that looked smooth but actually wasn't, gave her nothing. Then Maggie heard a murmur of voices and Jack and Riley strode into the room.

"ME's here," Jack said to Maggie.

Grace stood. She spoke calmly, though her voice quavered in spots. "You can let me go, or you can pour me another drink," she said. "Those are the two choices."

The cops absorbed this. Then Jack clapped his partner on the shoulder and said, "Detective Riley will be happy to finish up with you. Maggie?"

As they left she heard Grace say, "Sure I can't get you a glass, Detective?"

"Don't tempt me," Riley grumbled back.

Jeremy Mearan's day had been off from the start. He'd had a trainee in to observe a sale and the guy had taken a bath in Axe body spray. The client they met had been an old lady complete with pilled cardigan, thick glasses, and plenty of equity in her slightly dilapidated house. Mrs. Wattle reeked of rosewater, so between the two people at his desk he had been skirting a migraine. But he had to show the new guy how they did it, so he gently explained to the old biddy how she wasn't alone, so many lovely older Americans were cash poor but equity rich, and he could make that money pile she lived in work for her. All she needed was to put a new roof on, but of course since the monthly payment would be practically nothing, she might want to take out extra money and pay off some bills . . . but she didn't cooperate with his spiel. She didn't need more money. Credit cards? Didn't have a balance. New car? She didn't drive. Dream vacation? She didn't like to travel. College tuition? Her children were long grown. Mearan had cast about with increasing desperation to find a reason to increase the loan amount and finally hit on her ne'er-do-well grandson, chronically in need of bail money and a good rehab program. Perfect. He got her to triple the loan amount, then left her to dream of saving both her home and her flesh and blood and excused himself to "check her credit score." He and the trainee moved to the espresso machine in a corner of the room.

The trainee bubbled over with questions, voracious and snapping. "What is—"

"Seven-eighty. It would be higher if she had more debt, but when she pays cash for everything—"

"That's good."

"Exactly. That's why I'll tell her it's 720. Maybe 700. You can't get too crazy in case they go storming off to a spouse or another family member to see who ruined their credit."

"But—"

"This regretfully pushes her into the next interest rate bracket. And increases the up-front points. But, I add, a good appraisal could lower them again."

"The appraiser—"

"Works for us. Different name on the letterhead, of course, but they're a trusted firm with whom we've worked for years; that's why we recommend them so highly. Ninety-five percent of the time they'll go with the first name on any list you give them. People are lazy. Just tell them what to do and they'll do it."

Instead of appreciating this font of accumulated wisdom the guy barely listened to Mearan's answers before asking more questions—which weren't even questions, more like check marks on his own invisible worksheet. The trainee came from an auto megastore— a used-car lot, in other words—and thought himself to be pretty hot shit. Every other sentence began with the phrase "At AutoGlobe we . . ." as if he had owned the damn place. His mouth opened to do it again but Mearan turned away and returned to the client.

He explained how she qualified only for a higher interest rate but that wouldn't be a problem with an adjustable rate mortgage and its low monthly payments. The rate couldn't go up more than 2 percent a year and could be locked in at any time. He didn't mention that the "lock-in" rate was a completely different rate, already at a higher number than if she simply got a fixed rate in the first place. He didn't tell her about the massive prepayment penalty.

Sterling loved elderly clients, who came from another time when banks didn't lie to their customers. They loved immigrant clients, who couldn't get through the wall of fast words thrown at them. They loved minority clients, who had been trained not to question authority. They loved clients who lacked the sophistication or experience to crunch the numbers themselves.

But again this widow didn't cooperate. Mrs. Wattle wanted to show the paperwork to her granddaughter, who had made her promise to do exactly that. *Before* signing.

Loans available changed by the day, Mearan told her, full of sincere concern for her financial well-being. By the hour. And their appraiser happened to have an opening that afternoon. They could get this taken care of today.

Mrs. Wattle chewed her lip. Her granddaughter had given her strict instructions.

Mearan understood. What a sweet girl she must be, looking out for her nana. But the appraiser's schedule stayed packed. . . . If they couldn't get this done now, it might be weeks. And according to an SEC report the interest rates were about to skyrocket. He would hate to see her miss this opportunity.

She signed.

He took his trainee off to the copy machine with a bottle of Wite-Out. Let Mr. AutoGlobe demonstrate his mad skills at fluffing up a client's income. Mearan hated getting white stains on his fingers, and the guy did have a deft hand at it, which only annoyed Mearan more. At least the guy didn't ask if the appraiser really had such a tight schedule (of course not) or how they'd get him to the property that afternoon (if he even bothered; either way a bonus hidden in Mrs. Wattle's closing costs would ensure a prompt report in the range they needed). He did ask which of the forms Mrs. Wattle would be taking home.

"The cover sheet showing her low, low rate," Mearan told him, "and our privacy policy."

"Nothing else?"

"Are you kidding? If that sweet, loyal granddaughter reads the fine print—screw that."

"Done deal." The trainee nodded his approval.

This irritated Mearan. He didn't need the guy's approval. "Our dear Mrs. Wattle is a grown-up, fully capable of researching her options. We're helping her achieve her goals."

"Yeah," the guy said. "Right. At AutoGlobe we—"

"Don't care," Mearan told him.

A completely routine morning, yet somehow everything had felt off, from Mrs. Wattle's deep brown eyes to the presumptuous trainee to the taste of the coffee. Maybe he'd known as soon as he looked through the walls and didn't see Joanna at her desk. Maybe he had a premonition.

Dead.

How could she be *dead*?

And how long would these idiots keep him here before he could get back to the office?

Chapter 4

Maggie walked with Jack to the other end of the building, through the gleaming hallway and past the empty rooms. They didn't speak, didn't make any reference to their shared history; they had no reason to. The situation had been laid out and nothing had changed. It had been thirty-five days since Maggie had been pushed off the cliff at the edge of her comfort zone and all she wanted was to claw her way back to the center of that space . . . except it didn't seem to be where she had left it and wouldn't come when called.

And the only person on the planet who shared the secret of her turmoil was the man who had created all this chaos in the first place. The man now walking alongside her.

But the past could not be rewritten, not by either of them.

She doubted this case would affect their delicate balance. Jack would not be gunning for the killer of Joanna Moorehouse, no matter how brutal. Even if he were a budding serial killer, the crazed and blatant monster who had done this would not escape notice for long. Jack targeted the career criminals, the ones who had left a long pattern of mayhem but kept up a human cushion of deniability that enabled them to escape prosecution time and again. Jack always gave the justice system several chances first. The psycho who killed Joanna Moorehouse would not have that defensive structure in place. Once found, he would be convicted.

Unless, she reminded herself as they joined the ME investigator in the room with the body, a killer who could walk away from a decimated corpse without leaving even a wisp of a trail had his own version of a defensive structure in place. One as brilliant as his exit.

Then, all bets might be snuffed out.

"How's the arm?" Jack asked her.

A few weeks before, her right shoulder had been dislocated in order to save his life. Since then he had studiously avoided her, and she him. "Peachy." Then she thought that could be interpreted as sarcastic so she added, "It's just fine."

The responding ME office investigator was a young man with black skin and a world-weary expression. He stood on the other side of the body, in between the sofa and love seat, on the corner of the Persian rug, making notes on a form attached to a clipboard. Maggie said, "Morning, Keshawn. How's it going?"

"Need my coffee."

"It's eleven o'clock."

"I know. I'm two cups behind. Why're you always bringing me this craziness?"

"I like to make your life interesting."

He paused in the notes to glance down at the corpse. "It sure made *her* life interesting. At least for a little bit."

He repeated all the work for his agency that Maggie had already done for hers, photographing every inch of the body, observing it from every angle. Then he poked and prodded it a bit, observing the stiffness of the muscles and the red patches of lividity. "Not much, since she bled out for the most part. Didn't leave much to coagulate at her low points. Rigor's full. I'd say twelve to twenty. It's cool in here, so that might slow things down. We got a last contact?"

"Left work nine-thirty last night. We'll have to get the alarm company to tell us when she deactivated the panel and take a look at her phone. According to the boyfriend, this fits the description of what she wore yesterday."

They observed the body once again.

"So," Keshawn began.

Maggie said, "She gets home from work, shuts off the alarm, is here long enough to kick off the heels and probably lose a suit coat, but not long enough to get ready for bed."

"Of course, she could be the kind that goes to bed at three and gets by on a couple hours of sleep. Don't understand that, myself."

"Cause of death?" Jack asked.

Keshawn eyed him. "You're kidding, right?"

"I meant other than the obvious."

"In this case the obvious is pretty damn obvious. Extreme trauma causing fatal blood loss would be my guess. Sure, it could turn out to be a heart attack, because watching someone hack my body open, I'd have a heart attack, too. But she looks a bit young for that. There's no sign of petechiae or trauma to the neck, other than the stab wounds, which probably severed her vocal cords and crushed her larynx, in case the lungs filling up with blood wouldn't asphyxiate her quickly enough." A muscle pulsed under his left eye. He crouched next to what was left of Joanna Moorehouse just as Maggie had, getting a closer, more methodical look. "Her state of undress is a bit concerning. Of course we'll do swabs. Maggie, you have everything you need before we move her?"

"Yes."

Riley guided the two ambulance crew—aka "body snatchers"—into the room and said to Jack, "I cut the cleaning lady loose."

"Grace," Maggie supplied.

"Yeah, her. In here every week for months and she doesn't know what the victim did all day or whether she had any family left in the world. She's either not real observant or not real curious."

Maggie said, "Maybe neither. The homeowner didn't leave a lot of personal stuff lying around—as in *none*. Whatsoever. What did the boyfriend say?"

"That he hasn't got a clue," Riley went on, slouching his bottom onto the arm of the far recliner and waiting for Keshawn to finish his notes. "They worked late with some other people; that was the last he saw of her. No reason to call. They didn't make a habit of texting nite-nite to each other; they weren't that kind of a couple. Lots of hot tempers at work, but that's normal for this business."

"The mortgage business?" she asked.

Jack said nothing, as usual, letting his partner do the

talking, so Riley nodded. "Big money in mortgages. Something about somebody wants to buy the company—"

"And she didn't want to sell?"

"No, she was hot to sell, but on her terms. Then there's some other buyer and lawyers and accountants gumming up the works—I couldn't make what he said add up to an actual sentence with a noun and a verb for the most part, so I'm sure I didn't get the full disclosure, but it sounded like one more day in the glittery world of high finance. These people chew Maalox for breakfast. But murder?"

"I saw her bank account statement in the office," Maggie said. "It looked pretty murder worthy to me."

"Yeah, to me too. But to these suits? They lose that much before breakfast without batting an eye. Sometimes the market goes up, sometimes it goes down."

Keshawn finally spoke. "This don't look like corporate espionage to me, anyway."

No one had to ask what he meant.

He had set the clipboard aside and now focused the camera's lens on the puncture into Joanna Moorehouse's cheekbone. "It looks like pure animal rage."

After he completed his photographs and asked the detectives approximately twenty-five more questions, he had the body snatchers stretch a transport sheet lengthwise along the victim's body to flip her onto. Maggie crouched next to him, camera at the ready, to see what lay underneath Joanna Moorehouse.

The snatchers pulled on the left arm as Keshawn pushed on the woman's hip, and the body, stiff as an I-beam, rolled onto its right side. Keshawn and Maggie snapped pictures, then took a closer look.

Nothing commanded their attention. Joanna Moore-house from the back appeared every bit as fit and toned as Joanna Moorehouse from the front. Most of it had been coated in red as her lifeblood had seeped out and around and under her, except in spots such as the center of her buttocks and her shoulder blades, where the liquid couldn't quite wriggle under the skin. But a few minutes' inspection established that there were no injuries; all the assault had taken place while the killer had been eye to eye with his victim.

The snatcher holding Joanna's arm let go, but just as the corpse would have settled back into its original position, Maggie's gloved hands shot out to grab it. "Whoa!"

"Whoa yourself," Keshawn said. He helped her support the upper back as the whole body started to slide away from them. "See something?"

Maggie stared at a swirling of blood messed up by Joanna's struggles to push off her attacker, struggling to hold the woman's body from falling back onto it. "Does that look like a fingerprint?"

Their heads bumped as they gazed downward at a feathery pattern at the edge of the blood pool, next to where Joanna's left arm had lain.

Keshawn made a doubtful mumble as the snatchers flipped the body over onto the sheet. Maggie still stared, moving her body in a deep crouch that threatened to overbalance.

Keshawn said, "Not trying to be, you know, obnoxious or nothing, but you pretty flexible, girl."

"Yoga," she explained, her voice muffled by her thighs. She let the snatchers move the body and waited until Keshawn left the dais to get a few last details from the detectives. If she could have gone into a sphinx pose and positioned her arms around the possible print to keep it safe without looking completely ridiculous—and getting someone else's dried blood on her shirt—she would have.

When the others were at a safe distance she got out the tripod for her camera, put an ABFO ruler next to the print, and snapped the tiny area at a variety of exposures and apertures. She used a digital SLR but this was not a point-and-click situation. The shiny white tile turned out to be both a blessing and a curse—as a background it created perfect contrast with the dark red print, but it also bounced back light from the flash and even the windows, making the print's ridges disappear in a blaze of unglory. Finally, she obtained a few images that satisfied her.

She returned to her car, passing the two detectives as they spoke to a handsome but harried-looking young man. The police IT guy stood next to the latter while holding Joanna's cell phone in his latex-gloved hands, comparing the call history while Riley took notes. The young man said, "Yeah, that's our in-house lawyer. He's working on the requirements violations. That's— let me see, I think that's one of Deb's numbers—yeah. She's with Ergo . . . Insurance, they're insurance. That one . . . I don't know who that is . . . let me see. . . ."

Maggie retrieved the Amido Black reagent and stopped in the kitchen to borrow a pitcher, which she filled with tap water, handling the faucet handle as gingerly as possible to avoid the black carbon she'd dusted it with. Then she appropriated a roll of paper towels and returned to where the body had lain.

Amido Black stained blood to a dark purplish black

shade and could bring out further ridge detail in her one lonely print. But it had to be rinsed—easily accomplished on a small object or anything vertical, like a wall. Quite a different stretch of road when gravity could not be your friend.

Less would have to be more. Instead of dousing the area, she used a disposable plastic pipette to drop the dark reagent onto the blood pattern, enough to cover the print and extend a few millimeters past its edges. The liquid formed a perfect blob and sat there. The floor must have been perfectly level. . . . Nice to know the quality of the construction stayed in line with its price.

Because it showed no inclination to flow, instead of pouring the water from the pitcher she used another pipette. Squeezing its bulb hard gave the water enough force to push the stain to the side, where she blotted it with the paper towels. Not exactly elegant, but it worked. The ridges darkened, other smudges and spots appeared, but no more prints. Only that one.

It could belong to the victim, but Maggie didn't think so. It appeared to be a simple loop but oriented upward, toward where her head had been, not downward where she would have put her hands to cushion a fall to the floor. Possibly she tried to turn to her left side, pushing off the floor with her right hand.

But it could also be from the killer's hand as he held his victim down in order to continue stabbing her. His hand slipped off her bloody arm and—wait, then he'd have to be holding the knife in his left hand, to free his right fingers to press on the floor. But the chest wounds seemed to skewer to the victim's left, which would be the killer's right. Plus that one puncture under the left cheek. It all put Maggie in mind of a right-handed killer.

Oh well. She'd find out soon enough when she got Joanna's prints from the autopsy. She packed up her equipment to tote back to her car, fighting the nagging feeling that there should be more she could do. Such a brutal murder, and such a dearth of evidence left behind.

Chapter 5

Jack stood in the shade of the weeping willow trees with Riley and Jeremy Mearan, but the branches couldn't shelter him from the humidity. Cleveland temperatures could vary wildly in the summer but the lake always kept the air hydrated. He and Riley had convinced the young man to loan them his phone so the IT guy could compare his e-mails with the ones on Joanna Moorehouse's laptop—which would be helpful, but keeping him from alerting the rest of the staff to their boss's demise would be *really* helpful. Usually the suspect list began with family, then friends. Coworkers ran a distant third. But this victim, from everything they could determine, had no family or friends. Virtually every communication on her phone had been from a business associate, and they had found no sign of a second cell or another computer or even a damn iPod. Coworkers catapulted to the top of the "automatically-suspect-these-people" list, and Jack was already forming a plan to infiltrate that pool.

But the separation from the electronic heart of his

universe was already giving Jeremy Mearan the shakes. "But I have to tell them. Joanna *is* the company, and the place is already in chaos because of this merger. They have to know she's not coming back!"

Maggie came out of the house with her usual comportment of awkward containers and crossed the drive to her car. Mearan was not too upset to forgo checking out her ass but kept on point. "I want to leave, and I want my phone back."

Riley brushed a leaf off his shoulder. "Of course. But we're going to need to talk to some of your staff anyway, so it would be better if that could all be done at the same time."

"Why? What difference does that make?"

Riley said something conciliatory but untrue, because simply put it would be better for the investigation to question people before they'd had enough time to compare notes, get stories straight, or resolve to speak no ill of the dead. Usually ill was what got the dead where they were, and exercising restraint in commentary of same often covered up important information.

The IT guy came out of the house with a square package in brown paper—certainly the laptop—and stored it in his car.

"There!" Mearan announced. "He's done. I've told you all I can, and I want to *leave*."

Before Riley could agree, Jack said, "Just give us five more minutes and we'll have you on your way."

"I don't—"

"*Look.* Someone took the woman you slept with and sliced her open like gutting a deer."

Mearan blanched. Puking seemed a definite possibility. "What do you mean, sliced open? You said stabbed—and I thought that meant *stabbed*. You mean they cut her more than once?"

Jack ignored this. "Do you care? I'm not asking if you loved her. But do you at least *care*?"

"Yes! Yes, I—" He seemed to realize that he meant it, and it came as a bit of a surprise to him. "I care."

"Do you want us to find who did this?"

Still pale, Mearan nodded.

"Okay. Then wait here."

He and Riley moved away, out of earshot. Maggie slammed her trunk shut and joined them.

Riley asked, "What are you thinking, partner?"

"We've got an opportunity here. Given this location, the doors locked—or at least we think they were—this is probably not random. This woman had no life outside her job. We have to assume she knew her killer and she knew him from work."

"So we burst into the office, announce that she's dead, and question everybody while they're still in shock?"

"Exactly. Then we ask for DNA and fingerprints."

Riley scoffed. "No way they're going to give us that. These sound like high rollers, not Sunday-school teachers."

Maggie waited between them, her gaze switching back and forth, as absorbed as a spectator at Wimbledon.

"They will, with all their coworkers around them. Their pals and cubicle-mates might wonder if Jake in cubicle three refuses to give up his DNA. They might start to wonder why. That sort of thing makes office parties awkward and promotions iffy."

"He said we're talking about twenty, twenty-five people, and we don't even know what this place looks like. If they physically scatter, there's nothing we can do. If they want to go home to weep into their hankies or play hooky with a sort of snow day, we can't stop them. It's not the crime scene."

"I know," Jack said. "But it's worth a try."

"And it might come as a shock to little Joanna's flunkies, but the guy who did it—*he* knows she's dead. He's not going to be shocked at all. He might even have called in sick today, just in case we pull such a stunt."

"He'll be there. He'll be calm and cooperative. He might even give up his prints, if everyone else does. He won't want to do anything that will make him stand out."

"How do you know that?"

Because that's what I would do, Jack thought. "Trust me."

Riley raised one eyebrow. That wasn't something Jack said often, or ever. He studied Jeremy Mearan, then turned back. "Okay. Why not? Like you said, it's worth a try. Maggie, you come too."

That surprised her. "Me? Why?"

She didn't want to be around him, Jack knew. Any more than he wanted to be around her. Each other's existence formed a personal sword of Damocles with the thread ready to snap at any moment. It didn't make for social comfort.

"In case my smooth partner here talks them into prints. We may have a window of about two and a half seconds before they change their minds and we'll want to be ready to go. You got stuff in your car?"

She shrugged. "Yeah, some."

"Okay, then." He nodded toward their subject. "Test run. Let's see you get him on board."

Jack cracked the knuckles of one hand and said with a confidence he didn't feel, "No problem."

They returned to the victim's sort-of boyfriend. Jack told him that they'd like to accompany him to his office to inform the staff and then gather as much information from same as they could. At first the guy blinked in confusion more than any sort of concern. "Sure . . . whatever."

"We'd like to be the ones to break the news, so to speak. To tell your coworkers of Joanna's death."

An expression of great relief flowed over the young man's face. "*Would* you?"

Obviously the kid had been dreading it, truly dreading. Jack jumped on this. "Of course. We've had a lot of experience at that, unfortunately. And from an investigation point of view, it would be best if we could que—talk to people before they get too overcome to remember events clearly."

This made no sense, but Mearan didn't care. As long as he didn't have to stand in front of a room full of people and tell them that the woman he slept with had been slaughtered in the safety of her beautiful house and, oh, by the way, the company will probably fold now and you'll all be out of your jobs, he would cooperate with any plan. He didn't even ask for his cell phone back. He gave a brief description of the office— second floor of a small downtown building, cubicles for the originators, four offices for the execs, conference room, a file room. Then he came back to, what was to him, the most important point. "And you'll tell them that she's . . . dead?"

"Yes."

"Are you going to tell them that she was murdered? And . . . how?"

"Yes, but perhaps not right away. That's why it's important that you say nothing and follow our lead, okay? *Nothing*. If anyone asks you for details, don't answer."

Mearan studied the cops, eyes narrowing. "Easy enough—I don't know any. You think whoever killed her works at Sterling. And that if you burst in there and don't give them time to think you can surprise them into giving themselves away?"

Jack said nothing. It sounded kind of ridiculous when the kid said it.

"But how do you know it's someone there? What if it was some random pervert or like the guy who cuts the grass or something?"

"Then we still get an unvarnished account of Joanna's recent activities."

Mearan didn't seem to hear him, lost in his own mulling. "How do you know it wasn't me?"

Jack made himself smile at the guy. "Then you'll give yourself away, sooner or later. And we'll be there."

The apple in Mearan's neck bobbed up and down.

Maggie drove the city's assigned forensic unit vehicle with spotty AC and a lingering smell of blood from the Moorehouse mansion to St. Clair Avenue, talking to her boss on the phone. She filled him in with every detail she could until he protested: "Okay, stop. I've got it, incredibly rich, lonely hottie gutted on her living room floor and the cops are chasing the staff at her company because they've got nobody else to look at?"

"Well, yeah—that's where we stand." She could picture Denny pinching his broad nose with long black fingers, mentally rearranging his staff's workload as she slowed at East 22nd and Euclid to avoid rear-ending a brake-happy van. She pulled around it. The driver also spoke on a cell phone. Some people could do both at once, and some couldn't. "They've still got the house sealed, so we can go back whenever we want. At least until the department gets tired of paying two officers to babysit the place. The IT guy is going through her computer, trying to find out what she's been doing and where she's been going *other* than work. Jack called this offshore bank to alert us if anyone tries to access Joanna's accounts."

"Who's Jack?"

She must be doing a better job than she thought of keeping her life compartmentalized. "Homicide."

"Oh, okay. And he thinks an office-full of people are just going to give up their vitals? In this day and age?"

"You know you sound really old when you say things like 'this day and age'?"

"That's because I am." Denny chuckled. He could manage a laugh now and then since his third child started sleeping for more than an hour at a time. Some days he seemed downright perky. "And they don't think it's the boyfriend?"

"No . . . they asked him to identify the body and he nearly puked at the thought. Then they unzipped the top of the body bag to show her face, and he caught a glimpse of the damage to her torso and nearly fainted."

"Okay, then. Do you need help? Josh is at a traffic."

He meant a fatal or possibly fatal accident, at which the crime scene technicians would assist the traffic investigators by taking the photographs. "Bet he's not happy about that, with his allergies."

"Carol gave him a Benadryl nondrowsy. Says it will keep him going through anything. Did Amy get there?"

"Yeah, she took over the scene for me."

A pause ensued. She was about to say good-bye when Denny said, "Maggie, a heads-up—you might be recalled in the Graham trial."

Prosecution could put on rebuttal witnesses after the defense presented their case and rested, in order to refute something brought up during the defense phase of the trial. Despite the boisterous trial activity portrayed on television shows, this very rarely happened. The defense could even recall prosecution witnesses during their own phase of questioning. "Okay. Why?"

"The prosecutor says defense is going to bring in an expert witness to argue the fingerprint ID."

"Oh. Well, good luck to them." That was their right, and they could parade in all the paid testimony they wanted. It wouldn't change the facts, and the facts were that Graham had left his prints on the murder weapon. Which had also been found in his house, under his bed, where the cops found him twenty minutes after the murder occurred. The case was, one might say, as solid as polished granite.

"I wanted to let you know. Keep me posted on your rich hottie. And keep out of the way if those Wall Street people start throwing chairs at each other."

Maggie slowed at her destination, a white marble building on St. Clair near 30th. "It's some sort of mortgage loan company. I doubt they're the chair-throwing types."

"You ever been around money people? I mean *real* money? They are a different breed, Maggie."

"You and Fitzgerald, on the same page."

"I'm not kidding. Chairs will be the most innocuous things they throw."

She looked up at the stone edifice. Pretty, probably historic, but not particularly intimidating in itself. A group of seven or eight people on its sidewalk carrying signs concerned her more. "You may be right."

The signs read PREDATORY LENDERS and something about stolen homes. That was all Maggie had time to catch before her car slid by. The protesters waved their signs at her, their voices rising, trying to call attention to their plight with desperate abandon. "Help the victims!" "Fraud took my home!" "Thieves!" Maggie turned right at the corner to find a place to park.

A small lot behind the building had a monitored lot, and it took her a minute or two to convince the attendant that she was with the two detectives in the previous car and thus would not be ponying up the four dollars per hour it cost nonstaff to park there. The older man *hmpf*ed and peered at her through heavy eyebrows and quite literally dragged his feet over to lift the gate for her, then stared at the back of her moving car as if to memorize the license number. Unauthorized parkers would not be allowed on his shift. *At least*, she thought, *when the cops ask him if anyone strange has been hanging about, he's going to know.*

She grabbed her camera and some swabs and swab boxes, an ink pad, and the few fingerprint cards she had in her trunk—perhaps four. If the staff actually co-operated she would have to use plain copy paper to roll their prints on. Not ideal, but workable. As long as the prints were clear it didn't matter if she rolled them on the back of a menu.

She caught up to the detectives on their way through the rear door with Jeremy Mearan. The young man seemed to panic now that the moment to face his friends had arrived. His hand trembled as he pulled open the heavy glass-and-brass doors.

They entered a lobby much more impressive than the exterior of the building warranted. Original marble covered not only the floor but the walls, its richly aged texture turning Joanna Moorehouse's mansion into a shoddy nouveau riche imitation. Leather sofas formed a waiting area and the receptionist's sweeping desk had been carved out of mahogany. A thick carpet runner in deep red muffled their footsteps as they passed through.

On the other side of the filmy curtains she could see the protesters on the front sidewalk milling about. They didn't seem interested in the lobby, more focused on shaking their signs at passing cars.

"Is that a piano?" Riley asked—not that the shiny black full-sized grand in a corner could have been anything else. Mearan didn't bother to answer, just nodded at the receptionist and pressed the button for the elevator. As the doors opened, Riley added, "Anybody ever play it?"

Mearan glanced at the piano as if he had never seen it before. "I don't think so."

Maggie shook her head as the doors closed. Denny had been right. The rich *were* different.

Or at least they pretended to be.

Two patrol officers, different ones from the crime scene, had joined them and the antique elevator barely held the whole group.

Maggie took a breath, feeling not only claustrophobic but oddly nervous. Give her dead bodies any day. Live ones always proved much more troublesome. She glanced up at Jack, who immediately hissed, "Stop looking at me like that."

"Like what?"

"Like I'm supposed to know what I'm doing."

Riley chuckled.

Chapter 6

The elevator opened into a noisy cauldron of sound and scurrying, despite thick rugs and a waiting area with a heavy antique coffee table and a chocolate-colored couch that Maggie wanted to dive into. The office cubicles weren't cubicles in the traditional sense but beautiful wood desks separated by live plants and cleverly disguised file cabinets, with ergonomic chairs on silent casters. Not even the stacks of plain buff-colored file folders and giveaway pens could hide their beauty. Natural light streamed in from all the windows, sometimes passing through the glass walls of private offices with even more opulent fixtures. But somehow none of this elegance soothed; instead, the traditional wood and the modern walls clashed instead of melding. Or that could be the effect of so many combined voices all talking at once, with no one listening.

Desk phones, cell phones, speakerphones were all employed. At least nine people sat at the twelve-odd desks in the open area, ringed by five of the glass offices. Two sat empty, perhaps Joanna's (the largest) and Jeremy Mearan's. The other three were occupied by two men and a woman, respectively, all talking on phones. Through another glass wall sat a long conference table with two people at each end, boxes and files unceremoniously piled onto the glossy wood. Even the file room had glass walls.

It seemed an unlikely place to plot a murder, or be able to keep any secret at all.

On the other hand, since no one seemed to pay any attention to anyone else, the murderer could have done his planning right there and still escaped notice.

A woman at one end of the conference table looked up just then and apparently pegged them as out of place. Without turning her head she stood, moved around the table, and walked toward them.

Jeremy Mearan let out an ear-splitting whistle, of which Maggie would not have believed him possible. He didn't seem like he'd had the upbringing for that kind of a talent.

Not everyone paused in their speech, but enough did for him to be heard. "Sorry to interrupt, but I need everyone to listen to this right now. Hang up, put the phones away. Tell clients you'll get back to them."

Most of the men—and they were mostly men—working the phones got a stubborn look, resenting the disruption, but when Mearan added, "I have bad news," in a voice beginning to tremble, even they made quick excuses and clicked off.

Of the three in the glass offices, an older man rubbed his face and swung his feet off the desk. The woman had hung up anyway but looked superbly annoyed, either at the interruption or at Mearan being the interrupter. The other man had his door shut and had somehow missed the whistle. Turned toward the window, he continued his conversation until the woman banged on his outer wall as she strode past.

As she did she demanded, "What the hell is going on, Jeremy? Where is Joanna? How could she—"

The young man waved a limp hand at the cops. "They're . . . they're going to tell you." Then he collapsed into one of the waiting-area chairs and hunched forward, chin in his hands, fingers over his mouth tightly enough to press white streaks into his cheeks.

Jack told them only that Joanna Moorehouse had been found dead.

Reactions ran the gamut. A man near Maggie simply said, "Huh." The woman from the conference room paled. The woman from the nice office frowned. A stocky man in the center of the room asked if Joanna had killed herself.

"We're still investigating the circumstances."

The man persisted. "Easy question. Did she off herself or not?"

Jack barely moved but somehow straightened into a steel-hard figure with a voice to match and repeated, "We are investigating the circumstances."

Maggie felt the stab of fear he could still arouse in her, but the people in the room had no idea how close they were to seeing the real Jack, the one who felt able to judge whether someone lived or died. The stocky man certainly didn't. He turned to the guy across the aisle from him and said, "I bet she killed herself."

A dam broke and the room erupted into similar speculation. Voices asked questions that no one could answer: What would happen now? Was the merger off?

Who would take over? To this, names were bandied and refuted.

Jack spoke over them, requesting that they remain to speak with the detectives. No one agreed but no one argued. They were more interested in talking with each other.

Everyone, as Maggie studied them, seemed shocked and surprised, annoyed and concerned, but not grieving—this was a business, not a family. Joanna's death created a vacuum in that business and it would have to be filled. No one—to her relief, since she stood in front of the elevator—seemed interested in leaving. No one apparently felt the need to, as Riley had suggested, go home to cry in their hankies.

"We will also need to collect your DNA swabs and fingerprints for elimination purposes."

That silenced the room. For about one full second.

"Say what?"

"No friggin' way."

"You can't make us do that."

"Only so we can eliminate any of your prints from prints found on items at her house and in her office. They won't be entered into any police database." He still looked commanding and more than a bit terrifying to Maggie, but still couldn't make much of a dent in this crowd's general paranoia.

"*No.*"

"You can't make us do that," the woman from the nice office repeated.

"No, we can't," Jack agreed. "It would be voluntary. If you don't wish to cooperate with our investigation, that is entirely up to you."

The woman glared, seeing the trap.

The expressions on some faces in the room changed to those of curiosity as their owners wondered how this was going to play out. Who would balk, and, more importantly, why?

Riley strode through them to commandeer the conference room. There didn't seem to be another option. Obviously it wouldn't be a good idea to parade an army of suspects through the victim's office, in case it held any evidence worth having.

"I don't believe that you won't put it in your database." The young man pulled his tie away from his throat. "You guys always say that but you never throw anything out."

Jack pointed at Maggie. "Maggie handles our AFIS. If she says your prints will be destroyed, they'll be destroyed."

Every pair of eyes in the room turned toward her, only for a moment, but long enough to make her want to run screaming for the stairwell. She didn't do this personal confrontation crap. That was why she had gone into forensics and not policing. Now *she* glared at Jack, who hadn't taken his gaze from the young man in the tie.

"Again, it's entirely up to you," he said. "If you're worried about it."

The stares of his coworkers forced the man back into his seat. He said nothing further. But one of the few women at the desks gestured toward the two patrol officers flanking the elevator. "But we can't leave until they do."

Jack said, "You can go any time you want. We are

asking you to stay and help us investigate the death of your colleague."

The office woman said to him, "This is the headquarters of a four *billion*-dollar national business. We're all very sorry about Joanna, but—"

"This is a murder," Jack snapped.

The room gasped, and Maggie could see him mentally kicking himself in the form of a vein bulging at his temple.

A new wave of shock rounded the room.

"What the crap?"

"Someone murdered her?"

"Are you sure? Are you *sure* she's not on a beach in Aruba with last quarter's profits?"

The woman recovered. "Well, that's—"

One of the older men from the private offices finally spoke. "Come off it, Lauren. You're not filling her boots just yet." To Jack, he said, "Whatever you need, say the word. You'll have our complete cooperation."

A very pretty girl with very dark skin at one of the desks nodded fiercely. "We owe it to Joanna." For some reason this produced some eye rolling among her coworkers. One muttered, "*Tyra*," with exasperation.

The older man said, more curiously, "Was it . . . really murder? How'd she die?"

"We're still investigating—"

"The circumstances. Got it. Help yourself to the conference room, which I see you already have. Okay, folks. Tell these guys anything they want to know. Otherwise get back to work."

Lauren said, "You're not filling her boots just yet either, Pierce."

He ignored her and returned to his desk. Maggie let out a breath she hadn't known she was holding.

Lauren marched up to Jack. "You might as well start with me."

She might as well have added, "Because I'm the most important person here," it seemed to be so strongly implied . . . but then again, it could be true. Maggie followed them into the conference room. Because of the glass walls, this interview would be completely visible to the sea of eyes they had passed through. It might encourage all interviewees to stay on their best behavior, or it might stifle any spontaneous admissions. Either way, it made an interesting setting for an interrogation.

The man and woman Riley evicted had gathered up their files and briefcases and booklets. The woman had an entire file box, and Maggie picked it up as she said, "Sorry about the disruption."

"Oh, don't worry," the woman said and gathered the rest of her items. "I wasn't making a lot of progress anyway." They carried their loads out the door. "I guess I'll take the waiting area. It's that or the floor in the file room, and I'm too old to do the cross-legged thing for very long."

She looked about thirty and perfectly flexible, but Maggie said nothing and followed her through the desks. The workers had reverted to their original state, on the phones, talking fast, wireless headsets bobbing as they typed at the same time. "Won't the noise bother you?"

"They're all like that. Financial firms, I mean." She set her files on the coffee table and motioned for Maggie to do the same with the box. Her fellow evictee had already claimed half of it. "I'm a regulator. From the

Fed—Federal Reserve. I go into these places to make sure they're conforming to the capital requirements and compensation limits, if any, the rate charges—anyway, that's what I do."

"Hence, the conference room."

"Yep. I'm a temporary squatter, like Dhaval here. He's from DJ Bryan, doing the due diligence before they buy Sterling." She waved at the dark-hued young man who had plopped his files on the other side of the coffee table. Happily the coffee table spanned at least seven feet end to end, so they had plenty of room, but he did not look remotely pleased about the new digs.

"*If* we buy Sterling," he said sourly, pulled out his phone, and took no further notice of them.

"How long have you been here?" Maggie asked.

"Huh. It's been about three years since I moved from DC—oh, you mean at Sterling. Two weeks, no, a little less. I've been here before, though, I think about seven months ago. I'm Anna, by the way. Anna Hernandez."

"Maggie Gardiner. I'm the forensic specialist."

"Cool. Is that guy waiting for you?"

Jack held the door to the conference room, watching them.

"I think he may be."

Sitting in on witness interviews was not her job, but she slipped into the room and took a seat as unobtrusively as possible. The detectives might want her on hand to take samples before the interviewees changed their minds, and having to call her in could interrupt the flow. An interview, or interrogation, often meant convincing someone to bare their soul, to dredge up events they hadn't noticed at the time, to confess to

things they didn't want to admit, even if criminally innocuous. A give-and-take would be created, weaving a
spell that if broken would not be regained. Maggie
never interrupted a detective's interview for any reason. So, since Riley and Jack seemed to want her there,
she sat.

The woman's name was Lauren Schneider, and she
was the regional manager for the western states, from
California to the Mississippi and including Alaska and
Hawaii. Leroy Sherman handled the east. Pierce Bowman was from DJ Bryan, the large investment bank
planning to buy them, and from his behavior you
would think they already had. Sterling Financial was a
mortgage banking firm; they originated loans that
they then sold to investors. The DJ Bryan sale was de-
sired by all parties, once details were worked out. Lauren had known Joanna Moorehouse since she had
come to work for her four years previously, and Lauren
had no idea who might have wanted to kill her. She
asked again how Joanna had been killed, a reasonable
question, and again Jack and Riley refused to answer.
They were welcome to collect her saliva and fingerprints. She had nothing to hide, unlike a few of the dis-
trict managers out there on the floor.

Riley asked her to clarify that remark.

The woman tossed her perfectly coiffed brown hair,
releasing a subtle perfume. Maggie wasn't much into
perfume but even she thought it smelled of exotic
places with hammocks on the beach and linen-draped
cabanas. "Oh, I don't mean anything really *criminal*.
But this is a cutthroat business. We're not a bunch of
kindly bankers helping ordinary folks achieve the
American Dream of home ownership, like we're wear-

ing scuffed shoes in the only two-story building on Main Street in Podunk, Nebraska—even though we *are* helping people achieve the American Dream much more than the small bank in Podunk. But we're also doing it for the profit margin." As Riley opened his mouth she added, "I meant that I wouldn't be surprised if some of the managers have a tax violation here or an illegal housemaid there. Their expense reports sure as hell get creative."

"So people come here to finance their home loans," Riley said.

"To one of our regional offices. This is our headquarters, where we oversee the regionals and train their managers. I know it's small—that's by design. Having too many chiefs only dilutes the profits—and, um, the product."

"Did Joanna have any enemies?" Jack asked.

"Sure. Bank of America, Freddie Mac, Fannie Mae, every mortgage originator in the country hates our market share, which grew again by two percent last quarter. That's why Bryan wants to buy us. But I doubt any of them would send an assassin to her home." She seemed to consider her own remark. "I mean, it wouldn't do any good. Joanna founded Sterling, but it's not like it's going to go away without her. It would be like killing one of you. The investigation would still go on, right?"

This seemed an odd analogy, though true. It was her utterly impersonal delivery, with an utter lack of hesitation over the word *killing* that stuck in Maggie's mind like a thumbtack.

She went on. "No, if someone murdered Joanna it—are you sure it wasn't a burglar? She showed me pictures of her house and it looked pretty spectacular. Not like mine, but really nice. I can't believe she hasn't been robbed already."

"It's a possible theory, but from the appearance of the scene we don't believe it's likely," Riley said, as if he was reading the line out of a manual. Lauren Schneider didn't seem to notice.

Maggie wondered at someone who described the Moorehouse mansion as "really nice." But then, she had only seen pictures.

According to her.

"Huh. Well, who knows what Joanna was getting up to in her off hours. She had always been tight-lipped about her personal life. She didn't tell and I didn't ask. Seems to me the only suspect from this office would be her little boy toy out there, Jeremy. He's employed here only because she found him useful in bed. He wouldn't know a decent tranch if it swallowed him."

"'Tranch'?" Riley asked.

Lauren blinked at him, then laughed, which temporarily softened her features. "Oh, sorry. Mortgage loans are sold in categories according to risk and return, called tranches. Think of it as slaughtering a cow. You get filet mignon, flank steak, and hamburger. They take bundles of these mortgages and chop them up. Investors in the first tranch get paid first, as the borrower pays on the loan. They make, say, six percent interest. The second tranch gets paid next, and they get nine percent. The third tranch gets paid last, but since it's the riskiest because the borrower might repay the loan early before they get their cut, they get twelve percent. Risk versus return is all investing is. The biggest risk is prepayment. Investors *want* a thirty-year mortgage to take thirty years, because that maximizes the interest paid."

Riley said, "So one man's debt is another man's—"

"Stream of income."

Maggie could see Jack's eyes glazing over, and he changed the subject. "Can you think of any enemies? Of Joanna's, or Sterling's?"

The woman hooked one thumb over her shoulder, pointing at the windows behind her. "Him."

"The protesters?"

"Their leader. Ned Swift is our local crusader against the big, bad companies that actually make money. When he isn't writing op-eds, he's holding press conferences and handing signs to those people he occasionally gets to show up. 'Ned versus the Fed'—no? You haven't—anyway, if you want an enemy, he's who comes to mind."

"Had he argued with Joanna?" Riley asked, making a note.

"Mostly via the press and blog sites. He'd call her constantly. . . . We kept changing her number but somehow he'd get it. This is the third protest he's staged—there was another last week, the first about three months ago. They think by blocking the front door they'll interfere with our business, but we come in the back and they don't dare tangle with Mannie. He'd eat them for breakfast if they tried to pass the gate." She appeared to take great satisfaction in that mental image. "And, as I said, customers don't come to this location anyway. He got a few minutes of film coverage and that was it. The housing bust is over, prices are going back up. Ned is old news and he can't stand it."

"Any of those protests turn violent?"

"Nah," she said, then remembered that she alone represented sophistication. "No."

"Well, we'll talk to Mr. Swift. Anyone else?"

She shook her head, but uncertainly. Riley repeated the question but she had made up her mind and insisted that everyone admired Joanna. There were no serious internal disputes.

The constant murmur of noise out in the desk pool ebbed and flowed. Lauren Schneider's gaze darted across that room constantly, looking for . . . what? Moral support? Opposition? That no one slacked off in Joanna's absence?

"What about this merger?" Riley asked.

"The merger is a great idea. It will open up our system to new markets. DJ Bryan is the largest and best investment bank in the world. We couldn't be more secure than to be part of their umbrella."

"Don't a lot of people lose their jobs in a merger?" Jack asked.

"Yes," she said without hesitation. "But we won't. Loan officers in some of the smaller regionals might become redundant, but no one here will be let go. Bryan will need us. We're the ones making Sterling so profitable."

She spoke confidently, but there seemed to be the slightest undercurrent, tremulous and worried, and Maggie noticed the woman's perfect manicure bite into one folded forearm. Mergers caused reshuffling. People always lost their jobs—and very often the people at higher levels, not lower. The business world was Machiavellian: Don't keep the old leaders around—they'll only divide loyalties and delay the conversion to the conquering group's way of doing things. Unless Lauren's job had been guaranteed in the merger agreement, she couldn't know what would happen. With or without Joanna.

It didn't seem to give her much of a motive to kill her boss, though.

Unless she believed those boots *were* hers to fill, and a position for Joanna's with DJ Bryan *had* been guaranteed.

"Your coworker Leroy Sherman? Will Bryan need him?"

"Leroy barely knows what the name of this company is. He had been a bigwig at Goldman Sachs and Joanna hired him just to get his name, and his credibility, on the letterhead. We don't need him anymore but he has six more months on his contract. When he's not playing golf he's at his desk scheduling tee times."

The detectives finished their questions and Lauren Schneider gave up her DNA and fingerprints, even though, she insisted, it would do them no good since she had never been to Joanna's house. She glared at Maggie as she conducted the indignity of swabbing the insides of Lauren's open mouth. Maggie tried to be as pleasant, downright obsequious, as she could. To roll someone's complete prints properly it is important that their fingers be relaxed and pliable. If the donor's body tensed up in an angry knot, it made the process that much more difficult. Lauren Schneider was nothing if not an angry knot. When they were done she looked at her ink-covered palms and then shot Maggie a skewering glance, as if Maggie had dealt a profound and deeply personal betrayal. Not even Riley's polite thank-you thawed her.

He held the door for her so she wouldn't have to

touch the handle with her darkened fingers. "Would you ask Mr. Bowman to come in?"

"I'll do whatever I can to help you catch whoever killed Joanna. That does not make me your secretary." With that she left the conference room, holding both hands away from her as if they now needed amputation.

Chapter 7

"Sweet gal," Riley summarized. "That was a bunch of nothing. Let's get this Pierce guy. What sort of a name is that, anyway? Pierce? Sounds like a Hallmark movie."

"You watch Hallmark movies?" Jack asked.

"Don't start no nasty rumors."

Jack said, "And their buddy Ned, too. Sounds like he has a different take on Sterling Financial's assistance in the American Dream."

"Ned Swift. And what kind of a name is *that*?" Riley left the room to retrieve the distinguished gentleman from DJ Bryan.

Maggie, now on the other side of the table where she had stood to fingerprint Lauren Schneider, studied the hubbub of the office. The pretty girl, Tyra, watched them, worrying one long fingernail between her teeth. Three other men huddled over a mahogany cabinet and shot glances at the conference room, obviously discussing the situation. No one else seemed to be paying any attention at all, back to constructing spreadsheets on their computers with a phone tucked under one ear, their fingers flying over the number pad on their keyboards faster than the wings on a hummingbird. In the waiting area, Dhaval stayed absorbed in his paperwork, but Anna Hernandez, chin propped on one fist, elbow on crossed knee, gazed back at Maggie.

"What do you think?" Jack asked her.

Startled, she said, "About the murder? I don't know. It seems like a mess, frankly—like we've either got no logical suspects or way too many."

"I'll say. Give me a plain drug dealer drive-by any day."

"Uh, yeah."

But he moved closer to say, "This killing certainly seemed more personal than eliminating a business rival or stopping a merger. And if the guy staged it to look personal when it wasn't he would have done a better job— left out wineglasses or something like that, not disappear like a ghost. But someone who had lost their house . . . people get very emotional about their homes."

"Or had lost their life savings in a fund backed by bad mortgage loans." His cologne or aftershave or whatever replaced Lauren Schneider's expensive scent. Maggie found that she preferred it.

"True."

Riley opened the door and ushered Pierce Bowman in, who promptly announced, "Let me guess. Lauren said she was Joanna's right arm and everything at Sterling Financial was hunky-dory."

Riley and Jack exchanged a look.

Riley said, "Won't you sit down, Mr. Bowman? And tell us all about it."

Inside police headquarters in the Justice Center on Ontario Avenue, Maggie's ex-husband, Rick, sat at his desk typing up his final reports on the "vigilante killer" who had offed three of Cleveland's worst. One of the worst had killed a young girl, too, so that made the whole investigation a mess. Most of it was Patty Wildwood's case, but the star of the department had moved on to other things. It fell to Rick to continue the search for the vigilante, who had disappeared like a wraith, blown out over the lake to other lands. Which left Rick scrambling to look busy in order to justify his paycheck. He typed slowly.

Another detective walked up and said, "Gardiner, there's some hot chick here to see you."

Rick eyed him warily. When cops said that they usually meant his ex-wife. Or someone who personified the utter opposite of "hot."

But "hot" described Lori Russo accurately. The Cleveland *Herald* reporter merely had to flick her blond tresses over one shoulder to make every man in the room sit up and take notice. And notice they did, as she wound her way back to Rick's desk. The conservative slacks and slightly oversized blazer did not dampen their interest in the least. There were two female detectives in the room, who didn't even bother to roll their eyes.

Rick sat up and straightened his tie, running one hand through his hair.

Lori took the chair next to his desk without waiting for an invitation. "Good morning, Detective. I've brought you that list of murders from Chicago, Phoenix, and Detroit. At the bottom I put that horrible elder abuse case in Phoenix that sounds similar to the one we had here, where the vigilante killed that woman."

"Uh—yeah." Rick forced himself to look away from her T-shirt to the two sheets of paper she placed in front of him. "This is what your contacts found out."

"Yes. I was hoping you could talk to the police in those cities to see if they noted any similarities to the murders that took place here."

"Sure. Of course. I have been doing that anyway, of course—checking with NCIC. That's the National—"

"I know. What have you found out?" She propped her elfin chin on one hand, giving him the benefit of her long lashes.

Rick tried to calculate how long he could keep Lori Russo coming around, and what he might be able to get out of her in exchange for tidbits of scoop. Bait the hook. "I've been working very hard on this, but I'm afraid I can't share that with you. As you know, this is an open investigation."

"Yes, but—"

Toss out the line. "However, I can tell you that I have confirmed the five Chicago murders were all done with a twenty-two caliber. Unfortunately, Chicago averages at least one homicide a day, so five lowlifes shot in the back of the head and the body moved, over a number of years—it's not much of a pattern. They were never connected, and no kind of suspect developed. Cops

there don't even have an approximate description, like
we have."

"But there's also Detroit and Phoenix."

"Oh yes, I'm going to check those out, too." Start to
reel. "Thanks for coming by the office here, but you
didn't have to do that. Maybe if I find something I can
tell you we can meet someplace quieter. There's a cool
place at Thirteenth and Euclid I've been meaning to
check out—"

"Cowell? It's fabulous."

"Great, maybe we can meet there—"

And the line snapped. "My husband loves it. I'll
bring him along, if we can find a babysitter. Thanks a
lot, Detective. I'll be fascinated to see what you can
find out. I think this guy's got a longer history than
anyone has guessed."

"Uh . . . maybe."

She sprung up from the chair, flashed him a brilliant
smile. "You'll call me as soon as you get some answers, right? I can't wait to hear from you."

He watched her firm bottom as she marched away.
*Yeah, sure, I'll be calling. But you're going to have to
give me more than a flash of a tight T-shirt if you think
I'm going to hand you your "breaking news"!*

A guy at the next desk smirked at Rick's expression.
Rick glared back. And if this vigilante guy had operated
in other cities before moving to Cleveland, so what?
Knowing where he'd been didn't tell Rick where he'd
go. How was he supposed to track one guy who had
moved from one humongous city to the next and then to
the next with nothing but a police artist's sketch to go

on? There wasn't a handy database of who went where and when. No doubt he had appeared and disappeared from those cities just as he had from Cleveland. And Rick was supposed to track him?

Feeling supremely sorry for himself, Rick went to get another cup of coffee.

"I'm an account manager at DJ Bryan. We're the firm everyone wanted to be bought by when the economy tanked a decade ago. Sterling Financial generated four hundred and fifty million dollars in net revenue—in other words, profit—last year. But Bryan generated five hundred and fifty *billion*. So whether we buy Sterling or not is a life-changing decision for Sterling but not for Bryan. We can afford to be picky. Joanna didn't get that."

"Didn't get that how?" Riley asked. Maggie could see his struggle to make sense of all the financial dealings and sound intelligent at the same time. Cops had to be chameleons, walking the walk and talking the talk wherever they went. Blending in, establishing rapport. Riley was better at it than Jack, so Jack usually stayed quiet, playing the "heavy backup" to Riley's "charmer." But this was a tough crowd, too specialized to give a crap about rapport. They didn't need the police for anything except finding Joanna's killer, a vague and secondary concern for them. The business came first, and the business wasn't even going to pause.

"Remember way back when banks used to issue

mortgages, knew who they were lending to and had incentive to make good loans? Then came computerized credit scores so consumers could shop around and get better rates. Then Lew Ranieri took these assets that weren't liquid—mortgages take a long time to pay back and you can't cash them out quickly—and turned it into something that could be bought and traded in the short term."

"Securitization," Maggie said.

The two detectives sent her funny looks, but Bowman barely paused. "Exactly. This wasn't a bad idea—even if housing prices fell in one city, they wouldn't fall in *all* cities. Until they did. But instead of spreading the risk, it dispersed the disease."

Bowman leaned back in the swivel chair, one ankle across one knee, then partially turned so he could look at the detectives, the sky outside, and the managers at their desks with only the slightest shift. "They based everything on the assumption that at the absolute worst defaults would hit six percent. They had historically been one percent. People get very attached to their homes."

"Ya think?" Riley said.

"So that even if the entire bottom tranch, say twenty percent, defaults, the two top tranches are one hundred percent safe. Except that housing had never seen the leaping increases that occurred in the first ten years of the new century. So historical data might not have been the best indicator, but no one wanted to think about that. People took out home equity loans or bought houses on spec based on the assumption that the value would *keep* shooting up. Construction workers and waitresses were trying to become real estate moguls. But every market eventually saturates, and defaulting on an investment is not as wrenching as suddenly being out on the street.

"So banks finally realized their mistake and a bunch of mortgage lenders went out of business or got bought by other banks and they all tightened up their lending practices. Well, when the dust settled, people still wanted mortgages. They still wanted refis and home equity loans. They looked around for lenders and found a vacuum. And you know what they say about a vacuum."

Jack glanced at Maggie as if expecting her to jump in, which for some reason made her smile.

"It sucks up the dirt?" Riley suggested.

Pierce Bowman laughed. "I was going to say nature abhors one, but yours is probably more apropos in this case."

Jack said, "And this has to do with Sterling because . . . ?"

"Enter Joanna Moorehouse, who goes right back into the subprime mortgage business that everyone else had just gotten out of. In no time at all she's trading into the billions with some decent tranches . . . but of course she also has a number of trades that completely suck. I'm interested in buying her good stuff, not the crap."

"And Joanna—"

"Said it was all or nothing. She's ready—she *was* ready—to move into the big tree in the Big Apple. But I wasn't biting."

"And Lauren and Leroy Sherman?"

"They were all for splitting the company, if that was what it took to shake the dust of Sterling Financial off their feet."

"But Joanna didn't agree."

"Vociferously. Sherman is one of those who keeps his head down and lets everyone else get shot first, but Lauren would get into it with Joanna. These glass walls look nice and fancy and 'aren't we all so honest,' but they don't block sound all that well. No secrets here."

Riley spelled it out. "So you think Lauren killed Joanna to get the merger done."

Bowman laughed. "No! Sorry, didn't mean to imply that. Lauren talks a good game but she's no Lucretia Borgia. She's not even a Joanna. Now if *Lauren* had been killed. . . ."

Riley said, "So you don't work for Sterling. But you have an office—"

"Just temporary. I evicted the in-house counsel—poor kid."

"How long have you been at this location, then? In Cleveland?"

"Two, two and a half weeks. It should only take another few days; then Dhaval and I will be done and out of here." He glanced out the window at Cleveland's downtown. "Thank God."

"And when you say 'done'—"

"After due diligence we'll have a finalized proposal of what portion of Sterling we're willing to buy and what they're going to have to dump. Then Joanna can—could—take it or leave it." He grew pensive and added, "I hope this doesn't delay things. I'm not sure exactly how their charter . . . I assume Leroy and Lauren take over, which will be good for me. They're on board and the deal will go through." His face cleared. Maggie could imagine him thinking "win-win for everybody."

Except, of course, Joanna.

Chapter 8

Beyond that Pierce Bowman had nothing to add. He hadn't known Joanna Moorehouse or anyone else at Sterling longer than the few weeks he'd been there, had no personal relationship with any of them, had never been to Joanna's house, and had no idea if she had any enemies other than the protesters outside. Even they did not rise above small-town antics to him. "You should have seen Wall Street during the Occupy movement days. I went to work every day waiting for someone to toss a grenade into our lobby or coat all our *Journals* in anthrax powder. Bastards."

To Maggie's surprise, he gave up buccal swabs and fingerprints without complaint. Perhaps he simply didn't want Lauren Schneider to show him up; as he elbowed the conference room door open he threw a challenging glance toward her office. Then he continued to the men's room with his hands balled into fists to keep the ink from brushing any part of his suit.

Riley leaned over the radiator cover, stretching out

his back and watching the people on the sidewalk. "I think they're breaking for lunch. Speaking of which—"

"You're hungry," Jack finished for him, as if this were a foregone conclusion.

"I was thinking that if our day traders out there get the munchies, we can't stop 'em. Our guy could go out for burgers and never come back."

"Yeah," Jack said. "But that officer standing at the elevator doors—with his required body cam we will have nice close-up shots of anyone who leaves."

"Thank you, ACLU," Riley muttered. "Those body cams work both ways."

They were tense, Maggie saw, and thought she could understand why. Being here at all was a gamble. These were the early hours of an investigation into a brutal murder, and if Joanna Moorehouse had been slaughtered by an ex-boyfriend or a long-lost child looking to inherit, then these hours would have been a complete waste of time. And looking at the people at their desks, so focused on interest rates and market shares, it was hard to believe any one of them could have plunged a knife into a human being again and again with the same intense drive.

The elevator *dinged* and a delivery boy—man— laden with a stack of white boxes emerged. Everyone looked, without pausing in their phone conversations, their gazes following the tower of sustenance as the delivery guy moved over to a large table in the corner and set them down with an assurance born of practice.

Riley said, "There. Munchies averted."

The very pretty young woman Maggie had noticed

earlier finished a call, went over and paid the man. They exchanged a laugh, he left, and one by one, managers took a break from the desk work to drift over to the salads and sandwiches. The woman came to the conference room and told the cops and Maggie to help themselves if they were hungry. Her name was Tyra Simmons, and she was Sterling's in-house counsel. "Seriously, we always have too much food. Most of these guys are like teenage boys. Some days they inhale the whole table, and other times they forget to eat altogether."

Riley asked if she could spare them a few minutes.

The smile wiped from her face, but she took a seat and explained her position there. Every investment firm had their own lawyer, particularly important in this day and age. Real estate and fiduciary laws varied by state and sometimes by city and, on top of that, changed often. Regulatory requirements from the Federal Reserve and SEC were a constant challenge. It kept her busy, she finished wearily.

Riley asked, "Are there any lawsuits pending against Sterling?"

"Right at the moment? About forty-eight." At their surprised looks, she said, "That's pretty average for this market share."

"What are they, um, regarding?"

She brushed a handful of long dark hair over one shoulder. "People not happy with the return on their investments. People not happy with their mortgage payments. People not happy with being evicted after they couldn't make their mortgage payments. Other companies not happy because we're taking their customers too easily. That sort of thing. Normal, unfortunately, in the business world."

"Let's talk about the suits right here in the Cleveland area," Riley said.

"Forty-eight," Tyra Simmons said. "Those are the ones in Cleveland. Nationally, I couldn't guess. Ninety-nine percent are nuisances with no legal merit."

"Any one-percenters that come to mind?"

She thought, a line forming between her perfectly shaped eyebrows, and drummed one set of long nails on the tabletop. "Ned sicced a class action on us regarding one of our power loans."

"Ned Swift?"

"The same."

"Was Joanna worried?"

Tyra shook her head.

"Any of this class action group get especially hyper, especially toward Joanna?"

"No. Just Ned. He showed up here a few times. He would demand meetings with me and her, but then he didn't have anything new to say so we started to refuse anything if it didn't happen in front of a judge."

"What happens to the suit now?"

She blinked. "Nothing. I mean, nothing changes. It was brought against Sterling, not Joanna personally. Though . . . she got some pretty ugly letters. Joanna would shrug them off but I could see they bothered her."

Jack's interest seemed to perk up. "Did she keep them?"

"I did." She spoke more surely now, perhaps glad to

have some concrete way to help. "I insisted. You never know what will help in a lawsuit."

The slender woman popped up without further warning and went to her office.

"There's something she's not telling us," Riley fretted.

"She's a lawyer," Jack said. "There's probably worlds she's not telling us. Like maybe Sterling Financial is as crooked as hell."

Tyra returned with a green hanging file. Maggie gloved up and took it from her; if they wanted to collect fingerprints from the pages it would be best not to add more of their own. But paging through the sheets with Riley and Jack looking over her shoulder, it seemed that processing wouldn't be necessary. The authors were not anonymous. They included their names and addresses as they told Joanna Moorehouse that she and Sterling Financial were "thieves," "hucksters," "economic vampires who sucked the lives from their already weakened prey." The effect of this somewhat elegant analogy had been ruined by a very less elegant illustration of a devil-like scourge supping at the neck of a prone stick figure. Drops of blood in contrasting ink added a finishing touch of drama.

"Let's start with this guy," Riley suggested.

But the next missive trumped the drawing since it described Sterling, and Joanna personally, as "a money-sucking leech whore who ought to be burned at the stake."

"That one kind of scared me," Tyra admitted. "I insisted we update our security system here. Joanna even said she had gotten one for her home, so I know it bothered her."

The low murmur of voices and activity outside suddenly bounced higher, into an excited waterfall. Riley crossed to the window and looked out. "Miss Simmons, is that Ned Swift?"

She moved to his side, lithe as a cat, and took one quick peek. "Oh yeah. That's him."

Riley and Jack exchanged a look, then mobilized without a word. They were stepping into the elevator before Jack noticed Maggie behind them.

"You stay here," he ordered as he punched a button.

What was she supposed to do there? "Why?"

"Can never be sure about a mob." The doors closed.

She stood there, stupidly watching the light move down the crack in the middle as the car descended. What did that mean? Were the irate customers going to attack the detectives with pitchforks and hand-lettered signs when they took away the group's leader? Would a riot ensue? What should she do?

She returned to the window, pressing her forehead against the hot glass in order to see the sidewalk below. From that angle the half closest to the building was lost, but she caught a glimpse of Jack's shoulders and Riley's thinning red strands as they approached a middle-aged man with curly hair and a lightweight plaid jacket. The cops spoke, the group of protesters hovered like agitated bees, Maggie watched, and then Jack moved toward the building and out of her sight.

Ned Swift turned out to be a wiry man with sandy blond hair, almost as tall as Jack, with round glasses and a few ancient acne scars marring an otherwise cherubic face. When the detectives emerged from the building he said only, "Did they call the cops on us again? We have a permit."

Riley straddled tough and friendly with this guy, telling him that they had no problem with the protest but would appreciate a few moments of his time, his words reassuring but his tone firm. Swift didn't mind. He agreed instantly and entered the cool lobby with a cheery wave to his acolytes, who, after a few worried looks, carried on wending through the sweltering morning without him.

The detectives settled on the leather furniture, next to the piano. The stone and glass of the walls nearly soundproofed the room and it was nicely quiet, save for the clicking of the receptionist's keyboard and the tinkling hush of a tiny Zen waterfall on the end table.

Riley flipped open his notebook. "Can you summarize for us exactly what your problem is with Joanna Moorehouse?"

"Certainly." Swift settled more comfortably into the soft armchair and straightened his jacket, releasing a puff of Axe body spray into the atmosphere. "If you remember the housing bust, 2008, thirty percent of Slavic village homes went into foreclosure, Cleveland led the country in vacant homes, etcetera etcetera?"

This time Riley said only, "Yes."

"Because mortgage originators like Sterling made loans to people they knew bloody well could never pay them. They set it up, collect their fees for doing a little paperwork, the investors get monthly payments, borrowers begin paying off their house, everybody's happy."

"So what's the problem?"

"You know how that Greek guy said everything had to be in moderation?"

"Yeah?"

"When there's money being made, moderation goes out the window. Even people with bad credit don't want to pay high rates and, obviously, don't have the money to pay high *payments*, so . . . creative math. Adjustable rates that you can 'lock in'—except the rate you're locking in is a completely different rate, prime plus whatever the bank feels like tacking on, so from day one this will already be *higher* than a thirty-year fixed. Low rates with balloon payments, which would work out fine if you know you're going to win the lottery in three years. Interest-only payments, in which you aren't paying a penny of the principal until the payment leaps up by one or two hundred percent in, say, seven years."

"But—" Riley began.

"Exactly. Why make loans you know are going to fail? Because Wall Street compensation is based on that year's performance. All the higher-ups get bonuses based on a percentage of profit—for CEOs this can be millions, double- and triple-digit millions. So when they will make more in one year than most people could make in several lifetimes, they don't think in the long run.

"These firms—Ameriquest, Long-Term Capital, Long Beach Mortgage, and now Sterling—they don't care if they falsify paperwork, whether they let their clients lie about their income, whether they flat-out defraud their clients by pretending to sign them up for a fixed rate and then fake the papers to put them in an adjustable rate—because by the time their monthly payment suddenly triples and they default, the original firm is long out of it and the borrower is arguing with a company that never knew them and only knows what the original firm told it." Ned went on, using both hands for emphasis, "Unfortunately, the sophistication of the American borrower had not caught up by 2008 and isn't much better now."

Jack tugged at his tie. Ned Swift seemed calm and scholarly with a good grasp of the facts. He also seemed to loathe Sterling Financial and Joanna Moore-house from the tips of his reddened ears to the raging tremor racing through his voice.

"People have to fight back. Cleveland and a bunch of other cities sued the lenders, but the mortgage banker's association donated a few million to the state political parties and the lawsuits were thrown out. The Federal Reserve, the SEC, Congress threw up their hands and said there was nothing they could do. In 2008 the music finally stopped and some dancers collapsed, the government bailed out the rest, and our lawmakers were supposed to make laws so this couldn't happen again."

Jack's legs twitched, aching to move, to do some-thing.

"Except with caps on their compensation the invest-ment banks and mortgage banks had plenty of money to keep up the kickbacks to the political parties, so the new laws wound up watered down into trickles."

"Wait," Jack said. "Are you protesting things that happened ten years ago, or things that are happening now?"

"The past is preface," Swift said, but wiped away the smug tone when he saw Jack's lack of appreciation for it. "The behavior I protested in 2008 slunk away for a while, laid low but never went away. Mortgage secu-rities were a cash cow, and just because we slaughtered the cow doesn't mean people lost their taste for milk. The big firms reined it in because no one, not even them, wants to go through *that* again, but little places like Joanna's saw opportunity. Have you noticed commercials for instant credit and cold calls from barely legal sharks offering anyone who answers a no-collateral, pick-a-payment loan? They're *baaack*—doing all the bad things they did before, but this time having the sense to get out before someone blows too hard on their house of cards. Why do you think Joanna's selling to DJ Bryan?"

"So you're saying Sterling knowingly made bad loans?"

The smugness returned and Swift spoke with exaggerated patience. "Yes. One of her victims—I have the copies right here"—he pawed through a battered leather carryall full of files and dog-eared pages—"wanted a refi to put a roof on her house. Eighty-five, and she's going to be kicked out of the home she raised her children in. Tina, a part-time waitress in Tremont told the loan officer she only made about three-fifty a week. Including tips. He said no problem and added a zero. A welfare mother on Quincy bought a three-bedroom, two-bath bungalow in Brooklyn. A guy named Kurt—"

Riley interrupted. "Okay. So Sterling is a predatory lender and you're organizing a class action lawsuit. But what is your relationship with Joanna Moorehouse?"

Swift put his files aside. "She's the head of the snake. She knew exactly what she was doing every step of the way."

"How long have you been acquainted with Ms. Moorehouse?"

Swift finally picked up on the oddity of Riley's questioning. "Our lawsuit is against Sterling. What, is Joanna whining about the protests, or the letters? Is she going to—"

"How did you know about the letters?"

He paused, but only for the briefest second. "She all but threw them in my face last time I saw her."

"And that was?"

He made a show of thinking, chin in one hand, staring into the distance. His gaze fell on the people on the sidewalk outside, and the lines around his mouth softened as when a mother looks upon her brood. "About two weeks ago. The gargoyle in the back lot knocks off at six and our Joanna tends to work late."

"So you laid in wait by her car?"

He frowned at the wording. "No! I just wanted to make sure she would personally be in court for the hearing the next day. Instead she shrieked at me about getting irate letters."

Jack tried to break up the guy's chain of thought. "Why is DJ Bryan interested in buying them if Sterling is an empty shell?"

"Ah, excellent question. Why are they? And why don't the investors who are buying these toxic assets know that they're toxic?" He didn't wait for them to answer. "One word: ratings."

The cops said nothing, mainly because they had no idea what he was talking about.

"Securities are rated according to their risk level. Triple-A is the best you can get; that should be a secure investment for anyone, mutual fund, Goldman Sachs, anybody. Most of Joanna's tranches were rated triple-A by Carter & Poe, an esteemed ratings agency."

"Okay," Riley said. "So they were good."

"No, they sucked."

"So why did . . ."

". . . they get a good rating? Excellent question." He gazed at Riley over steepled fingers.

"How about you answer it, then?" Obviously Riley had had enough of MBA school. So had Jack. Perhaps they could get the white-collar unit to take on a murder case . . . nah.

"Carter & Poe's have about eight thousand employees, eleven of them here in Cleveland. The one assigned to Sterling drives a Porsche and lives in Gates Mills."

"Is that unusual?"

"A little bit," Swift said as if he found this amusing. "Their staff makes good money—*everybody* who works in the financial world makes money that the rest of us can only envy—but I have a friend at the IRS who says he doesn't make *that* much."

"Does your friend often violate privacy laws?"

"Every chance he gets. Actually, I'm exaggerating—I don't know what Mr. Fourtner's paycheck totals. But he's either very bad at his job to screw up a rating that badly, or he's very good at getting side work."

Riley said, "You think Joanna paid him off."

"I do indeed."

Riley switched tacks again. "When did you go to her house?"

Swift frowned again. "I never went to her house. I don't even know where she lives. Why—why all the questions all of a sudden? I've been trying to get someone to pay attention to Sterling's thievery for months now."

"Where were you last night?"

"I left the law center about seven, met friends for dinner, went home to my wife. Why? Someone key her car?"

"She's dead."

Swift looked surprised, or gave a good imitation of looking surprised. "*Dead*? How?"

"Last night," Riley answered without answering, "who were the friends at this dinner?"

The man remained silent, running through the implications of this question. "She was *murdered*?"

"We're still determining the circumstances. What makes you assume that?"

"I don't think you'd be asking me for an alibi if she got in a car accident. Was it—suicide? Are you sure she's even dead? This deal with Bryan is dragging—if they're actually doing due diligence for a change. Maybe they found that Joanna is in bed with that nice boy from Carter & Poe. Bryan is too big to fall into that trap again. It would be every bit Joanna Moorehouse to cut and run. She's probably on a yacht in Malaysia."

"I can assure you she's not on a yacht in Malaysia."

"Huh. Well, that's . . . interesting. Doesn't really change anything as far as the lawsuit goes, but Joanna would have been great to put a face on the company. Any jury in the world would hate her on sight. Though Lauren's nearly as unlikeable." He gazed again at the protesters on the sidewalk, now worried for their future. For Joanna Moorehouse's lack of same, no worry at all. But then, they'd hardly been friends. Not at all.

"Can we have the name of the restaurant?" Riley went on.

"What, you mean you're actually going to check—like I'm a *suspect*?"

"We're actually going to check."

This still seemed to amuse him more than anything, and he gladly gave up the location, the names of his friends, the name of his wife, and their home phone number. But fingerprints and cheek swab, no. Not a chance.

Of course, they had no grounds to insist, so the cops and the rabble-rouser parted ways amicably enough. At least on his part.

"What do you think?" Riley asked as they stepped into the elevator.

"He talks a good game."

"People who spend their time suing other people usually do. But I'm not ready to count him out."

"Me neither," Jack agreed.

Chapter 9

From the window above Maggie watched the protesters restart marching in a loose circle. No cries of foul arose and none started using their signs as weapons, so apparently Ned Swift was only too happy to discuss Sterling Financial and Joanna Moorehouse with Jack and Riley.

Tyra Simmons had returned to her desk. Maggie flipped through the rest of the letters, saw nothing too outrageous. Her stomach growled but she was stuck—she couldn't leave as long as the detectives might need her, for more prints or in case Ned Swift turned out to have a knife injury on his hand where his fingers slid down the bloody hilt as he stabbed Joanna Moorehouse. If Denny needed her he would call, so she had no reason to insist on leaving. But she also had no reason to starve herself. The lunch break had wound down, and as Tyra promised, a number of containers remained on the table in the corner. Maggie left the conference room, padding silently past the absorbed managers.

The containers were labeled, a variety of salads and sandwiches, all with the logo "Totally Fresh!" in swirls of green.

"Help yourself." Anna Hernandez appeared at her elbow. "They always overorder. I've taken leftovers home for dinner practically every night this week. Believe it or not, for alpha types like these guys, it's pretty healthy stuff. Maybe they think the antioxidants counteract sitting at a phone all day."

"Thanks." Maggie selected a salad topped with grilled chicken.

"You're on a break?" Anna snagged a sandwich and a can of iced tea.

"Sort of. The detectives are downstairs talking to Ned Swift."

"That jerk. I hope they arrest him."

"Why?" They wandered back to the sitting area, Anna shoving her binders aside so they could set their drinks on the coffee table. Maggie didn't normally lunch with murder suspects or witnesses or family/friends, but if she went back to the conference room she would eat with her face plastered to the window to make sure Jack and Riley weren't being lynched from a light pole.

And large chunks of forensic work involve waiting. Waiting for search warrants, waiting on ME investigators, waiting for firemen to douse the flames, waiting for EMS to extract a driver from their T-boned car. She was used to waiting.

The young man from DJ Bryan had earbuds and seemed to be listening to music as he worked. It probably helped with his concentration to block out the hubbub. If he noticed Anna and Maggie, he didn't acknowledge them.

"He hates us. The Federal Reserve, I mean. That's his actual slogan, 'Ned versus the Fed.' Ridiculous. Like the whole 'audit the Fed' movement. We're already audited by the General Accounting Office, always have been." She chewed thoughtfully. "But he can get traction because most citizens don't understand what the Federal Reserve does. It's probably like how people react to you, at the police department, because you can't stop all crime. Everyone believes 'the government' is this omnipotent, consistent block of law when it's really a conglomeration of stuff that has grown up over time. The too-big-to-fail banks that got the bailouts? Only half were overseen by the Federal Reserve—JPMorgan, Wells Fargo, Bank of New York Mellon, Bank of America—and half of those didn't even *need* the bailout, but they had to go along to avoid stigmatizing and causing a run on the ones that did. Okay, BOA and Citigroup did, mostly because BOA had bought the disaster known as Countrywide—sorry, I'm losing you."

"No, go on. I find this interesting," Maggie assured her. What the heck, she had time to kill, and dwelling on ten-year-old events kept Anna from asking her questions she couldn't let herself answer. Such as how Joanna Moorehouse's intestines looked while spread across her marble floor.

"My point is the others—Merrill Lynch, Goldman Sachs, Morgan Stanley—were regulated by the SEC. AIG was an insurance company. Lehman, which of course didn't get a bailout, was SEC. Fannie Mae and Freddie Mac were under the Office of Federal Housing Enterprise Oversight, which Fannie and Freddie kept gutted of any real power because they had a take-no-prisoners stranglehold on Congress. All those sub-prime mortgages? Only about twenty percent were from banks under Fed regulation. Okay, I have a plastic Ben Bernanke on my dashboard and I think Janet Yellen is the bee's knees, so yes, I'm biased. But prior to the crash no one had heard the term *bubble*. Only thirteen percent of mortgages were subprime and the fixed rate subprime was doing fine. Not one bank failed in 2005, for the first time since the institution of the FDIC in 1933. And of subprime mortgages only twenty percent were at banks regulated by the Fed. All the others were SEC, Office of the Comptroller of the Currency, Federal Housing Oversight—which was part of the problem, of course."

Maggie curled herself into the leather couch and dug into the salad. It had some kind of dressing, to her initial dismay, as she avoided dressings of any kind. Then she took a tentative bite. "Oh my gosh, this is good."

"Told you."

"It tastes like they just picked it out of a garden."

"Yeah, they're right up the street. You've never been there? You're in the Justice Center, right?"

"Yes." *Keep the conversation away from you.* "So what went wrong? With the securities?"

The young woman tucked her feet up under her legs, making herself comfortable on the leather sofa. "Wall Street is like the mafia when it comes to skimming. Every time a financial product changes hands, someone takes a cut. The money is in the fees. Kind of like airlines these days, or medicine. That's why doctors order a boatload of tests that you probably don't need—maybe they're being safe, and maybe they're purposely racking up the hospital system's bill. It's a volume business. Suddenly there was a price war in the mortgage business. Adjustable rates, teaser rates, balloon payments—any way they could get those first few payments, sometimes only the *first* payment, as low as possible to get people to sign on the dotted line, they'd do it. They'd call up their investors at JPMorgan or Merrill Lynch and ask if they'd buy ninety-five percent—loans where borrowers were only putting five percent down. Yes? What about ninety-seven? What about one hundred, no money down, no income verification? Insanity, right?"

Maggie speared a cucumber slice and agreed.

"Except they'd look around at their fellow firms who were making money by the boatloads and they'd say, yeah, I guess we'll do that. They weren't stupid— these are really smart, really tough moneymakers, but risk assessment is all about history and subprime mortgages didn't have much of a history. As a significant section of the loan market, they hadn't been around that long. Anyway, back to the Fed. Computer trading and statistical models made trading so fast and so complicated that no one knew how bad their exposure was. So when some banks finally got nervous about their subprime exposure and tried to pull it in a little, that was a pinhole in a very weak dike. Banks started dumping their subprime securities, the value of the securities dropped because everyone was selling them at once, and it all devolved into a shame spiral. Banks who had been loaning money to everyone and their brother stopped loaning it to anyone, even each other."

"A panic," Maggie said.

"An old-fashioned panic. That doesn't happen at reg-

ular old depository banks anymore because the FDIC
insures our deposits. But investment banks, bank holding companies, insurance companies aren't regular old
depository banks. Their investments can only be insured using other investments, and when they all went
down the tubes—"

"Crash."

"Every economy in the world came to a screeching
halt in September 2008. And many other countries
don't have comprehensive deposit insurance like the
FDIC. 'Cats and dogs, living together, mass hysteria.'"
She finished with the quote from *Ghostbusters*, and
drained the last of her iced tea. "And according to Ned
it's all our fault. I shouldn't joke—I'm not joking—it
was decidedly *not* funny. DC was like the land of the
walking dead, only not the slow-moving out-of-it zombies, the superfast man-eating kind. If I had ever
thought I had any genuine friends there, I quickly got
disabused of that notion."

"You spent a lot of time there?"

"I lived there for twelve years," Anna said. "Just a
little girl from Kansas, I thought I'd made the big time.
Bright lights and monuments. One year I even got to
go to the Jackson Hole conference. But fortunes eventually shifted and I got exiled here."

"Oh." Maggie spoke without inflection.

"And discovered there was a place left on earth
where real human beings did real work and really cared
about other human beings. People picked dinner com-
panions without thinking about which political party
happened to be waxing or waning at the moment. I
could live downtown without maxing out my credit

cards. I found a boyfriend who actually seems to have a soul. Hell"—Anna slumped until the back of her neck rested on the top of the sofa—"I'm never going back."

"I'm glad to hear that," Maggie said. "Cleveland has a little bit of a self-esteem problem."

"Hah! Try being from DC. Everyone else in the country hates you on principle."

Maggie set her empty container on the coffee table. Riley and Jack had not reappeared. She didn't want to break her don't-interrupt-police-interviews rule in case they were getting somewhere with Ned Swift, but she still might be able to make herself useful. "And this week you're here with Sterling Financial. What did you think of Joanna Moorehouse?"

"A coldhearted snake," Anna said promptly, then sat up in surprise. "Oh, that's terrible! I shouldn't talk about someone dead that way."

"It's okay, she won't hear you. And the truth is more important than platitudes right now."

Anna nodded, but took some time to think over her next words. "Of course, I never saw her anywhere but here, and never discussed anything but which records I needed to review and how long it should take me. So who knows—she could have fed the homeless and played with kittens and thrown marvelous dinner parties in her spare time, but all I got to see was a totally focused, all-business CEO in no uncertain terms. She made decisions instantly and unilaterally, never any comments about needing to discuss something with her staff. She would give me only what I needed and exactly that—needed by her terms, not mine."

Maggie steered back to the murder at hand. "But Joanna wanted this merger to go through."

"Oh yeah. She seemed . . . excited. It's the only time I've seen any animation out of her—a sort of humming tension to her body is the only way I can describe it. But a happy tension. That's what passed for emotion, I guess, for a—"

"Coldhearted snake."

"Yeah. That *is* mean. I know nobody likes seeing regulators on their doorstep. We disrupt, interrupt, take up space. But most places at least pretend to be friendly. Joanna never pretended anything."

"What about the other people here? Anyone *against* the merger?"

Anna gazed out at the floor. "Don't seem to be. I've heard some of the more junior managers griping about it, worried that jobs will be cut and those jobs will be theirs, which is probably true. But certainly no one sounded upset enough to kill over it. How was she killed, anyway?"

Maggie coughed.

"Oh—you can't tell me that, can you?"

"No, sorry."

"That's okay. I get it. . . . Are you sure it wasn't some crime of passion thing? I can't see little Jeremy offing anybody, but who knows what other kind of people—Joanna *must* have had some personal life, didn't she? Doesn't everybody?"

"You'd think so." But if Joanna Moorehouse had had secrets, lies, and passionate entanglements in her life, she had kept them very well hidden—*so* well buried that she may have helped to cover up her own murder.

"Your friends are back," Anna pointed out, as Jack and Riley emerged from the elevator.

They interviewed everyone else in the office; most conversations went quickly. The managers simply worked there; they weren't personal friends of Joanna and she didn't talk to them much except to tell them they were doing something wrong. But the job paid well and only that mattered to them; they didn't need pats on the back. A few argued with Lauren frequently over this deal or that, but conflicts were purely business and murdering Joanna wouldn't have resolved any of them. Three young men—the same three Maggie had seen huddling over their desks—banded together and refused to give up either DNA or fingerprints. If they'd hoped for a dramatic stand on civil rights they were disappointed; the detectives merely shrugged and said that was entirely up to them. They did, however, make careful note of their names and general description. Still photos could be seized later from the patrol officer's body cam. Meanwhile, Maggie helped herself to the copy machine's store of clean paper to finish the fingerprinting.

Jack grew tired of hearing about banking and deals and capital requirements but couldn't shake the feeling that the reason for Joanna's murder sat there somewhere, visible through those glass walls, if only he could get a handle on the motive or if someone would give themselves away with a tiny slip or a furtive look. Nothing happened, and the Medical Examiner's office called to say the body had been prepared for autopsy, and did they plan to attend.

"Yes," Jack told them. Then he left the offices of Sterling Financial with the sickly feeling that they hadn't yet learned a damn thing about who had murdered Joanna Moorehouse.

Chapter 10

The autopsy suite smelled as it always did, like a very clean slaughterhouse, wafts of disinfectant swirling around the stench of blood and offal. It was not bad, relatively speaking. Postmortems on the day's other victims had been completed and Joanna's corpse had the room to itself. Decomposition had only just begun, her flesh still firm and white; but the opened stomach and intestines smelled rank. The air-conditioning was functioning properly today, so all in all, not the worst visit to the morgue Maggie had ever experienced. Relatively speaking.

She had come hoping to collect some hairs and fibers from the victim's clothing—obviously this crime had been up close and personal, and she hoped for some transfer from the suspect—but that idea had been quickly dashed. When the killer had cut open the shirt, pants, and underwear they had flopped to the side and soaked up the blood and fluids seeping from the body. They were now stiffened, saturated planks. The trace evidence specialist had attempted to "tape" them, and passed the tapes (affixed to sheets of clear acetate) over to Maggie, but even with the naked eye she could see there wasn't much there. Any loose fibers from the suspect were now welded to the late Joanna's clothing.

But the pathologist had already completed more than half the autopsy, so Maggie figured she might as well stay for the rest. No surprises cropped up. Cause of death was, as expected, exsanguination—Joanna Moorehouse had bled out, and rather quickly. Before they'd been sliced and diced the stomach had been empty and the lungs had been clear. The liver showed no signs of cirrhosis. Toxicology results would take a few days, but it seemed that Joanna Moorehouse had been a healthy woman with no signs of alcohol or drug abuse.

"Not exactly an athlete, though," the doctor muttered, poking at the musculature with one gloved finger. "I wouldn't say she worked out. She probably kept her figure by simply not eating."

"That makes sense," Maggie said. "I didn't see any workout equipment at her house. I don't think she even owned a pair of running shoes. Highly fashionable Mephisto hiking boots, yes, but without even a scuff on the soles."

"She worked in an office," Riley said, visibly wincing as the diener—the assistant—took a scalpel and sliced the scalp open from ear to ear. Then he took a chisel and separated the flesh from the skull, flopping it open so the cranium could be sawed in half.

Joanna Moorehouse would never be beautiful again.

"Ever seen anything like this?" Riley asked the doctor.

"Had a woman stabbed last month, pretty bad, nothing like this but pretty bad. They thought her boyfriend did it, but his pals covered for him."

"One in spring," the diener added. "Chick in Maple Heights. One wound, but it almost took her head off."

"Sounds like the mob," Riley said.

"Or some foreign shit."

"This woman has to have some relatives somewhere," Maggie burst out, apparently startling the detectives, who turned to glance at her. "Have we even found next of kin yet?"

Riley said, "No one has a clue. That Lauren woman said Joanna had never, ever talked of her family, not where she was born, not where she went to school. She had Duke University listed on her CV, but that's as far into her past as she went. We can hope IT finds something in her electronics, a text, an e-mail, anything."

"Why?" Jack asked her.

Maggie shrugged. "It seems . . . a little pathetic. This woman seems to have been the envy of anyone who saw her, but here she is being sli—autopsied— and no one on the planet seems to give a crap."

Riley agreed. "Even Jeremy didn't seem to regard her as anything more than a good deal. Hot, *and* the boss."

Jack said, "She made her choices."

Maggie looked at him. The words sounded harsh, but the tone didn't. . . . More regretful. Was he picturing himself on that slab? That someday he would die among strangers, such as herself, who didn't even know his real name? Who if they knew a few of his secrets, such as herself, might feel only relief?

We all make choices, she thought.

The pathologist said, "Hmm," interrupting the ruminations of everyone else in the room, who then demanded to know what he meant.

"Hematoma to the back of the head." He prodded a large dark red mass along the inside of the scalp, between the flesh and the bone of the skull. "Somebody socked her a good one."

"Would it have knocked her out?" Riley asked.

The pathologist sighed. "Why do you always ask me that? There's no way to tell. It wouldn't have killed her, I can tell you that. It didn't get a chance to swell enough to endanger anything and . . . it didn't crack the skull." He peered at the bone, running bloody but gloved fingers over the rounded surface. "I don't think so, any . . . maybe a little tiny one, a hairline crack . . . maybe not."

"So he hit her with something," Jack interpreted.

"Dunno. It seems pretty unformed. No defined edges . . . a very blunt blunt object."

Maggie pictured the gleaming living room. "What about the floor? Marble tile?"

"Mmm, yeah. If he had smacked her backward good and hard. Or maybe she slipped, feet went out from under her. It could be that simple. I had a grandmother slip on a ceramic tile floor . . . was mopping it in her bare feet. . . ."

He murmured on but Maggie stopped listening. Joanna Moorehouse could have been running away from her attacker—the house had so little furniture or other décor that someone could have chased her through those rooms without disturbing anything. Or the victim could have been in the living room backing away from him and tripped over the dais steps. Or they could have been having a quiet conversation until he abruptly shoved her backward onto the marble tiles. The blow might not have knocked her out, but she could have been dazed, seen stars or simply reacted to the pain. And in that split second, he was on her, stabbing and slicing.

"Any sign of sexual assault?" she asked.

"Don't see any. We took swabs, of course."

No apparent motive. No apparent beneficiaries. No apparent suspects.

Very strange, Maggie thought. Very, very strange.

The next morning Maggie felt refreshed. She had gone to bed at a reasonable hour after a short conversation with her brother, Alex, currently playing in the San Antonio area. He and Daisy had taken the kids to see the Alamo and bought them cowboy hats. That, he had assured his sister, did not mean his musical genre would be taking a turn toward the cornfields.

"Maybe you should consider it," she had told him. "You might get to meet Taylor Swift."

"That *is* incentive," he had agreed. "Did you get the bowl I sent you?"

"I did. Thank you so much. I put it on the table next to my door." She smiled as she said it, to inject some enthusiasm into the statement as she glanced at the large item on her tiny table, an overbalance waiting to happen.

"Do you like it?"

She glanced at it again, her gaze automatically moving to the door to be sure she had locked it—which she hadn't. A shadow moved along the crack at its bottom, one of her neighbors returning home. "It's . . . heavy."

"It's basalt," he said proudly. "Densest stone there is. The girls are learning about density. Cost me thirty dollars just to ship it, so now they know something about postal rates too."

"That's really cool, bro. I'm not sure how it goes with my décor—"

"You have décor?"

"Very funny." The shadow hadn't moved, oddly. The hallway doors were staggered so it couldn't be someone waiting to enter the apartment across the hall. Maggie stood up from the couch.

"But you like it?"

"Love it totally." Because it came from Alex. If anyone else had given it to her she'd think it a monstrosity of angles and a complete impracticality of houseware. She *snicked* the dead bolt into place, then, feeling silly, put her eye to the peephole. But the sliver of hallway within its range stood empty.

Meanwhile a satisfied Alex rang off to help his elder daughter with her math homework. Daisy homeschooled the kids on the road, darned her husband's stage outfits, and kept them all healthy. Maggie thought her sister-in-law had the patience of several saints melded together.

The touring kept Alex too busy to notice how Maggie spoke less and less of her job. She was afraid to, afraid to let something slip in an unguarded moment with her lifelong confidant. She had to think in two worlds now: the one she shared with other people, and her inner one, where only she knew exactly what she had done.

Well, she and Jack.

But Jack would be gone soon and nothing . . . bad . . . had happened. No unexplainable homicides had turned up, no one shot in an alley or some new and equally untraceable method of killing surfaced. Jack had kept his end of their bargain. Murders in Cleveland had continued, of course, but even the current unsolveds had strong suspects with none of them a mysterious vigilante. Rick seemed to have given up on the case, as he usually did on anything that proved too difficult. Her lab stayed calm, she and her coworkers worked to further the cause of justice, and Carol had new photos of her twin granddaughters. The sky outside bulged with heavy clouds but she had made it to the station without being soaked. So this morning all was right in Maggie's world.

Her outer world, anyway.

Then her ex-husband walked in.

Not a big deal, certainly. They were on amicable terms and got along well now that they no longer had to live together. Despite that, her heart still sank a little every time he showed up, especially when he wore the grumpy face that meant he'd shortly be yelling about something. Usually at her.

"Morning," she said. "What's up?"

He pulled over a task chair from the next bench and dropped himself into it, then pulled himself up to the high table she bent over with the latent prints from Joanna's crime scene. Her heart sank a little more at the idea he planned to stay a while.

"I was upstairs with the Graham trial," he said. "I interviewed one stinking witness, and I gotta go testify about it."

"That sucks."

"Everything about court sucks. Then they took my granola bar."

The non sequitur startled Maggie away from her fingerprints. "What?"

"I'm first on, so they want me there at eight, right? No time for my usual bagel, so I grabbed a granola bar that someone left on the counter in the report-writing room and took it up there, made it on time. Went through the metal detector, my keys set it off, they pat, find my breakfast and confiscate it. Turns out our poor innocent killer has a peanut allergy, so they have to make sure you don't even open a bag in the courtroom. The bailiff told me he thinks it's a ploy to put Graham in segregation at the jail. He thinks he's tough with his women, but general population would make mincemeat of that douche."

"Crazy."

"Yeah, the Latin Kings can't kill this guy but Mr. Peanut can wipe him right out. Go figure. Meanwhile, my stomach is rumbling. Want to get some lunch?"

"Sorry, I'm pretty swamped here."

"Besides, you just brown-bag an apple and yogurt, right?"

She had to smile. "Yep."

"Figured. Okay, well, I stopped in because I'm still working the vigilante killings."

"Yeah?"

She took the picture of the bloody print from under Joanna's body and placed a jeweler's loupe on top of it, which kept her from having to look at him.

"Is there anything you haven't told me about this guy? Any little detail?"

"No, of course not." Maggie figured it was reasonable to sound annoyed. She had gone through her story a number of times with all the detectives, and more than once with Rick and his partner. She had filled out a lengthy statement. She had completed all her required visits with the department psychologist. She had done her best to imitate a trauma victim trying hard to put it behind her.

"You said you didn't see his car."

"No. Only that woman's car, and I didn't really look at that."

"And the gun?"

"Twenty-two. I think, anyway. All black, no chrome."

"Ruger? Smith & Wesson?"

"Big and loaded. That's all I needed to know right at that moment." She gave a tiny shudder, a real one.

But Rick asked more. "A scar? An accent? A smell?"

"Smell? Seriously?"

He shrugged. "I'm grasping at straws here. I've got some damn reporter nagging me about other murders, kinda similar ones. I know she's trying to embellish a story but . . ."

Maggie carefully placed a set of ten-prints, rolled at the Sterling offices yesterday, next to her photo of the bloody print. She kept her voice level, polite. "Other murders?"

"Chicago, and Phoenix. Maybe Detroit. It's probably fantasy, I know. Finding gangbangers shot in alleys is a daily occurrence everywhere."

Maggie adjusted her loupe. "How many altogether?"

"I dunno. Twenty, maybe. That we know of."

Twenty. She had never asked Jack. She hadn't wanted to know and he wouldn't have told her anyway. He'd told her nothing of his life before they met. Hell, he'd told her nothing of his life *since* they'd met. They were hardly drinking buddies.

Twenty.

And she could solve them all, if she simply opened her mouth.

She looked up, opened her mouth—

"The guy's a killing machine, in other words," Rick went on. "And yet he didn't ki—hurt you. He left a witness who could identify him."

"Yeah?"

"You have to ask why."

"No, *you* have to ask. I'm just glad to be alive."

Her ex held up a hand. "Not trying to make you feel bad or anything. I know this isn't fun to talk about. But why did he let you go? It couldn't be because he wanted to get in your pants."

Which is the only reason any man would show her courtesy, she supposed. "You've asked me that. The shrink asked me that. Everyone, in one way or another, has asked me that. Because I didn't fit his criteria. He may be . . . crazy . . . but he has a code. I didn't fulfill it. There weren't any others? Witnesses in other cities? Ones who got away?"

Rick shrugged and said he didn't know before returning to his previous topic. "The only real interesting one is Phoenix, because they also had a woman running an illegal nursing home, left the people there to rot. Just like here."

Maggie's jaw clamped shut. Maria Stein. Jack had been on her trail but she had slipped away to come to Cleveland and spread her poison among the innocents there. If anyone had ever deserved to die . . . but "deserve" didn't enter into it. Maggie had to stay silent now because if she told the truth she would go to jail.

too generic. But that was okay—if she could
entify someone, tell the officers "I think it's
ut I can't swear to it," it would give them a
tart. If nothing else about that person fit the
n they would be cleared. But it was worth a
e as if a witness had seen a white Ford pickup
e scene so the detectives went out and ques-
owners of white Ford pickups. It didn't mean
ite Ford pickup owner had committed the
that the witness even saw a Ford and not a
ut if during an interview they discover that
Ford pickup owner lived nearby and had had
rgument with the victim the previous day,
e questions would therefore be warranted.
wever limited, the print had been the only
y the killer, and she would work it until her
ut.

one rang, startling her.

And she didn't want to spend half her life in prison on
behalf of Maria Stein.

"Really. And the person who did that was killed?"

"No, she got away. But the reporter looked for circumstances similar to our spree, I guess. I'm checking
with departments in Chicago and Detroit to see if they
had anything like that. They nearly laughed me off the
phone at first, since their homicide rates make Cleveland look like Disneyworld, but they're putting their
crime analysts on it. They're searching both methods
of murders and types of victims. And elder abuse."

"Oh," she said. "Good."

It would be normal, Maggie reminded herself, to be
curious. After all, she'd been both saved and "nearly
killed" by this mysterious vigilante. She abandoned
the prints entirely and gave her ex-husband her full attention. "So you think he was following that horrible
woman?"

"Yeah, it would make sense. Who knows? But this
reporter is going to keep making a stink until I come
up with something. I need to find out where he went.
Then I can point her there and it can be some other
city's problem."

Maggie nodded. "Unfortunately, he didn't share his
plans with me. Other than the description and sketch I
already gave you and that he probably owned a cat, I
can't help."

He studied her, gazing at her with more intensity than
she remembered from their brief marriage. "You're
sure."

"Yes! Yes. You've wrung every last detail out of me.
Believe me, if there was anything else I could tell you,
I would."

This was, of course, a bald-faced lie. But Rick had never been attuned to anyone's thoughts but his own. He wouldn't start now.

Would he?

She didn't like the coolly appraising stare. Rick didn't do cool appraisal. He did noise, force, bombast.

"Okay," he said at last, and she had to physically restrain herself from puffing out a held breath.

"Let me know what you find out," she said.

"What? Oh . . . okay." He got up to leave, but then turned back. "In that murder room. The one on Johnson Court."

"I remember." She wasn't bloody likely to forget.

"Did you see his car outside when you went in?"

She plunged her face back into her matching loupes, staring at the prints as if the dark flowing lines would give her a picture of what to say. She tried to remember the details of her original statement. She had a copy in her drawer for that exact reason. "Um . . . what I said before, dark sedan with one busted taillight. It was parked farther up the alley, so I didn't pay a lot of attention to it."

"Huh," Rick said. "Okay."

She kept her eyes glued to the small lenses until she heard his steps leaving the room, then let her forehead rest on them for a brief moment. Lying was hard. No wonder detectives simply kept asking the same questions until their targets slipped up. It would happen, eventually. It always did.

She couldn't change the past, couldn't take back her decision. She told herself to focus on what she *could* do, such as find Joanna Moorehouse's killer. The bloody print would not be easy to compare—the ridges

were clear, but generic, proba
of the finger where the patter
lines coming from one side an
middle to lower parts of a fing
more distinctive patterns: loo
the attendant deltas where th
roughly triangular shape. Abs
bloody print lacked a particu
close-knit combination of, say
a short ridge—that could give
for in the sets of ten-prints, an
efficiently eliminate possible n

The generic quality of the p
searching it very difficult. It
palm, but she didn't think so. T
or other patterns around it ma
finger. At least Maggie could
belong to Joanna Moorehouse.

She had run it through the A
the system had dutifully offere
matching patterns. Its first cho
of a young man named Damo
fectly, except for a scar that s
one side of the bloody print. T
placed Bruce Duffy next. His
fectly except that a feathering
ridge could have been a bifur
sponding ridge in his right mid
there.

Even if she found a match
rect, based on years and year
prints every day, she still mig
swearing to it in a court of law

print was
at least i
this guy
place to s
crime, th
try—sam
leaving t
tioned all
that a wl
crime, or
Chevy, b
one white
a bitter a
well, mor

But, he
clue left
eyes fell

Her ph

And she didn't want to spend half her life in prison on behalf of Maria Stein.

"Really. And the person who did that was killed?"

"No, she got away. But the reporter looked for circumstances similar to our spree, I guess. I'm checking with departments in Chicago and Detroit to see if they had anything like that. They nearly laughed me off the phone at first, since their homicide rates make Cleveland look like Disneyworld, but they're putting their crime analysts on it. They're searching both methods of murders and types of victims. And elder abuse."

"Oh," she said. "Good."

It would be normal, Maggie reminded herself, to be curious. After all, she'd been both saved and "nearly killed" by this mysterious vigilante. She abandoned the prints entirely and gave her ex-husband her full attention. "So you think he was following that horrible woman?"

"Yeah, it would make sense. Who knows? But this reporter is going to keep making a stink until I come up with something. I need to find out where he went. Then I can point her there and it can be some other city's problem."

Maggie nodded. "Unfortunately, he didn't share his plans with me. Other than the description and sketch I already gave you and that he probably owned a cat, I can't help."

He studied her, gazing at her with more intensity than she remembered from their brief marriage. "You're sure."

"Yes! Yes. You've wrung every last detail out of me. Believe me, if there was anything else I could tell you, I would."

This was, of course, a bald-faced lie. But Rick had never been attuned to anyone's thoughts but his own. He wouldn't start now.

Would he?

She didn't like the coolly appraising stare. Rick didn't do cool appraisal. He did noise, force, bombast.

"Okay," he said at last, and she had to physically restrain herself from puffing out a held breath.

"Let me know what you find out," she said.

"What? Oh . . . okay." He got up to leave, but then turned back. "In that murder room. The one on Johnson Court."

"I remember." She wasn't bloody likely to forget.

"Did you see his car outside when you went in?"

She plunged her face back into her matching loupes, staring at the prints as if the dark flowing lines would give her a picture of what to say. She tried to remember the details of her original statement. She had a copy in her drawer for that exact reason. "Um . . . what I said before, dark sedan with one busted taillight. It was parked farther up the alley, so I didn't pay a lot of attention to it."

"Huh," Rick said. "Okay."

She kept her eyes glued to the small lenses until she heard his steps leaving the room, then let her forehead rest on them for a brief moment. Lying was hard. No wonder detectives simply kept asking the same questions until their targets slipped up. It would happen, eventually. It always did.

She couldn't change the past, couldn't take back her decision. She told herself to focus on what she *could* do, such as find Joanna Moorehouse's killer. The bloody print would not be easy to compare—the ridges were clear, but generic, probably from the upper part of the finger where the pattern settles out into simple lines coming from one side and exiting the other. The middle to lower parts of a finger usually contained the more distinctive patterns: loops, whorls, arches, and the attendant deltas where the ridges diverged in a roughly triangular shape. Absent all that activity, the bloody print lacked a particular "starting point"—a close-knit combination of, say, a bifurcating ridge and a short ridge—that could give her something to look for in the sets of ten-prints, an anchor from which to efficiently eliminate possible matches.

The generic quality of the print made comparing or searching it very difficult. It could even be part of a palm, but she didn't think so. The lack of any smudges or other patterns around it made it seem like a single finger. At least Maggie could establish that it did not belong to Joanna Moorehouse.

She had run it through the AFIS system already, and the system had dutifully offered up its ten most closely matching patterns. Its first choice, the left index finger of a young man named Damon Martini, matched perfectly, except for a scar that should have snaked over one side of the bloody print. The system's logarithms placed Bruce Duffy next. His ridges also matched perfectly except that a feathering at the end of one bloody ridge could have been a bifurcation while the corresponding ridge in his right middle finger did not divide there.

Even if she found a match she believed to be correct, based on years and years of looking at fingerprints every day, she still might not feel comfortable swearing to it in a court of law. The information in the print was too generic. But that was okay—if she could at least identify someone, tell the officers "I think it's this guy but I can't swear to it," it would give them a place to start. If nothing else about that person fit the crime, then they would be cleared. But it was worth a try—same as if a witness had seen a white Ford pickup leaving the scene so the detectives went out and questioned all owners of white Ford pickups. It didn't mean that a white Ford pickup owner had committed the crime, or that the witness even saw a Ford and not a Chevy, but if during an interview they discover that one white Ford pickup owner lived nearby and had had a bitter argument with the victim the previous day, well, more questions would therefore be warranted.

But, however limited, the print had been the only clue left by the killer, and she would work it until her eyes fell out.

Her phone rang, startling her.

Chapter 11

Tyra Simmons's home couldn't have been more different from Joanna Moorehouse's. A small bungalow on the near east side that she had obviously renovated and decorated with care, it nearly burst with furniture and accoutrements and mementos of people Tyra Simmons loved. She had an expensive leather sofa but with a well-worn crocheted afghan scrunched in one corner. Her closet held designer clothes but also comfy T-shirts and a box of Barbie dolls and other childhood toys. Her bookshelves contained more than her law school textbooks—plenty of novels and a myriad of framed photographs, candid shots of the friends and family in Tyra's life. The two women did, however, share a fondness for takeout.

She had even kept an old-fashioned address book, as well as entries for "Mom" and "Dad" in her cell phone. It made notifying the next of kin much easier.

Her body, however, formed nearly a mirror image to Joanna's. Lying on her back with her clothing and then her torso splayed open, the knife having carved up deep sections of skin and organ, her face turned toward the ceiling with the utter hopelessness that came from feeling one's life slip away. But Tyra hadn't given it up easily. Her arms flopped open at her sides and bore numerous cuts and gashes. One finger had been nearly severed. But still her attacker came, slashing and stabbing until she went down and stayed down.

Maggie usually spent very little time feeling sorry for the victim. With only one chance to get everything at the crime scene done right she usually had too many other things to think of, things that would benefit the dead much more than her sympathy. But when she had met Tyra the day before, the vibrant, intelligent, concerned, *alive* Tyra, it became impossible to look at what had become of her without an almost crippling sense of sorrow.

So she took a deep breath and tried to push all those feelings to the side. It didn't quite work.

As with Joanna, the actual conflict had taken place in a relatively small area, in the opening between the front foyer and a formal dining room. From the lack of blood elsewhere in the house and the lack of items disturbed, Tyra had not run through the house to get away. She had not been restrained—no chafing on the wrists or ankles—and showed no signs of beating, though any bruises might not have had much of a chance to form without blood flowing. Half of her throat had been cut to the bone and blood loss would have quickly stopped the heart. The dining room floor had a thick carpet in a deep red color, so it likely did not do the damage to the back of Tyra's head as the marble had done to Joanna's. Though perhaps that explained why Tyra had more time to fight back before consciousness faded.

"Who found her?" Maggie asked.

"Another chick from the office," Riley said. He nudged the front door closed with his toe; no one wanted to touch it until Maggie could process for prints, but he also wanted to keep the air-conditioning in and the neighbors' prying eyes out. "Tyra's car has been in the shop—foreign job, so it takes a while to get parts. This other gal has been giving her a ride every day. Arrives this morning, knocks, no answer, calls Tyra's phone, no answer, peeks through the window next to the front door and loses her breakfast."

"She lives alone?" The deep gash in the victim's throat would have kept her from screaming. Strands of her long waves lay scattered on the pile, probably caught by the knife at the same time.

"Nobody but one of those little froo-froo dogs." Riley looked around, as if the animal might choose that moment to gnaw on his ankle. "Which has made itself scarce."

"He did it again," Maggie muttered.

"What?"

"Walked away from this bloodbath without leaving a trail." The color of the carpeting did not make it easy to see blood, but still, with a flashlight and close inspection she should be able to see *something*. There were plenty of impressions from heavy feet between the body and the front door, but those would be from EMTs, cops, and herself as well as the killer.

Jack spoke. "He wouldn't necessarily have a lot of blood on the bottoms of his shoes. They'd be pointed away from the activity while he was straddling her."

Maggie agreed that the carpet made the situation different from Joanna's house. It would have brushed off the soles of the killer's shoes as soon as he stood, unlike marble tile, with no absorbency. There were a few small smears around the body, which could be the edges of his shoes or, more likely, his hands as he wiped them or simply pushed himself up. He might have been shaky after the ferocious attack.

But not shaky enough to leave blood on the door-knobs as he exited the property. Maggie had already checked the three ground-floor doors.

"Shoes aside, this guy has to be covered in blood. He walks outside and gets into his car? Not worried that neighbors or joggers might notice a man walking around stained in red?"

"Late at night," Riley guessed. "No one out of doors."

"It wasn't that late." Tyra had changed into comfy clothes: yoga pants and a worn T-shirt, athletic bra, and cotton panties. Yellow ankle socks seemed to sum her up, Maggie thought—young, bright, *alive*. "Not quite pj's, though I doubt this is what she'd wear for a date. I'm guessing quiet weeknight at home. So why did she let the guy in? Or did she not lock her door after returning home and he just walked in?" There were no signs of forced entry. Tyra had a home alarm system but it used only motion sensors; she wouldn't have it on while home.

Jack said, "Maybe one of these two women forgot to lock their doors. But both?"

"They knew him," Riley agreed. "Maybe he wore a Tyvek suit. That's why there's no blood. He stands up, takes it off, he can tuck it under his arm and stroll out of the house all spankin' clean."

Maggie argued, "And she lets a guy wearing a Tyvek suit into her house? Or stands here and watches him put it on?"

"She doesn't let him in. He gets in somehow, surprises her."

Maggie stood next to the body, her gaze roaming the room as if she could picture these different scenarios playing out. "But gets close enough to stab her without her running away, bumping into things, snatching up an object to use as a weapon. Maybe she started to run and he struck her in the back—we'll know more when we can turn her over—but Joanna didn't have any injuries there."

"She knew him," Jack echoed.

Riley had a thought. "Maybe it's the alarm company guy."

"Different systems."

Silence descended again as they puzzled this out, broken only by the electronically produced shutter sound of Maggie's camera as she documented the scene. The garish light of the flash illuminated every inch of Tyra Simmons's broken body. Riley, in particular, didn't seem able to tear his gaze from the corpse. Finally, he said, "Do you think my girls would object if I told them they could never live alone?"

"Probably," Jack said.

Maggie frowned at him, then said to Riley, "As long as they don't work for Sterling Financial, I'm sure they'll be fine."

This did nothing to reassure the concerned dad. "At least not without a security system, infrared cameras . . . a gun taped to the bottom of a table in every room . . . and a Rottweiler."

Jack said, "Natalie's only thirteen. I think she'll be living with her mother for a while yet."

"Don't know. She wants to start *dating*." He made it sound as if the little girl had decided to join a cult in Timbuktu.

Maggie cast about for something to distract him from envisioning one of his own daughters slaughtered on her own floor, and something he had said came back to Maggie. Having become more acquainted with the victim's circle than usual, she asked, "Which other woman at the office found the body?"

Riley fumbled for his notebook, then decided not to bother. "Hasn't been there that long, but says she's the regulator, whatever that means. Good-looking girl. She's out in my car."

Maggie stopped taking photographs. "Anna Hernandez?"

"Uh—yeah, that was it. Why?"

Maggie explained that they had spoken the day before. "I'm going to see how she's doing."

She finished her photos of the living room, then set the camera down on an end table. She left the detectives to continue their canvas of the house and went out the front door. Pieces of cobalt sky peeked out between clouds that lowered the temperature but also fostered the humidity. Birds sang along with the low hum of traffic on nearby Chester. Everywhere else in the city, it was a nice day. Not so much for Tyra Simmons.

She went to Riley's battered Crown Vic and opened the back door, where Anna Hernandez had been staring straight ahead. She turned to Maggie with relief, clasping her hands as if they had been friends for twenty years. Oddly, it felt as if they had.

"This is terrible. Who is doing this? And why Tyra? I mean, I'm sure Joanna had lots of enemies, but Tyra was such a sweet girl."

Maggie realized she shouldn't discuss the case or anything about it, though that probably wouldn't be possible. "I just wanted to see how you were doing. I'm sorry you have to wait. If you want to go home—"

"I don't mind, honestly. Anything I can do to help. I mean I barely knew Tyra—never met her before this assignment. But we got to talking about her car and I drive right by here on my way in so . . ."

"I know it must have been a shock."

"Shock doesn't begin to cover it. Is that what Joanna looked like? Is that how she was killed?"

Maggie said nothing, but of course her silence created confirmation.

"Who is doing this? Why? Who declared war on Sterling Financial, and even if they did, why Tyra? Why not Lauren? She's next after Joanna. Tyra was just in-house counsel and I don't think they ever listened to her anyway."

Maggie should stick to neutral topics. Pat her hand and get her a drink of water. But she couldn't help asking, "What makes you say that?"

Anna's racing thoughts had already leapt forward, so she had to stop and retrace. "Because Tyra said so. I think that was how she introduced herself to me—I'm in-house counsel, not that Joanna ever listens to me anyhow. A joke, you know. Self-deprecating sense of humor. But then on our morning commute she'd be bubbly and ready to go, and then on the way home I could barely get a word out of her. She seemed frustrated. And worried."

"About what?"

"No idea. And honestly, she could have been like that all her life, for all I know. We've only been commuting partners for four or five days. She *did* seem high strung on a general basis."

"Did she—" *Not your job, Maggie, not your job.* "Please tell the detectives anything you know about Tyra, if she had worries or concerns, especially about people in her life. In the meantime, can I get you anything, a drink of water?"

"No, thanks. I think I'd throw up anything I swallowed. Oh—I called the office and told them. I was in such a daze, I didn't know what else to do. I don't know any of Tyra's family or anything so I didn't know who else to tell."

"It's okay. We understand."

"And I told them how she . . . looked. I hope that's all right."

"Of course," Maggie said. Not ideal, but you can't control everything. Officers always preferred to hold back some details from public consumption, but that had gotten increasingly more difficult in the modern age. Amazing, Maggie thought as she retraced her steps to the house, how cell phones had changed nearly everything about their lives. And deaths.

Then she put aside such philosophical reflections to process the rest of the crime scene.

* * *

As it turned out, their efforts didn't yield much. Nothing else in Tyra's house appeared to have been disturbed other than her body. Her laptop sat charging on the kitchen counter next to a curdled bowl of cornflakes and her purse, with its wallet intact. Her phone had been plugged in on the end table next to her bed, still neatly made. Jewelry, real and costume, filled the wooden box on her dresser, and a fairly current video game console sat tucked under the large flat-screen in the living room. Robbery had not been the motive.

At least not the garden-variety kind. Tyra's briefcase yawned open on the kitchen table with papers fanned out beside it—impossible to tell if Tyra had been working while munching on her cornflakes, or if the killer had been looking for something and then possibly took it with him. Maggie photographed and then studied the pages, but they might as well have been written in Greek—mostly numbers, listed with acronyms that meant nothing to her. Next to those entries there were columns labeled "R factor," "10 y proj," and finally something she could read: "rating." The ratings ranged from A to AAA.

"Must be a list of Sterling's financial products," she said to Jack, who stood reading over her shoulder.

Another page had been ripped from a legal pad and covered in handwriting—Tyra's, Maggie assumed. In looping letters she had repeated the first two columns of letters and numbers but then written in her own R factors and ratings. She had not graded the products as highly—CCs and Cs.

The next page had been printed by a computer. The

heading read "Carter & Poe," but then the rest of it devolved into the same hieroglyphics as the first two.

"I have no idea what this means," Maggie confessed. "This could be completely normal take-home work for her."

"Maybe not." Jack summarized Ned Swift's allegations about Joanna's cozy relationship with the ratings agent from Carter & Poe. "Maybe Tyra had her suspicions, and made her own calculations about what rating Sterling's products actually merit."

"Could she even do that? She was a lawyer, not an accountant."

"An investment bank lawyer. She'd have to know at least the fundamentals."

Maggie nodded. "And if she got suspicious, started crunching some numbers herself, then whoever killed Joanna to keep this a secret might have come after Tyra."

"And went all Ginsu on them to keep from paying a slap-on-the-wrist penalty to the government?" Riley interjected, coming up behind them. "Stripped these girls naked and cut their guts out in the name of corporate espionage?"

Maggie remembered something else Anna had told her. "Financial firms like Sterling pay year-end bonuses based on that year's profits. These can figure into the millions."

Jack said, "So if a bad report comes out and their products are devalued, the bonuses this year could be short a few yachts or private islands along the equator."

Riley said, "People have had their guts cut out for a lot less. Hyper little Tyra was a straight shooter and might spill the beans once she cottoned on. But if Joanna was paying off the ratings agency to overvalue her stuff, she's not going to tell anybody, so why kill Joanna?"

"More year-end bonus to go around?" Jack said.

"She had an attack of conscience?" Maggie suggested. "If she fessed up it would kill the deal with DJ Bryan and Sterling would stay small-time?" But she knew that didn't sound right. Every description of Joanna didn't seem to include a conscience.

"Or Tyra was in it with Joanna," Jack said. "That's why she'd been nervous, worried that DJ Bryan's due diligence process would find it. With discovery imminent, a coconspirator needed to cut ties."

"Or Mr. Pierce Bowman of New York discovered their little subterfuge and went into a rage that they dared to screw with the venerable firm of DJ Bryan. I could see that guy slicing a woman open and then going out to play nine holes." Riley glanced toward the dining room, where most of Tyra's body could be seen from the kitchen table. "I don't know. It still seems like . . ."

"Overkill," Maggie finished.

"In every way."

"We need to talk to Joanna's favorite Carter & Poe rater," Jack said.

"Absolutely," his partner agreed.

But first they had to finish up at the scene of Tyra Simmons's murder. Jack freed Anna Hernandez from the back of their police car. Maggie and the IT guy examined Tyra's electronics. Her phone didn't have a passcode, and neither did her laptop, and with guidance from IT they had checked her e-mails, voice mails, and texts. No threats, no warnings, no pleas. She had sent her last text at eight-forty the previous evening, to her mother, to remind her of an aunt's upcoming birthday. She had missed calls from people in her contacts list at nine and nine-fifteen.

E-mails were routine. She had both a business account and a personal one. The recent business communications consisted of a lunch order and the current Sterling stock prices, a daily newsletter of changes and updates in federal and Ohio laws and regulations. Her last e-mail from Joanna simply asked for a "fact sheet" regarding a possible expansion in New Mexico. Nothing that waved a red flag, nothing that indicated a motive for murder. Nothing that told Maggie why someone had come into Tyra Simmons's home to brutalize her.

Maggie's processing had reached the bathroom, the most intimate place in a person's home. It didn't reveal any dire secrets either. A few indications of a male presence remained—a bottle of aftershave in a drawer, a pair of boxers much too big for the slender Tyra at the bottom of the laundry basket—but they didn't seem consistent or permanent. A boyfriend but definitely not one up to live-in status yet. Tyra's only prescription meds were birth control pills; otherwise her medicine cabinet held Advil, cough drops, and Band-Aids. Maggie shut the mirrored door to see Jack's reflection staring back at her.

"Jeez!"

"Find anything interesting?" he asked.

"Nothing. Tyra seemed to be a sweet, hardworking girl."

He grimaced. "Yeah, unfortunately what she worked on is incomprehensible to mortal man."

Maggie turned her back on him and opened her fingerprint kit. She brushed black powder across the porcelain sink, on the off chance that the killer had used it to clean up.

"We're going to talk to the ratings guy," Jack said, leaning over her shoulder to peer at Tyra's cosmetics before retreating to the doorway. "Swift alleges bribery, says Carter & Poe have to be in on it."

Nothing useable on the sink. She moved on to the tub.

"You think the killer did a Lizzie Borden? Killed Tyra in the nude, and then took a shower?"

"I doubt it. It's hard to wash blood off in a snow-white bathroom without leaving some trace. And he'd still have to get from her body downstairs to here without a trail, so no." She continued to brush powder, though, "just in case." Cops were huge on "just in case."

"Swift has a point about the rater."

"How so?"

"Mortgage companies like Sterling have customers' deposits like banks, so they use short-term funds, uninsured funds, money market, pension funds, and interbank lending overnights."

"Mearan mentioned overnights," Jack said.

"The collateral for those funds can be mortgage-backed securities—the tranches Lauren described. The ratings agencies weren't keeping pace with these very complicated funds so their value started to falter when the housing market finally saturated and prices began to fall instead of skyrocket. Suddenly everyone realized that they didn't really know what their securities were worth. If you know something is worth zero, you know what to do. But if you don't know *what* it's worth, you're paralyzed. If the economy is an engine, credit is the gas. The banks began to refuse credit to other banks and the investment banks were stuck with money going out but none coming in. They tried to sell the collateral, the mortgage-backed securities, but when everyone was trying to unload them the value fell even further. It was like realizing there's a bee in your car. All you can do is bail out. So everyone bailed out."

"And the world fell apart," Jack finished.

"But if credit is the gasoline, liquidity, that is, cash, is the oil. Without it, the engine seizes. That's why banks have to keep a certain amount of cash on hand for just such emergencies. But because of categories of certain funds—I won't even get into all that—about every institution in the country didn't have the cash reserves they should have had. Everything froze. The economy can handle inflation, it can handle deflation, it can handle stock crashes. But it can't just *stop*. People lost jobs, retirement accounts, and homes." She lifted a palm print from the edge of the tub; it probably belonged to Tyra, unless their killer had small, delicate hands, like his victim. "Houses are extremely illiquid assets. Unlike crashed stocks they take a long time to clean up. They can't sit there until the value comes back up like your share of Apple.com. They have to be maintained, cleaned, the grass cut, etcetera. So kicking all the loan defaulters out of them only created new problems. Banks still had no payments, and now they had a chunk of real estate that no one wanted." She smoothed out the wide tape with the print on a glossy white card. "The scary thing is, at the start house values had only lost four percent. But when investors withdrew from risk and lenders from lending, they forced up costs and rates for entities that were perfectly stable with good credit, like auto and credit card loans, the 'good' prime mortgages, and so on. It became a big downward spiral so that by 2009 we'd lost 6.2 million jobs. No stopping the spiral then. We're still recovering over ten years later. My point is—"

"I was wondering."

"—that a good rating on a security isn't a bonus, like getting a gold star from your teacher for extra credit. They are a globally accepted measure of a bond's value. They're important. And when they can't be trusted, bad things happen."

She could feel his gaze boring into her back as she finished powdering the white porcelain. "How do you know all that?"

"I read the papers," she said gently. Cops had very tricky egos. One verbal misstep could make her working life difficult—which, where Jack was concerned, was already difficult enough.

Jack said nothing while she gathered her equipment and closed up her fingerprint kit. Then he asked, "Maggie, who played in the Super Bowl this year?"

She blinked at him in bewilderment. "I don't know. Why?"

"Just checking." A corner of his mouth flicked upward, which in Jack passed for a smile.

But a moment later a sudden wail made them both start; it sounded as if a wounded animal had been set afire. "What—?"

Jack turned away. "Sounds like the family has arrived."

Chapter 12

Someone at Sterling had been close enough to Tyra to alert her parents, who had rushed to her home with various siblings on their heels. There is no good way to learn that your child is dead, but standing on that child's front lawn in the harsh light of a beautiful summer day while her eviscerated body cools inside had to be one of the worst. Her mother collapsed onto the grass, sobbing. Her husband slumped more gradually, but joined her there. Two sisters did their best to physically envelop their parents while one of the brothers made a dash for the house, only to be caught by the emerging Jack. He restrained the strong young man without apparent effort, and Maggie could suddenly understand how he had dumped all those dead bodies single-handedly.

She watched from the high window of Tyra's bedroom, feeling like the coward she knew she was when it came to grieving family. Tyra had opened the window to the cool night air and now Maggie heard Jack say, "Do you want us to catch who did this? Then you have to let us do this right." He guided the brother back to his family, now and forever minus one.

Watching the sobbing group, Maggie couldn't help but feel that between Tyra and Joanna, Tyra had been the lucky one. At least Tyra had had people in her life who cared deeply for her. Joanna's circle hadn't shed a single tear.

Maggie turned away and went back to work, feeling not only guilty but ineffective. As at Joanna's—although at Joanna's it had been more difficult to tell because of the sheer lack of items present—nothing indicated that the killer had even entered the second floor. At both locations it appeared that the killer had entered the house without needing to *break* in, killed its occupant, and left again without either cleaning up or leaving a trail of blood out the door.

How?

Maggie returned to the body. Joanna's house had been isolated in a thicket of trees and space that money could buy. She could have shouted for help all night and no one would have heard her, but Tyra lived in a tight neighborhood of cute homes with small yards. Only the one upstairs window had been open, but still, she must have screamed as she fought her attacker, as he put deep gashes in her arms on the knife's path to her chest. But if he had been smart, and focused, and learned from Joanna, that slice to her throat may have been his first. Take out the vocal chords and then he could work without fear of alerting the neighbors.

Maggie still crouched next to the body when the Medical Examiner's staff arrived.

* * *

Jack and Riley moved the family to the backyard, where Tyra had a small patio set in the shade of a maple tree. Obviously they couldn't use the front porch, where anyone could look through the sheer curtains to see Tyra's body. The budding leaves weren't full yet, but the branches were better than nothing against the sunshine. The day grew even more humid and airless, or perhaps it only seemed that way. The dazed parents were settled in chairs, their children flanking them like overprotective Secret Service operatives. Riley opened his notebook and plunged in with the standard questions.

No one had seen Tyra the evening before, but she had e-mailed one of her sisters around dinnertime and spoken with her mother around seven p.m.

"She'd come by at least a few times a week," her mother said, as her husband nodded in agreement. "We'd usually go shopping together on Saturdays. But we'd talk every day whether she stopped in or not."

Tyra had sounded tired and a bit stressed but had only said that work had been "crazy" that day and she couldn't keep up with everything that was going on. "I took that to mean she had some project she didn't think she could do, some deal where she had to check the laws in other states and she might miss one. Tyra never failed at anything but always thought she would. I told her she'd figure it out. . . . I always said that. I don't suppose I paid a lot of attention; Tyra always got uptight when she didn't have any cause to. I should have listened better." The older woman abruptly burst into a geyser of self-recrimination.

Her husband rubbed her back. "Not your fault. Tyra fussed about her job every day."

"But this time she said, 'I don't know, Mama. I don't think this can be fixed,'" the woman wailed.

"Do you know what she meant?" Riley asked, in his handling-the-family-gently voice.

"No! I should have listened."

"I don't think she liked that job," one of the brothers offered. "But it paid well."

"What didn't she like about it?"

For some reason five members of the family turned to stare at the sixth, a sister a few years older than Tyra named Sophie.

"What?" she squeaked.

"She always talked to you about it," her father said. "Did she tell you anything she didn't tell us?"

Sophie sighed, then explained to the detectives, "I'm a lawyer too, in-house counsel for AIG insurance. Tyra and I talked shop a lot, shooting the breeze most of the time. Sterling's had some lawsuits over predatory lending and insurance companies always get sued, so we'd trade strategies sometimes."

"Anything specific? Recently?"

Sophie appeared to make an effort to think. Jack could see the family resemblance between her and her pretty sibling. "She mentioned a case coming up, a guy named Kurt Resnick. He had taken out an ARM with a balloon payment and lost his shirt. His wife committed suicide. Tyra knew they'd lose in court—no jury is going to look at this grieving father of two and side with the evil corporation. But huge judgments are usually reduced or even vacated in appeal, so we talked about a plan for the second round, but . . . Tyra was too damn softhearted to be a lawyer. That's why she went into white-collar stuff instead of trials, but still . . . it really wasn't the job for her."

"She wanted to be like you," her mother said softly.

Sophie began to cry, and Riley moved to other questions to give her some time.

They had no idea who could have meant Tyra harm. She had always been popular and sweet, beloved by everyone. She had an on-again off-again boyfriend she had met in law school. He worked at a firm downtown that handled estates and corporate law—nothing to do with mortgages or investment banks. "A very nice boy," the mother said. "A player," the father sniffed. The other sister rolled her eyes and said that the guy would run back to this controlling bitch of a girlfriend, then come crying to Tyra when it didn't work out yet again. They had encouraged Tyra to end it once and for all and she would go out with other men, but never quite gave up on her ex-schoolmate. Someone without the backbone to stand up to the other woman seemed an unlikely candidate for this kind of slaughter, but Riley dutifully recorded the name of the controlling bitch girlfriend. Except that wouldn't explain—

"Do you know Joanna Moorehouse?"

The men of the family looked blank. The other sister said, "I think that was the woman she worked for." Sophie and her mother nodded. When asked what, if anything, Tyra had told them about Joanna, words spilled out.

"She'd gotten filthy rich," the mother said.

"She was the opposite of softhearted," Sophie said. "She told Tyra that people make their own decisions in life, and intelligent adults should do their homework before they agree to the largest purchase they'll ever make."

"She's shady," the mother said. "Tyra had a party once, when she bought this house, right? Maybe about a year and a half ago. And she invited people from work too, and introduced me around, and I remember asking if her boss lady was there and she said she hadn't asked her. 'We're not friends,' she told me. 'We get along okay, but she doesn't have friends.' I said then maybe she *should* invite her, this poor woman with no friends; me being a mama and all I'm picturing this lonely little girl. But Tyra said something like that woman is as shady as the day is long, and I don't want to get any closer to her than I have to."

Riley asked, "Did Tyra ever explain what she meant by that?"

"No."

He looked at Sophie, who had calmed enough to explain, "She thought Sterling had a lot of unethical practices. *Lots.* But they were all legal, and she felt it her job to keep it that way and prove that in court when necessary. Every company does scummy things. That's just life."

"Tyra wouldn't have let her do anything wrong," her mother asserted. "Tyra would never help someone break the law."

"Of course not," Riley soothed. "But maybe that's

why Tyra worried so much about work, because she thought Joanna *was* doing something wrong?"

"Maybe," Sophie said. "But honestly? Probably not. Tyra took things too seriously. She always did."

This did not seem to be getting them anywhere. Jack said, "Can you remember anything else she said or did about Joanna Moorehouse? Specifically?"

They all shook their heads.

"Did she tell you Joanna has also been murdered? Yesterday?"

This news stunned them. All six family members stared at Jack as if he had begun dancing on the tabletop.

"What?"

"Murdered like Tyra? The same way? How *was* she killed? Shot? Stabbed?"

"Wait a minute—you think Tyra was killed over *work*? What she did at *work*?"

"Why didn't I talk to her more last night?" her mother wailed again. "I should have asked more questions. She sounded upset—"

This latest shock had pushed the family over the edge into complete bewilderment. What could Tyra's death have to do with a boss she didn't socialize with and didn't even particularly like? The boss had never set foot in Tyra's house, and it didn't sound as if Tyra had ever been to hers.

Beleaguered, Sophie explained again that Tyra had not confided anything more about Joanna or Sterling than she had already told them. Sterling's legal troubles were routine for the industry, and unlikely to cause it any real difficulty. The merger with DJ Bryan would almost certainly go through and Tyra looked forward to it, thinking it would be just as well if her position was eliminated or the entire office moved to New York. It would force her to quit a job she didn't really like that much anyway, and perhaps find a client more suited to her sensibilities. Maybe even someone in the public sector, a charity or an NGO.

Riley wrote down the names of Tyra's close friends while Jack played waiter and brought them bottles of water from Tyra's fridge. Riley needed to keep them talking until the victim's advocate arrived to walk them through the process of what happened next and to help them make arrangements for Tyra's funeral. This would also keep them out of the way and blocked from view while the ME staff removed their very much loved Tyra's body from where she had been slaughtered on her dining room floor.

Jack and Riley returned to the bustling offices of Sterling Financial, which didn't seem any more affected by Tyra's death than they had been by Joanna Moorehouse's. Managers fidgeted at their chairs, phones glued to their ears as they pecked at their keyboards. Perhaps, Jack wondered, they were trying to impress their possible new boss from DJ Bryan with their industriousness in times of stress, but Pierce Bowman didn't appear to notice. With his chair swiveled toward the window, feet propped on the desk borrowed from Tyra, he had his nose buried in that day's *Wall Street Jour-*

nal. Jack entered his office without knocking while Riley took a phone call in the lobby.

Bowman glanced up. "Yeah, I heard."

"Heard?"

The guy finally swung his feet down and faced him. "About the in-house counsel. Too bad—sweet kid, not to mention gorgeous. Her and Joanna both. You got anybody in mind? Never mind—can't tell me, right?"

Jack said, "One theory is that Joanna might have been engaging in illegal activity and Tyra knew or found out about it. You've been looking at this company pretty closely because of this merger."

"Purchase," Bowman corrected.

"Have you found any red flags?"

Bowman sighed. "Have a seat, Detective. You don't have to loom over me like some sort of avenging angel."

Jack resisted for a moment, purely because he really didn't like this guy, but then told himself not to be stupid. If the guy was willing to talk, let him talk. He sat.

"Dhaval, my quantitative analyst, has gone over their books thoroughly, verified accounts, even called in favors in other cities. What Sterling says it has, it has. They even meet their capital requirements, which is where most places fail their stress tests. There's nothing wrong with Sterling. No red flags. If Joanna and Tyra were keeping some dark secret that some third party murdered them over, I don't know what it could be. Believe me, I would have no problem with killing this deal and heading back to New York if I found something I didn't like."

Unless it made money, Jack thought to himself.

"What about an ethical problem, rather than a financial one?"

"Ethics?" He didn't appear to know the word. "What do you mean?"

"If Joanna engaged in tactics that were not actually illegal, but shady."

He stopped there because Bowman chuckled. "Sterling is a mortgage loan origination firm. *Everything* they do is shady. Banks don't loan people money because we're nice guys who care about increasing participation in the American Dream. We loan money because it makes us money and, in addition, gives us capital to play with. We gamble with other people's money, your money. If things go well, everybody wins, but mostly us. If things don't go well, we still get year-end bonuses; they just won't be as big."

"Speaking of bonuses . . ." Jack pulled a copy of Joanna's Panamanian account out of his jacket pocket and passed it across the desk. "Do you recognize this account?"

Bowman gave it a close but not terribly interested look. "No, but there isn't much here to go on. Let me ask Dhaval."

He pulled out his phone, of course, instead of getting up and walking the fifteen feet to the conference room, where the quant toiled. At least he didn't text but barked a summons into the phone's tiny speaker.

This sucks, Jack thought as they waited in silence, *having to rely on members of the suspect pool to interpret our evidence.* But he didn't see an alternative.

The serious Dhaval arrived to study the printout

with mild curiosity. "What is this? I never saw this." He added absently, "This is a lot of money."

Bowman got intrigued enough to get up and read it again, over his subordinate's shoulder. "Joanna was skimming." A statement, not a question. It didn't seem to surprise him much.

Dhaval asked, more to himself than his boss, "But where did it come from? This account number . . . possibly the capital deposits . . ."

Bowman said, "I knew that bitch was up to something."

Jack asked if this would affect the merger.

"Purchase. Not so much. It only shows that Sterling is more profitable than we even knew, if she could skim this much and not miss it." Bowman shrugged. Then a pleasant thought seemed to occur to him. "Plus, Sterling gets it back, because it actually belongs to Sterling, right? We can work that out with the Panamanians. A boatload of cash always sweetens a deal."

Glad you're happy, Jack thought. But what if this didn't come as a surprise to Bowman? What if Joanna had put that money aside as a personal sweetener to the deal, and it had been meant for him? Or, as they had originally thought, what if it had been Joanna's escape hatch for when Bowman found out Sterling was a house of cards? Which, according to Bowman and Dhaval, it wasn't.

Jack ground his teeth.

Just then Riley poked his head into the glass box and told him they had a situation.

Jack abandoned the two money managers. "Tell me

it's not another dead body. Though that might be prefer-able to all this white-collar stuff."

"Got a guy in the lobby named Kurt Resnick. He had been out there waving signs with the protesters, then walked in and made the receptionist call us."

"Yeah?"

"He says he killed Joanna Moorehouse."

Chapter 13

Kurt Resnick fidgeted in a folding chair that the help-ful receptionist had installed in her supply closet to give the cops some privacy. They could have taken him downtown, but when a subject is in a mood to con-fess it's best to go with it. Breaking up the flow could give him time to rethink his decision. They had dallied only long enough to get the digital voice recorder out of Riley's car.

About forty-five years of age, Resnick had an un-ruly shock of medium brown hair, medium brown eyes, lean arms, and a wiry build. Dressed in a tidy pair of jeans and a generic polo-type shirt, he was nice looking in a studious way. Definitely not threatening. Definitely not easy to picture fileting Joanna Moore-house open like a freshly caught walleye.

"Mr. Resnick," Riley began, calm and courteous but with that little edge that said Kurt had better not be wasting their time. "You wanted to talk to us."

Jack sat in the third folding chair. The walk-in closet was truly a closet, with only a small AC vent that could keep up fine with paper clips and spare toner but not the combined body temperature of three adult males. All three men were much closer to each other than they would have preferred. Their knees nearly touched. Cozy, a real estate agent would say. Jack did not care for cozy.

"Yes. I killed her."

"Joanna Moorehouse?"

"Yes." The man nodded emphatically.

"Okay. Why'd you do that?"

The man rubbed his palms on his thighs. "Because she killed my wife."

"Can you explain?"

"I certainly can. I've been explaining for years, but no one would listen. That's why I killed her."

"How did your wife die?"

"She took my thirty-two that my brother had given me, put it in her mouth, and pulled the trigger."

"Your wife did?" Riley asked in surprise. "It was suicide?"

"Yes. Because of Joanna Moorehouse."

Riley gave Jack an "*oh hell*" look and took out his notebook. "Okay, let's do this right and start from the beginning. Name?"

The detective dutifully recorded Kurt Resnick's middle initial, his address—a motel on Brookpark Road—and his lack of a phone or phone number. He had been out of work for two years but recently began a position with a small construction company on the west side.

"And what do you do there?"

"Bookkeeper." He laughed, and the painful, desperate sound of it made the hair on Jack's arms stiffen. "I'm a bookkeeper. You'll see why that's ironic."

"I'll take your word for that. Now, Joanna Moore-house."

The man plunged in with quick words. "It was four years ago. I needed a mortgage. I had good credit—at least I thought I did. I had a good job at an architectural firm down here." He meant downtown. "But I was . . . in love."

"With Joanna Moorehouse?"

"No! God, no! With my wife. Let me—okay. My first wife and I did nothing but argue, things were not good, the boys were getting into their teens and old enough to handle it. I took a vacation to Los Angeles, to visit my sister and think things over, planning to start divorce proceedings as soon as I got home. I went to high school there and they had an alumni function one night and my sister kept asking me about my marriage, so I went in order to avoid talking to her. Ran into Rose. We hadn't even dated in high school, just friends, we'd talk. I never saw her again after gradua-tion. But . . ."

"Yeah," Riley said. "We get it. You reconnected with a childhood sweetheart and—"

"*No*. We connected in a totally new way, adult way. She was radiant, vibrant, strong. Everything I hadn't had in my life for a long, long time. The end of her own bad marriage had been finalized and her ex took everything in the divorce. All she had was a condo in Irvine and custody of her three girls."

Riley tried to steer him. "Okay, second chance at love. How does Joanna Moorehouse—"

"We planned for her to move here as soon as I could find a place. My wife got a shark lawyer who made me

buy out her half of the house, which she got to keep—
don't ask me how that worked, but by that point I
would have paid anything to get away from her, cheap
at the price in order to start life with a clean slate. I had
a good job, and Rose made even more than I did as a
gym manager. We'd be fine. I needed only a modest
home with five bedrooms, so that her girls had space
enough to make up for moving away from LA and my
boys had a place to stay on the weekends. The future
looked, well . . . rosy. That's what I kept telling her,
my little joke. Rosy. . . ."

His voice trailed off and he stared at the floor. Jack
wondered how much more they'd have to hear about
the star-crossed lovers before getting to the crime. But
Riley, who could pollute the air with curses at a driver
who took a split second too long to make a left turn,
showed infinity-plus patience with a confession. Especially a confession that could wrap up this whole un-
wieldy case.

"I found a perfect one. In Bay Village, only a block
from the lake, adorable bungalow that had been kept
up to perfection by the same family for two genera-
tions. I knew it was right, but so did a bunch of people
I had to outbid. When I called Rose and told her to quit
her job, list her condo, and start packing, it was the
happiest moment of my life.

"Of course, I needed a loan. A guy at work had refi-
nanced his house through Sterling, told me about them.
It didn't occur to me to check around—low interest
rates, a personal recommendation, I was in a hurry
and, hey, I know numbers. I'm a friggin' bookkeeper,
right? It's not like I don't know what I'm doing."

Riley nodded. Jack tugged at his tie. There wasn't

much airflow in the closet and he wished he could open the high, tiny window. But he'd sweat for a while if it meant they could close the Moorehouse case.

"Only I didn't," Resnick went on. "I thought because I had good history and a job, I'd have a great credit rating. But the money I owed my wife each month took half of my paycheck, I had credit card balances from living in a hotel after I left her, and I couldn't include Rose's income because we weren't married and her name wasn't on the house, because she wasn't here and I needed to get the stuff signed and I didn't think it was important. So on paper I became 'subprime' as if I were a part-time Uber driver who declared bankruptcy the year before. See?"

"Not really," Riley admitted. "What does this have to do with—"

"Sterling offered me a pick-a-payment option and I leapt at it, figuring I could keep the payments low for a year or two, Rose would sell her condo and find a job here, maybe I could find a better lawyer to renegotiate what I was paying my wife, and then I could make the full payments and whittle it down. I had it all figured. Because I'm a numbers guy, right?"

"But something went wrong," Riley prompted.

"I didn't even look at my copies of the loan forms. I didn't notice that they had added a digit to my monthly income, which made up for the payments to my wife. Or that I had to pay a list of fees for flood and tax certificates, appraisals, documents, etcetera, all arranged in-house by Sterling because it was so convenient. But what could I say? I needed the loan. I figured a little creative accounting wouldn't hurt anyone in the long run. I didn't want to think that a company faking their own paperwork *might* be sort of a red flag. I started making payments on my no-money-down, fictitious income loan with the adjustable rate and payment. Oh, and on the bill I got every month, they made sure the first number I saw was the interest only payment, the lowest amount I could pay. It's a bad loan to people with bad credit, but, I told myself, these people must know what they're doing."

He paused to swallow hard, as if his mouth was dry. Jack felt the same, as if he might suffocate before they reached Joanna Moorehouse's part of the story. He wished for a bottle of water. Then he wished for a glass of bourbon. Lots of ice.

"Meanwhile, housing is still a buyer's market and Rose couldn't find a buyer for her condo. She left it on the market and moved here, with the girls. We moved into our five-bedroom honeymoon cottage and planned a wedding. My boys came over on weekends. The girls weren't happy about leaving the glamorous West Coast so we tried to soften them up with smartphones and the new iPads for Christmas. About then my company, the architectural firm, which had been holding on by their nails during the post–building bust years, finally let go, dissolved, and I was out of a job. Rose, who could have managed Dulles International given the opportunity and had overseen the largest chain of gyms in southern California, couldn't find a job. At *any* salary, certainly not one that would support our finances. Gyms aren't quite as numerous in Cleveland as they are in California and the clients aren't as well heeled as the Hollywood crowd."

"You went broke."

"We weren't merely broke, we were in a deep dark

pit of broke and still digging, paying for everything with credit in order to eat and keep clothes on our backs. A friend of mine took me out for beers one night and let me cry on his shoulder for an hour or two. Then he suggested refinancing. We're money guys, remember? Moving around dollars is a hobby to us—only usually it's other people's dollars. He said I could refinance for enough to pay off my credit cards *and* my ex-wife—a higher payment, of course, but it'd only be for about three months. Without those debts my credit score would improve and I could get a reasonable mortgage with a lower payment and start fresh. The key was to get all the debt paid off and make sure the refi didn't have a prepayment penalty. Sterling called it a power loan."

"I thought this office didn't deal with customers," Jack said.

"No, it was all done over the phone, as with the first loan. They e-mailed me the documents and I brought them here, because, well, I couldn't afford a FedEx envelope. We paid everything off, my credit score improved, and I came back to Sterling for the second refi, the third loan. Up to this point I didn't blame Sterling for anything; I blamed myself. But when I asked to refinance Sterling balked, because, of course, they hadn't made enough money on the second loan. They didn't want to give up that sweet interest. So the guy on the phone said he'd crunch the numbers and e-mail me the documents. He did—except the monthly payment came out way too high. By this point in time and largely out of sheer desperation I had learned to read *everything*, so I knew what the payment should be. I protested. Next they got the payment down but added all sorts of nonsense fees and premiums. Kind of like 'dealer prep' and 'restocking charge'—they mean nothing, but companies charge them because they can. They added a prepayment penalty. I protested again, e-mailed a copy of my copy of the second loan's paperwork that clearly stated *no* prepayment penalty. They e-mailed back their copy, which made no such notation and showed that the extra interest I paid was for some sort of mortgage insurance. In other words, fraud. They must have thought I wouldn't say anything since I hadn't argued when they 'adjusted' my income on the first loan."

"Sterling doctored your loan paperwork."

"Yes. I'm making these crushing payments, we're eating by virtue of the credit cards again, and Sterling keeps dancing around and around. I complained to the Better Business Bureau. I complained to the SEC. I complained to HUD, Fannie Mae, anyone I could find an address for. Most didn't even respond. Finally, I sued Sterling, and Joanna Moorehouse in particular. Until then, I'd never heard her name."

Finally, Jack thought. *Maybe Riley is right. Patience pays off.*

"Rose was making minimum plus commissions selling clothes at the Galleria. Her girls went back to live with their father and she felt miserable without them, worried about them partying in LA with no supervision. I had to discourage my boys from coming on weekends because we couldn't afford to feed them and my ex made noises about getting sole custody if I couldn't even handle occasional visits. I represented myself in the lawsuit because I couldn't afford a lawyer, and if I won I couldn't afford to split the settlement. I *wanted* to settle, either get enough to keep us going or to get the loan payment I was supposed to have, that's all. I did not have the strength for a drawn-out battle by that point. But Joanna wouldn't budge. That was the only time I saw her, in court." He came to an abrupt stop and shook his head, as if still amazed at the complete train wreck his life had become.

"And when was that?" Riley asked.

"About six months ago. Rose and I both missed paid work time to be able to put our case in front of a judge. Moorehouse breezed in with some young guy and this pretty black girl. . . . She laid out the fake documents, and since all I had were e-mailed copies, it looked like hers were the originals and I had tried to alter mine. I said to her, right there in court, that all she had to do was call it a mistake, a typo, anything. I wasn't the SEC, I wasn't interested in getting her slapped with a fine. I didn't want to get out of paying what I owed, I just wanted the loan I was supposed to get. In a court of law she said, 'I'm sorry you can't pay your bills, Mr. Resnick, but that's hardly my fault.' Rose burst out crying. Rose was the strongest person I've ever known, and she started crying right there in the courtroom. She didn't care about being strong anymore. When we got home she locked herself in our bedroom and I heard the shot."

His eyes filled with tears, but they didn't spill over. He didn't have enough left for that. "We had never even gotten married. Couldn't afford a place, a dress, or even flowers. Nothing."

They waited for him to continue, but he kept staring at the floor until Riley prompted, "So then you . . ."

"Decided to kill her. Joanna Moorehouse. What the hell, I had already lost Rose and my kids and every

penny I had or would have for the next twenty years."
He leaned forward, elbows on knees, and ran his hands
over his face and through his hair. The two cops leaned
back as far as possible to give him room.

"And how did you do that?" Jack asked. Something
about Kurt Resnick didn't seem right.

"What? Decide? It wasn't difficult."

"How did you kill her?"

Resnick gave him an odd look. "You were there.
You saw."

"We need you to tell us."

"Oh, right. I stabbed her. Again and again."

That had not been released to the press.

"Where?" Riley asked.

"All over."

"No, I meant where, geologically?"

"Geographically," Jack corrected quietly.

"Oh! At her house."

That had been in the paper. "Where in her house?"
Riley persisted.

"I don't know. I didn't care. I stuck the knife into
her a number of times—I can't be more exact than that
because it's all sort of a blur. I couldn't believe I was
doing it. There was blood everywhere."

"How did you get in?"

"I rang the bell. I said I wanted to talk about my
lawsuit and she laughed and turned away. I guess she
wasn't afraid of me, figured she already won so there
was nothing more I could do. I wanted to show her
there was a *lot* more I could do."

"What time was this?"

"In the evening."

"We're going to need the details, Mr. Resnick. Please be as specific as you can."

"Um, okay. I went over to her house—"

"How did you get there?"

"Bus."

Jack pictured the narrow, elegant street and took a guess. "Buses don't go anywhere near her house."

"I took the fifty-five and got off at Clifton and 117th."

"Oh," Riley said. "Okay. What time?"

"About eight-thirty."

"The fifty-five stops running at seven."

Now Resnick gave Riley an odd look. "No, it doesn't."

"Sorry. My mistake, then."

If he could see that the cops were trying to poke holes in his confession, it didn't bother him. "I rang the bell and in a minute or two she opened the door. She didn't even remember me at first, but then she did. I told her Rose had killed herself."

He choked on these last words.

"And then what happened?" Riley asked.

"She said, 'Who's Rose?' And then I stabbed her."

"Right there in the doorway?"

"No—she got scared when I pulled out the knife. She turned and ran." Now his gaze switched from one detective to the other, no more staring at the floor, as when he recounted his near-marriage.

Judging his effect? Jack wondered. *Or looking for cues?*

Riley pressed, "So where did you stab her?"

"I told you, I'm not sure. I wasn't looking at the house."

"Where on her body did you stab her?"

"All over."

"All over *where*?"

"All over! I don't remember! All I could see was this red haze and her *mocking* face through all of it! Nothing mattered except making sure she could never do this to anyone else. Ever."

"So she died."

"Yeah," he said, puffing out as if he had been sprinting. "She died. And I was glad."

"Then what?"

"Then I left. Went back and took the bus back ho— to the hotel where I live now."

"And the other people on the bus didn't notice you were covered in blood?"

This suggestion surprised him. "I wasn't."

Riley pointed out, "You said there was blood everywhere."

"On her. There wasn't much on me."

That didn't seem likely. Yet the killer had left the house without either cleaning up or leaving traces of red anywhere, so it could be true. Blood did funny things.

"Plus I had an outer shirt, a flannel shirt that caught most of the spatters. I took that off, used it to wipe my hands."

"Do you still have it?"

"No, I stuffed it in a garbage can on the way back to the bus stop. The next day was garbage pickup. Everyone had their cans out."

Jack remembered swerving around a garbage truck on their way to the crime scene and felt his reservations soften. The specific bus line, the trash pickup day, the time of death . . . they all fit the facts. "Which address?"

"I have no idea. Harborview Drive, that's all I remember."

"Then how did you find the right house?"

Again, he seemed surprised at the question, as if it should be obvious. "I'd been there before. I'd followed her home a few times, trying to get up the courage to confront her. Back when I still had a car."

"And you'll sign a statement attesting to all this information, when we write it up," Riley said.

"Yes, of course. It's true. All of it."

"One more thing, Mr. Resnick," Jack said. "What about Tyra Simmons?"

Kurt Resnick blinked. "Who?"

Chapter 14

"What do you think?" Riley asked Jack after they booked the very cooperative Kurt Resnick into a holding cell, pending arraignment.

"I don't like it."

"Me neither. He's too sketchy on details. Every time we get to specifics like what room of the house, whether lights were on or off, what she was wearing, then the memory gets fuzzy."

"Which does happen." Not to him, but to other killers. They locked on their quarry with tunnel vision that blotted out the rest of the world.

They certainly *wanted* Kurt Resnick to be telling the truth. Confessions were a gift and usually provided cops with a deep sense of satisfaction to know that they had it right, that the suspect did indeed do it and the case had indeed been solved. Refusing such a gift felt fractious and unsettling and greatly foolish. Yet accepting with significant reservations could turn out to be lazy at best and corrupt at worst.

For the moment they would take Resnick at his word. On a probationary basis.

Jack said, "I looked up those two stabbing cases the doctor mentioned. Both still unsolved. They figure a boyfriend for one, but his alibi's holding up."

"Any connection to Sterling?"

"None whatever. Nothing to do with real estate, banking, big bucks, or each other. Both worked downtown—that was it. And no disembowelment or ghost-like exit. Whoever did these left plenty of blood trails all over the scene."

"Not like our guy."

"Nope."

They crossed the atrium of the Justice Center, which occasionally flared with spotty sunshine from the glass above. As always, it thronged with agitated citizens either on their way to the courtrooms upstairs or on their way from, whose worried faces contrasted with those for whom this was just another day on the job. The combined voices of the people milling about bounced off the soaring ceilings and glass windows, so Riley and Jack kept their tones low; they didn't want their conversation echoing to the assorted attorneys and bail bondsmen who perpetually haunted the area. Riley said, "Yeah. I still don't like it. And where does that leave Tyra Simmons? It had to be the same guy who killed them both. The bodies are practically identical."

Jack clutched the stiff piece of paper with Resnick's fingerprints, which they had collected in the booking area. If he had killed Joanna Moorehouse then the bloody print under her body should match one of his fingers; there could be no other explanation for that print, and that would wrap up their investigation with a neat bow. He pressed the button for the elevator. The bank of moving cars would be impassible minutes before nine a.m. when the court sessions began, but just before lunchtime they had plenty of personal space and the car to themselves. "So if Resnick killed one, he had to kill the other. But why deny it? He's ready to post Moorehouse's killing on Facebook with a celebratory emoticon, so why the total blank on Simmons?"

"If anything, he'd have *more* motive to kill Tyra. She was the lawyer, she was the one who won the court case that ruined his life. But he didn't even recognize her name."

Two floors passed by. Jack said, "Suppose he killed Moorehouse and someone else killed Simmons."

"But the bodies were cut the same way. And no one saw Joanna's body except us."

It took only half of another floor for them to have the same, simultaneous thought.

"Jeremy," Jack said.

"Except for Jeremy," Riley said. "Our little boy toy ID'd the body for us. He got a peek at his ex-girl's chest in the body bag."

"So he didn't kill Moorehouse, but grabs the opportunity to off Simmons in the same way, knowing we'd assume the same killer."

They mulled that. The elevator stopped, the doors opened, and neither one of them moved.

"Risky," Jack said. "He had no guarantee that we would clear him of Moorehouse, which we didn't, officially. Not until Resnick walked in."

"And why kill Tyra at all? He could have a much better motive to off Joanna. She's tired of him, tells him he'll have to start doing a real job or find another boss to slip it to, and he goes off."

As the elevator doors closed again Jack said, "He doesn't know we know about the Panamanian account. With his girlfriend gone he has access to it, or can get access, but the lawyer knew about it, too. He has to get rid of her before she can have an attack of conscience, which would be like her, and tell the IRS or DJ Bryan or whoever about the slush fund."

"So he slices up Tyra to make her look like Joanna. Doesn't necessarily get suspicion off him, though."

"Unless he has some sort of alibi for Tyra," Jack said.

"I guess we need to find out. Time to have a chat with the grieving lover." Then Riley looked up at the position indicator light on the elevator panel. "Where the hell are we?"

Maggie sipped coffee as she listened to Jack's very brief explanation of Kurt Resnick's confession. She sat at an examination table with her loupes for examining fingerprints, the lighting and the table height adjusted to make the process both efficient and not too hard on the neck. Carol bustled in the DNA lab and crime scene tech Amy argued quietly over the phone with her boyfriend. Denny had gone home for lunch and it was Josh's day off. "But he says he didn't kill Tyra?"

"His exact words were, 'I don't know anything about that.' Didn't even seem to know who she was, which doesn't track either because if she was Sterling's lawyer he should have seen her name on paper a whole lot of times and in the courtroom. But apparently he focused on Joanna Moorehouse. Anything come back on *her* prints?"

"Nope. If she's ever been arrested, it wasn't in Ohio."

"Of course, she's only been in Cleveland about four years. The IT guy got nothing from her computer—she didn't have an e-mail or a Word doc that wasn't Sterling related. She wasn't on Facebook, Twitter, or even LinkedIn," Jack said, sounding frustrated. "She didn't post pics of her decorated cupcakes or her new drapes on Pinterest. As far as her electronic footprint is concerned, Joanna Moorehouse didn't exist until four years ago when she founded Sterling. How can you drink coffee in this heat?"

"Caffeine knows no seasons. You think it's a fake name?"

"It's not, actually. Joanna Marie Moorehouse was born in Crossing, Iowa, to a single mother. She lived there until twenty or so, went to the community college. Next thing she's in Los Angeles working for a real estate broker. All the Ivy League schooling on her resume is fake, she got a slap on the wrist in LA for falsifying her broker's license, and in a special spot of irony her house there went into foreclosure, but her name is her own. The victim advocate had to work backward from the real estate records. It took her all night, but she said it made a nice change from letting family members cry on her shoulder while she helps them pick a funeral home. She spoke with a sister, who said they hadn't seen or heard from Joanna in at least ten years."

Maggie said, "So she did have a family. She didn't spring, fully grown, from Zeus's head."

"Don't know, maybe she did. Her birth certificate reads 'father unknown.'"

"Huh. That's intriguing. So many business wunderkind types have daddy issues." Maggie caught herself and added, "Or maybe she was really smart and made up for a lack of resources with hard work."

"I don't care why she did what she did. I want to know why it got her killed." Jack rubbed one eye. "The Graham trial."

She blinked at the abrupt change in topic. "Yes?"

"You're going to be recalled, I heard."

"Yes."

"Watch your back. Graham may be in jail, but his clan isn't."

Bizarre on so many levels—her personal foil/nemesis/albatross expressing concern for her safety. Not unappreciated, yet she doubted the average defendant ever learned her name. "Meaning what? They're going to come gunning for me?"

"You're the whole case, Maggie. The ballistics from the casing at the scene implicates him, but your fingerprint ID slams the door on his cell. Without you—"

"Without me, Amy testifies. She verified my identification."

"You think these guys understand the finer points of forensic procedures?"

"You're serious?" She still couldn't wrap her head around it. Ten years in this field and she had never been threatened with physical peril . . . until, well, a month and a half ago when she'd met Jack Renner. Since then it had become commonplace without exactly being his fault, like two different pressure systems that were harmless until combined. Then, tornados.

"Yes, Maggie," he snapped. "I'm serious."

"Okay, then. I'll watch my back." What did that even mean? She had neither a weapon nor a black belt and couldn't afford to hire a bodyguard.

Jack must have come to the same conclusion because he didn't look satisfied. "Just knock off the midnight rambles for a while."

She liked to pace the city streets—the main, well-lit, occupied downtown streets—in the evenings, especially when things in her life were frustrating her as badly as this case was. Her turn to be unhappy. But she agreed, in order to pacify him as well as usher in a topic change of her own. She double-checked the lab to make sure none of her coworkers were around. "Speaking of . . . murder . . . Rick is still investigating the vigilante killer."

That was hardly news. "Yeah? So?"

She cradled the coffee mug in her hands, heart beginning to pound. "That reporter from the *Herald* is nagging him to look at similar crimes across the country. He said he had found some in Detroit, Chicago, and Phoenix. And apparently she . . . she had been in Phoenix."

If Maggie sought some bizarre kind of reassurance, she didn't find it. Jack's face might as well have been carved from basalt for all the reaction he showed. "So let him. Let her. It's not a problem."

She didn't ask if he was sure; he ought to know what kind of trail he had left or not left in those places, and there had not yet been the slightest suspicion that the killer could be a cop. There would be no reason for

Rick to think in that direction. But Maggie couldn't quite let it go. "Twenty."

Jack raised one eyebrow.

"He said there were at least twenty victims."

Jack didn't respond, and the scalding cup of liquid did nothing to warm her.

"Are there twenty, Jack? Thirty? Forty?"

He didn't look away. "Do you really want to know?"

This was not a rhetorical question, and it didn't take her long to answer. Her heartbeat slowed.

"No. I don't want to know."

"Then why—"

"Because I felt I should admit that I don't want to know." Anything less would be cowardly.

Jack leaned forward, as if to impart a confidence, and she automatically came closer as well . . . an odd reaction, when she thought about it later.

But he only said, "Stop feeling compelled to admit things, Maggie."

They stayed frozen like that, for a moment longer, his face only inches from hers. Then she withdrew with a sigh, annoyed without knowing at what.

She set down the coffee and turned back to Resnick's inked fingerprints. By their side she put the photo of the bloody print from under Joanna's body underneath one magnifying loupe, and refamiliarized herself with its ridges and pattern. Or rather lack of same.

She went through all ten of Resnick's fingers, explaining to Jack how the simplicity of the pattern in the bloody print made it extremely difficult to compare, and that she may only be able to identify a possible suspect, not convict him.

"But the computer made matches?" Jack asked.

"The computer brings up its ten best. Only human beings decide if they match—you know that."

"Yeah, but . . ." His voice trailed off before she had to remind him that there was no *but*. Computers did not *match* fingerprints, or DNA, or bullet casings. Only human beings could make those decisions.

So this human being went through the prints again. Examined the tips of each finger. Examined the assorted curving areas of the palms in case she'd been way off and the print under Joanna actually came from a tiny patch of palm rather than a finger.

"Maggie," Jack complained.

She ignored him. This could not be rushed. She went through them all again.

Deciding a latent print *matched* a set of known prints was actually much easier than deciding one *didn't* match. One felt peacefully content when every ridge lined up. But when they didn't you could never feel quite sure— were they completely different, or were you just not looking in the right place?

Jack shifted his weight again.

"I don't think so," she said.

"What? It's not his print?"

She sat up, distinctly unhappy. But this was her job, to establish the facts, and everything she could see established one single fact: the bloody print by Joanna's body had not been made by Kurt Resnick.

Jack's shoulders sank a little. "Shit."

He didn't sound surprised.

"So we're back to square one," Riley moaned. "Then how come Resnick knew she was stabbed? And how did he know the exact bus route to her house and that it was garbage day? And why did he friggin' *confess* to it, if he didn't do it?"

"I don't know." They were on their way back to the Sterling offices, the streets busy as lucky people who had time for lunch got to go eat theirs. "Maybe he'd been stalking her, trying to get her to talk to him. Maybe he had an accomplice and the print belongs to said accomplice."

Riley brightened. "Maybe the wife didn't really commit suicide—she's actually alive and she killed Joanna and Kurt is taking the blame so she can escape to Aruba."

Jack stopped for a red light and glanced at his partner. "You do watch a lot of TV, don't you?"

"You, on the other hand, probably don't even *own* one, am I right?"

"Do too." He didn't add that it had a nineteen-inch screen and spotty color.

"Never underestimate what a man will do for a woman."

Jack glanced again. He didn't often hear such a grim tone in his partner's voice. He wondered briefly what had caused the man's marriage to break up, and wondered if he would ever loosen up enough to ask.

Maybe. But not today.

If Riley noticed this scrutiny, he ignored it. "Let's say our little Kurt did have an accomplice who actually did the murder, told him about the bus and the garbage cans. Kurt confesses, uses the trial to showcase Sterling's predatory lending practices, then at the last minute with a Perry Mason flourish pulls this unshakeable alibi out of his ass and gets off. Not guilty."

Jack refused to say so, but that would not be the craziest thing he had seen in his long career as a cop. It had a ruthless logic to it. He pulled into the Sterling parking lot under the piercing glare of the attendant. "This accomplice—assuming it's not his not-really-dead wife, would probably be another one of those protesters or someone who also brought a lawsuit against Sterling."

"How about Ned Swift?"

"It would explain Tyra, too. The predator's lawyer would definitely be on the chief rabble-rouser's list. Resnick's blank on her could be faked, another block in his not guilty platform."

Riley pulled himself wearily out of the passenger seat. "We've got some hot leads now, boy. But first let's see what the office gigolo has to say."

Chapter 15

Jeremy Mearan had managed to hang on to his private office, even without his boss/girlfriend's protection. Perhaps he was more than just a pretty face. Or perhaps Lauren Schneider had more important things to do in the wake of Joanna's death than play musical chairs. Joanna's office remained untouched as well. Dhaval and Anna Hernandez had moved back into the conference room, taking up positions at opposite ends of the vast table. Dhaval's dark head bent over various folders, but Anna ignored the ones in front of her. She stared out the window at the blue Ohio sky. Jack wondered if she saw Tyra's ravaged body.

The rest of the office workers plied their phones and keyboards in a sort of unchanging bloc. Jack could probably fire a round into the ceiling and everyone would pause, look up, and then go right back to what they were doing.

Mearan seemed busy as well, his desk a sea of folders and printouts. Whoever thought we'd evolve into a paperless society, Jack thought, had jumped the gun by a couple of centuries. He and Riley opened the office door and entered without knocking, which didn't seem to surprise the kid or even annoy him; from what Jack knew of Wall Street types, politeness did not concern them overmuch. Indeed, he seemed relieved to see them. "Hell of a thing about Tyra, huh? So the same person killed both of them?"

"That's how it appears," Riley said, helping himself to a seat. Jack did the same.

"But why? That's what I can't figure out." He let his pen drop to the desk and ran a hand through silky black hair.

"When we first spoke to you yesterday," Jack said, "you assumed Joanna had been worried about going to jail. You never quite explained what her legal troubles were."

Mearan's eyes widened as if a teacher had caught him cheating on a test. Normally Jack loved suspects who lacked a poker face, but this guy's seemed almost too perfect. And his expression went on and on as his brain searched for a way out of this conversation. "Um—"

"There's no point in lying to us, Jeremy. Joanna's dead, it's not going to matter to her, and anything you two cooked up is going to be found within the week, either by us or Pierce Bowman. So bothering to lie to us is like telling the hangman his shoe is untied."

Perhaps not the best choice of analogy. Mearan's skin paled and he made a slightly choking sound. Jack had meant to shock him into fight or flight, not the third option: freeze.

But the kid sucked in a few breaths, maybe to make sure he still could, and said, "Okay . . . I think . . . I'm not sure, but . . . I think she might have been worried about the CDOs. There might be a problem with the CDOs."

"Uh-huh." Jack fervently hoped this explanation would be conducted in English.

"Those are collateralized debt obligations, right? Financial products? It's our mortgages, which we chop up into tranches."

"We know tranches," Riley said, with a slight touch of pride.

"The default rate on the mortgages goes into making up the CDO's rating. Rating is what makes investors buy them." He paused.

"And?" Jack prompted.

"Defaults were rising."

"To what percentage?" Riley asked, and Jack had to face the slightly bruising admission that his partner seemed a lot more savvy on this topic than he was himself. But then he took the same advice he'd given Maggie: Stop feeling compelled to admit things. It never helped the situation.

Mearan pulled at his collar even though, as usual, he didn't wear a tie. "Thirty-five percent."

Now Riley did the wide-eyed thing. "Thirty-five?"

Apparently that was a lot, Jack thought.

"That's a worst-case scenario estimate," Mearan immediately backpedaled. "At the rate we're going . . . and it may be a bubble. Housing had been coming up for a long time; it's normal to backslide at periods. It will readjust."

"And if it doesn't?" Jack asked.

Mearan looked ill. "Then Sterling's investors will lose money."

"But Sterling wouldn't."

Mearan nearly rolled his eyes. "Until the investors sell all their other Sterling products and new investors are scared off. Financial firms are like sharks. If they stop moving, they die."

"Why did Joanna let this happen?"

Mearan thought. "Same reason every other mortgage firm did it before the crash. Because it makes a ton of money. And it works—until it doesn't."

"And when it doesn't, you can kiss a merger with DJ Bryan good-bye."

Mearan's expression changed again, but to what Jack couldn't put a name to. "Not necessarily. Bowman wants us to split the firm—basically spin the riskier mortgages off into a subprime specialty shop. Which, to be honest, would eventually fail, especially if this recent . . . difficulty . . . is any indication. The regular, quote unquote, mortgage business would stay in a different firm, the one Bryan would buy."

"Yeah, Bowman told us that. But Joanna said no."

Mearan shook his head in agreement. "She said it had to be all or nothing. She didn't think Bryan would come up with enough money to make the advantage offset the cost of dissolving the bad stuff. She thought Bowman kept implying that he knew about the default rate increase—which he couldn't—"

"Why not?" Jack interrupted.

Mearan's hands fidgeted with every word. "Because that's my department. All the default cases come to me, so I'm the only one here who knows how many they add up to. Me and Joanna. I . . . kept it off the books. Lauren and Leroy don't even know."

"You hid them to keep DJ Bryan's price up."

Mearan's gaze darted toward the back of Bowman's

head, as if the man might be able to absorb the conversation through the glass. "Yes, because Bowman would use it to lowball their offer, give us way less than Sterling is worth."

"But Sterling *is* worth less," Jack pointed out.

"No," Mearan insisted, without a trace of irony. "Sterling is worth every penny we're asking for it."

Riley said, "But if you split into two companies, then you'd have a reason to get *more* out of DJ Bryan."

Mearan threw out his hands in frustration. "Thank you! That's exactly what I kept telling her. But she wouldn't hear of it. They don't get to pick and choose, she said."

Jack said, "So only you and Joanna knew about this default rate?"

"Yes."

"What about Tyra?"

The hands got even more agitated. "Oh, we could *never* have told Tyra. She'd have all sorts of problems with disclosure and due diligence. . . . For a lawyer she was bizarrely . . ." He searched for a word.

"Honest?" Jack suggested.

"Impractical."

The detectives said nothing, Jack pondered why, if Tyra hadn't known about this problem, she had been killed.

Maybe she'd found out. Maybe she had been threatening to expose Joanna, and—assuming Mearan really was as guileless as his face suggested—there *had* been another person who knew about the growing defaults. Someone willing to kill Tyra to keep her silent . . . but then why kill Joanna, who certainly had no reason to expose them. And Joanna was killed *first*.

Riley apparently reached the same dead end. "And this is why you thought Joanna might be worried about going to jail?"

"What? Yes . . . well, no. As I said, fudging the default rate wasn't exactly *illegal*. . . . If it adjusted in the next quarter we could have explained it as corporate strategizing. Anyway, what can get you in trouble is the ratings. Our CDOs are still rated triple-A, which is why investors pick them. Ratings are everything."

"Yes?" Riley prodded, when Mearan took too long to formulate his next words.

"Ratings agencies are hired and paid by the very firms they're rating. That brings up some conflict-of-interest issues."

"And now? With Joanna?"

"After the crisis changes were made that were supposed to result in more realistic ratings. I guess what I'm trying to say is a decent ratings agency, certainly Carter & Poe, should have been able to figure it out."

"And they didn't."

"*He* didn't. There's one guy on the Cleveland mortgage desk. His name is Sidney Fourtner. He kept slapping a triple-A rating on our stuff even when, in my opinion, it didn't deserve it."

"You think Joanna was paying him off?"

Mearan shrugged, his expression much less guileless all of a sudden. "That's my guess. Playing around with default rates, that wouldn't have worried her. That can be explained. Actual bribery . . ."

"That's the kind of thing people go to jail for," Riley said. "Or at least they would in a well-run criminal justice system. Out here in the real world she'd probably get a fine or a few months at Club Fed. So you're suggesting we look at Mr. Fourtner."

Mearan shrugged again, in an unconvincing show of nonchalance. "You asked why I assumed Joanna would have been worried, and that's what I had assumed. I have no idea if I'm correct or not. She never told me. Maybe Mr. Fourtner is incompetent."

Jack wondered. Mearan had every reason to shift their attention away from himself. Of course, that didn't necessarily make him a liar. "There's another question we have, about Joanna's Panamanian account."

"Huh?"

Jack pulled out the statement showing Joanna's $600,000,000 worth of deposits in the Banco de Panama. He passed it over the desk and asked if Mearan knew where the money in that account had come from, or where more than one half of it had gone.

The young man's gaze darted over the simple form, top to bottom, then top to bottom again. The skin of his face turned a dark red; his body tensed; and he exploded both physically and verbally, leaping up from his chair and pounding the surface of his desk with one fist so hard it should have cracked the mahogany. "That *bitch*!"

Before they could visit the ratings agency, Jack and Riley had an appointment at the Medical Examiner's office, for which they were late. The autopsy on Tyra Simmons had already worked through the torso and reached the skull. The detectives had requested the same pathologist, all the better to note similarities and differences between the two Sterling victims, but that had not been possible. That doctor had Wednesdays off, and the county never, save for extreme circumstances, paid overtime. So they got a small woman with jet-black skin and a perfect bun of graying hair who said she had reviewed the Moorehouse report.

"Death is the same," she told them in sparse language. "Exsanguination. Specifically, the stab wound that sliced open the aorta. She'd have been dead within seconds after that."

"But she'd struggled first," Jack said, more of a statement than a question, given the wounds on Tyra's arms.

"Oh, yeah. She held him off for a very short time, even with the choking. But once he breached the heart, it was all over."

"Choking?"

The pathologist peered at him over Tyra's exposed skullcap. "She had a large hematoma over a partially crushed larynx."

"He hit her in the throat?" Riley interpreted.

"Very hard." She shouted over the bone saw.

"With a weapon?"

"Can't tell. It didn't leave any distinct patterns on the skin, like a gun might. Could be a billy club. Or the side of his hand, if he's in good shape. The throat is a much more delicate area than people realize, easily damaged. This bruised the cartilage, would made it swell quickly."

"So she couldn't scream?" Jack asked.

The doctor shot him a reproachful look as she gently separated the top of the cranium from the brain. "I can't say that, though it certainly wouldn't have been easy. The swelling might have eventually suffocated her if the blood drain hadn't done it first. Huh."

"'Huh'?" Riley demanded. "What's 'huh'?"

"Bruise to the back of the head."

"Would she—" The pathologist eyed him. Riley plunged ahead anyway. "Would she have been unconscious? Don't yell at me. Anything? Best guess? I promise I won't quote you at trial."

"Detective—"

"Wild guess, then."

"If it will make you happy—"

"Deliriously."

"It's a bruise. Nothing life threatening. It would have hurt but there's no real damage."

Jack had been mulling all this over. "Tyra had close neighbors. That's why he had to punch her in the throat, to keep her from screaming."

Riley followed along. "With Joanna, it didn't matter. She could have screamed all night and no one would have heard her."

"Tyra's head landed on the carpet. A thin carpet but—"

"Still nothing like solid stone."

The pathologist let them chatter while she carried Tyra's brain to the counter. She set it on the thick plastic cutting board and sliced it with what looked suspiciously like a bread knife. Apparently she found nothing of interest, now and then only cutting off a sliver to keep for possible future testing. These slivers she dropped into the quart container of formalin sitting nearby.

Jack moved closer to ask her, "Anything in the stomach?"

"About three hundred mil, somewhat digested, so she'd eaten shortly before. Something with grains and possibly milk—like cereal."

"Any abnormalities?"

"None. This girl had been a perfectly, *perfectly* healthy young woman until someone did this to her." The petite doctor looked up at him. "Find that someone, Detective."

"I intend to," he assured her.

Though I have no idea if I can accomplish that, Jack thought as they left the building, hence his wording. A desire to succeed has never guaranteed success. After all, the road to hell is paved with good intentions.

He ought to know that better than anyone.

Chapter 16

The receptionist at Carter & Poe told Riley over the phone that Mr. Fourtner was out on a "site visit" but expected back at three. In the meantime they returned to Joanna's mansion to gather every paper they could find regarding the Panamanian account.

"So, girlfriend was holding out on Mearan," Riley said as he pulled into the winding drive of the huge house. "It seemed to hurt his feelings."

"Was he more angry because she had made plans that didn't include him, or because that money could have paid off their toxic assets and sealed the DJ Bryan deal?"

"Oh, I think his pain was all for himself. Girlfriend intended to retire to a beach in Aruba without taking the boy toy along, 'cause, you know, no matter what they say"—Riley parked the car and opened the door—"they really *don't* respect you in the morning."

The house had been "sealed," which meant that tamper-proof evidence tape had been used over the front door. If broken it would be immediately obvious, and this was deemed "good enough" security so that the department didn't have to waste two patrol officers to guard the property twenty-four hours per day. Of course, anyone could simply enter by another door or window; with such a huge estate the officers hadn't sealed every single opening, even on only the ground floor—more out of concern for the heirs than from laziness. The tape was hell to clean off. It wasn't a perfect system, but few things are in practice. At any rate the front door had not been opened since they'd left the day before. Jack used the keys they had in custody and reset the alarm.

The detectives split up and did a quick exam of the surroundings. Joanna's blood still marred the white marble floor of the living room and the air had grown a bit rank, but there were no pry marks on any windows or doors. The office's controlled chaos remained unchanged from their last visit. If the killer had returned to the scene of the crime, he had left no sign of it.

"Six hundred million," Riley muttered as he searched the desk drawers for more Banco statements. "I can't even wrap my head around that kind of money. I could send my girls to Harvard with that. If they didn't have the grades—which they would, you know—"

"Of course," Jack agreed.

"At least Natalie would. Hannah, I might have to take a page from Joanna's book and bribe the admissions office. But then I'd buy a yacht and sail around the world."

"You don't know how to sail," Jack guessed.

"Doesn't matter. With that kind of money I'd have a crew of twenty . . . a captain, a navigator, a babe in a corset whose only job would be to bring me a beer whenever I wanted one."

Jack paged through the contents of the small filing cabinet, again, looking for anything related to defaults, bank accounts, or Carter & Poe. "And leave the PD? You'd miss it."

Riley laughed uproariously at that one. "Sorry, partner, but I'd be out of that place so fast I'd litter the linoleum with skid marks. I'd call my pension rep from the marina to get the paperwork started. I might leave a Post-it on your desk to say good-bye."

"What, I'm not invited on this yacht?"

"Sure you are. Anytime. It looks like she'd been making steady deposits to this account, nearly every month. This could be her salary, you think? Bonuses?"

"Mearan certainly didn't think so."

Riley moved on to the credenza. "Boy toy may not have known as much as he thinks he did."

"Lauren Schneider disavowed any knowledge as well," Jack reminded him.

"That type would disavow having been born. Though if it were legit she'd have no reason to. Besides, Joanna had her salary directly deposited into this account"—he held up a form—"at Ameritrust. Regular checking, regular savings."

"But how could Joanna embezzle that much from her own company without anyone knowing it? Yeah, she was the boss and yeah she was a control freak, but—"

Jack heard the click of a closing door, somewhere in the house. He and Riley both stared at the open doorway; in unison their hands fell to gun butts and holsters unsnapped. Jack moved toward the hallway, his steps silent and quick. If someone had come in, the same someone who had brutally murdered two women, they needed to exercise extreme caution. If someone had just left, then he was getting away while they dawdled.

The department's victim advocate suddenly appeared in the doorway, startling them both.

"Sorry," she said, a small woman with bird-like movements and uncontrollably curly blond hair. "The door was open. I didn't mean to scare you, you big, tough homicide detectives."

"Super tough," Riley confirmed, resecuring his weapon. "We chew bullets for breakfast."

"I've got the victim's sister here."

"Here?"

"She appeared at my desk practically the minute I set the phone down. Says she was passing through the state anyway. She wanted to see the house, so we were going to do a drive-by . . . but then I saw your car and that the seal had been broken. Okay if I let her in? Do you guys want to talk to her?"

"Yes, we want to talk to her," Riley said.

"Her sister's blood is all over the living room," Jack warned. Victim advocates didn't usually play chauffeur, but this one had a particularly soft heart.

"I'll put her in the kitchen, then," she said, and disappeared again. The detectives looked at each other, dropped their papers, and followed.

But the sister from Iowa had not waited on the porch. They found her in the living room, gazing down at the blackened, flaky blood that had spilled from her sibling's macerated body. Jessica Moorehouse had the roots of Joanna's dark hair as well as her sister's eyes and pale skin and height, but Jessica's frame seemed more wiry than slender, and she had, not recently, bleached the dark tresses to a dried-out straw color. She didn't quite have her sister's flair for simple designs, wearing instead blue jeans with a complicated pattern of deliberate tears and bright new ballet flats. From the breast pocket of a print T-shirt both plunging and tight enough to restrict breathing she pulled a white handkerchief trimmed in lace. "Is this where she died? My sister?" she asked as soon as they entered the room.

"Yes," Riley said. "We're sorry for your loss."

She pressed the handkerchief to her nose.

"If you're feeling up to it, we'd like to ask you some questions about Joanna."

"Have you arrested anybody?"

"No, not yet."

She glanced at the floor again, then around the room. Abruptly she moved away from the bloodstains and circled around the leather sofa, eyeing the areas that hadn't been stained. Next she moved over to the vast windows and their view of the shore. "How does that work with lakes? Does she own all the way to the Canadian border?"

The victim advocate exchanged a look with the cops. "Just the waterfront, I believe."

"And this is Joanna's outright? No mortgage?"

The VA said, "No, she paid cash. Somewhat ironically for a woman who founded a home mortgage business."

Jessica Moorehouse turned from the window with a deep breath. "Well, Joanna always said real estate was the best investment a body could make. I'll be happy to tell you anything I can, Officers. I want you to find who killed my big sister."

They settled her in the kitchen, on the other side of the house. The VA got her a glass of water and then went out to her car to return some phone calls. Jessica Moorehouse sat at the head of the large table, showing a brave face to the detectives but unable to keep her gaze on them. Instead it darted to every inch of the kitchen as if memorizing the space, from the granite countertops to the intricate light fixture.

"Thank you for getting here so quickly," Jack said.

"Oh, no prob. As I said, I was passing through anyway, on my way to visit a cousin in Maine. I'd been thinking of dropping in on Joanna, since I hadn't seen her in a while. But I didn't have this address. This new address." Looking down and giving a little sniff, she added, "I guess I was too late."

"The VA said it had been ten years since you'd heard from Joanna?" Riley asked.

"I'm sure it hadn't been *that* long. Maybe five, probably less. She'd call—we'd call each other once in a while. But we hadn't visited in a number of years, no. We're not a very good family for keeping in touch. Too busy, I guess."

"When was the last time you spoke to her?"

"I really couldn't say."

"Ballpark. One year, four years?"

"I really couldn't say," she repeated, and pressed the handkerchief to a pair of eyes that, Jack now realized, were utterly dry.

"Okay. Whenever it was, what was going on in her life? Did she express concern about any aspect of it?"

"No . . . the usual sister chitchat, you know." She seemed fascinated with the stainless steel side-by-side with the subzero drawer.

"Did she talk about her boyfriend?"

"Joanna was never the kiss-and-tell type."

"What about Sterling?"

She drummed the chewed fingernails of one hand on the tabletop. "Who's Sterling?"

"Her company," Riley said through gritted teeth.

"Oh, of course! Sorry, my brain was still on boyfriends. She didn't talk to me about work—I never had a head for figures. Except my own," she said, and gave them a good look at what there was of it as she abruptly stood. "Joanna and me . . . we didn't grow up in a place like this. Hell, we couldn't have *imagined* a place like this. I was ten before Mama had the cash to buy half a trailer—before that it was falling-down motels and abandoned buildings. We lived for three years in a condemned hotel. Believe it or not, that was the nicest place I remember. Somehow one of the guys who lived there—we weren't alone, the place was full of families—kept the water turned on no matter what the water company did, and sometimes we had electricity. Joanna and I caught the school bus on the next corner even though we weren't on the driver's roster. They weren't so fussy about those things back then. We didn't leave until the city tore the place down. The trailer," she continued as she began to open cabinets, examining their contents, "we had to share with another lady and her two boys. They were younger than me and Jo but tough little shits, made picking on us their purpose in life. Jo and I finally caught the older one alone and dragged him out into the woods, beat half the life out of him. He told his mama some boys had done it, wouldn't admit it was girls. But they stopped teasing us. We even got to be sort of friends after a while." She pulled a heavy plate out from a shelf, held the plain white saucer in her fingers, smoothing a thumb over the surface. "He probably would have been my first baby daddy if his ma hadn't died and they had to go live with their dad. Who promptly kicked them out anyway."

"And Joanna—" Riley prompted, trying to speed up this trip down hardscrabble memory lane.

But Jessica didn't seem in any hurry, exploring each cabinet as if they held royal jewels instead of pots and pans, some with the price tags still attached. "Jo got old enough to get a job at a grocery store. She started bagging but then worked in the office."

"How old was she?"

"Fourteen. She looked a lot older. She figured that was why the manager hired her, but he never tried any funny stuff, she said." She laughed, fingering a coffee mug. "She'd have cut him in half if he'd tried. Joanna might have been tough, but she was no slut. She could have ruled our little town if she wanted to, could have gotten the mayor into her bed with a glance, but she didn't care about that. All she wanted to do with our little town was get the hell out of it." She shut the last cabinet. "Can't blame her for that. I wanted that too, but where did I go? She always was stronger than me." She ran her fingers along the polished counter, feeling its hard surface. "But, on the other hand, I'm still alive."

None of this seemed helpful. Jack said, "So she moved to LA?"

"Headed west. Only she didn't care about getting into the movies, just getting a job. I don't know how she came here, to Ohio." She opened a drawer and loose silverware rattled, adding, "I'm sure she told me, but I don't remember."

"Can you remember anything she mentioned about her life, about Sterling Financial, any legal issues?"

The dark roots quivered as her head came up. "What legal issues?"

"That's what we're trying to determine, if she had any worries in her life."

"No. Nothing. We . . . we mostly talked about family things. Our cousins. Kids we went to school with, that sort of thing."

And how were you talking, Jack thought, *when there were no Iowa area codes in Joanna's call history, no family e-mails, and she didn't have a Skype or Facebook account.*

Unless she had a second phone that the killer had taken with him. "What phone number did you call to talk to Joanna?"

"I . . . can't remember the number offhand. I had her in my contacts."

"Can you show us? We need to make sure that we're aware of all of Joanna's telephone numbers."

A hand went to her left butt cheek as if to protect the rectangular piece of electronics resting there. "I got a new phone a few weeks ago. The contacts didn't transfer right, so I've actually lost Joanna's number. . . . That was one of the reasons I planned to stop by on my way to Maine."

Except that she had neither an address nor a phone number to "stop by" to. "Uh-huh."

Jessica peeked into the garage, scanning that area. "Have you . . . found . . . ?"

"Who killed her? We're working very hard on that."

She faced them, handkerchief forgotten. "A will. Did Jo leave a will?"

"We haven't found one. But then we weren't looking for one."

"She didn't marry, had no children, right? That lady told me that."

"As far as we know, but that's up to the probate court to determine."

"But without a will this all goes to next of kin, right? That's me."

"Your mother," Riley said, standing as well. They might as well give up on this interview. Obviously Joanna had had no contact with her sister since walking out of the family trailer ten years earlier.

"*And* me," Jessica repeated, examining the alarm panel. She opened the hinged door and peered at the controls.

"I believe Ohio law says next of kin is parent, before sibling. But as I said, that's probate's department."

Jessica closed the alarm panel with a *snap*. "Didn't I tell you? Mama passed," Jessica assured them. "Not very long ago."

"Sorry for your loss," Riley said automatically. Jack said nothing.

"Thank you. You're so kind. So there's this house, and that Beamer in the garage, and—what about bank accounts? How much did she have in the bank?"

"I really couldn't say," Jack told her, and if she

caught the sarcasm she gave no sign. He didn't even have to signal his partner to know that they would not be mentioning the remaining millions in the Banco de Panama. If it had been illegally siphoned from Sterling it would have to be repatriated. No point letting Jessica Moorehouse salivate over a sum she may not receive. "Again, that's up to the probate court to research and determine."

She rolled her eyes. "How long will *that* take?"

Riley said, "We don't know. Thank you for your time, Miss Moorehouse."

"Okay," she said easily. "Good-bye."

"I'm afraid you have to leave as well. We're not authorized to turn over the keys—"

"But this place is mine now," she stated, in a voice turned to stone.

"Not officially, I'm afraid. We have not released it as a crime scene, and after that it's up to the Medical Examiner's office. They will let you know when you can take possession."

Anger pushed aside all pretense of grieving. "But this is my place now. I need to stay here. I'm not paying for a hotel when there's this huge house all empty. Where's the sense in that?"

"We're trying to find who murdered your sister," Riley reminded her. "This is still a crime scene. We can't allow you to remain."

Her face flushed, but she had been beaten back often enough in life to know which battles to pick. "All right. Fine. Just snap it up."

She stalked past them without another word and marched out to the driveway, her new shoes making snapping sounds along the tile and concrete. The victim advocate now stood in front of the car but Jessica ignored her to throw herself into the passenger seat.

"You didn't make a friend," the VA observed.

Riley said, "I think she expected to haul her suitcase up the front steps as soon as we left. She said the mother is dead."

"She is? I didn't see a death certificate while checking vitals. When?"

"Miss Jessica didn't say. Frankly, she didn't say much. How quickly did she get here after you called?"

"I swear it was overnight. I didn't locate a number for her until after quitting time, and she showed up at my desk bright and early this morning."

"How long does it take to drive from Iowa?" Riley asked Jack.

"Never been there," Jack said, which wasn't entirely true. Actually it wasn't true at all, but that would be another memory lane that did not need a stroll right this minute. "It would depend where in Iowa, but she could probably do it overnight."

Riley said, "Or she was already here, stops by like she says to look up dear old sis, realizes dear old sis has been holding out on her and isn't interested in letting country-girl sibling hone in on her new sophisticated lifestyle. They argue, baby sis knows exactly who's going to inherit. . . . I can totally see this chick getting funky with a butcher knife. She's probably slaughtered hogs by the dozens."

The VA laughed. "Okay, living in Iowa doesn't automatically mean living on a farm."

"Do me a favor anyway—you talked to the deputies in that town, to make the notification?"

"Yes."

"Call them back. Ask them if Jessica was in town yesterday, and if Mama is, in fact, dead. If she's still breathing then they need to seriously consider protection before Ma has an accidental fall or eats some bad toadstools."

"That's a bit . . . imaginative."

Riley threw a dark glance toward the car's occupant. "Hog slaughterer."

"And," Jack said, still reasoning out the homicides, "how would she even know Tyra? Or have any motive to kill her?"

"To cover the motive. Make it look like it's all about Sterling and that missing six hundred million."

"*How* many million?" the VA asked.

"Never mind. Just make sure we know exactly where baby sister is staying, her current address, everything. Please. I don't want her disappearing."

The VA nodded toward the mansion's facade. "She thinks she's going to inherit *that*. Take my word for it, we couldn't budge that girl out of Cleveland with a crowbar and baby oil."

Chapter 17

Maggie drove back from the Medical Examiner's office, where she had picked up Tyra Simmons's fingernail scrapings and clothing tapings. The clouds had parted without actually raining, leaving the baking earth with a sense of incompleteness.

Her route took her past Sterling's offices, where the usual group of about fifteen protesters thronged the sidewalk—with two additions. Ned Swift stood at their forefront, facing a pale Anna Hernandez. The chat did not look friendly.

Maggie hesitated. She needed to get back to the lab and spare some time to prepare for whatever Gerry Graham's defense attorney decided to throw at her—she could *not* let some fast-talking shyster bamboozle the jury. But before she knew it she had pulled the car to the curb and joined Anna, the sun and the protesters' stares equally glaring. They were hot, tired, and frustrated.

Thus, she entered the argument in the middle. ". . . rewarded fat Wall Street firms by bailing them out," Ned finished.

Anna said, "Would you have preferred to jump back to the early thirties, when thirty-eight percent of banks failed because credit dried up? Everyone knows recessions are even worse when people and businesses already have high debt levels. Collapsing consumer spending sent production and employment reeling. Someone had to spend, and that was the government."

"Which you violated the Constitution to do!" Ned moved closer to Anna. Maggie moved closer to Ned, without any idea what she would do if he threw a punch or, God forbid, the crowd joined in. They seemed ready, pushed to the brink of the abyss by fear and desperation.

"Oh, make up your mind—we were too far removed from investment banks to be able to legally loan to them, or we were supposed to control even the non-Fed-regulated banks so this wouldn't happen in the first place?" This momentarily silenced him but she didn't seem to notice. "And Section 13(3) of the Federal Reserve Act says we can loan to anyone in unusual or exigent circumstances, and the circumstances couldn't get much more exigent."

"The Fed acted way outside its powers," Ned insisted. The protesters were a mix of average colors, genders, and ages, but two men of greater than average musculature flanked Ned Swift. They looked ridiculous trying to stare down the petite Anna, but Maggie had no faith that the traditional disdain for picking on someone smaller would apply here. Surely the indignity of "beating up on a girl" didn't seem to occur to males of the modern age.

Anna said, "Don't fool yourself that the bailouts weren't sanctioned. Your congressmen and -women knew exactly what the Fed and the Treasury were going to do and exactly why. They agreed it was necessary, behind closed doors. But put a camera in their face and then it's all hand-wringing and outrage. They voted TARP down to look good in front of their constituents, until those constituents saw their pension plans shrink like plastic wrap under a hair dryer. Then Congress grew a pair and passed it. Reed, Pelosi, and Dodd *asked* the Fed to loan to GM and Chrysler—"

"Never mind GM," a dumpling of a woman interrupted. "What does this have to do with the people here foreclosing on my house?"

"Forget it, Mrs. Davis," Ned sneered. "Our government is only interested in helping their Wall Street pals."

"Wall Street *is* Main Street," Anna said, more vitalized than cowed by this confrontation. A true believer. "If credit is choked off growth goes down, unemployment goes up. Congress wanted to wait until the damage got huge, visible, and irreversible . . . and the money lent to those Wall Street pals, incidentally, was repaid with interest in six years, putting a profit of four hundred and seventy billion back in the government's coffers."

Ned said, "Only so the banks could get around the executive pay restrictions."

"Does it matter why, as long as the US got its money back?"

"Pay restrictions should have been made permanent!"

"You want to nationalize the banks? Have private enterprise taken over by the government?" Anna all but purred. The crowd of staunch mideasterners turned to look at Ned.

"What? No!"

"That's what it would take. It's not practical otherwise—if conditions are too onerous the firms wouldn't participate."

"Fine," Mrs. Davis said. "Can I have some of that four hundred billion?"

"Sorry," Anna said, sounding genuinely regretful. Her color had not returned, the shock of Tyra's death obviously still with her. And having to talk a mob out of a riot wouldn't help, Maggie thought. Maggie needed an opening to break in, get Anna, and leave with her. She felt 95 percent sure that this incident represented only posturing by Ned Swift, but also 95 percent positive that his motives wouldn't matter if the crowd decided to act.

But Anna kept talking. "The profit we make on loans like that and T-bills, once our operating expenses are deducted, goes to the Treasury to reduce the deficit."

"I need *my* deficit reduced." But the woman's voice had calmed.

"I'm sorry the Fed couldn't save the economy, and your economy, entirely. This wasn't just the worst financial crisis since the Great Depression—it was the worst *ever*. We kept a recession from turning into a depression. It was the best we could do."

Mrs. Davis patted the young woman's arm, commiserating over a suddenly shared sorrow, and Ned Swift's face reddened. Maggie calculated how many steps lay between her and her car. Between her and Anna and her car. Sweat trickled down her back, not entirely from the humidity.

Maggie said, "Anna—"

A young man popped up with a sarcastic tone. "One more time—why are we talking about what happened ten years ago when *this* year Sterling lied to me about my loan?"

"Ask Ned," Anna said. "He brought it up."

Swift opened his mouth as if his next words would be at earsplitting decibels, but nothing came out. He had exhausted his diatribe and gotten nowhere, and it made him angry. Angry men could turn violent within a nanosecond, something Maggie knew only too well.

"This isn't helping," Maggie said to the crowd. "She can't help you. The woman you should be haranguing is already dead. Come on, Anna." She laid a hand on the young woman's rock-hard bicep and tugged, hoping the person she tried to rescue wouldn't turn against her. That could happen, too.

But Anna slowly moved.

"Good luck with your lawsuit," Maggie told the crowd, which seemed to soften enough of them that she got herself and Anna across the street and into the car without any epithets or thrown missiles. As she started the engine she watched Ned Swift on the opposite curb, his eyes narrowed against more than the sun.

In front of his own people he had failed to skewer the enemy in a battle of wits, and now he looked as if he wanted to skewer Anna with a set of sharp knives. And Maggie, too. She drove away.

Chapter 18

Anna finally spoke. "Thanks for the ride. And—thanks."

"No problem. Where were you going?"

"Lunch, I guess. I had to get out of the office. I couldn't sit still and crunch numbers. No one there gives a crap about Joanna and even less about Tyra. And I keep seeing her lying there. . . . I should have gone out the back way but I didn't think . . . why did you stop?"

"I thought they were going to lynch you."

"So did I."

"Have they ever gotten violent? Against people at Sterling?"

"Not that I know of. Ned seemed to be all talk. Until today."

Maggie squinted. She had forgotten her sunglasses. "Where should I drop you?"

"Right here." Anna pointed, and Maggie pulled into Totally Fresh!'s small parking lot. "Would you join me?"

She needed to prep for the Graham trial. She had evidence in the car. But Anna, despite the resolve she'd shown the mob, trembled from hairline to ankle. And Maggie felt hungry. Starving, actually.

Maggie left the scrapings and tapings in the car. She locked the vehicle; only she had the keys, the items were to be stored at room temperature anyway, and the odds of the killer or some random vehicle burglar breaking into the car to steal what had been found under Tyra Simmons's nails had to be astronomical. Besides, the diner had only a small lot and she could see the car from the window. This should, she believed, constitute sufficient chain of custody. And she really *was* hungry.

The air-conditioning greeted them with a welcome blast of chill. The restaurant had room for only six tables along a spotless tile floor. The equally spotless kitchen stayed in full view, where hair-netted employees in sparkling white smocks assembled lunches for the healthy-food crowd. The peak lunch hour had faded yet customers still filled the order-line rails.

Don't talk about the case, Maggie reminded herself as they waited in line for the nice-looking delivery boy from the day before to take their order. *Don't share any police information, don't ask anything that could be construed as an interrogation, and* don't *tell her you're on the way back from Tyra's autopsy.*

"I had to get out of there," Anna said again when they sat. "Two people dead in two days, and all they care about is market share. The . . . surrealism got to me and so . . . I decided that nothing counteracts surrealism like chicken and almonds with rice noodles."

"Absolutely," Maggie said, just to say something.

"Although I think mac and cheese would be even more antisurreal. Maybe a good bloody hamburger with bacon and cheddar."

"Comfort food."

"Yeah." It didn't seem any amount of food could comfort Anna. She picked at her noodles.

Say something, Maggie ordered herself. *Something that's not about dead bodies of sweet girls.* "Why does Ned blame Sterling's habits on the Federal Reserve?"

Anna gave this some thought before answering. "Used to be, banks were careful about loaning because if the borrower didn't pay the loan back, the bank lost. Problem was, sometimes banks assumed people were bad risks because they were the wrong color or gender or had had a period of low earnings. Plus they were the only place to go for a long-term loan so they could afford to be picky. Credit needed some democratization, and one White House after another, regardless of party, wanted to up home ownership in the United States. Home ownership makes citizens more stable, contributes to overall economic stability, etcetera. America's always been more sentimental about home ownership than other countries. So presidents encouraged financial firms and especially their own Fannie and Freddie to make more loans—there's nothing wrong with legitimate subprime lending—and investors got hooked on mortgage-backed securities. Meanwhile, the Internet and computerized credit scores made it easier to examine and approve borrowers, regardless of whether you had a branch in their city or not. Good for borrowers—now *they* could be picky, and go for better rates than the snooty bank. They could go to mortgage loan originators, like Sterling, and other firms that only did loans. I know what you're thinking."

Maggie had been thinking that she should have stuck to a more general topic. Like the weather. But at least Anna now ate her noodles instead of pushing them around on her recycled paper plate.

"Why aren't I in Ned's corner, wanting to publicly crucify Sterling? Practicality. The whole financial crisis started with Bear Stearns—they had a lot of mortgages, too much uncollateralized paper, and they tried to fix it. But once a run on them began, no one would lend to them even with T-bills—totally safe—as collateral."

Maggie remembered to check on her—or rather, the city's—car but the Taurus with the faded paint rested comfortably in the parking space, windows and doors intact, Tyra Simmons's fingernail scrapings undisturbed.

"Bear wasn't too big to fail; it was too interconnected . . . like a chain-link fence. Each wire is only one wire, but pull on it and the whole fence wobbles. It's been ten years, but still this country can't afford another wobble," Anna said in deadly earnest. "I want the Sterling problem to be quietly and discreetly dealt with by merging with Bryan. That is my top priority here, not, unfortunately, helping those poor people whom Sterling cheated."

"You think Sterling did?" Maggie asked, before she could stop herself.

Anna finished the last of her noodles. "I can't prove it. Here's the life of a regulator: Firms are supposed to open their books to us, so we can check that they're meeting their capital requirements and that their reported incomes and outgoes are on track with what they're reporting. Simple, right? Except we're getting the information from the very people we're regulating. I guess it's like a criminal investigation. You can't open up a suspect's head and look inside. You can only find out what they're willing to tell you. And if it's like, oh yeah, I stole that car, they're sure as hell not going to tell you. Lauren has a habit of waving away my requests as 'confidential' and Joanna simply ignored me. Jeremy continually gave me printouts that were outdated. The guy who had them before me . . . not a bad guy, but he had short-timers' syndrome, ready to retire and his brain had already chartered a fishing boat in the Keys. Definitely not about to challenge anything or anyone in any real way."

"You think he let stuff go?"

"I think he let a *lot* go. Their capital requirements had been underserved for years before I got there."

"So you're—"

"Hamstrung. All we can hope is that the firm is either sloppy, so that you find the important stuff anyway, or that they're actually honest and aren't doing anything bad. And a little courtesy is great, too. Most firms do a great job of faking their complete cooperation, but some are stupid enough to be dismissive or hostile. In Fannie and Freddie's heyday they treated their regulators like absolute dirt, because they had so much pull on the Hill they could get away with it. But our power to interfere in business dealings is limited— by design. We have a capitalistic society and it's been working pretty darn well for over two hundred years."

"What *can* you do?"

"Write my report as best I can. Point out what else I need to see and that requests for same have been denied. Complain to my superiors. Same old same old. Supervisors promise to look into it, maybe even report to the relevant congressional subcommittee, people murmur, political parties make more contributions, resolutions get adjusted, parties make more contributions, and somehow it all gets lost in the shuffle. You make noise, you eventually get drowned out. You make too much noise, you get transferred or fired. In this day and age of short attention spans, contributions to parties and super PACs are like water in a watering can. It keeps washing the harsh parts of the legislation away until the cliff of legal versus illegal has been eroded into a gentle slope. Dodd-Frank was enacted years ago, but it's still being rewritten. Congress wants to gut the Consumer Financial Protection Bureau and fund it through congressional committee instead of directly through the Fed. Funding is everything. Once they hold those purse strings they can bring even a bulldog to heel. That's how Fannie and Freddie got away with so much for so long."

"Wow." Maggie had only finished half her salad, so fascinated by this portrait. "That really sucks."

"Yeah . . . I guess it's like your job. You battle the crime, but you can never make it stop. All you can do is keep trying to fight the good fight. You can't change anyone's integrity but your own."

Hardly a new thought, but it struck Maggie with a force she didn't expect. Was that what she was doing? Fighting a good fight? Jack had killed people and she had looked the other way. *She* had killed someone and looked the other way. What the hell did *that* say about her integrity?

Just when she began to think she had coped, she had put all past events in a box in her head where they could stay quiet and stop screwing with her sense of the world, they burst out with teeth bared and claws flying.

"You okay?" Anna said with concern. "You suddenly look . . . um . . ."

"Yeah, fine. I thought of something, that's all," Maggie lied, as she had been lying to everyone around her for thirty-seven days. She had gotten good at it. "Thanks for explaining all that, though. I find it interesting."

"Happy to. Usually I bore people to death."

Maggie smiled but her stomach churned, now rejecting the delicious lunch. At least Anna looked better. Her color had returned and the trembling was gone.

Standing, Anna said, "Thanks for the physical and mental rescue, too. We'll have to do lunch again. Next up in the series of lectures by Anna Hernandez: derivatives and what they mean to you."

"I look forward to it."

They emerged into the hottest part of the day, reflected sunbeams wafting up from the city's asphalt. Despite the temperature Anna wanted to walk back to the office and Maggie didn't argue; she knew how a brisk stride with no company save your own could help to clear one's head. But as she unlocked the driver's door, Anna standing only a foot away, the rear driver's-side window exploded into a thousand tiny shards of glass.

For a split second Maggie could only stare, her mind dumbly wondering why a pane of glass would suddenly decide to self-destruct, and hope that none of the shards now piercing her forearms would find their way into her eyes. Or Anna's.

Then she let go of her keys, grabbed Anna Hernandez, and shuffled them both into a crouch behind the rear bumper before she even registered the tuft of stuffing coming from the rear driver's-side headrest inside the shattered window. The shot had come from the car's ten o'clock. She needed to get the bulky metal object in between her and Anna and the shooter.

Elsewhere on the street, excited voices raised, brakes squealed, other tires accelerated in fear or escape. The two women clutched each other. No more shots came, but Maggie didn't intend to take any chances. She dialed 911 with one trembling thumb and kept Anna huddled behind the car until the cavalry arrived.

Chapter 19

"Not even a make?" Riley asked her in disbelief.

"I didn't even turn and look," Maggie said, embarrassed and miserable. She sat in the back of an ambulance in the Totally Fresh! parking lot, more for protective cover than out of medical need. "I grabbed Anna and ducked behind the bumper. It could be anything from a pickup to a bicycle for all I know. He might have been on foot, though that sounds awfully risky."

The detective said, "All right, don't beat yourself up about it." But it sounded like a suggestion to beat herself up about it, at least a little.

Jack hadn't said a word yet. He watched the EMT pick the last sliver of glass out of her left elbow and gazed pointedly at the small pile of bloody gauze accumulating in the biohazard trash can. None of the cuts were deep, but they were legion and included a few in her chin. Clothing had protected the rest of her body. Anna had fared only slightly better. As if the poor girl hadn't already been through enough for one day, Maggie thought.

Riley said, "Patrol grabbed what passersby they could corral and a few helpful drivers stuck around. With luck they'll come up with something."

Jack interrupted, as if he had held it back as long as he could, "I told you to be careful."

"What?"

"Graham made threats against several of the witnesses in his trial. You were one. I told you that."

"They weren't shooting at me." She refrained from adding *you idiot*, but could hear the words in her voice. "They were shooting at Anna."

"You don't know that."

"As I had rescued her from a mob only a half hour before, yes, I pretty much do. It had to be one of Ned's gang. Those people are frustrated and angry way, way past desperate."

"So is Graham. He never intended to go without a fight."

"How would anyone in Graham's gang know where to find me? I've never been here before and had no plans to stop. Anna and everyone else at Sterling frequent this place every day."

Jack wouldn't let up. "They followed you."

"No, they followed *her*. I'm so far down on Graham's list of enemies they wouldn't get to me until next year. They'd take *you* out long before me."

"You're the whole case. The prosecutor believes that, so you'd better trust the defense team does as well."

"Criminals don't assassinate forensic scientists! That kind of thing only happens on TV."

"Distressed home owners don't assassinate Fed regulators, either! Anna doesn't even work for Sterling."

Riley held up both hands. "Kids, kids. Let's agree to disagree on the theory of this and—"

"They can't figure that out, and even if they can they may not care. You didn't see this group up close and personal. Their lives have been decimated. They are ready to get blood on their hands."

Jack said, "You need to—"

"I don't even blame them," Maggie continued, and to her horror she heard the tremble in her voice that told her tears weren't too far away. "Sterling is horrible. They prey on people over and over and have no remorse. They're doing the wrong thing and they know it and they do"—she looked at Jack—"nothing. They don't stop."

He shut his mouth with a snap.

Maggie tried to shut hers, with less success. But she forced herself off the topic of personal responsibility to say, "As if Anna hasn't had enough shocks today. First she finds her friend's mutilated body."

"Mutilated?" the EMT repeated, with some interest.

"Then she's nearly lynched, now this. It's a wonder the poor girl is even coherent." To the EMT she advised: "You should prescribe a sedative."

"Thanks for the confidence, but I don't have the authority to write script. Not an MD."

"That's too bad." She knew she was babbling in the aftereffects of shock, but she couldn't help it.

"My bank account thinks so, too."

Not willing to concede an inch, Jack said they would

drive her back to the station. In cuffs if necessary, his tone implied. They would pull up their car to the end of the ambulance to lessen the distance—

"No! Not until I get some stuff out of the car."

"It will be towed. Your purse and camera will be—"

"Tyra's tapings and fingernail scrapings," she told him. "I'm not leaving without them."

Rick Gardiner had his feet up on his desk, coffee cup on his blotter, chair tilted back, a legal pad in his lap, but despite this relaxed stance he might actually be getting somewhere. Scribbles appeared on the pad as he asked questions of a homicide detective named Daley who worked out of the Maryvale precinct in Phoenix, Arizona. After being transferred around by a few brusque types, Detective Daley ("no relation to the Chicago Daleys") seemed willing to chat at length about the run of vigilante-type killings they'd had roughly four years before.

"Of course at the time we didn't know they were connected. Just seemed like lowlifes shooting lowlifes, you know?"

"Sure. Here too."

"Between the meth labs and the coyotes and the flow of drugs over the border, we've always got plenty of guys turning up dead. It actually used to be worse, back before the housing market bust. When it did, I think a lot of our more fringe-type transient dwellers moved on and the homicide rate went *down*."

"Yeah? Here too. Well, first it went down and then when the economy sucked it went up and now it's down again."

"But the woman with the elderly people—that was weird. Not in the normal pattern of dealers and cartels. An outlier, that's what they call that. I never forgot those old people—who could?—but we didn't connect her case with these murders."

Rick noticed his captain in the hallway, in conversation with a lieutenant, and swung his feet down before the captain turned.

"These people were like nothing I've ever seen. Human beings left to rot in place while they were still alive. I've worked child murders that didn't freak me out as much as that place did. I'd been kind of on the outs with my son—he's my only kid—but after that I called up and mended ways. Took a while, but someday I'll need someone to give a shit if I have a bedsore eating through my leg, you know?"

"Yeah. Do you have a description of this woman?"

"A vague one. There was one old lady there still coherent—she hadn't been there that long—and she said white female, thirty-five or forty, long dark hair, brown eyes, maybe five-six. It took us four days to get that out of her, plus a name: Ethel Barrios. But if such a person existed she did it without a legitimate driver's license, a credit card, or a phone."

"How'd you find them?"

"My old buddy Anonymous Tipster."

"Female or male?"

"Male, nine-one-one said. Low voice, no accent. So this dark-haired bitch wound up dead in your city?"

"Looks that way. Right next to our victims, who sound like carbon copies of yours. Now I'm looking for the guy who shot her."

"When you do, pin a medal on him for me."

"I'm okay with that. You said you had about five cases that maybe sounded like the same guy?"

"Only in that all five took three twenty-twos to the back of the head and were found outside. Their pals and their enemies all disavowed any knowledge, but of course they would. I worked one of them, and . . . was weird, I'll admit. Another outlier."

"Why?"

The captain entered the maze of detectives' cubicles and Rick hunched over his legal pad, making notes about things he didn't even need notes on. He wrote ".22" and "5 cases—Daley." Always best to look busy when the captain was around, even when the man had ridden a desk most of his career and wouldn't know how to catch a bad guy unless you hog-tied said bad guy first and erected a big red arrow next to him.

"This one dealer turned up dead. Really bad dude, made El Chapo look like Hello Kitty. But his inner circle would never have had the guts to move against him, and if they had they would have bragged about it and used it to cement their position as the baddest mother. Instead, his guys seemed lost without him. The gang fell apart, and their territory absorbed into other groups. And his enemies—again, if they had done it they'd be twirling signs on street corners to brag about it. Nothing quite seemed to fit, you know?"

"Yeah, I do. Any hints of who the shooter had been? If it wasn't one of the usual group?"

"Not a peep. Everyone on the street seemed even more clueless than we were." Rick held the phone away from his ear as the guy coughed hard enough to macerate a lung. "Sorry. Don't believe them when they tell you this dry air is so good for your sinuses. The dryness just means you breathe in more dust. Anyway, meant to say after your reporter called, we pooled our suspicious cases and found one where there might be something sorta like a witness."

He'd be leaving the reporter's role out of his report, Rick knew. Then he perked up and not only for the captain's benefit. "A witness?"

"We had a coyote—obviously, in my area, we have a lot of them, a guy who sneaks people over the border. Sometimes they simply do the job, sometimes they hold up on one side or the other until the crossers or their families cough up more money—"

"I know what a coyote is," Rick snapped.

If Daley noticed the pissiness he didn't give any sign. "So this guy took money from the illegals, brought them over a section of border that's in the middle of nowhere in a four-wheel pickup that he and a buddy had modified. They put extra shields and super-tough stuff along the undercarriage so this thing could go over the desert like a tank, but they could ride it on the streets and it would look like a totally ordinary truck. Except with crappy gas mileage."

"And he—"

"He'd bring the illegals and dump them out at a city park—or at least he'd dump the adults and the kids who belonged to them. But there're always a few un-accompanied minors, you know, whose parents shove them into the chute to get them out of whatever hell-hole they're living in. They're supposed to hook up with relatives on this side or tag along with their fellow crossers. So this coyote would say he had friends who worked in legal aid, specializing in getting children classified as abandoned children and political refugees, etcetera, put them on the path to getting legalized. But it only worked for abandoned children, no adults or families, blah blah. So the other crossers scatter like coues and he's left with a few unattached kids."

"Cooze?"

"Coues. They're deer, white-tail deer. Only found in this area."

"Huh," Rick said. "Can you hunt them?"

"Yeah, in season. They're small, though, not like those horse-sized things you guys have up there. Anyway the crossers go off and leave the kids with this nice coyote, see?"

"Not good," Rick guessed.

"You could say that. He locks them in his basement, in these cages. Rapes, starves, screws with them in every way possible mental and physical, like they're his own personal ant farm and he's got the magnifying glass. Boys, girls, he don't care. The ones we found were between nine and fourteen. The people they crossed with, they'd be off trying to make their own lives, not hanging out with this coyote, who might come to the attention of authorities at any moment. If family members in Mexico ask questions he'd say the other crossers found a family to take them in but he didn't know where. Even when the kids' families got suspicious what could they do? Call the police and tell them they were having trouble with their personal smuggler? We figured one of them took care of him themselves. It would hardly be the first time."

"That sounds more logical than—"

"Except all the cages were full. If a family member had offed the guy, surely they would have come back to spring the kids and skip a nine-one-one call to the PD."

"Did the children give you anything?"

"Not much. Most of them wouldn't say a word in any language, but one did. Not right away. Department of Child Safety took the ones who couldn't or wouldn't give us someone to contact in either country, and this one little girl got comfy enough with her caseworker to tell her about a man who had come to the house and taken the coyote away. She said the coyote showed him the cages, sort of bragging about them all friendly-like, but then the man pulled a gun on the guy and they went away. Next thing she knows the cops are break-ing in the doors and she never sees the coyote again."

Rick said, "That's our guy. Kills the coyote and calls nine-one-one for the kids."

"A real humanitarian."

"This girl got a look at him?"

"They came right up to her cage. But she was only about seven then, without a word of English. She said he was a big guy, white, with brown hair. That was it. And since she barely weighed forty pounds I'm pretty sure every man in the universe would be 'big' to her."

Rick thought fast. "Can you get in touch with her? This girl?"

"No idea. I can check with DCS, see if they know where she went. But it's been five years—she's proba-bly bounced between ten different relatives by now, might even be back in Mexico."

Rick didn't give him more time to talk himself out of it. "I'd really appreciate that. If you do find her I can e-mail a sketch."

"You've got a sketch?"

"Yeah." He didn't bother to explain it came from his

ex-wife. "If this girl could take a look at it, confirm or deny that it's the same guy, it would help a lot."

"That's a long shot. She'd be twelve or thirteen by now, might not remember much."

"Long shots are all I've got at this point," Rick grumbled before ringing off. He left his hand on the phone, drumming the fingers of the other on his face, realizing that even if he could confirm that his guy had been in Phoenix, it didn't necessarily help him find where the guy was *now*. But it would justify his salary and, therefore, and most importantly, would be good for Rick.

"Getting somewhere, Gardiner?" his captain asked. The guy had stopped next to his desk; Rick had been so involved he hadn't even noticed.

"Maybe so, Cap," he told the idiot ass-kissing social climber, with no little amount of satisfaction. "Maybe so."

Chapter 20

Mr. Fourtner had returned to the rather plush offices of Carter & Poe and could see them now, but still Jack and his partner had to wait ten-plus minutes in the small reception area. Riley, who never passed up anything free—candy, coffee, snacks, or especially alcohol—had promptly availed himself of the Keurig-type machine. He chose the most exotic-sounding dark roast and opted for the heavy porcelain mug instead of to-go paper. Jack paced a slow circle around the soft leather couch; its color matched the coffee. He had a bad feeling they were about to waste more time. Sidney Fourtner rated Sterling's financial products, which allowed Sterling to easily sell such financial products for a healthy profit. Several sources had said those ratings were not justified by any facts on this plane of reality. To reconcile those two sides, Sidney Fourtner would no doubt launch into the same sophisticated gobbledygook that all these types used for one reason and only one reason: to hide the truth of where the money came from and where it went. And maybe the even worse truth that they weren't sure themselves. They could bet Fourtner wouldn't admit that Joanna Moorehouse had bribed him to give her securities triple-A ratings when they didn't deserve them.

And why, Jack asked himself, had he and Riley been giving Joanna's second-in-command, Lauren Schneider, a pass? If she really was Joanna's right hand, then certainly she knew about bad loans defaulting right and left and the arrangement, if there had been one, with Sidney Fourtner.

As soon as they were done there, he intended to head right back to Sterling. Joanna and Tyra had both known something that got them killed. If Jeremy did not make up the third point of a conspiratorial triangle—and he might—then surely Lauren had to be the most likely candidate for the slot.

Meanwhile, he puzzled over the shot fired at the two women. Perhaps, *perhaps*, Maggie was right and it had been intended for Anna. The theory had a lot going for it. But he didn't want her counting on it. Maggie tended to think that no one noticed her, when the truth was *everyone* noticed her. She tended to think that because she worked in forensics that made her invisible, that even if cops had targets painted on their backs every minute of the day it would never affect her. He knew her to be wrong. But what could he do and, reasonably, what could she? She could hardly stop coming to work, might even be more vulnerable alone at home. He kept pacing, his mind ping-ponging between the horns of this dilemma.

"Detectives," said a voice, and Jack turned. Sidney

Fourtner immediately struck him as a fair-haired version of Jeremy Mearan: young, handsome, a body toned in the gym. But Fourtner strode with a confidence that Mearan didn't yet have, and his cool appraising stare belied an arrogance that Mearan hadn't yet developed. He was a Westminster blue ribbon winner compared to the puppyish Mearan. Jack disliked him instantly, the way any not-so-handsome guy dislikes a pretty boy, for whom the world opens like an oyster offering a pearl the size of a basketball.

That Fourtner welcomed them with a gracious hello only made it worse. "Please come in. Have a seat. Excuse my office, it's a bit cluttered." By this he meant two or three thin manila folders on the glossy wood of his desk. The rest of the spotless area was all tasteful décor and expensive furniture. A narrow but tall window showed them the Flats as well as a curious pigeon, looking in at them.

"What can I do for you?" Fourtner asked as soon as they settled.

Riley explained that they were investigating the two murders at Sterling. Surely he had heard about them?

He had. "Terrible. And bizarre—women to be attacked in their homes like that. Do you think it's a serial killer?"

"It's highly unlikely that he would randomly pick two women from the same company."

"No, I wouldn't expect that to be random at all. But it could still be a serial killer, some psycho who works at Sterling."

"Do you have anyone particular in mind?" Jack asked, to see what he would say.

"No . . . I rate their financial products. I don't spend a lot of time in their office."

Riley said, "Or with Joanna Moorehouse?"

He didn't blink, didn't hesitate. "Joanna was more than a client. She was a friend. I'll miss her."

"Is that allowed? To be friends with the head of a company you have to rate?"

Fourtner smiled, with a touch of what seemed to be real sadness. It only made him more handsome. Jack wondered if money hadn't been the only thing swaying him to Joanna's wishes. "In a perfect world, no. But this is a relatively rarified field, especially in a smaller city like this one. Everybody knows everybody; you can't help it. So yes, Joanna and I were friends."

"Or more than friends?" Jack suggested.

"Did we date? Yes, occasionally. Not recently."

"Did you have a falling-out?"

"No, not at all. Joanna . . ." That touch of sadness again. Either the guy was really good, or somewhere in there he actually felt an emotion or two. ". . . kept her feelings to herself. She never let anything interfere with business. We had a good friendship, but we had a great working relationship."

"So we heard."

Fourtner raised one eyebrow but didn't take the bait.

Riley pulled out his notebook. "When was the last time you saw Joanna Moorehouse? Either personally or professionally."

"I hadn't seen her personally in months. I stopped in at Sterling last week to pick up the April stats."

"You spoke to her?"

"Yes, sat in her office—you've seen their offices?"

The detectives nodded.

"A fishbowl. We chatted, I was there for about ten minutes, I left. Before you ask, Joanna didn't confide any worries or fears to me. There were some protesters on the sidewalk but I went in the back. I asked if they were causing her any problems but she said no—or rather, she said 'nothing I can't handle.' I said, 'They haven't invented what you can't handle,' and she laughed. That was the last time I saw her." His face grew cold, giving Jack a preview of what he would look like as an old man. "Who killed her?"

"That's what we're trying to determine. When was the last time you were at her house?" Riley asked.

He shrugged. "That mausoleum of hers? Quite some time. Four months, maybe?"

"Do you know the alarm code?"

"I don't remember her having an alarm."

"Spare key?"

He shook his head, dislodging a blond lock so that it swept one eyebrow, which simply reinforced the *GQ* look. "No key exchange, no drawer full of stuff in her bathroom, and I never met her parents. It wasn't that kind of relationship."

Riley asked, "What kind was it?"

"We are adults who enjoy—enjoyed—each other's company. That's all."

"What about your relationship with Sterling? What exactly do you do for the company?"

Fourtner explained that securities, bonds, and other financial products were rated according to safety and stability—judged largely by historical returns—so that investors could make quick decisions about whether the products' estimated earnings were a good deal compared to their risk.

"But you're paid by the people you're rating."

"Yes. Is that a conflict of interest that's gotten the system into trouble in the past? Yes. That's why there're all sorts of requirements and hoops we jump through today to make sure that our assessments are impartial. But we provide a business service for business investors. There's no reason to make the taxpayers pay for it," he said this last in a pious tone.

"Tell us about Sterling's ratings," Riley said.

Jack mentally chafed as Fourtner launched into another round of explanations regarding subprime mortgages, tranches, and CDOs. He decided to cut to the chase. "We know there's a problem with the CDOs."

This did not seem to concern Fourtner, or even startle him. "And that problem is?"

"They're derivative products based on Sterling's mortgage loans. The default rate of those loans is ten percent and rising."

Riley stared. Fourtner fiddled with the corner of his desk blotter; for one of the high-tech generation he seemed to actually use the calendar printed on the blotter pad, with appointments and reminders jotted in every square. Save for the weekends. All work and no play . . . "Some fraction of loans will always default, even under ideal circumstances, and the circumstances of the economy are much improved but hardly ideal. What we used to consider standard is now abnormal, and the abnormals are now standard."

Jack didn't believe a word of it. It sounded like pure BS, and not even highly rated stuff. "And yet you say all their bonds are triple-A. I mean you, personally, rate them that way. Yet the Sterling regulator is taking a closer look."

"She can look all she likes. Joanna's products have always been solid. What will happen under Lauren, I have no idea, but Sterling has always been able to satisfy its investors."

Still run-of-the-mill BS. "How?"

"I beg your pardon?"

Riley sipped his coffee. The pigeon pecked the window. They both watched this conversation as if it were a fight in which they hadn't a dog. "*How?* The CDOs are based on the mortgage loans. The tranches may be chopped into risk categories but they're still stacked on the backs of borrowers. If those borrowers stumble, the entire tower comes down."

"Interesting analogy." Fourtner must have realized that condescension might not be the best course when one is on the list of suspects in two murders, and went on. "That would be completely true if the CDOs were the end of the line. They're not. The CDOs are insured, in a sense, by the CDSs. The credit default swaps."

Shit, Jack thought. *Something* else.

"CDSs are completely misnamed, because they're not swaps at all. They're insurance policies in case the customers default. Sterling buys a credit default swap from Ergo Insurance for a fee. If the borrowers keep paying, nothing goes wrong, Ergo keeps collecting its fees. You've met the rep, Deb Fischer? If too many borrowers in a certain tranch default and the security loses its value, then Ergo gives Sterling enough money to cash out their investors. Simple."

Jack and Riley were silent, trying to spot the catch. There had to be a catch.

"CDSs got a bad rep during the crisis. Some critics, including a lot of congressmen who were trying to look good to their constituents by going to a televised hearing and asking oh-so-tough questions of the Wall Street baddies, said that with CDSs banks and mortgage companies were actually betting on their borrowers to fail. It skirts the line between, on one hand, hedging your bets so that your bank doesn't lose a lot of money and hurt your investors or shareholders or customers who utilize your products, and, on the other, simply trading products to make a profit for the *bank* on the backs of the customers you're supposed to be working for. Violating fiduciary duty, in other words. Plus you could buy a CDS on a bond when you didn't even own the bond, which meant you could bet on other banks' CDOs. That's kind of like buying a life insurance policy on someone you don't even know. It's creepy, but it's legal."

"Okay," Jack said. Maybe Sterling's products were solid plus shored up by an insurance policy, and maybe Jeremy Mearan had pointed them toward Fourtner out of sheer jealousy . . . or maybe Fourtner was a very smooth talker.

"During the financial crisis everyone had taken CDSs too far—that was the problem, relying on them to be a safety net and a cash cow at the same time. And, for a time, they were. But a safety net that saves you when you jump from the third floor isn't going to stop you when you jump from the eightieth. AIG got way too far into CDSs and it nearly killed them because insuring

CDOs wasn't regulated the same as insuring people's lives or homes. The funds didn't maintain sufficient capital. Then once people looked at the collateral—the housing market—in these collateralized debt obligations and saw it dropping like a stone, AIG needed even more money to make up the difference. Eventually the government had to come to the rescue with the bailouts." He stared pensively, either at his reflection in the window or at the pigeon behind it. "Insufficient capital was the core problem in the mid-2000s."

"Sterling has sufficient capital?" Jack asked, having run out of intelligent questions. All he wanted to know was whether Sterling deserved its triple-A rating, and this guy sure as hell wasn't going to tell him if it didn't.

But, to his surprise, Fourtner hesitated. Then he said, "Yes."

Just "yes"? No long-winded explanation of some esoteric financial product? "Where is it? This capital? In cash?"

"Not only cash—tangible assets have to be at least six percent of total net worth, that's all. That includes property, equipment, accounts receivable. There's no point in keeping a lot of cash these days, not with interest rates at rock bottom."

Joanna Moorehouse apparently hadn't gotten that memo, Jack thought. Because she had a crap ton of cash and he wanted to know if this guy knew about it, but had no way to find out other than to ask. "Did you know about Joanna Moorehouse's account at the Banco de Panama?"

Fourtner didn't react. "I'm sure Sterling has a lot of accounts. I don't audit them. I simply rate the bonds they sell."

The hell with this. "And your ratings are suspiciously high. Why is that?"

"Suspicious to whom?"

"How much did Joanna Moorehouse pay you to get those triple-As? Or did she offer you some other form of payment?"

"Are you suggesting that I took bribes from Joanna?"

"It's not a suggestion. It's a statement."

"Made by whom?"

Riley set his porcelain mug with its complimentary coffee on the edge of Fourtner's desk. "Everyone involved with Sterling."

For someone accused of a crime he seemed remarkably sanguine . . . but then, he probably always looked that way. Jack could see why he and Joanna made the perfect friends-with-benefits couple—no worry that either one of them would ever evidence a shred of human feeling. Nothing mattered but the bottom line. Feelings were only a distraction.

Exactly, it occurred to him, as he lived his life these days.

The accumulation of indignation dissipated like a puff of breath on a cold day.

"I assume you mean Anna Hernandez and morons like Ned Swift," Fourtner was saying. "Most people have no idea how money actually works, how a financial firm actually makes a profit. It's not their fault—most of it is rather opaque. All I can do is assure you Joanna never bought a rating from me, not with her body or her money or anything else. I won't even waste your time going on about how much I resent the implication."

Just as well. They had wasted too much time already.

Jack stood up and Riley followed suit. They thanked him for his time and left. The coffee mug stayed on the desk. The pigeon didn't budge from his window. Both seemed to serve as one final indication of how little effect the cops' visit had had on Sidney Fourtner's day.

Chapter 21

"Thank heavens you're back," Carol exclaimed as soon as Maggie, her arms coated in antibiotic ointment, walked through the door with Tyra Simmons's samples.

"I didn't realize you'd miss me so much. I'd have left you my charm bracelet to remember me by."

Carol didn't even run with the joke, having noticed the myriad of small cuts and the deep smears of blood on Maggie's shirt and pants. "What happened to you?"

"Long story. The main point of it is that the car's going to be out of commission for at least a day. What did you need me for?"

"Were you in an accident? Are you okay?"

"No and yes. I'll tell you the whole story if you tell me why—"

"You need to talk to Denny about this Graham trial. The defense brought in some hired whore to poke holes in your fingerprint identification."

Maggie dropped the manila envelope on her desk and slung the strap of her small purse over the back of the chair. "Well, that's called getting a second opinion and they're welcome to it. We have to trust the jury to know a hired gun when they see one. And to know a guy who shot his girlfriend to death just like he shot his last girlfriend to death and probably the one before her when they see *him*."

"Yeah, well, talk to Denny. He's worried."

"Of course I will. But when *isn't* Denny worried? I think it's in his job description."

She took a step in that direction but the middle-aged Carol lifted a hand, palm out. "Wait."

"What?"

"You have a charm bracelet?"

Denny did, indeed, appear worried, and even more so when she gave him the briefest possible rundown of the incident.

"Wait, wait. Someone shot at you?"

"No, at Anna. I happened to be standing there."

"How do you know they were aiming at her? I'm not trying to freak you out, but—"

"Do I look freaked out?"

Denny, always honest, said, "Yeah, a little. Sorry, but . . . there it is. Anyone *would* be. Especially with this Graham trial and talk of a hit list—"

Maggie rubbed her forehead; every movement of her arms made the skin feel tight and creaky. She had gotten the right shoulder healed from its dislocation and now the arms, especially her left, felt skinned. "Not you, too."

"It doesn't help that the entire sum of evidence is this one print on this one gun."

"Which was found under his bed and whose bullets match the slug found in the victim."

"The slug hit bone. It got pretty mashed up."

"The general characteristics match. That's evidence."

"Circumstantial."

"And a witness."

"Her five-year-old daughter. She did great on the stand, but the jury is going to remember their own kids and judge accordingly. At five my son insisted that the neighbor had a robot that drove his car and that our dog could talk."

"Are you sure it couldn't?" Maggie couldn't resist asking.

"I'm just saying."

"Yes, children aren't always reliable but they're also amazingly observant. Plus there're statements from his very grown-up cronies and her friends about how much they fought and that he had pistol-whipped her the day before and how she had been planning to leave him."

"Most of which have already been recanted since each one of those witnesses has a criminal record that dates back to their teens and they know how snitches fare in jail when they find themselves back inside for violating probation. It's been child's play for the defense to skewer them." He settled back into his chair, hand to chin.

Maggie sat back as well. At least her back didn't hurt. A defense challenge didn't worry her—the facts were what they were—but she hated the idea of being recalled to court. She hated the idea of going to court in the first place. Few tortures more nerve wracking were permitted on U.S. soil. Confined to a chair while someone did their best to make you look either incompetent at best or corrupt at worst for as long as they chose to continue . . . only a pure masochist, or perhaps an adrenaline junkie, could enjoy that. She was neither. "Who's the expert witness?"

"Some guy from Idaho. The prosecutor says he wrote a statement that the ridges don't line up and your report lacks all detail and fingerprint science can't satisfy all the Daubert requirements."

"Wow. Everything but the kitchen sink."

"The prosecutor is bouncing off the walls. If this case is lost it's going to look bad for the city and worse for the department. Graham has killed at least three women, and his last right-hand man vanished into thin air a few years ago, all for fun, and at least twice that many on gang business. It's not as if he tried hard to cover his tracks—he practically posts the news on Facebook with a smiley emoticon."

"That wouldn't surprise me." She had glanced at him once or twice in the courtroom—with having to divide her attention among the prosecutor, the defense attorney, the judge, and the jury, she could very often leave the stand with no recollection of what the defendant looked like. But Graham, she remembered.

A very ordinary-looking man, white skin, light brown hair, a trimmed goatee, heavy biceps under his dress-for-court shirt, the kind of guy you could picture grilling burgers over a backyard pit, the kind who might curse at the pull string on his mower and make every peewee ball game his kid played. Until he smiled, which he did often.

Then the crooked tilt to his lips seemed to reflect an

unholy glow into his eyes, and his brows would knit with an intensity that made one wish, beg, plead to the heavens, "He's not looking at me, is he?"

But he had been, watching her every breath from the time she had approached the witness stand until she passed through the audience pews to the door at the back of the room. As she had pulled it open she had noticed him still watching, turned completely around in his seat and ignoring the prosecutor as he called the next witness. He had caught her eye in that instant before she gratefully slipped from the courtroom, hoping never to return.

It got under her skin. She didn't like what she'd seen there, a salaciousness, a freedom, a promise—of what, she didn't want to imagine. Maggie had encountered plenty of killers before Graham and usually found them subdued and dull. Not him.

Apparently this creepiness didn't translate through the camera because he had plenty of women writing to him in prison. His attorney seemed fond of pointing out how many marriage proposals he had received since his incarceration. Graham liked to read them to the reporters during breaks in the trial. It mystified Maggie to know there were some human beings who when everything told them that something was X they would insist it was Y. Maybe it made them feel smart or special, in that like a conspiracy theorist they could see what no one else could. Maybe they had been so wronged in life that they automatically mistrusted everything told to them. Or maybe, she thought, they were really, really stupid.

"All I can suggest," Denny was saying, "is bone up.

On current studies, statistics, Daubert points, your resume, proficiency testing, everything. Who knows what this guy will pull out to throw at you."

"Sounds like fun," she said wearily. "I'll do my best."

"You always do. So what is up with these two women? We haven't seen a case that violent since they found that little foreign girl in the cemetery. And even she wasn't, like, disemboweled."

"I don't have any idea. There's a mind-boggling amount of money involved, but it goes in all different directions and these corporate types aren't going to confess to anything shady—"

"Doesn't sound like a business thing, anyway. Nobody disembowels over money, unless that money is in the form of fifty kilos of Colombian snow. *Then* maybe."

"I don't know," Maggie said. "Did I mention this is a *lot* of money?"

"Don't they have someone in jail anyway? He killed the women because they repossessed his house or something?"

"He only confessed to the first victim, and his story isn't exactly hanging together."

"Still, if you're looking for something more personal . . . home is as personal as it gets."

"I know." She stood, wearily. "That's why Anna almost got shot an hour ago."

"That was a waste of time," Riley muttered, stepping too hard on the brake for the light at Euclid. "That guy could lie until the end of time without batting an eye. I think Joanna bribed him with everything she had and he knows we can't prove it. Money people know how to hide a money trail."

"Absolutely," Jack agreed. "But it doesn't give him any motive. Why kill the golden goose? It gives both he and Joanna a reason to off Tyra, if Tyra found out and had too much conscience to ignore it."

"But with both Joanna and Tyra gone, he's doubly safe. And I could picture that guy carving up a human being like a Christmas turkey and then walking away without a hair out of place. He and Joanna must have made quite a team. Like something out of those puppet porno movies."

"I don't even want to know why you're familiar with those."

"And why are you familiar with CDOs and derivative products? You've been holding out on me, partner. Here I totally bought your glassy-eyed act."

"It's not an act. But just because this stuff bores me silly doesn't mean I wasn't listening."

"You make me nervous when you do that," Riley said without inflection, glancing over at Jack as he stopped at another light. "Makes me wonder what else you're holding out."

"Only a Katy Perry fetish."

Riley raised an eyebrow.

"Light's green."

Riley drove on toward the Sterling building. They had called Ergo Insurance looking for Deb Fischer, only to be told she was at Sterling. Two birds, one stone, since they wanted to do a follow-up with Lauren Schneider as well.

Jack kept his hands balled into fists to keep himself from drumming his fingernails on the dashboard. They had two extremely dead women and no real leads and now bullets flying and he couldn't even be sure at whom. He felt like everything they had done since Joanna's death had gotten them exactly nowhere. The answer had to be at the Sterling office, but Riley was right—experts in a field were also experts at hiding their path through that field. They would never find it without help. Or a whole lot of luck.

Deb Fischer now shared the conference table with Anna Hernandez. Dhaval and Pierce Bowman had returned to New York, temporarily, to formulate the final offer for the purchase of Sterling. Technically this meant that two of their suspects had left the state without so much as a good-bye, but Jack didn't feel either to be a flight risk. With his lengthy resume Bowman had certainly weathered more intense investigations than this one, and Dhaval merely crunched numbers with no personal stake in whether DJ Bryan bought Sterling or not.

Of course, if the sale could be considered a done deal with Joanna out of the way, that provided a motive for Bowman, Schneider, and Mearan.

Anna Hernandez began to gather her papers, willing to voluntarily exile herself to the waiting area again, but Deborah Fischer could not contain her curiosity and demanded to know what they wanted. A short, somewhat portly woman with a head of unruly curls, she didn't look like Sidney Fourtner's type but agreed with him completely. "Sterling has plenty of insurance in CDSs."

"Is that normal?" Jack asked, wondering why banks

would buy insurance in case their loans turned out to be bad decisions. Wouldn't it be more effective to not make the bad loans in the first place?

"Oh, sure. CDSs have been around for decades—went from twelve billion in 2000 to sixty-two trillion in 2007. They used to be super cheap because no one thought a CDO would default. But it's a double whammy when the value of the CDOs falls, because that means your income, the loan payments, goes down at the same time your insurance costs are going up because obviously there's a problem with defaulting or your value wouldn't be going down."

"Spiraling disaster," Riley said.

"That's why Ergo is much more careful postcrisis. It had been insuring these risky tranches and investing in them as well, but without the oversight and restrictions that banks have. Everyone was totally complacent about risk. Things had been too good for too long. But guidelines are tighter now, and the ratings agencies have been straightened out so we can make a more accurate assessment."

"Speaking of which—" Jack began.

"If anything Joanna had overinsured, but hey, I work for Ergo so of course I'm not going to complain. She bought another batch of CDSs from me two weeks ago."

Jack pulled out his copy of the Panamanian account, showing the $350,000,000 disbursement to Ergo. "You mean this?"

She checked it out. "Yep."

Jack had forgotten Anna Hernandez's presence until she dropped her files back onto the glossy table. "Wait, that's not what I've been finding."

Riley asked what she meant.

"According to the books Joanna gave me, Sterling was woefully *under*insured. Somehow it hadn't concerned my predecessor, but then it seems not much did."

"It's a recent purchase," Deb said. "Maybe she hadn't updated you yet."

"Why didn't you tell us that?" Riley asked Anna.

"Because it's not a crime, technically. . . . It's a regulatory requirement. I'm preparing a report for my supervisor and he will have to decide whether sanctions are taken." At the cops' skeptical look she tried to explain further. "The laws are in a state of flux about CDSs. In one way it's betting on a firm's own loan clients to fail. The Senate hearings raked Lloyd Blankfein over the coals for doing exactly that at Goldman Sachs. It's a very gray area right at the moment."

Jack tried to put some pieces together. "Except that Sterling's triple-A ratings are *based* in part on having the CDSs to be able to counteract any defaults."

Anna saw his point. "Somehow Carter & Poe issued ratings based on CDSs that didn't exist."

"But they did exist. I sold them to her," Deb said.

"Her," Jack repeated. "Not Sterling?"

"But Joanna—" Deb began, then stopped, obviously replaying events in her mind. She opened a binder she had brought and frantically flipped pages. "The application page—you're right, it reads 'Joanna Moorehouse.' I didn't think about it, if I even looked at it. . . . These purchases are so routine—"

Riley made a choking sound. "Three hundred and fifty million is routine?"

"At these levels? Yes. But all companies have various accounts so it still could be legit. You'd better confirm with Lauren that Sterling truly doesn't have these CDSs on its books."

"And if they don't?"

Deb Fischer said, "Then Joanna was betting on her own customers to fail. Betting heavily."

Jack asked, "Did you tell Pierce Bowman this? Or anyone from DJ Bryan?"

"Heck no. I don't work for DJ Bryan. Whether they buy Sterling or not has nothing to do with me. It wouldn't be bad for me if they did, though. . . . They're more conservative, they'll be more likely to stock up on the CDSs. . . . Oh, I see what you mean!"

Jack hadn't been aware they'd meant anything. He threw out questions like multiple fishing lines, hoping that one would accidentally snag something he could use. And in order to sound as if he knew what the hell he was talking about.

Riley must have been wondering as well. "What we mean?"

"Why didn't this person kill me? If Joanna was underinsured, playing fast and loose with the company's assets, and had some falling-out with whoever had been in on the plot, that person killed her. Then Tyra found out about it so she had to die, too. I might have wound up in their sights—shit, what a thought!—but I have a husband and a big dog so no one's going to be sneaking into my house to stab *me* to death. The dog would scare any killer away. The husband, okay, not so much."

A thought occurred to her before she went any further with this theory, however. "Of course, it wouldn't make much sense to kill me. All the CDSs are on our books at Ergo. If I died any replacement of mine could simply look them up. There's nothing hidden at *my* office."

"Unlike Sterling," Riley said.

My thoughts exactly, Jack thought.

Chapter 22

Lauren Schneider looked up in annoyance as they entered her office. "What now? Are you getting anywhere? Two of our people slaughtered in two days, and—?"

Jack had planned to hit her with the Panama account, hoping Mearan hadn't already told her, and the information they'd gotten from Deb Fischer, but instead Riley asked if the merger had progressed.

"Yeah," she said in confusion, then corrected herself. "Yes. Bowman expected me to cave without Joanna, but he's starting to come around. He needs to offer a higher price now that we're spinning off the riskier tranches, not lower."

"So Sterling is going to split? Even though that's not what Joanna wanted?" Riley asked.

"Joanna is dead," she said without hesitation, and without much regret either. "It's the best plan for Sterling, our investors, and our employees."

"But Bowman is still lowballing you?"

"That's what he was doing in New York, apparently,

trying to talk Hernandez's supervisor at the Fed into an extra discount if Bryan buys Sterling. But Sterling— while we've done incredibly well for our size—is hardly in the too-big-to-fail category and the Fed is out of the bailout business. According to Hernandez, they told him to hoist his own petards. No, Bryan gives us a fair price, we pay off the lower tranches and we're good." She gave a very human-like sigh and rested her head on the back of her ergonomically designed leather desk chair. "And we don't have to do the whole going public thing. I hate IPOs. Total chaos. Why are you asking?"

"We want to ask you about the account at the Banco de Panama."

A slow blink of her long lashes. "Which account is that?"

"It's an account of Joanna's. A personal account, apparently, in her name alone."

She promptly lost interest. "I wouldn't know, then. If it's a personal account then it's her personal business. Her executor will have to help you."

Jack doubted she could fake the indifference, which meant that Jeremy Mearan hadn't shared his information yet. He probably hoped to find a way to get his own hands on it and didn't need any competition.

Lauren said, "Does she have an executor? Who gets that house? I'm just curious."

Another trait of fallible humans. Lauren Schneider seemed to be letting her guard down. Perhaps getting out of Joanna's shadow would be good for her.

"Probably her family," Riley said. "Miss Schneider—"

"*What* family? Joanna never mentioned family."

"Miss Schneider—"

"Mrs., actually. Unlike Joanna I *do* have a family, a husband and even a set of daughters."

Superior, again, to Joanna Moorehouse. Not quite out of that shadow yet. Riley said, "We spoke with Deb Fischer and Anna Hernandez about Sterling's CDSs."

"What about them?"

"Anna seems to think your CDOs are underinsured."

"Well, she's a regulator. It's her job to find something wrong."

"You weren't concerned?"

"I'm sure Joanna had an appropriate level."

"She did. But they paled in comparison to the boatload she'd bought for herself." Jack showed her the Banco de Panama statement.

Lauren Schneider glanced at the paper, then pored over it. Her face grew cold. "Excuse me. I'm going to get Deb in here." She stalked off to the conference room.

"So we're thinking Joanna used the cash in her Panama account to bet against her own company," Riley said to Jack.

"Which she was about to sell."

"But the CDSs were for the CDOs. Whose name is on the masthead wouldn't change that."

Jack said, "Look at you, using the lingo and stuff. So she hides the default rate until Bowman buys Sterling, makes money from the sale. Maybe she resigns. Then the truth about the defaults comes to light, the CDOs crash, she cashes in the CDSs and makes even more money."

"Or even starts another company since the crash will happen on Bryan's watch. Maybe that's why she opposed splitting the company."

"She screws her own customers and employees and still keeps her reputation as a moneymaker extraordinaire," Riley said as he watched the action in the conference room, where Lauren, Anna, and Deb Fischer had an animated, three-way discussion that none seemed to enjoy. "No wonder somebody wanted to kill this woman."

Jack's phone rang. The voice of a harried dispatcher told him, "You'd better get out to the victim's house—Moorehouse's."

"Why?"

"Apparently there's some sort of riot going on, and they're threatening to break into the house. Our sealing tape isn't going to keep them out."

Maggie held her breath as she unfolded the white piece of paper containing Tyra Simmons's fingernail scrapings, not out of any psychological anticipation but to keep from blowing any tiny fibers or broken hairs away with her expelling breath. Fingernail scrapings were one of those exams that seemed as if it should be done much more scientifically than it actually was. The underside of the nail was scraped, *gently*—they didn't want to pick up more of the victim's own skin cells than could be helped—with a plastic pick, and the contents were dropped or wiped onto a piece of sterile filter paper. All fingers of the right hand in one paper, the left in another. The papers were then folded into druggists' folds so that nothing could escape and sealed in a clean envelope.

Then people like Maggie would unfold the paper under a stereomicroscope (which functioned as a large and powerful magnifying glass) in the hopes that something useful would be present, such as blood or skin that didn't turn out to be the victim's, or some terribly distinctive fiber that would inexorably point to the killer. But people like Maggie usually found only blood and skin and fibers that belonged to the victim; or generic, uninteresting fibers that didn't point to anyone in particular; or dirt.

She heard a rustling at her elbow as Carol settled into a task chair at the nearby counter, and the clink of her coffee cup as she set it down. This meant that, elsewhere in the lab, DNA samples were replicating themselves in tiny plastic tubes and Carol had until her timer went off to relax and chat. "Are we having fun yet?"

"Mmm."

"Doing fibers?"

"Mmm." Maggie tilted the paper downward to herd the tiny shreds of evidence inside it into a drop of water on a glass slide. Then she covered the drop with the razor-thin cover slip and breathed normally. A wet mount remained delicate—the cover could slide off at the slightest provocation—but it would also be much easier than sticky, viscous mounting medium to remove if she saw something in the scrapings that needed chemical testing. And she could breathe without blowing her evidence away.

"I had my time on the sunny rock with the snake representing the other snake," Carol said, and after a moment Maggie sorted this out to mean that she had testified in the Graham trial.

"Has the state rested?" Maggie asked, adjusting her microscope lens. Her skin ached a bit from the tiny cuts but in simple discomfort, not pain. They would heal quickly. Meanwhile Carol and Denny had avoided the topic, letting her be the one to bring it up. Which she hadn't.

"Uh-huh. I was supposed to be the grand finale. More like a sparkler that won't stay lit."

"I'm sure you were totally grand."

"My firework personality can't make up for getting only a partial profile off the trigger. Sure, the alleles are consistent with Graham but they'd be consistent with a lot of people. I said that. Defense kept asking if I was saying that this DNA conclusively matched Graham. 'No,' I said, 'I'm *not* saying that.' A few more questions, and he'd come back to 'So you're saying this proves my client' and on and on."

"Ad nauseum."

"It certainly gave me nauseum. Got anything good there?"

"Nothing on the tapings from the clothes. Under the nails I've got a pink fiber that looks like the same color as her T-shirt. And a bundle of fibers . . . white . . . thin."

"Cotton? Fab. Nothing better than white cotton."

Which was so ubiquitous as to be useless. "Sarcasm is not becoming in a woman of your stature. Besides, it's not cotton. Or not *all* cotton."

Carol went back to the Graham trial. "But for you, by the way, he's calling in an expert."

"Denny told me."

"I think he thinks there's no way he's going to convince this jury that not only did someone else use the gun but that he did so without leaving his own fingerprints *and* without smudging Graham's. This jury is dying to convict; you can see it in their faces. Scumbag's lawyer is going to have to try everything."

"Huh." The bundle of fibers seemed like a clump of clear and dirty white tendrils of varying diameter and cross sections. A hot mess, frankly, but somehow familiar. She switched to the polarized light microscope.

"Wear your big-girl panties."

"I'll be sure to." Maggie pulled a long plastic box out of a drawer. It held part of her reference library of synthetic fibers.

"What are you doing?" Carol asked.

"These fibers are weird."

"Please don't say that in court. Especially in front of Graham's attorney."

"But I think I've seen them before." With the slide of Tyra's fingernail scrapings on one stage of the double microscope she began to put slides of the known synthetic fibers she had mounted over the years on the other. "It's not polyester, or nylon, I can tell that from the polarization, but—"

Carol's timer beeped in her pocket. "Gotta go. My microtubes are calling me."

Maggie murmured a response and continued to try different slides, finally settling on one that seemed to copy the characteristics of Tyra's clump in every respect. She checked the label. Tyvek.

Huh.

Tyvek made a lightweight but not terribly breathable wrap, used to protect houses under construction and make envelopes for overnight express mailings. It also formed booties, lab coats, aprons, sleeves, and full-body suits for forensic or medical personnel, to keep them from contaminating the scene and keep the scene from contaminating them.

Riley had joked that the killer may have worn a Tyvek suit in order to get away without leaving a trail of blood, and Maggie had responded that either woman would not have opened her door to someone suited up like a CDC member responding to a mass epidemic. Maggie still believed that, especially in Tyra's case. After Joanna's murder the young lawyer would have been on edge.

And among the many things made out of Tyvek for forensic use were the small drawstring bags used to protect the hands until the nails could be scraped or gunshot residue could be collected. They were slid over the hands and the strings pulled and tied around the wrists and were much easier to use than paper lunch bags. One of Tyra's long nails had probably caught on the inside of the bag during this process.

That must be it.

She moved on to the other minuscule items on the wet mount. Aside from the Tyvek and the pink fiber, a clump of something green appeared to be vegetation and a small piece of animal hair. It lacked a root and had a very thin diameter. The medulla—the central channel in the hair—separated into a distinct series of rounded boxes, the "string of pearls" look characteristic of animal fur. These were the soft, fuzzy hairs that provided warmth and softness and, unfortunately, often looked alike in cats, dogs, rabbits, and many other mammals. The thicker, coarser guard hairs were more easily distinguished.

The piece of vegetation didn't provide much help, simply seemed to be a tiny part of leaf. It could be anything from a maple leaf to a piece of lettuce to a blade of grass.

She wrote up these vague and unhelpful observations and carefully set the wet mount aside. When the water evaporated she could scrape the items back into their paper. Something might come up in the meantime that would make her want to take another look.

For the moment she got a fresh stick of gum to chew off some of her frustration, then looked up to see her ex-husband stride into the lab. As always her heart sank a little and she reminded herself not to be unfair. Rick was not a bad person, only a tedious one. But they got along fine now that she no longer had to serve as his personal flunky, so she summoned up a smile to greet him.

"Good news." He collapsed into the task chair Carol had vacated and explained how a detective in Phoenix told him about a pedophile coyote who might have been a victim of their vigilante, and how the only cooperative witness had been this seven-year-old girl. "And this Daley guy found her! She's almost thirteen now, still in the area, got adopted by a couple of bleeding hearts, learned English, and remembers this whole drama like it happened yesterday. Still wakes up screaming now and then."

"Poor kid." *A witness.*

He didn't mention the shooting, so the news must not have filtered back to him. Her lab coat covered her arms and she kept her chin tilted down toward her work.

"Yeah. So anyway I e-mailed that sketch you gave the artist and Daley's going to see if the girl can ID him."

"Oh." The girl wouldn't, of course, because Maggie had described a slightly obscure but favorite actor of hers, Michael Ironside, as the vigilante killer. But that might be a good thing if the sketch *didn't* match the girl's recollection, breaking the tie between Jack's work and the deaths in Phoenix. Maria Stein's abuse of the elderly would remain a weird coincidence. On the other hand, perhaps the girl would believe her sketch matched the man—she had only been seven, traumatized, and maybe any intimidating-looking male could be made to fit the horrible memory. That would be good, too. It would confirm Maggie's story in a way nothing else could, put her firmly on the side of the very honest angels. Here was a serial killer and he had pulled the trigger, not Maggie. In case anyone had any doubts.

Anyone like Rick. "What's the matter? I thought you'd be excited."

"Well, it's interesting. I'm not sure how it's going to help, though—it's been, what, five years now? This one little traumatized girl, even if she can positively ID him—does that really get you closer to identifying him?"

"Maybe not. But it'll be confirmation that he had operated in that area. We can reopen all the similar unsolved and see if they had anything in common, how he's picking them. Even if not we could still get a free trip to Phoenix out of it."

She nearly swallowed her gum. "We?"

"Sure! You're my only witness. I might be able to

wheedle the budget into sending us so you can look at mug shots, maybe even compare notes with the little wetback."

"Rick!"

"Fine, Hispanic child. People in this city have not forgotten about these killings, which means the captain isn't about to let *me* forget. If I don't come up with something he's going to think I'm twiddling my thumbs and transfer me back to property crimes, where I'll be chasing smash and grabs until I retire. Besides—look, I ain't trying to get back together or anything—this is a legitimate lead."

"I know that, I . . . of course I'll do anything the department needs."

"Besides, I remember how much you like to travel."

She made herself smile. "Guilty. But Arizona—I've heard it's awfully hot. Like, really, really hot."

"Yeah, but it's a dry heat." He studied her suddenly, with a new and uncharacteristic sharpness. "What gives with you? Since when do you not jump at the chance of an expense-paid trip? You always moped because your brother was in San Francisco or Houston or Miami or Timbuktu and you weren't."

"I didn't mope."

He leaned forward, nearly falling out of the wheeled task chair. "You think I'm some kind of bumpkin who can't see past his own front yard, some idiot who couldn't find a clue if a Hooters waitress handed it to him, I know."

"Rick—" she said, and stopped, since on the whole she *did* think that.

"But I know you, Maggie. I know you better than you think."

His words chilled her. Words that would have sounded comforting and even endearing under other circumstances only produced a sense of inexorable dread. She could feel her eyes widening and turned her face down. *Breathe. Carry this off.*

She faced him again, firmly, having decided to play the trauma card. "Because I still wake up at night too, okay? I'm used to coming onto crime scenes after everything is over, not being part of one. It's taking some . . . adjustment."

Weak and vulnerable should work on Rick. He had never realized that she had held their household together, that she had all the self-discipline he lacked. But it didn't seem to be cutting through his misgivings right now, so she added, "However, I can handle it. If you need me to go to Phoenix, let's go. I'll just pack lightweight clothes."

He gave a smile that didn't quite reach his eyes. "That's my girl."

"I'm not your girl, Rick." She went back to her microscope, gazing through the lens at nothing, adjusting knobs that didn't need to be adjusted. "Keep me posted."

She listened to his footsteps leave the room.

Chapter 23

Jack and Riley pulled up behind a knot of cars parked willy-nilly in the wide drive of Joanna's mansion and stepped onto the grass. Most of the vehicles had seen better days, some with plastic taped up in lieu of windows, and in the midst of them sat the Channel 15 mobile news team van. Off to the side a perky female reporter faced the camera, her back to the twenty or twenty-five protesters milling about the drive that curved along the porch. One pounded on the front door when the mood struck him. The entire assembly seemed oblivious to the gathering rain clouds overhead.

Jack had seen most of the same protesters in front of the Sterling building on previous days, but now they moved with more agitation. A few signs read, KURT RESNICK MARTYR TO PREDATORS and FREE KURT and MOOREHOUSE WAS THE REAL MURDERER. In the midst of them stirred Ned Swift.

The reporter stopped Riley as they circled toward

the crowd, her black skin glowing with the hum of energy all reporters possess. Underneath her trim dress she wore Reeboks—feet don't appear on the camera, after all. "Hey, Detective. How about an interview about what's happening here?"

"Good morning, Shanti. How about you tell me what's up? I just arrived."

She obligingly turned and waved at the crowd. "Newsworthy Ned called and told us about the guy you arrested for Joanna Moorehouse's murder. The victims of Sterling are here to support him."

"Let me guess. They say he's innocent."

"No, no, they told me he did it but it's justifiable homicide."

"Seriously," Riley said. It wasn't a question.

"I don't make the news," she told him with a shrug. "I just report it, and it's been a slow week. Ned's plan is to petition the court for the money from Joanna Moorehouse's estate to use for Kurt Resnick's defense. And also to pay all these people back for losing their homes."

"Good luck with that," Riley said. "Why are they knocking on the door? Do they expect her ghost to answer it?"

"Oh, someone's home. A woman poked her head out once and yelled at them to go away. Ned says, anyway. That was before I got here."

Riley exchanged a look with Jack. There were only two women likely to be in the house, and they doubted Grace the cleaning lady would set foot on the property for any amount of overtime. They moved toward the steps.

"Be careful, Detectives," Shanti called after them. "These people aren't in a reasonable mood. Why do you think I'm standing over here?"

She was right. The crowd had seen them pull up and were now waiting for them, a tight cordon between them and the front door. Ned Swift waited on the steps, supervising from the lofts.

The two cops went to walk around them, but as a group they shuffled to the side like a single awkward organism. It was almost comical. Almost.

Riley held up a hand and announced that he and Jack were not there to deal with their protest, but simply to continue the murder investigation.

"Let Kurt Resnick go," a middle-aged woman said.

"The bitch deserved to die," a younger man said.

"He didn't do it!" said a voice from the back.

"But if he did then we all did," said a man off to the side. "I only wanted a second mortgage to put a new roof on my house. I had perfect credit. But Sterling got a hold of my wife and me and gave us a line of crap about how the interest rate didn't matter, only the payment, except the payment doubled and they never told us that—"

"You're arresting the wrong people!" a young woman cried.

Jack could feel the adrenaline running through the crowd, infecting anyone who breathed it in. He hated mobs, he hated crowds, and he wasn't even that crazy about people one-on-one. They were too unpredictable in groups, using the support and implied anonymity to put their brains on hiatus and meld into a mindless hive.

"We're not here to arrest anyone," Riley pointed out. He sounded calm but Jack could see sweat gather on his neck even though the large trees protected them from the sun. The second most dangerous types of police calls, after domestics, were crowds. "We're trying to do our jobs."

A fiftyish black man said, "Sterling talked my mother into refinancing. She only had a monthly pittance from Social Security, left over from my dad, and when the payment went up it took all of that. She starved to death because she didn't want to ask me for help."

"They're animals!"

"Then you want us to continue investigating, right?" Riley reasoned.

"You don't care about us! You're trying to hang Kurt Resnick!" a thirtyish soccer mom type insisted. Behind her a short but powerfully built man spooned her back until he forced both of them into Jack's personal space. He tried to step back but a paunchy and graying man had crowded in and Jack's foot landed on his toes. The man didn't move and neither did Jack, letting all the weight of his six-foot-four bulk come to a focus in one heel, and abruptly that area developed empty space.

"You turn a blind eye to places like Sterling because they have all the money."

"We're investigating a murder," Riley said again. "That's the job of this detective and me. We need you to let us do our job. We have no authority over questions of loans and mortgages."

A fortyish woman with long gray-streaked hair who

looked as if she could bench-press Riley's entire body blocked the detective's path. "So you ignore it? While crooks throw us out of our homes?"

"Sterling defrauds and extorts. That's criminal court. You need to arrest *them*," a man chimed in. He didn't look old enough to own a house, but ages got tougher to estimate the older Jack got. How close the kid hovered to throwing a punch wasn't hard to estimate at all.

"Regulatory agencies are already investigating Sterling," Riley said. They weren't listening.

Jack could feel the ground crumbling at the edge of a violent abyss. It could give way at any moment, swallowing them whole. The sky rumbled with disquiet as well. He asked the crowd, "What about Tyra Simmons?"

A pause. Most of the people blinked at him with total lack of recognition, but a few recognized the name. One man said, "She deserved it too. She got my case thrown out on some technicality."

The man who had spoken of his mother said, "She did Sterling's dirty work."

"Lawyers are always the worst," one man muttered.

Jack's patience, not hefty to begin with, faded completely. "What do you want us to do? Right here. Right now."

That quieted them again, because, of course, they didn't know. They only wanted to vent their frustration, their desperation, their rage at how their perfectly reasonable and ordinary lives had been turned upside down until they—employees, parents, citizens—had been turned into hate-spewing zombies.

"Let Kurt Resnick go," one said.

Another immediately disagreed. "No, don't let him go. He needs to go to trial so he can tell the world about what Sterling did."

"Arrest Sterling," a young woman said.

Riley said, "Sterling is a company, not an individual."

More people spoke up. "Arrest Joanna Moorehouse!"

"She's dead, you moron."

"Try her in absentia, then."

"Excuse us," Riley said, and gently pushed forward.

Ned Swift, seeing that his band had lost the battle of both will and wits, descended from the heights to intervene. "We don't want to hold you up, Detectives, but it's important that these people be heard."

"You've got Channel 15 in the driveway as requested," Riley pointed out.

"Has Mr. Resnick been arraigned yet?"

"In the morning. What made you come out here instead of your usual spot in front of the Sterling offices?"

"This building belongs to us now. We're petitioning the court to seize Miss Moorehouse's assets to reimburse the people she bilked."

Riley made a show of brightening. "Sounds great. You'll want us to wrap up this murder investigation then, so the location can be released."

"Uh—"

"Thanks." Riley pushed past him. Jack did the same on the other side. He felt, rather than saw, the crowd try to follow, but Swift must have nixed the movement.

When they reached the front door he glanced back. The cordon remained, but Ned now selected a few members to approach the pretty reporter.

The seal on the door had been broken. Riley selected the key with the evidence tag from his pocket, but it proved to be unnecessary. The door opened inward as soon as they stepped up to it, and Jessica Moorehouse's weathered face appeared.

"Can't you make them go away?" she hissed.

"Well, well, Miss Moorehouse," Riley said. "How did you get in? Seeing as we have the only keys to the door."

"Just because I'm from the country doesn't mean I don't know a few tricks."

"You misunderstand. That wasn't banter—I want to know how you got into this house."

She gave a toss of distressed hair. "Get used to disappointment. This is my place now and you have no right to keep me out of it."

"Miss Moorehouse—" Riley began, but she pivoted and headed for the kitchen. As they followed Jack noticed that she wore a chiffon peach blouse and a pair of dark capris a size too large, no doubt borrowed from her dead sister's closet. Simple logic, he knew—as Joanna's only heir Jessica would own all of it very shortly. So why shell out her limited resources for a fleabag motel when this mausoleum and its closets sat unused?

Except they still hoped to find some clue to Joanna's killer among the dead woman's effects, which her sister had now usurped and possibly compromised. Or simply thrown away.

And if Sterling's crimes demanded reimbursement from the estate, the long-lost sibling might be in for a crushing reduction in benefits.

"At least," Riley whispered to Jack as they walked, "the VA found out the mother really is dead. We don't have to worry about her being shivved in the root cellar by darling daughter."

"Good to know," Jack agreed.

Apparently Jessica spent a lot of time in the kitchen—one of the few rooms with furniture other than the blood-spattered living room. Takeout containers littered the counter along with Jessica's recharging cell phone and some odds and ends from elsewhere in the house. Little sister had been taking inventory of her newfound estate.

Riley sounded as if he was still rattled from the near-riot outside, his voice tight. "We do have a legal right, a legal responsibility to keep you out of this house. Not only is—was—it a sealed crime scene, *it doesn't belong to you*. We could arrest you for trespassing right now."

"But you won't." She slumped into a chair, pulled her knees up to let her bare toes hang off the seat, and crossed her arms over her shins. "You know why?"

"Why?"

"Because I've got something you want."

"And what is that?"

"Evidence." She spoke with the cocky brassiness characteristic of her, but this didn't seem to be a brazening-it-out effort like her lace handkerchief and dry tears. She seemed genuine, which both worried and intrigued Jack. He hoped they had damn well gotten anything worth collecting at their last visit because Jessica had no doubt been over the house with the finest of fine-tooth combs, touching, moving, and altering every single inch of it.

"Evidence of what?" Riley was saying.

"That's your job to determine. I only know it's important."

"But what is it?"

"Can I stay here? Can you make it okay with the probate court or whoever that I stay here until it's all legally settled?"

Riley rubbed his forehead and turned in a slow circle before saying, "Let me get this straight. You have a piece of evidence and you're holding it for ransom?"

"Yes," she said.

"How about we arrest you for obstruction?"

"Obstruction of what?"

"Evidence."

"And what is this evidence?" She smiled. "I know something about arresting people. You have to have a warrant. And in this warrant you'd have to explain exactly what it is I'm obstructing you from. And you can't because you don't know."

"I think I'd have to write that down to make sense of it," Riley said. But he saw it, and so did Jack. She knew something but they couldn't prove she knew it because they only had her word for it. She might be bluffing, but if so they could always throw her out later. And there wasn't any hard-and-fast mandate regulating when to turn over keys to the next of kin.

It was a measure of how much this case sucked that Jack and Riley didn't even look at each other before they said, in near unison, "Okay."

Jessica smiled. "I knew you'd see it my way."

Riley dangled the house keys from one finger. "So let's see this evidence."

Jessica didn't move, merely swung her head from side to side as if stretching her neck muscles. "It was sitting in plain sight all the time. But you guys looked right past it."

The cops said nothing.

"Not your fault. You kind of have to know the story or you won't understand it." She got to her feet and slowly wandered around the edge of the table. "When Joanna and I were kids, we didn't have much. But one year, right after Easter, our mom got a halfway decent job at a department store. It didn't last—somehow her jobs never did. But they had half off Easter merchandise so she bought us both piggy banks. Only they weren't piggies." She halted her meandering gait and brushed aside a Burger King bag to pick up a blue porcelain rabbit from the counter. Jack remembered seeing it in Joanna's bedroom, an incongruously unsophisticated item for that house, a cheap, inexpertly painted item that only a small child could love. "Mine was pink. Bunny banks—the Easter theme, you know?"

She rotated the porcelain object in one hand to show the coin slot at the back of the head and the rubber stopper in the hole at the bottom, which one was supposed to remove to get the money out.

"I picked that up," Jack said. "It was empty."

"It didn't have any coins in it," Jessica corrected.

"As I was saying, we didn't have much, so we used our bunnies to hold what we *did* have. Pictures we'd cut out of magazines. Letters we'd write to ourselves about what life would be like when we grew up. Sure as hell never imagined *this*, though." She waved a hand at the ceiling. "When we got older they held cigarettes and notes from our boyfriends. So, you see, you needed me to come here. Because I understood the significance of this little blue blob."

"Are you telling us that there's something in there?" Riley asked.

"That," she said, pulling the rubber stopper off the bottom, drawing out both her words and the drama, "is what I'm telling you."

Jack found himself holding his breath to watch this bleached trailer park resident pull a wad of something white from the violated bottom of a chipped porcelain rodent, and berated himself for doing so.

Jessica stepped to the kitchen table and spread out the tissue that had been in the rabbit. Nestled inside the tissue sat a black SD media card, its gold teeth grinning up at them.

"What is that? What's on it?" Riley asked of her. Media cards were usually popped out of cameras and a card reader was used to transfer the photos to one's computer, but increasingly they could be used as tiny USB drives holding everything from videos to documents.

"I have no idea," she confessed cheerily. "I don't have a camera and apparently neither did Jo, and you took her laptop so I had no way to view it. But I can tell you one thing: If she kept it there, it was important.

Like, *really* important. The most important thing she had."

"Because of the bunny," Jack said.

"Because," she assured them solemnly, "of the bunny."

Riley handed her the house keys.

Chapter 24

"So you told her she could stay?" the captain demanded.

Riley said, "Who's going to complain? As far as we've been able to determine, aside from one 'work flunky with benefits,' there *is* no one else in this woman's life. The victim paid cash, so even if sister trashes the place, there's no bank to lose money on it. And her theory about the importance of this SD card makes sense."

"Because you found it in a bunny."

"Exactly."

Jack slipped the card into the reader tethered to his computer. "Though how it could be more important than an account with over six hundred million dollars in it, I don't get. And she left the statement about *that* sitting in open view on her desk."

"Okay, let's find out what's more important than six hundred million dollars," the captain said. He only knew of the story because he had been wandering through the unit upon their return and happened to ask where the investigation had taken them.

"Love?" Riley suggested.

"You are such a softy." The captain laughed. "We're going to have to start calling you Care Bear or something."

Riley scowled at the prospect. "I'm guessing what the *victim* may have thought important. Love was the only thing she didn't have, and supposedly you can't buy it."

"I beg to differ. We have a whole unit that deals with people selling it."

Jack ignored them both and clicked his mouse a few times. A video began to play.

"That's Joanna's office," Riley said, after peering at the screen.

"Are those walls *clear*?" the captain asked.

Joanna sat at her desk beneath the high-resolution though slightly fish-eyed camera lens, which must have been perched on one of her bookcase shelves. They had searched her office but of course hadn't pulled down every financial tome and reference book on the higher shelves, and one of them must have housed the camera. Its view covered nearly all of her office space and reached a short way into the center pit, where the brokers and managers usually sat. As they watched Joanna brushed a wave of black hair over one shoulder and shoved two manila folders out of the way with a quiet *swish* of sound.

"Girlfriend bugged her own office," Riley breathed.

Jack asked of no one, "When did she film this? When is that place ever empty? Those brokers gave me the impression they never sleep."

"Like sharks," Riley agreed. "In more ways than one."

On the screen, Joanna looked up from her laptop as her office door swung open. Pierce Bowman came in and sat across from her without a greeting. He leaned back, crossed one ankle over the opposite knee, and said, "So, what do you have?"

Joanna leaned her arms on her desk, one hand draped over the other. She sounded utterly calm, her voice low and unaccented. Jack listened to the dead woman speak, Joanna Moorehouse sounding exactly as he had expected—cool, steady, focused, and completely unemotional.

"I have ten million for you, to be transferred to any account of your choosing. Once the sale is finalized, the other ten million will be yours."

Bowman hardly jumped at the offer. In fact, he scoffed, "Twenty? I made that in bonuses last year."

"But you won't this year. You've been slacking, spending too much time on the golf course while the young lions took your market share. It's understandable—you're ready for retirement. So am I."

"You mean I won't make a bonus after Bryan figures out what a ton of crap Sterling is."

Joanna didn't bite. "There's nothing wrong with Sterling. But I'm not willing to risk another run like Lehman and Bear suffered—"

"It'll happen once your default rate comes to light. This new Fed girl isn't going to sleep at the wheel like the last guy they sent."

"There won't be a run if Sterling is under the Bryan umbrella. That will be enough to reassure investors."

Bowman hesitated, then spoke clearly: "You'll have to step down as CEO. One of our own guys will run it."

"I know." She spoke without regret, and that seemed to confuse Bowman. Jack figured in Bowman's experience people didn't give up power that easily. But then Bowman didn't know about Joanna's Panamanian nest egg.

On the screen, Bowman studied her, determined to make her squirm a bit before he agreed to the deal. "You won't admit it, will you? You still won't admit that you ran the company into the ground, and now you're going to pawn off the empty husk, grab the pay-off, and disappear."

"As are you," she pointed out. "Let's face it, we're both biting the hand that fed us. Now, do you want the twenty million or not?"

He hesitated, still waiting for that squirm. It didn't come. Joanna met his gaze with her own steady one. He could walk away, tell his employer not to touch Sterling with a cattle prod, and still have his very lucrative position. Twenty million seemed to be pocket change in his world. But Joanna had summed him up—growing older and tired of the financial brawling that came with the territory. Ready to get out and give his own higher-ups one last finger while he did so.

"Okay," he said.

She did not waste even a second on gloating or an I-told-you-so smirk. "Do you have your account numbers?"

Silently he pulled a small piece of paper out of a breast pocket and slid it across the desk to her. She tapped the sequence into her laptop and, a moment later, said, "First ten million is in. You can confirm at your leisure. Would you like an e-mail confirmation?" She asked this with a smile that made Jack see why she had young bucks like Fourtner and Mearan locking horns for her attention. Joanna Moorehouse had been exciting, enticing, mysterious, and flat-out hot. She wasn't classically beautiful in life, her nose too prominent, cheekbones not very high, sharp chin. It was her inner stillness, her complete mastery over her own mind and body that captivated.

"Very funny," Bowman said, and pulled out his cell phone. Apparently he used an online app to check his balances in whatever offshore account he had given her. He nodded in satisfaction, stood up, and walked to the door. There he half turned as if trying to think of a zinger for an exit line, couldn't, gave up, and left. Joanna watched him go.

She kept smiling, only for herself now, and lounged back in her chair, rocking a little. She didn't get long to enjoy the afterglow since her door opened again and Jeremy Mearan walked in. He flopped into the chair that Bowman had evacuated and asked, "So we're a go?"

"The sale is assured. He could still screw us, but I don't think he will. I truly don't," she emphasized, enjoying her private joke.

"I wouldn't count on it," Mearan grumbled. Apparently he didn't know about the camera any more than he had known about Joanna's slush fund. "Tyra better not find out about this."

"She won't."

"Are you going to take her with us to New York?"

Joanna shook her head. "She'd never leave here. She has family."

"Yeah, that's true." He also slumped back in his chair; the hour must have been very late indeed. "What about you? You have any family?"

"Not a soul," Joanna stated, without a trace of regret. "I'm all alone."

"That's not true." Jeremy Mearan stood and slid off his suit coat. Then he moved around to her side of the desk, unbuttoning his shirt and sliding his belt out of its loops. "You have me."

Joanna didn't bother answering. Perhaps she preferred to keep her lies to a minimum. But she swiveled her chair to face him, leaving her back to the camera.

The three cops watched Mearan's passionate but somewhat clumsy seduction and Joanna's vague response for another few seconds until Jack hit the *Stop* icon. He said, "So she recorded this to be able to keep Bowman in line in case he tried to take her payment and then back out. But if she intended to take her money and run, why did she care what happened to Sterling?"

Riley said, "It was her baby, in every sense of the word. The company seemed to be the only thing in the world she cared about. She wanted it to have a good home. Besides, if she ran off we might, or DJ Bryan might, look closely enough to find the missing funds. If she simply resigns with a fare-thee-well, the business only looks forward and not back."

"We'd better watch the rest of this video," the captain said. "There might be more, um, admissions made."

Jack said, "What if Bowman came back from his HQ and said it's no good, New York knows about the default rate and they're not going to buy at any price. She either wants her money back or tells him to try harder because she has him on video accepting a bribe to screw over his own employer."

"So he kills her to get the tape? SD card, whatever?" Riley said.

But that didn't make sense either. "If he had, he would have torn that house apart to search for it, and we would have known. Unless he was really, really good and left the place looking as if it hadn't been touched."

"Nobody's that good."

"Then the place hadn't been touched. No one killed her and then searched for that card."

"Besides," Riley added, "if he'd have found that statement from her Panama account, I bet he'd figure out a way to get the money from it. I think all you need is the account number. If he were willing to screw his bosses for twenty million, I can't imagine what he'd do for six hundred million."

"Two-fifty," Jack reminded him. "After the disbursement to Ergo."

"Still, ten times more than her offer."

"We need to start the video back up. Maybe there are, uh, more people involved," the captain suggested.

"Without a damn time stamp we have no idea when she recorded this," Jack said. "It could have been the night of her murder. It could have been a month before."

Riley said, "A lot could happen during a gap. Somehow Tyra got involved, or at least someone thought she was involved."

"Why would anyone assume that, though? Joanna's hardly going to tell her lawyer she committed bribery."

"Tyra could have stumbled on half a dozen red flags. In addition to this bribery there's fraud—keeping the default rate under wraps—and Joanna's nest egg. People have been killed over much less."

Jack said, "What we do know is that Mearan knew. And he's still alive."

"Grab your coat and hat," Riley said. "Time to have another talk with the lad."

"I could watch the rest of this video for you," the captain offered. "See if they say anything else that implicates, um—"

Jack knew, as every working stiff knows, to throw your boss a bone as often as possible. "Would you, Cap? That would be a big help."

"No problem," the captain said with an expansive wave, and settled himself at Jack's desk. The two detectives headed for the elevator.

As the doors closed, Riley said, "You might want to disinfect your chair when we get back."

Jack said, "Ew."

Chapter 25

Maggie entered the courtroom, not at all happy about being in that place and at that time. She had been taking another look at Joanna's fingernail scrapings, as blood-caked as they were, and trying to send the bloody fingerprint from under her body to the FBI database—doable but complicated. Unlike forensic units on television she couldn't just hit a button and search the warehouse of ten-print cards the bureau had accumulated for the past century. It required online forms and protocols and queuing. Plus, she had Rick and his Phoenix trip on her mind, with nightmares of Rick strolling past a unit photo and catching sight of Jack in the back row. Rick declaring, "Hey, I know that guy, he's at our department now." The Phoenix cop saying, "Oh yeah, that's so-and-so." Rick saying, "No it's not, it's Jack Renner." "No, his name is Bill" or Jerry or Oswald or whatever he'd been going by then . . . maybe even his real name. She hoped it wasn't Oswald.

"Raise your right hand," the court reporter said loudly,

startling Maggie out of her reverie. She'd nearly walked by the woman without stopping. She swore herself in, her healing arm under cover of her suit jacket, and then stepped up onto the dais with the witness chair.

Plus, she hadn't had nearly enough time to prepare for whatever Graham's attorney decided to throw at her. Maggie had worked with fingerprints long enough to feel completely comfortable with her conclusions, but she couldn't keep up with every study, research project, and court decision regarding fingerprint science. And she found it very difficult to explain in words what was essentially a picture.

Gerald Graham sat at the defense table, staring at her as before. She told herself that she was part of the process of putting him in jail for the rest of his natural life, so one could hardly fault him for taking an interest in the proceedings. That his stare seemed abnormally intense and his smile downright creepy changed nothing. She straightened her back. And even though she truly believed Anna had been the target, she tried to telegraph: *Shoot at me, will you?*

His attorney came out swinging with a tricky, and entirely reasonable, question. "Ms. Gardiner, how do you know when a fingerprint matches another fingerprint?"

She gave the pattest answer she had. "When they have a sufficient amount of information in common and I would not expect to see that amount of correspondence in prints from two different sources."

"What information are we talking about?" The attorney, a rather nice-looking middle-aged man with a tiny coffee stain on his power tie, spoke from the podium. This particular judge didn't hold with attorneys "prancing all over the courtroom like Lipizzaner stallions."

"As I explained last week, information in the ridges themselves, what patterns they make, where they end and divide, other things like scars, incipient ridges, and pores. We take notes of all these characteristics and their spatial relationship to each other and compare them to the corresponding characteristics in the questioned print."

A fancy way of saying "We look at them and see if they match."

"And where are these notes?"

"I beg your pardon?"

Graham continued to stare, now licking his lips at her. His attorney's cochair, a bear of a man, neatly blocked him from the jury's view so they could not witness this behavior. But right now Graham could play all the mind games he wanted. The fear of looking like an idiot in front of the jury kept her focused on the attorney asking the questions.

"Your report is a few mere sentences. You compared these prints, found them to be the same. Where are the contemporaneous notes, the checklists, the descriptions of each print?"

"You have our worksheet. I believe it's exhibit number—"

"The worksheet doesn't have much more than the report. Columns with the numbers of the latents and a single space with some symbols about the quality of the print. My client's freedom may depend upon the quality of this print, this single little partial print that *you* say matches his. And you try to hang him with a single sentence?"

She had heard this before, too. "A detailed written description of both prints could be pages long but still wouldn't tell you whether or not I am correct in saying that the prints match."

"So a long report would be pointless, is that what you're saying?"

"Yes."

This brief answer temporarily stopped him, and she went on. Graham had gotten bored with trying to freak her and now paged through a notebook on the table in front of him.

Maggie said, "You have blown-up photographs of his fingerprint and the print from the gun. If you like we can put that back on the projector and—"

"But your conclusion is subjective, correct?" the attorney interrupted. He might be able to convince the jury that she had erred if they didn't spend too much time looking at the fingerprint themselves. "It's only your opinion that these prints match?"

"An opinion based on the evidence and confirmed by a second examiner."

"But comparing fingerprints isn't really a *science*, is it? It's just you looking at pictures of things and deciding that they 'match.'" While his attorney made contemptuous air quotes around the word, Graham pulled a pink envelope from his notebook and seemed to smell it, peeking at Maggie over its top edge.

"Fingerprint conclusions are repeatable and repro- ducible and have been so for about two hundred years. The national database contains fingerprint sets from over one hundred million people and latent prints are searched against it all day, every day. Errors by human beings, when divided into these numbers, average in the one-hundredths of one percent. If that's not sci- ence," she added boldly, "I'd like to know what is."

She wondered when he would get around to his hired expert and assert that his expert had declared the latent print from the gun a nonmatch to Graham. Per- haps, she thought hopefully, the expert had refused to act as a hired whore and was *not* challenging her iden- tification. The thought buoyed her.

Graham slipped a finger into the pink envelope and ripped the top open.

The attorney switched tracks again. "Let's get back to how this print got on the gun. Even assuming that the print does match my client's, it doesn't prove that he shot the victim, does it?"

"No," Maggie agreed. Again this short answer seemed to surprise the attorney.

"So it's completely possible that someone else stole the gun from my client, shot the victim"—he didn't name the dead woman, keeping the image of her as a human being as far from the jury's mind as possible— "and then put the gun under my client's bed." He had to stick with this scenario since Graham had stupidly told the police more than once that he hadn't touched the gun in weeks. He should have said that he discov- ered it in his room before they arrived with the search warrant—then the print would, or at least could, have been meaningless.

As Graham began to read his pink letter, after sniffing it again, Maggie summed up: "So you're asking if your client could have touched the gun, then someone took it, shot the victim without disturbing your client's fingerprint that was already on the gun, and then brought it back to his apartment and left it under his bed."

The attorney paused. It did sound pretty ridiculous when she put it like that. Everyone knew what a gun looked like and how it was held in order to shoot—using it without touching the front of the grip would be pretty damn impossible. But he had no other avenues. "Yes."

His client smirked at Maggie from between two pink sheets of paper as if even he found the mental picture hilarious, of the "real shooter" holding the gun with a fairy-light touch in order to preserve a fingerprint he couldn't have known was there and still managing to pull the trigger accurately enough to kill.

"I have no idea," Maggie said.

"So it's perfectly possible," the attorney insisted.

"I have no idea."

Graham began to cough, and wheeze in between the coughs.

"You can't say that didn't happen, because fingerprints can't be dated, can they? You can't tell us when my client's print was deposited on that gun, can you?"

"No," Maggie said. Fingerprints could last for years if left undisturbed in cool, not too dry conditions—though she doubted that applied to the underside of Graham's bed.

"Now, as you are surely aware, Ohio requires the Daubert standard for allowing testimony in court."

"The testimony of my fingerprint match has already been entered into the court, but go ahead," she couldn't resist saying. *Not a good idea. I am a forensic scientist, not a lawyer*, she told herself. *Don't try to out–lawyer-talk him. You will not win.*

"Then tell us about why there is no error rate associated with—" The attorney finally gave up trying to talk over his client's coughing and apparently decided to use the moment to perhaps garner a shred of empathy from the jury. He moved behind Graham and put a fatherly hand on his client's shoulder, despite the fact that his client was several years older than himself.

But Graham kept coughing, nearly doubling over. He tried to shove his chair back with such force that the table nearly overturned and the large cocounsel had to grab it. Graham's face had turned red and now faded to gray pallor as the coughing subsided to a strangled gasping. The attorney, who had jumped out of the way as if his client might have the plague, called for a doctor, a medic—anyone. "My client is having a medical episode. We need help!"

Maggie stayed right where she was. Neither a doctor nor a medic, she knew it would not help the situation—or the security in the courtroom—for everyone to crowd the defense table. She would do the bailiffs a favor and stay out of the way. The prosecutors did the same.

The spectators in the pews, however, did not feel so compelled. The entire audience rose as one and strained for a better look. The jury fidgeted, dying to do the same as long as it would not violate the dignity of the jury box.

The judge told one of the bailiffs to get the jail doctor on duty up from the building next door. He did not seem overly concerned, no doubt having seen a number of "medical episodes" inside his courtroom. He did order the jury removed. As they were leaving, the defense attorney had a thought.

"The EpiPen!" he cried to his cocounsel over Graham's twitching form. "This must be anaphylactic shock!"

"It's probably a heart attack," the prosecutor said.

"He's choking on something!" someone in the galley shouted.

"Let him die," a man intoned. Maggie had seen him before and felt fairly certain he was the father of the victim, grandfather to the orphaned five-year-old. Two print reporters immediately leaned in from a back pew and asked him for a statement.

The defense attorney's voice cut through the hubbub. "*Where's the EpiPen?*" he screeched with such desperation that Maggie felt sorry for him, a man she would have happily speared only a minute before. His palpable fear spurred everyone else in the courtroom to higher levels of adrenaline and a tremor ran through the room as staff conveyed a message to the hallway outside; the call for the EpiPen went out. The cocounsel, meanwhile, began CPR, a chancy idea since he outweighed his client by at least a hundred pounds and could probably have broken all of Graham's ribs with one compression.

The court reporter had stood up for a better look, but stayed next to her seat, hovering in front of the witness box. As loathe as she felt to intervene on behalf of the habitual killer, Maggie suggested to her, "Wouldn't he have the EpiPen on him? Like in a pocket or something?"

The woman shook her head. "They won't let him carry it because he could use it as a weapon. The deputy assigned to his guard duty keeps it with him. Besides, if it is a heart attack wouldn't an EpiPen make him worse?"

"Quite possibly," Maggie agreed. "Where is the deputy?"

The court reporter looked around. "I don't know. Once Graham's in the courtroom he can take a break, because the bailiffs are here to handle security. So he pops out now and then."

She shouted these last words for Maggie to hear as the room devolved into full-tilt chaos. The judge, sensing that this would be a lengthy interruption, ordered the bailiffs to clear the court. The spectators didn't want to leave the biggest spectacle since the trial began, so while wise enough not to refuse they certainly weren't in any hurry. And if the deputy on EpiPen duty had been strolling in the hallway, they now blocked his path in. But more likely he would be in the side entrances, the doors flush with the wall that entered the room directly from the walkways hidden behind the court's walls, where judges, juries, and police personnel could arrive from separate and more secure entrances. Yet no epinephrine appeared.

The large cocounsel kept up chest compressions.

His more excitable partner seemed on the verge of tears, his voice cutting through the noisy hubbub. "He's going to die! He's dying! What can we do?! Somebody's got to do something!"

His panic infected the room. Every person in it, including Maggie, hummed with agitation. Unfortunately, all the *wanting* to do something didn't translate into what, exactly, should be done.

The man at the source of all this consternation had grown quiet. Maggie no longer heard his wheezing breaths, and from what she could glimpse of his face and one arm, both lay still and flaccid.

A uniformed deputy cut through the crowd from the rear as if slogging through waist-deep snow, adroitly diverting one of the reporters who had stepped into his path. Maggie saw her calling a question to him, but the words were lost in the babble. When the man pushed open the railing gate into the well it seemed as if a dike had collapsed and the gallery members went after him like a following sea. Or a tsunami.

The deputy rushed to the fallen man. Maggie finally stood; from her elevated position in the witness box she could see even over the heads of the spectators. There seemed to be frantic discussion among the two attorneys and the deputy about where and how to inject the EpiPen, and this made sense: Medic duty was not part of the deputy's job. He had merely been supposed to hang on to the thing and pass it to the prisoner to inject himself, should it become necessary. But the prisoner now lay completely still and uncaring. The deputy stabbed the pen into unprotesting flesh.

"Ms. Gardiner."

Maggie turned. The judge, who seemed to have sprouted a few more gray hairs in only the last few minutes, spoke to her.

"You may be excused from the stand now."

Chapter 26

"But what happened?" Carol asked. Quitting time had come and gone, but she had taken one look at Maggie's face and brewed some hot, sweet decaf for her younger coworker. Maggie didn't know why. She was not upset and certainly not traumatized. She felt more confused than anything, and said as much.

"Doesn't matter," Carol said, blowing on her own cup. "It's a human reaction when someone drops dead right in front of you. Instinct. Nothing raises one's survival instincts like seeing a member of the herd roll over and give a death rattle."

"I'd really like to think that me and Gerry Graham weren't members of the same herd."

"You'd like to, yes," Carol said.

"That's supremely unreassuring."

"So he had a heart attack or an allergy attack?"

"No idea yet. I'm sure it will be in the paper tomorrow, and frankly I can wait."

"Did he clutch his heart or his throat?"

Maggie thought. "Throat."

"Allergy. Was he eating something right before-hand? He's not allowed to eat in the courtroom, right?"

Maggie pulled her knees up to her chin, balancing precariously on the seat of her chair, and pictured the scene. "No, he was reading a letter. Pink. I figured it had to be from one of his mail-order sweethearts. I'm guessing it was even . . ."

Carol waited, then prompted. "What?"

"What would happen if you had someone with se-vere peanut allergy and you ground up peanuts to dust and then coated a piece of paper in them? Wrote a long, appealing note so they'd keep holding it. Scented it with perfume so they'd take a good whiff as well—"

"Death," Carol said. "That's what would happen."

"Murder by mail. Not tough to find out the jail's address. High-profile case, he probably gets a lot of correspondence. All you have to do is disguise your handwriting."

"There's no shortage of suspects. Any family mem-ber of the people he's killed, maybe even his ex-wife, his kid, people who wanted him to stay in jail. The de-fense has been making such a show in the news, maybe those he terrorized were afraid he'd get out."

"It's iffy, though. He might have opened the letter in jail, where the guard with his EpiPen would be right there."

"Depends on how often they do rounds."

"He's in some sort of isolation *because* of the peanut allergy. The guard probably wouldn't be too far away. It's coincidence that he opened it in a courtroom when his epinephrine was in the pocket of a guy down in the cafeteria. And when the deputy did arrive, he used the pen right through the shirt into the arm. I think he'd seen too many old *Star Trek* episodes where they go right through the shirt. The thigh is the most effective spot."

"Yes," Carol said. "Thigh. So bad luck contributed to his death—aww, what a pity. Now we have an untraceable murder weapon and lots of suspects. How hard should we even look? The whole city wanted the guy dead."

Including, Maggie thought, *Jack*.

And me.

"I'm depressing you," Carol said, patting the younger woman's knee. "And you look worn out. Go home and go to bed, right now."

"I'm okay. I'm only wondering if it's terrible that my foremost thought is for how I don't have to go back into that courtroom and explain error rates."

"I wouldn't beat yourself up over *that*," Carol advised.

Maggie had indeed gone home and gotten into bed, pausing only long enough to send a good-night text to her brother and strip off her clothes before collapsing onto the sheets. It had been a very busy couple of days and she felt besieged. *Tomorrow*, she had thought, *my brain will sort out all the facts it has accumulated and the murders of the two women will make sense. Yes. Of course they will.* The apparent murder of Graham might not, but she decided not to worry about that or to spend much time picturing Jack's face when he spoke of the prolific killer. Graham might not even have had an allergy, using the story as a way to get himself a private cell. She would shelve that question for when she had more reliable information. Or maybe just shelve that question for good.

Yet she found herself lost in a dream in which she entered the courtroom to find Jack disemboweling the still-alive Graham when the phone rang. A third woman had been murdered. In her home, with her torso flayed open. Maggie hadn't wanted to ask any more, the nightmare still bright in her mind, and she arrived, bleary eyed, at an apartment building on East 12th Street twenty minutes later. The ground floor of the building contained darkened businesses, a small lobby leading to the upper apartments, and sat catty-corner to a small park. Not quite midnight but the streets were already deserted and she had no trouble parking the city vehicle in front of the curb. She could have gotten there quicker if she had walked from the police department, but schlepping all the equipment up several alleyways in the middle of the night with a looming thunderstorm didn't appeal to her.

A few raindrops gave her head some light pats, as if the sky released only what it must, holding the rest for a greater, coming battle. Jack and Riley loitered on the sidewalk with their own vehicle, finishing up some radio communication and appearing equally bleary eyed.

"He's getting bolder," Maggie said by way of greeting. "First an isolated house, then a house in a close-knit community, and now an apartment? There isn't a doorman, security cameras, nosy neighbors?"

"No, maybe, and not that we've found," Jack summarized. "There's a camera on the front door only and the superintendent is trying to figure out how it works."

"Oh joy. And the victim is from Sterling? Who?"

"The Fed regulator," Riley told her. "Anna Hernandez."

Chapter 27

Perhaps it had simply been one shock too many in a short period of time, a combination of the lack of rest, the gnawing concern over her ex-husband's investigations, a defendant dying ten feet from her, but Maggie's knees went out and her bottom smacked against the Crown Vic's front fender.

"Hey," Jack said, and grabbed her arm.

"What's the matter with you?" Riley asked.

When she found her breath again, Maggie said, "She was nice. Anna. I—I liked her."

"Yeah, that's tough," Riley said, his voice conveying "It's a truly rotten break," not "Too bad, suck it up."

Jack still studied her. "Are you going to be okay? Can you work this scene?"

"Yes," she said without hesitation. She had been at the first two murders, knew what to expect and what might be alterations in the pattern. No one would tear her from this crime. She owed it to Anna.

She pushed herself off the car and made herself straighten up. "Let's go."

"There's more," Riley said. "We're holding the guy who found the body because he also works at Sterling. Jeremy Mearan."

"Mearan." Maggie felt her forehead crinkle into a deep frown.

"That's the same reaction we had. What connection would Mearan have to Anna Hernandez? We've got no clue, but as soon as we have a chance we're going to ask him. And he'd better have a damn good answer." He held the door for her as she carted her camera and two toolboxes inside the lobby.

This would be the first time Maggie had to investigate the murder of a friend, even a brief one. She hoped it would be the last.

The building at 1675 East 12th Street had a clean, pleasant lobby with a small waiting area; a panel to buzz apartment intercoms; and a small, creaky elevator that smelled of Murphy's Oil Soap. And nothing else. The hallway leading to Anna's fifth-floor apartment likewise sported pleasant décor and relatively fresh carpeting, but on the whole it underscored the difference between public- and private-sector incomes, particularly once Maggie had crossed the threshold into the small foyer with Anna's jacket hanging by the door. Joanna had lived in a mansion that would rival those of A-list actors, whereas Anna rented a two-bedroom with a galley kitchen. Honest work did not pay as well as the other kind.

Though it usually came with fewer risks. Usually.

At first it seemed as if nothing was amiss. From the door Maggie saw a dining area and the small kitchen to

her left. Anna had not been a neatnik. Assorted mail
piled up on the dining table and dishes sat in the sink.
A half-table under the clothing hooks held a metal
bowl with a key ring and Anna's slouchy, many-pocketed
purse. On the floor below it sat her briefcase, made of
worn but real leather and bulging with papers, booklets, and stapled reports, one handle fixed with an oversized paper clip.

But to Maggie's right, a sofa, coffee table with a
balcony beyond it, the lights of the city twinkling behind panels of sheer fabric, and Anna's bare foot lying
on the carpet. Maggie took another step past the foyer
wall and saw the rest of her.

Anna, like Tyra, had changed for comfort, into a
camisole with a soft shelf bra and thin cotton pajama
pants. Those had been shredded, along with her skin
and the organs of her torso. She lay on her back, arms
flung out, palms upturned, with deep gashes in all
those surfaces. Her head had landed near an armchair,
and the wooden foot of it kept her head tilted to one
side, looking away from Maggie toward the wide windows and the city lights, with an expression of both
concern and sadness. No fear, no agony—only a mild
perplexity and a deep disappointment.

In what? Maggie wondered. *In the brevity of her
young life? In the identity of the killer? In me? I let her
assume that I would keep fighting the good fight just as
she did, that I would do something about the deaths of
her coworkers. I didn't tell her the truth: Whatever
fight I'm in, it isn't good.*

I am no longer on the side of the angels.

"You going to be okay?" Jack asked, cutting into her thoughts. "Are you sure you're going to be able to do this?"

"Yes," she said, as firmly as before. "Stop asking."

"I have to. You don't look so good."

She didn't answer, but with exaggerated precision she balanced carefully to slip booties over her shoes. Then she removed her camera from its case, attached the large flash, and began to document the scene.

She kept the rest of her equipment in the hall until all the preliminary photos were taken. Two patrol officers kept guard out there, standard procedure for crime scenes, to handle crowd control, minor canvassing, and any criminal elements who might decide to return to the scene of their exploits. But all five personnel kept their voices low, nearly whispering, and not out of concern for the neighbors' beauty sleep. They didn't need a bunch of curious looky-lous stopping by. As Maggie bagged and tagged items of evidence she kept them right inside the apartment door.

It seemed a clear repeat of Joanna's and Tyra's murders. In her brief photographing of the rest of the apartment, nothing else seemed disturbed. A single glass of wine with a half inch of Moscato left in it sat on the counter. The spare bedroom had been outfitted with a desk and bookshelves, knickknacks, and an opened laptop that, when jostled, came back to life to reveal an e-mail to someone named Wayne, never sent, bearing a single sentence: "How about Lola for dinner tomorrow night?" Because it hadn't been sent, Maggie saw no way to tell when it had been written. Maybe the IT department would have a way, but she didn't and did not intend to touch anything on the keyboard to try to find out. The electronics specialists had one simple rule for the collection of computers, cell phones, tablets, GPSs, and any other digital evidence. The rule consisted of: "Don't touch anything!"

The spare room also had a litter box on the open closet floor, and from the smell it had been used recently.

"Where's the cat?" Maggie asked.

"What cat?" Riley asked.

It had found a hiding space during the terror, no doubt. The animal lover in Maggie resisted the urge to search for it. It would come out when it wanted, or when it got hungry enough.

Satisfied that nothing else in the apartment presented an obvious clue to the intruder, and with no indication that he had progressed past the body, she returned to the entryway. She used a paper cone and a can of spray powder that could give much better results on doorknobs than a brush, but found nothing but smudges on both the inside and outside knobs. The doors' surfaces also had nothing but smudges except for one fairly clear set of prints from a left hand on the inside edge, where someone inside the apartment would push the door shut. She tried the metal bowl, the table it sat on, poked around in the purse, where the wallet, cash, and cards Anna had carried remained in their tidy compartments just in case Anna had made a note of a meeting, a phone number, anything to indicate who had arrived at her apartment that evening. She brushed powder on the walls and the kitchen floor, even though the investigators had probably obliterated

any shoeprints, and photographed any that didn't belong to Riley, whose shoes she demanded to see.
Jack's, for some reason, didn't leave marks on the tile.

Of course they don't, she thought crossly.

When she had exhausted the entryway she started
on the living room area, and Anna's still body. The blood
pool around her hadn't even finished drying.

This time Maggie didn't let herself stare, or pause,
or even think about breaking down. She didn't want
more inquiries from Jack or anyone else. So she got
her numbered markers and her measuring tape and her
clipboard and began to sketch the small living room.

"What was Mearan doing here?" she asked of no
one in particular.

"That's what we're about to go ask him," Jack said.
"As soon as the EMTs clear. Apparently finding the
body shocked his system."

"She had mentioned a boyfriend. Could that be
Mearan?" She couldn't quite picture Anna with Joanna's
boyfriend.

"Don't know," Jack said.

"They kind of looked alike," Riley observed. "The
two women, I mean. Skinny, dark hair, same age. That
could be his type."

"Totally different personalities, though," Maggie
said, as her eyes fell on a framed photo next to the television.

"Maybe personality isn't as important to him as a
good pair of—um, physical characteristics," Riley
said.

Maggie picked up the photo, which showed Anna

and an unfamiliar young man, faces pressed together blowing out candles on a cake that read, "Happy Birthday Wayne." "I'm willing to bet this is the boyfriend."

She passed it to the detectives. Riley wondered aloud why Anna was also blowing out candles and said perhaps she and Wayne were fraternal twins. Jack said that in that case the cake would read, "Wayne and Anna," and Maggie said according to the e-mail they had a dinner date the following evening—tonight, actually—at Lola on East 4th and Anna hadn't mentioned having any family living in town.

Riley asked, "Any idea of a last name?"

"An e-mail address."

"Wayne will be in her phone," Jack said. "IT can get it for us."

"We'll check him out, but my money is still on Mearan. Maggie, you need anything else from us before we go downstairs for a chat?"

She shook her head.

"Call if the ME investigator turns up something earth-shattering. Otherwise we'll be back sooner or later, depending on what the boy toy tells us."

They left and she turned to the unpleasant task of doing what she could with Anna's decimated body. She took more close-up photos of the torso, the hands, the area around her. The clothing, as before, had been ripped from neck to ankle with something very sharp and then flung open. Both hands had wounds, a deep stab in the center of the right palm and a slicing cut along three of the left fingers. Her left bicep and right forearm had slashes. One, from the position, seemed to have been postmortem, in line with a stab to the outside of one breast. The knife must have slid down a rib and continued into the arm. Anna's breasts had taken a great deal of abuse; her chest was now a mass of torn skin and blood. Once the rib cage ended it got worse.

The stomach had been pierced and the contents filled the air with a smell that the neighbors would be complaining about once they started leaving for work. Colon, small intestines, all had been breached, and a sickly brownish fluid mingled with the darkening blood in the peritoneal cavity and on the floor. The liver glistened with a dark red color. It was such a *mess*, Maggie thought with unwelcome despair. She could see no way to determine what came first or second or last. And what did it matter anyway? Someone had come in and stabbed Anna to death before she could do anything beyond throwing up her hands in self-defense. The blood loss came too fast and too severe; her life force flowed away before she could . . . what? Grab a phone? Scream?

How *had* he managed to completely and quickly overpower a healthy young woman in a populated apartment building? It happened in the evening, obviously. People were home. These were nice apartments but not luxury condos and couldn't be *that* well soundproofed. Maggie gazed at Anna's throat and thought she could detect a slight bruising in the parts that weren't smeared with blood. She would need the pathologist to tell her more, but it wouldn't surprise her to learn that he had silenced Anna with a blow to the throat, as he had done with Tyra.

It seemed an iffy way to keep someone quiet, hugely risky in a busy building.

Maggie took copious photographs of Anna's throat and used her superbright flashlight to examine it, her face coming way too close to her new friend's drying bodily fluids. But she did not see finger marks or prints in the blood on Anna's neck. It seemed to have been dabbed on here and there by contact with bloody clothing, either the suspect's or her own, not by his hands as he choked her. Her face had stayed clean except for a few drops of red spray. Perhaps he had choked her into unconsciousness before the carnage began. Maggie would like to think so, but then why were her eyes open? More likely he had managed to damage the larynx enough to keep her from crying out, from shouting for help to the people to the sides, above and below, while her killer plunged a knife into her body again and again.

Why? What could someone gain by killing these three women? Joanna and Anna had been on opposite sides of the business. It had been Anna's job to force Sterling to toe the regulatory line, and Joanna evidently felt it had been her job to move that line to her own advantage whenever possible. Tyra had been in the middle, an honorable girl working for a less than honorable client. Who could be working against all three simultaneously?

She got out her handheld crime scene light, a flashlight with a vaguely gun-like shape. The combination of wavelengths emitted would cause a number of things to fluoresce and glow—fibers with certain opti-

cal properties, luminescent paints, bodily fluids such
as semen and, to a lesser extent, saliva. She didn't expect to find much. Swabs from Joanna and Tyra had
not shown any sign of sexual contact. Or rather, Maggie corrected her thought, they had shown no reaction
for semen, which was not the same thing.

Wearing a pair of orange goggles, she warned the
two patrol officers outside that she would be dousing
the lights in the apartment. She would leave the apartment door open, however, to give her just enough illumination to keep from stumbling around.

"You're going to work in a dark room with a dead
body?" one of them asked her.

"It will hardly be the first time." She hit the switch.

Blood did not fluoresce by itself; it had to be treated
with a product such as luminol or Bluestar first, and
then it did not need a light source to glow. Instead it
absorbed the ultraviolet rays from her light and turned
even darker, so that parts of Anna's body seemed to
disappear into a vast background. Other parts, like the
few sections of unstained skin, appeared quite ordinary. There were a few spots of fluorescent light; some
errant fibers, the tag inside her pants, the elastic in her
underwear all glowed—as well as a spot about the size
of a dime on the thin carpet next to Anna's right thigh.

That it might be from the killer seemed too much to
hope. It could be a cleaning product, or if it was semen,
it could be from a boisterous but past encounter with
the absent Wayne. Still Maggie wasted no time in getting a sterile scalpel from her kit and cutting a square
that included the stain from the carpet. She dropped it
into a manila envelope, sealed it, and then used a fresh
scalpel to cut another square a few inches away and

unstained from the carpet as well. That would be their reference sample to show that whatever the glowing stain turned out to be, it could not be intrinsic to the carpeting itself.

She still worked in the dark. She hadn't wanted to take a chance on losing the spot or getting too close to it with a Sharpie, and the hallway lights gave her enough illumination to work. About to stand up and flick the switch, she caught a brief glance of two small glowing orbs watching her from the kitchen.

"Well, hello, kitty," she said.

Chapter 28

Jeremy Mearan sat in an empty apartment on the second floor that the building manager had donated to the cause of American justice. Mostly, Jack figured, to avoid loaning them his office, with its precisely ordered desk accessories and vintage Indian memorabilia. The vacated efficiency, however, still had coffee rings on the laminate counter from the former tenant, and said tenant's parakeet had let a pile of down accumulate in one corner. No furniture remained, but the manager, determined to make the space workable, had scrounged up three folding chairs of varying condition. Jack's wobbled. So did Jeremy Mearan's, but he didn't seem to notice. In his current state he wouldn't notice if the ceiling were abruptly removed by alien life forms.

He sat with his face in his hands, straightening only when Riley shut the door behind them with an audible *clack*. He still appeared to have stepped from the pages of a magazine but in an ad for more casual clothes, with his faded jeans, clean T-shirt, and perfect five o'clock shadow, but without the poise and sense of entitlement models radiate in those posed photos. The two cops took their places across from Mearan. Riley read him his rights and had him sign the Miranda card.

"What were you doing at Anna Hernandez's apartment?" Riley asked.

Mearan kept one fist propped against his chin as if his head were too heavy to keep upright otherwise. He wore an expression and spoke in a tone of utter hopelessness. "I went to see her."

"We could have worked that out for ourselves," Riley said, his tone even.

"I had . . . decided to give her the book."

"The book?"

Talking seemed to require great effort on his part. "The employee manual. For Sterling Financial."

Jack said, "You went over to the Fed regulator's home late at night to talk about Sterling's company policy? Is that what you're saying?"

"Yes."

"And when you did, you just *happened* to stumble over her dead body?"

"The door wasn't shut all the way. When I knocked, it opened a crack and I could see—her."

He looked as if he would throw up. Jack kept up the questions, partly to avoid the puking. "Did you see anyone else? In the hallway, the elevator?"

Mearan shook his head.

"Did you go into the apartment?"

"*No!* I . . . couldn't . . . get any closer to her. I left the door where it was and called nine-one-one from the hallway."

"Anyone in the lobby? On the street?" Mearan kept shaking his head. "Where did you park?"

"At a meter on the next block. The spaces are free this time of day."

"I'm aware of that, thanks. How often do you pay a visit to Anna Hernandez's apartment?"

"Um . . . this was maybe the fourth time."

"Does her boyfriend know?"

"No. No one knows." Mearan ran his hands through his short hair. Weirdly, mussing it only made it more perfect.

"Did Joanna know? Was she angry?"

Mearan seemed to pale even further, which shouldn't have been possible, at the mention of his ex-boss-slash-girlfriend. "She'd have killed me. But Joanna's *gone*. That's why I finally decided to do it. No one else at Sterling deserves my loyalty."

Riley guessed at some math. "But you'd been carrying on with Anna before Joanna's death. Did she know, or suspect? Is that why you killed her?"

Mearan seemed to need a minute to work through those two questions before arriving at bafflement. "Kill who?"

"Joanna."

"I didn't kill Joanna!" He seemed stunned at the very idea. "I loved her. That's why I couldn't give Anna what she wanted . . . until now . . . because it didn't matter anymore. Without Joanna, there's no point. . . ."

"Anna, then," Riley moved on. "Why did you kill Anna?"

"*What?*"

Jack said, "Wait. What did Anna Hernandez want?"

"The manual," Mearan said.

"The employee manual."

"Yes."

"You came to her apartment late at night to bring her an employee manual? Why couldn't you have given it to her at the Sterling offices, where, by the way, you both happen to be all day long?"

"I didn't want anyone to know."

"Where is this manual?" Riley demanded. "You're not carrying a book."

"It's on the thumb drive. I handed it to you with my cell phone."

Riley glanced at the clear bag for personal property sitting on the coffee-stained counter.

Jack said, "Let's get this straight. Were you having a sexual affair with Anna Hernandez?"

"No," Mearan said, his voice suddenly very normal. He sounded like a tween girl offered broccoli for dinner. "Of course not! Why on earth would I be doing that?"

"Why not? She's young, very attractive. . . . In fact she looked a lot like Joanna."

Either they had woken the upstairs neighbor or that tenant had a very early whistle because footsteps creaked the ceiling over them. Meanwhile Mearan said, "Maybe. But she wasn't."

"Attractive?"

"Joanna."

"Did you kill her?"

"No!"

"Do you know who did?"

"No! I . . . don't think so, anyway. It has to be someone at Sterling."

Jack thought. "Why?"

"Who else would know about the manual?"

"*What is this manual?* How can it be so important?" Riley asked in exasperation.

"Because it's illegal."

The two cops exchanged frustrated glances. Jack said, through partly gritted teeth, "Start from the beginning, and explain your relationship with Anna Hernandez."

Another run of the hands through the hair, and Mearan sat back to give it his best shot. "When Anna first started as our regulator, she told us to feel free to pass on any concerns we had and she would respect our privacy—a polite way to say that if we wanted to do any whistleblowing, the Fed would protect our identities. I ignored her. I think everyone did. But on her second visit I—I had just been attacked in the parking lot by a guy I had put into an ARM a few months before. The intro rate had run out and his payment had doubled. He wanted to refinance but we'd have lost money on the loan, or rather not made enough."

"Imagine that," Jack said.

"Hadn't the loan been sold by then?" Riley asked, with visible pride in having gotten the hang of this.

"No, with power loans we milk the interest for at least six months."

"So what did he do?"

"He waited on the sidewalk outside the lot and reamed me out, swung at me, but I jumped inside the building and locked the door. I felt pretty shaken up. I immediately went to Joanna, but she basically told me to suck it up and shoved me out of her office. I mean . . . I respected Joanna's focus, but I couldn't even pour myself a coffee because my hands were shaking. It freaked me out, this guy. His face got so red, I don't know who I felt more scared for, me or him. In fact, it was that guy—that Resnick guy."

"Kurt Resnick?"

"Yeah, him."

"The current face of mob violence against Sterling? And you didn't think to mention that before?" Riley demanded.

Mearan blinked at him.

Jack got it. "Because his experience is commonplace, isn't it? Sterling has screwed so many people that they all melt together. Right?"

Mearan considered this question as if it were a piece of modern art. "You tell yourself that they can afford it, that they deserve what they get for not doing their own due diligence, that they're poor anyway and this won't make their lives a lot different, but . . . that's not really true."

"You don't say," Jack drawled.

"We steal. We rip people off right and left. We make up fees, charge them much higher interest than they could have gotten elsewhere and tell them that's the best they can do. We encourage them to lie on their income verification, and when they don't, we do it for them. We tell them they're getting a fixed rate and then change the paperwork to make it adjustable. We do exactly what Ameriquest and FAMCO were doing in the early 2000s. We are crooks," he said wearily. "We are beyond crooks. And suddenly I couldn't do the mental gymnastics to hide that fact from myself anymore, all because Joanna didn't want to listen to me whine. If she hadn't shoved me out of her office, she could have talked me down. That woman could talk me into anything."

"And Anna Hernandez?" Riley prompted. "Did she listen to you whine?"

"Exactly. She noticed my hands, poured the coffee for me. I couldn't help telling her what had happened."

"So another dark-haired beauty—"

"Not like that," Mearan immediately corrected. "There was never anything between me and Anna except her investigation. I told her about that particular case, only that, but dropped a few hints that situations like his might be widespread. We kept in touch after that. I fed her the grunts a couple times."

"What does that mean?"

"Like I told her I saw Joe McKinnon faking a W-2 form with Wite-Out and a copy machine, because he's an asshole anyway."

"And what did she do?"

"Nothing. She's gathering information to ask for a full-scale investigation of Sterling. That takes a while. Things have to be pretty egregious before the feds will investigate. Anna knew I was hedging my bets, and she hedged hers, gathering what she could, trying to pull me into being a whistleblower. At the same time I tried to keep her on line to use against Joanna if she tried to go to New York without me."

"You do have a way with the ladies," Jack said before he could help it.

"I'm a shit, okay?" Mearan snapped. "You think I don't know that?"

Riley pulled them back on track. "How many times had you been to Anna Hernandez's apartment before?"

"A couple of times. The last about two weeks ago. I told her a few more things about Joe McKinnon, and Artie switching the papers on a duplex, and Helen convincing a guy that a credit score of 650 only qualified him for eleven percent. But she was getting tired of my dancing. I couldn't make up my mind what I wanted to do—turn myself and everyone else in, or double down and throw in with the devil for good."

"So Anna—"

"She wanted the manual. It's used for training new account managers. We have a weeklong orientation at a conference center in their area. The newbies usually have a sales background, cars, insurance, not usually real estate, so they don't have much to *unlearn* before they can learn our way of doing things."

"The shady way," Jack said, just to clarify.

"Exactly. It's a little insane to have stuff like that written down, okay, but it creates consistency. Our people move around a lot, especially at the managerial level, so we need to have everyone on the same page."

"And if this manual fell into the wrong hands—such as Anna Hernandez's and the Fed's—it could be used against you," Riley said.

"It would sink us. It's predatory lending written in stone."

"And Joanna knew about this manual?"

Mearan snorted. "Joanna wrote it. Of course, she copied most of it from the Ameriquest one. It's amazing what you can find online these days."

"Does Lauren know?"

"Are you kidding? She *runs* the on-site training."

"And you have it, this manual?"

"Joanna had it on her laptop. I copied it to my USB one night while she was sleeping."

Jack could picture the comely Joanna tangled in the sheets, while Mearan tiptoed down to her kitchen or her office to steal a file from her computer. He wondered if Joanna knew. . . . The odds of Jeremy Mearan putting something over on Joanna Moorehouse seemed slim. Jack would have bet the woman had slept with one eye literally open. She might have let Mearan have his little intrigue, knowing all the while that it didn't matter what he did. A merger, a clingy boyfriend, a federal investigation—she would be escaping from all of them, into the arms of her offshore bank account plus whatever profit the CDSs made.

Perhaps that's what had made Mearan so angry when they told him of the Panamanian account.

"And you gave this manual to Anna?" Riley was asking.

"No. Like I said, I hedged. I thought if Jo tried to dump me before the move to New York, I'd blackmail her with it, threaten to give it to Anna if she didn't make me an assistant director at least."

What a charming relationship. "And you argued?" Jack asked.

"With Joanna? No. It never came up—we were still working on the merger and then . . . she got killed." He stopped dead, staring at nothingness, an expression of not only sadness but utter hopelessness on his face. Their lives had been hard-core sociopathic but he had been in genuine love, or something very much like it, with Joanna Moorehouse.

"So why did you come to Anna Hernandez's apartment tonight?" Riley asked.

"To bring her the manual," Mearan said, as if that should be obvious. "Without Joanna, protecting Sterling didn't make any sense. I guess you could say I finally made up my mind. I called her, told her I would bring it over. She said fine."

Riley asked, "She say anything else? That she'd be out, or in, or had someone over? Voices in the background?"

"Nothing." He said he had arrived around 9:30, knocked on the door, saw the body, called 911.

But hapless Jeremy Mearan had still appeared at the site of two brutal murders of women he had known well. When all the smoke cleared, those were facts not easily pushed aside.

But if he had killed Anna Hernandez, how did he do it without a single drop of her blood flying back onto himself? Mearan's T-shirt remained immaculate. The jeans had faded to a light blue and had no dark spots; neither did the worn loafers. His arms were clean, the nails manicured. He would have had to bring a change of clothes, moved into them—perhaps inside Anna's apartment—then disposed of them and returned to Anna's door, all without being seen. Jack made a mental note to check the building's garbage chute and Dumpster but didn't expect to find anything.

Jack's gut instinct said Mearan did not kill the women, but gut instinct could go badly wrong.

"What about Tyra Simmons?"

Mearan blinked.

"Did she know about this manual?"

The guy shrugged. "She knew *of* it. But we let her think it was more an oral structure than a written document. She'd have told us to get rid of it. To a lawyer, writing down how you instruct your employees to lie and defraud, well, you might as well shoot yourself."

"So why is she dead?" Jack asked.

Mearan blinked harder. "I have no idea. You think they've all been killed over the *manual*?"

"Why not? It could have put the whole lot of you in jail, right? People have been murdered for less."

"But the manual has been around for years. It's not that big of a deal."

"Wholesale fraud is not a big deal?"

"In this line of work," Mearan assured Jack wearily, "it's nothing that hasn't been seen before."

"So then why *are* they dead?"

"I don't know." Mearan leaned forward, letting his face fall into his hands again. His muffled voice escaped, both hopeless and desperate for hope. "I just don't know. And it's killing me."

Chapter 29

Jack returned to the apartment in time to see the body snatchers zipping up a body bag with what remained of Anna Hernandez inside. They had to strip off their bloody gloves and don new ones to do so—there had been no way to neatly remove her from the pool of bodily fluid surrounding her form like a sick aura. The ME investigator stood making notes on a clipboard. Two plastic crates full of brown paper bags, numbered but not sealed—she would do that at the lab—had been stacked neatly on the dining room table, and all the furniture now sat slightly out of place, evidence of Maggie's obsessive searching for something, anything, that the killer might have left behind. Maggie herself waited next to the coffee table, her gaze on the body bag being hefted onto the gurney. She held a mottled brown tabby cat in her arms and cried.

Jack looked again.

Yes, Maggie was crying. Very subtly, of course, the way she would, but her cheeks were definitely wet and a new tear rolled down them as he watched. He hoped for a moment that it could be sweat, but the temperature had fallen with the sun and a clammy breeze rolled through an open window.

This irritated him greatly. Maggie remained a threat to him. Their uneasy truce had held so far but it could dissolve at any moment. It only required Maggie to have one wrong moment of remorse or conscience or too much to drink with too close of a confidant or melancholia like that that had obviously struck her now, and his carefully constructed world could blow up. And he had no way to predict that, no method of monitoring her in order to have an early warning. No time to pack up and get out.

He was the fool, he suddenly realized. If Maggie posed such a threat—and she did—the only thing for him to do was to leave town, to resign, say his good-byes, invent a girlfriend who lived in Wyoming or something and get out while the getting was good. Then Maggie could weaken all she wanted, or needed. He would be out of reach.

He had failed to take the necessary steps, not her.

He snatched a napkin from a dispenser on the table, crossed behind the gurney, and wiped her cheeks, not too gently.

She looked up at him in surprise but at least shrugged out of the cloak of sadness enough to ask, "What did Jeremy say?"

It took his mind a moment to refocus. He summarized, and they were right back where they should be. Working the crime scene, two professionals, nothing on their minds but the murder of Anna Hernandez.

"She *could* have been killed over this manual, but Mearan swears no one had any idea he planned to turn it over. It would make more sense for someone to have killed Mearan. I see you made a new friend."

She glanced down at the cat, now getting a little bored with being held. "I'll take him home until we see if the boyfriend wants him. Patrol made contact—he's in Atlanta on an overnight trip."

"Animal Services can hold him."

"No," was all she said, in a tone that advised him not to argue.

"You look like crap," Carol told Maggie two hours later.

"Thanks. And thanks for coming in."

"No prob. I love coming to work in what is technically the middle of the night. Traffic is so much lighter than it is at reasonable hours."

Maggie handed her a manila envelope, now properly labeled and sealed. "I did an acid phosphatase and it's positive."

"Semen?"

"It may be nothing. It may be everything."

"I'll get right on it. But you know, if Denny argues about my overtime, I'm pointing him straight to you."

Maggie didn't even smile.

"You okay?"

Maggie shook her head. "No, not really. I—I liked her. I think we could have been friends."

Carol leaned against the counter behind her. "And

we're not used to meeting murder victims before they
become murder victims."

"Yeah. But it's not just that." Maggie ran her hands
through her hair, which would make it more unruly
than usual but, as usual, she didn't care. "Someone has
killed someone every day and we are no closer to knowing who or even why than we were when the cleaning
woman found Joanna's body. We have *no* clue. And
anyone at Sterling who does is not telling. There's missing money. There's a bribe. There's fraud. There're
damning documents that could take a whole lot of people down. There's a love affair and cutthroat competition. You want a motive? Pick one."

"And normally we can't find any."

"Instead we have too many. Any one of which could
be walking up to these people, slicing them up to—to
shreds—and walking away. Without a witness, without
a scream, without a footprint. How?"

Her voice raised too much on the last word, let too
much anguish escape into it. Carol gave her a look
shading from concern to alarm. "You need to get some
sleep. The cops are working on it and you can't save
the world by yourself."

"I'm not worried about the world. I'm worried
about the one person who, if the past few days are any
indication, will die tonight between dinnertime and
bedtime on their own living room floor." Maggie stood
up. "I'm going to call the feds, see if they expedited
my latent request. Can you run that piece of carpet
right away? Like—"

"Like now," Carol nodded. "On it. But promise me
that at some point today you'll go home for a nap."

"Of course," Maggie said.

They both knew she lied.

By noon Maggie had called the FBI twice and talked to a kindly older man. He had indulged her rush jobs in the past and now assured her he would call the moment the search results came through. She had examined every inch of every item she had collected from the apartment and run all the prints she had lifted through the database without much hope that any of them belonged to the killer; none of the surfaces or items she had dusted had given her any reason to think that the killer had touched or moved them. As before, he or she seemed to have entered, murdered, and left. She went to the autopsy purely to collect the fingernail scrapings and to see if what had been done to Anna coincided with or diverged from what had been done to the other two victims. She still felt a pang to think of her potential friend as she had been in life but didn't feel a compulsion to stay with her body through the outwardly horrific process of autopsy. Anna, the *essence* of Anna, had moved on and would not feel any concern or interest in the processing of her bodily remains. Maggie felt as sentimental about life as the next person but had long lost any sentimentality about death.

At least that was what she told herself.

"What are you doing here?" Jack asked as she entered the autopsy suite. The smell of blood promptly assaulted her senses. There were three bodies on three tables and the air felt overstuffed with putrescence.

"Fingernail scrapings." She reminded him of the Tyvek fibers. "What did the boyfriend say?"

"Went to pieces," Riley answered for his partner. "Sobbed, then said she griped about her job but never gave him the specifics. He's some kind of designer, graphic arts, says he never understood what she was talking about anyway so she gave up telling him about it."

"But she hadn't seemed afraid of anyone," Jack added. "More annoyed."

The pathologist, an older man who seemed medically thorough but also thoroughly cantankerous, glared at them. He didn't care for chattiness in his autopsy room. Unfortunately, he could not influence the other two tables, where the doctors and dieners engaged in a lively, four-way debate over the Cavs and the NBA playoffs and glares in their direction went unheeded. In his defense, given the damage done to the late Anna Hernandez, it took a great deal of time and concentration to determine, delineate, and document every gouge and slash mark. This also gave Maggie and the two detectives plenty of time to—quietly—compare and contrast every fact at their disposal. Not that it helped much.

Riley told her, "Mearan confirmed the bribe to Bowman—still in enough shock that he didn't even ask how we knew about it, so we didn't have to let him know how his little lap dance has probably been viewed by half of the police department by now. I'm sure that would embarrass him more than relatively minor bribery. It's amazing what these people consider business as usual."

"Aorta," the doctor muttered. The policemen asked him to clarify.

The pathologist spread his gloved hand behind one of the many slices in the skin that had covered Anna's left breast. "This wound severed the aorta. There's no coming back from that. It may have still been beating up until then, even with the other wounds, but that made the fat lady sing."

"Not the gash to the throat?" Maggie asked.

"That managed to sever the vocal cords without nicking the carotid. Of course, then she sucked blood into her lungs, so eventually she would have suffocated, but it looks like the breach to the heart soon made that irrelevant." He finished sectioning the heart, cutting the organ into thick slices with a bread knife. Then he spread the damaged aorta out on a light gray board and bellowed for the photographer to come and get a snap.

Maggie pictured Anna Hernandez trying to pull air into her lungs through a blood-filled hole in her neck, her body burning with piercing wounds, unable even to scream. Maggie had been there, had been flat on her back with a crazed, overpowering weight on top of her doing his best to plunge a knife into her chest, already bleeding from the slash to her throat—a mere scratch compared to Anna's wounds, now only a thin white line between shoulder and ear. Maggie's breath grew heavy; her heart began to pound.

"What about the prints?" Jack suddenly demanded of her.

"Huh?"

He had been watching her closely, which seemed

odd for him to do where others could see. "The prints. From the apartment. Anything?"

"Um—no. No hits. I'm guessing most of them are Anna's and Wayne's, and apparently neither of them have a record. At least in Cuyahoga County. The blood print from under Joanna's body—my guy at the Bureau promises to call me as soon—"

Her phone rang. Area code 304. She moved out into the hall. The kindly older gentleman at the FBI told her what he could. The print hadn't been that great, which, of course, she knew. He could give her a top ten and e-mail the individual sets of ten-prints, but she could decide for herself whether any matched or not. He didn't have time to do it for her.

She thanked him profusely and offered her first-born child, should such a being ever exist. He turned her down, saying he already had three of his own and they were more than enough.

"So?" Riley asked when she returned.

"We have possibilities," she told them. "He gave me a list of names, but whether they look anything like our blood print, I can't tell you until I get back to the office and download the ten-prints."

"Okay, who?"

The pathologist had finished with the heart and now removed the lacerated larynx. Cutting through the tough cartilage produced a crackling sound like crushing a bag of potato chips.

"First up, Maxwell Jacob Demuth, black male, date of birth ten twenty-two ninety-three. Second up, Patrick Jason Caldwell, white male, date of birth four fourteen ninety-six. Third, Aaron Michael Modesto, white male, date of birth six twenty-seven eighty-one. Any of those ring a bell?"

Both detectives shook their heads, disappointed. "None of them work at Sterling," Jack said.

Riley pulled out his phone. "Mick has been running down all the protesters. I'll see if he's got anybody by those names."

Jack said, "It could be someone at Sterling using an alias. I'll bet at least half those guys have criminal records. You have photos?"

"Not on my phone."

"We can check the names in the car." All cop cars had laptops, which could connect to the law enforcement databases for driver's license information and mug shots. As a civilian, Maggie had neither a laptop in her car nor access to that information.

The pathologist now had the photographer taking photos of the bloody cylinder that had been Anna Hernandez's airway and form of human communication. "Yep. Right through the cords."

"He must be getting really good at this," Maggie said. "To do that without severing the carotids."

The pathologist disagreed. "Just lucky, would be my guess. No one could get that close to the arteries on what I presume was a moving, struggling victim and not hit them if it weren't sheer dumb luck."

Riley got off the phone. "Zero. None of the names match our protesters or one of Ned Swift's extended group. And those people will be using their real names since they're home owners with lawsuits and bankruptcies and documentation behind them."

"So who the hell are Demuth and Caldwell and

whoever else?" Jack asked. "And what do they have to do with Sterling Financial?"

Maggie said, "They might not match the print at all. I won't know until I can sit down with the ten-prints."

"So—" Jack obviously wondered why, in that case, she still stood there talking.

"I want to see if she had a blow to the back of the head. Like Joanna and Tyra."

Anna's neck rested on a very uncomfortable-looking metal stand, which lifted her head off the table so the diener could cut through her scalp to the bone. Then he would scrape the flesh away from the skull and flip the hair down over the face. This was the most dehumanizing part of the autopsy, when the most personal part of the human anatomy seemed cast aside as unimportant, when the person most ceased to appear as a person and became nothing more than a slightly interesting object. Maggie took a deep breath and steeled herself against the shrieking whine of the bone saw as it removed the top of Anna's skull.

After it stopped, the pathologist moved in, running his fingers over a glossy blot on the inside of the flesh. "Yeah, someone bapped her on the noggin here."

"Bapped?"

The pathologist glared at the implied challenge to his terminology. "It didn't have time to swell much. Probably wouldn't have done any real damage. Would have hurt, but that's about it."

"Just like Joanna and Tyra," Maggie said. "He smacks her backward immediately, before there's any time for a struggle or even a scream. Then he's on top

of her, stabs her in the throat. Then he's got time."
Time to rip her body open, seam by seam.

She felt Jack's hand on her shoulder. "Go back to
the office," he said. "Tell us whether that print matches
somebody or not."

"Walk me out," she said. "I have a question for
you."

Chapter 30

Jack left Riley hovering over the pathologist and followed Maggie with a sense of foreboding. They tried never to have private chats, even on the phone. Normally they had nothing to say to each other.

But in the middle of the small parking lot at the Medical Examiner's office, with the oppressive humidity increasing the offal smell still in his nostrils, Maggie turned and asked him, "Did you kill Gerald Graham?"

This startled him. He looked around for potential witnesses. "Why are you asking that?"

"It's an obvious question," she pointed out. Obvious because she knew who Jack was.

"Do you really want to know? Or are you compelling yourself to ask?"

The breeze lifted her hair away from a somber face. "I want to know."

He could argue, or lie, or blow her off, but she would see through that. "Yes."

"*Why?* He was in court. He was going to be convicted and executed—"

"So I streamlined the process. So what?"

"Why? Why couldn't you have left it alone?"

"Because he might have gotten off if his attorney's expert could twist the jury's mind with that stupid fingerprint—"

"That wouldn't have happened." She kept her voice low, wisely, but it trembled with rage.

"You couldn't be sure of that. This is sure."

"You didn't trust me to handle it!"

He considered her. "Is that what you're pissed about? Not that I executed someone a bit early in the process but that I disregarded your professional abilities? Are your feelings hurt?"

"This isn't about me!"

"Apparently, it is. I didn't realize you were so sensitive." He tried to bite off the sarcasm and stick to the facts. "And you haven't realized that whoever shot at you two yesterday wasn't aiming at Anna. We've had two different informants finger one of Graham's—"

He broke off as a secretary exited the back door and stalked across the lot to her car, phone glued to her ear.

Maggie breathed in and out, heavily, obviously trying to keep herself under control. But her next words surprised him in their desperation.

"I can't do this, Jack. I can't."

"It's not up to you."

"It *is*. Because all I have to do is tell the truth, what I should have done in the first place—"

He grabbed her shoulders. "Stop. Just stop. You

can't control me, Maggie—accept that. You can't control much in life. Few of us can."

The truth was it hadn't been her he didn't trust—only the influence of a paid whore. Who knew what that attorney might have convinced the jury of even though everyone in the courtroom knew the guy was guilty as sin. But he'd be damned if he'd tell her that. Getting Graham off the planet was more important than coddling one by-the-book forensic scientist. "You can't prove I killed Graham, you can't even accuse me. The other cops would never believe it and it would only ruin your life, and you have too many good things to do with your life."

She pulled herself away. "You're not even making sense."

"I am, but you don't want to listen to it. There's no point in churning your brain up with this. It isn't going to go anywhere, and you know it."

She glared. Mightily.

But she had pulled a trigger herself once and couldn't expose him without exposing herself, so let her glare. He was done justifying himself to Maggie Gardiner.

"I can't keep doing this," she said again. Then she turned on one heel and left him standing there, wondering what she meant by that. Or if she even knew herself.

A rumble sounded in the distance.

"You look—"

"Don't say like crap," Maggie warned him.

Denny said, "Wasn't gonna. You look, um, tired, that's all."

"Look at this instead of me." She gestured at the screen, where she had used a comparison program to put her blood print on one side of the screen, and one of her ten-prints from the FBI on the other. Colored doodles marked the various information in the prints. "I've got an ending ridge, ridge, bifurcation, ridge, ridge, short ridge, ridge, ridge, two bifurcations—"

"Looks good," he said cautiously. But, like her, not enthusiastic. The tops of fingers are fairly generic areas compared to the middle of a fingerprint pattern, where all sorts of turns and stops and curves usually exist.

"This bifurcation starts a little to the right of where this one does," she pointed, touching the monitor's screen.

"Yeah, but that's not significant." Skin, pliable and flexible, stretched more or less depending on the surface it touched and how much pressure the finger applied to that surface. That's why photos of prints were never superimposed on each other—they would never match perfectly, nor should they.

"There's a little gap right here."

"That could be dirt."

"This short ridge here is pretty compelling."

"I think so," Denny said. "So who's our lucky winner?"

"Patrick Caldwell. Of Omaha, Nebraska. Served three years for raping his girlfriend. Used a knife—"

"That fits our crimes."

"—but didn't cut her, only threatened. Because of that he made parole. This is him. The FBI sent me their mug shots, too."

They both stared at the photo of a young man with

pale skin and black hair. His eyebrows seemed to over-power his eyes and a full, bushy beard covered his face from the top of his cheekbones on down. Maggie felt sure she had not seen him working at the Sterling offices, or in the group of protesters outside the Sterling offices, or on the bus or the news or in the courtroom.

Denny frowned. "And what is Patrick of Omaha doing at a Cleveland crime scene?"

"I have no earthly idea. Hence, my lack of exultation at this possible match."

Denny sighed, then straightened. "Well, it is what it is. You going to tell the guys what you have?"

"Yep. Along with my reservations."

"Okay. Good job. And then—get some sleep. That's an *order*."

She summoned up a smile. "Okay, boss."

Denny shuffled off toward his office and Maggie picked up the phone. She didn't want to talk to Jack, so she called Riley. He, of course, wanted a positive answer, but she made her ambivalence clear. They could consider the print an investigative lead, but not a positive identification.

Then she moved on to the fingernail scrapings.

They were full of Anna's blood, of course, but several fibers were caught in the dried red material. She tried a dry mount, then a wet mount. The water leached away some of the red so that she could see the fibers a bit clearer. A mess of white and dirty white fibers of varying thickness with some clumpy glue binding them together.

Tyvek.

Just as with Tyra.

She called Riley back. "He's wearing Tyvek. Probably a whole jumpsuit. That's how he gets away from their houses without some passerby calling the cops about a guy in bloody clothes."

"But why would these women open their door to someone in a Tyvek jumpsuit? Anna had a peephole in her door and had found a body earlier that day. She had to be jumpy."

"It had to be someone they knew."

"I thought you said the fibers probably came from the hand bags? I mean, the bags the body snatchers put on the hands at the scene."

"Not this time."

"Why not?"

"Because I asked Nick to use paper bags on Anna. For precisely that reason."

"Huh," Riley puffed. "Okay, then. Our guy's using Tyvek to walk away blood free. Does that mean he works in a lab?"

"You can buy Tyvek jumpsuits at Home Depot. Paint department."

"Oh." He sounded disappointed. "Okay. Well, let us know if you find anything else."

She hung up. Like so much forensic evidence, interesting, but not particularly helpful.

Riley relayed the information to Jack, who from the passenger seat spoke to the Nebraska Department of Corrections regarding the whereabouts of one Patrick Caldwell. Nebraska, it seemed, didn't know. He had been released, dutifully followed up with his parole officer for several months, and then disappeared. He didn't check in, didn't return for his final paycheck at the grocery store, and supposedly had not contacted his aunt or sister. To their relief, they said.

DOC could only give a rudimentary background for him. Apparently he had been a decent student from a tumultuous home and briefly held jobs in commercial construction, assembly line, and food service positions, where employers had always been satisfied with his work. Nothing to do with mortgages or loans. White collar wasn't really his thing.

Riley pulled into the Sterling parking lot and wondered aloud, "Could our video guys do anything with the mug shot? Maybe erase the beard? See what he'd look like with a haircut?"

"Last time I asked them to do that, they laughed me out of the office. Said I might as well ask if someone has a mole on their butt underneath their clothing."

Riley got out of the car and slammed the door. "Bet they could do it on TV. Why is Maggie calling me instead of you?"

Jack nearly stumbled over a curb. "What?"

"She always calls you. It's okay, I don't take it personally; you've got all that rugged manly-man appeal going on. But what happened? You two have a tiff?"

Jack lied best when he had time to prepare. He didn't excel at ad lib. So as he pulled open the lobby door— the front sidewalk now inexplicably clear of protesters— he took out his phone and checked the call history. No call from Maggie, but he told Riley that there was, that he hadn't picked up because he'd been talking to Nebraska.

"Oh," Riley said as they piled into the elevator. "Glad you didn't have a fight."

He didn't ask what the private chat in the ME's parking lot had been about. Pointedly so.

Jack tried to think of ways to say that he and Maggie hadn't argued, though they had, and that they weren't in a relationship, though they were in a weird, messed-up way. When the doors opened at their floor he still hadn't come up with anything.

Nothing, it seemed, affected the Sterling offices. Jack thought if the killer worked his way through their entire workforce, the last man would be at his desk, on the phone, alternately cajoling and threatening his regional directors to do more, produce more, make more loans, and bring in more fees. "You only did a million and a half last month," he heard one man, who barely seemed old enough for a legal drink, shout into the receiver. "That's nothing. Your counterpart in Lansing did three. And this month it's going to be four, or you know what? I'm going to fire him. So what do you think I'm going to do to you if you're not at least at two by next week?"

No one appeared upset over Anna's death. True, Anna had not been one of them; she had worked largely by herself and had been there only for a few weeks. And she had been an enemy of sorts, working to uncover whatever dirty little secrets the Sterling clan preferred to keep. In that way Anna's death was a boon for them—now the merger would be over and done with long before a new regulator could be brought up to speed.

Lauren Schneider certainly hadn't paused to grieve. She hummed at her desk as if her body were a finely tuned violin string. The small amount of papers on her blotter had grown to messy stacks and a legal pad in front of her had been covered with elaborate scribbles of to-do tasks. She spoke quickly on the phone while glowing lights on its console spoke of two calls holding. And she seemed more animated than they had ever seen her. She seemed happy. She seemed ecstatic.

She didn't even look annoyed when the two detectives entered her office without knocking.

"Triple-A. That's what I said, triple-A. Call Carter & Poe if you don't believe me. Look, Bob, I have to go. Say hi to Jeannie. Bye. *Bye.*" She hung up. "Do you have him? Whoever's been killing us?"

"Not yet," Jack told her. He didn't sit, uninvited or otherwise. "Do you know a Patrick Caldwell?"

She blinked, thought. "No."

"We'll need to check your employee rolls. Especially from Nebraska."

She didn't argue, still processing the implications of a name—any name. "Is that who it is? The killer? How do you know?"

"It's the name of someone we'd like to speak to."

"Is he one of Ned's crew?"

"We checked that. We need to know if he is or has ever been an employee of Sterling," Riley said.

"I can have my assistant check."

"Or a client."

"I can do that," she said, and immediately began typing on her keyboard. Lauren Schneider wasn't stupid. Three people from the Sterling office had died and, Jack realized, they had all been women. Females were scarce at Sterling—cutthroat loan brokering remained largely a man's game. Aside from a petite blond manager at a cubicle in the main room and Deb Fischer, with her husband and big dog, Lauren was the only woman left.

Maybe the guy didn't feel confident about going up against someone his own size, Jack thought. Or maybe he just liked killing women.

"We did a refi for a Patrick Allen Caldwell in Cheyenne," Lauren said. "Last year."

"No, it was Patrick . . ." Riley paused.

"Jason," Jack supplied.

She scanned her screen. "Patrick Jason Caldwell. Home equity line in Sarasota. Male, black, married . . . sixty-eight years of age."

"Not our guy," Jack said.

Lauren shrugged and searched again. "I have a Patricia Caldwell in Nebraska. Lincoln. Caucasian, schoolteacher . . . seventy-two."

"Mother?" Riley speculated.

Lauren said, "Refi with line of credit . . . defaulted . . . huh."

"What's 'huh'?"

"Says here the local Legal Aid brought a lawsuit against us for not disclosing the payment bump when the intro rate ran out. But Mrs. Caldwell died before the case got to court."

"Could be a motive."

Lauren stared at him. "For *killing* people?"

Riley said, "If someone ruined your mom's life and drove her into an early heart attack? Yes."

"There's no evidence that happened. She could have had cancer, for all we know," she scoffed.

"Any mention of a son or husband?" Jack asked.

"No. Only what I told you."

"Any other Caldwells? Past clients as well as current?"

"This is everybody." She nodded at the screen. "We have a number of Caldwells, but no other Patricks. Two in California, a LaVerne, widow, seventy-eight, and a John and Maybelle, both eighty-one."

Jack pulled out his phone and showed her the mug shot Maggie had e-mailed. Lauren stared carefully at the image, frowned, and continued to frown.

"You know him?" Jack asked.

"No . . . I don't know. I don't think so." She placed a finger across the phone's small screen, blocking out the lower half of the man's face with its bushy beard. "Something about the eyes—no, honestly, I don't know if I've ever seen him before. He certainly isn't someone I *know*."

"We'll need to ask the rest of your staff. Everyone, down to the parking lot attendant."

A sharp exhalation passed for a chuckle. "Good luck with that. But go ahead—ask any one of my employees anything you need. This has to be resolved, if this merger is ever going to get done."

"And if you want people to stop dying," Jack added.

"Yes," she said. "That too."

Just to be thorough they went through the same process with Maxwell Jacob Demuth and Aaron Michael Modesto. Demuth and Modesto being less common surnames than Caldwell, it didn't take as much time. Sterling had no employees named Demuth and only two clients, a Connie in Utah, black, widow, sixty-nine, and a Thomas in Atlanta, white, widower, seventy-seven. A few more Modestos, but they proved no more suspicious. Most were elderly.

"You do like to help out those senior citizens, don't you?" It was Riley's turn to scoff.

"Older people are often house rich but cash poor. We help them use their assets to maintain a healthy standard of living," she said primly.

He said, "Is that from page five of your manual? The section on catchphrases and rationalizations?"

She didn't react to the mention of the manual. She either didn't care or assumed his question had been rhetorical. So Jack got specific and asked her if she knew of the existence of the manual. She denied it. He asked if she knew that Jeremy Mearan had been about to hand it over to Anna Hernandez. The quick widening of her eyes told him that she had not known and now that she did she felt pretty damn ticked off about it, yet her mouth told him she didn't know anything about any manual and certainly not what Jeremy and Anna had been up to on their own time.

Meanwhile the tightening of those lips said that Jeremy Mearan had better start looking for another job. Immediately.

Jack couldn't believe they had hit another dead end. He felt fairly certain they had the guy's name and picture, and they were still floundering in the dark.

On their way out the door he turned back. "Ms. Schneider, do you live alone?"

"No. Husband and two daughters, remember?"

Jack hadn't. "Tell them not to answer the door tonight. To anyone."

At first she didn't seem to understand him. Then she did, and the blood drained from her already pale face, turning it a ghostly, translucent white from her expertly supported cleavage to her slight widow's peak of dark hair.

He shut her office door.

"You love me," Carol said to Maggie.

"Always," Maggie said, looking up from her microscope. She had spent the past fifteen minutes gathering fiber samples from the lab's supply of booties, sleeves, jumpsuits, and disposable lab coats to see if she could tell a difference between manufacturers. So far, not so much. "But why in particular at this moment?"

"I pushed our semen through CODIS."

Maggie sat up. "Already?"

"What can I say? I have mad skills. I also promised to send a guy in Virginia a full pan of cinnamon rolls. Have you ever had my cinnamon rolls?"

"Got a result? Does it match?"

The older woman held out a sheet of paper like a velvet-clad herald reading a decree from the king. "Results of CODIS database search number C-L-one-five-one—"

"Carol!"

"Patrick Jason Cald—"

"Caldwell," Maggie said. "Patrick Caldwell. Date of birth four fourteen ninety-six."

Carol pretended to pout. "Please don't tell me I have

to make cinnamon rolls for nothing. Those suckers are not easy. You have to baby the yeast—"

She broke off as Maggie leapt up to throw exultant arms around her.

"Ooof. You're welcome."

Maggie snatched up the phone.

Chapter 31

"But I thought there wasn't any sign of sexual assault," Jack said into the phone as Riley drove to Ned Swift's headquarters.

"A tentative conclusion because the autopsy didn't find semen." Maggie's excitement bled through the super-professional voice she was using with him At least she had called him and not Riley, which should allay his partner's sidelong glances for another day. "But he cut all their clothes off and sliced up their breasts and uterus."

"And heart and lungs and—"

"Still. Of course it had a sexual motivation. We've been saying that from the start—no one kills like *that* over money. I figure he wore a condom, but at Anna's it slipped, spilled a little when he removed it."

"Along with the Tyvek jumpsuit."

"Exactly."

"It's still speculation," he warned her. Jack did not speculate. In his personal endeavors he did not move until he had proven every accusation, established every fact, down to the last detail. "Patrick Caldwell could be an ex-boyfriend."

"Of both Anna's and her boss's?"

"Possibly. Joanna got around, apparently."

"If his print was only at her place, yes. But his print was in *blood*. That can't have an innocent explanation."

"You can't be positive it *is* his print."

"True," she said. "But still it defies imagination to think even *possible* evidence of him could turn up at two different crime scenes."

"I agree. We'll start a dragnet for Patrick Caldwell." He hung up as Riley pulled up to the curb along the side of the sagging storefront on East 40th near Chester. "Let's hope these guys can give us a line on who the hell Patrick Caldwell is."

"Even if they know, do you think they'll tell us? They rallied around Kurt Resnick."

"Kurt Resnick is their victim-of-predatory-lending poster child," Jack said as he got out of the car. "Patrick Caldwell is an escaped rapist. They'll figure it out."

"You, partner of mine, are an optimist."

"Hardly," Jack said, and slammed the door.

Maggie decided to go home. The rest of the city's occupants were eating dinner and she needed some recharging as well. She had done all she could for the moment, or so Denny kept telling her. The BOLO (Be On The Lookout) had been put out for Patrick Jason Caldwell along with his photo, and every cop in the city would be looking for him. She had written up her reports on the fingerprint and the Tyvek fibers. Carol had made up a preliminary finding on the semen stain from Anna's carpet, and the detectives had an arrest warrant signed. Now all they had to do was find the son of a bitch.

In the meantime, weariness tugged at her muscles and brain cells, forcing her to finally admit that she could do no more. She returned to her apartment—more easily because she knew that a meowing ball of fur would be waiting for her. Maggie wasn't sure her apartment building even allowed pets, as it had never been an issue before. Just a temporary arrangement, anyway.

She had brought a bag of dry food, a jug of scoopable litter, and a few toys from Anna's apartment to set up the currently nameless cat. She hoped Alex wouldn't mind if he ever found out that she used the basalt bowl—densest stone there was—he had paid so much to ship as a cat feeder . . . but most of her other dishes were in the washer and the cat wouldn't be able to scoot this one all over the floor. Densest stone, after all. A bowl of water, a flat cardboard box to hold the litter and the animal had spent a leisurely day in Maggie's apartment. At least it didn't seem to be complaining when she returned. She dumped her purse and lunch bag and cardigan on the couch and sank to the ground.

"I think I know who killed your mistress," she said, stroking the tabby's head. "But I have no idea why. Or where he is now."

The cat listened, staring into her eyes.

"Even if Patrick Caldwell is one of those loan officers and thought Anna, and maybe Tyra, were a threat to Sterling, how could he think of Joanna that way?

She had every reason in the world to protect Sterling until her last breath. And if he had been screwed over royally by Sterling, maybe lost his house, ruined his life, why would he blame Anna? She tried to help the little guy." The cat crawled into her lap, purring, and seemed to frown as Maggie kept speaking. "Maybe he thought she didn't do enough. Like abused children, they often blame the nonabusing parent more than the violent one. Maybe he didn't even know what Anna did, simply saw her there in the offices and assumed she worked for Sterling. Or maybe"—she looked down at the cat, the cat looked up at her—"he just likes killing women."

The cat meowed.

Maybe Jack just liked killing, too. Maybe that was why he couldn't resist taking care of Gerry Graham, a man who had already been taken care of, who sat in a courtroom about to go to jail. Maybe Jack truly hadn't trusted her ability to get the job done. Or maybe he enjoyed murder, not as a benign protector of innocents but as bloodthirsty and voracious as Patrick Caldwell.

And her silence kept Jack free, instead of putting him in a cell next to Caldwell, where he belonged. Where *maybe* he belonged.

She looked at her phone, sitting on the coffee table near her outstretched feet. All she had to do was pick it up and dial Denny, or the homicide unit, and tell them she had to amend her statement.

She could call Rick.

Rick would believe her. He had been with the department much longer than Jack and would be able to convince the other cops to take her word over that of a fellow officer. He could even help her construct a narrative that might keep her out of jail, some story in which she and Jack struggled over the gun and by accident shot someone directly in the center of the forehead, instead of the truth, that she alone quite purposely aimed the barrel. He could help her put an end to all this.

But what would he want from her in return?

Nothing gross like sexual services. He might hint but he wouldn't exactly blackmail—not even Rick would do that. But he would expect any forensic requests of his to be moved to the top of the pile. He would expect her full attention when he wanted it. He would expect any favor requested, *short* of sexual services, to be instantly granted. Forever.

There was no way she'd give her ex-husband that kind of power over her. Not to mention that forcing the burden of her secret onto his shoulders wouldn't be fair to him, either. Not that Rick had ever felt lying to be much of a burden.

No. If she did this, it would be without Rick. Maggie scratched the cat's ears, considering the same options that had churned through her mind for weeks.

She would simply have to tell the truth—the whole truth, and nothing but. She could play up the trauma and fear and fish-out-of-water bewilderment involved in her pulling of that trigger. It might sway a jury. It might not.

Outside, the thunder rumbled in the distance and the cat snuggled itself more deeply into her lap.

She could not tell a soul without accepting life, or a good chunk of it, in prison. She could never tell Rick or Denny or Carol and certainly not Alex such a thing and then ask them to keep her secret. That would be relieving some of her own burden by shifting it to them and she could never do that. The only person she could talk to, *really* talk to, in this new reality was Jack Renner. Who would only tell her to stop talking. The only alternative included hard time.

But all to avenge the murder of Gerry Graham? No, hardly. It was to do the right thing *despite* Gerry Graham, despite the fact that he had been a scourge on the earth and, in or out of jail, would continue to be. She could see no downside to his death—not for the taxpayers, not for his fellow inmates if he remained incarcerated nor his fellow gang members if he were set free by exceptionally clever lawyers. No doubt colleagues had already stepped up to fill the employment gap in his absence and might have fatally argued a demotion if the system released him.

Great, Maggie. You're using the well-being of thugs as a justification for accessory to murder. A new low.

She needed to pick up that phone. She forced her hand toward it.

The cat, resenting the interruption to its needs, dug its claws into her thigh.

"Ow! You might have warned me you still had those before I took you on as a roomie." She leaned over the cat and snatched the phone off the table.

The claws dug in again, as if both a warning and a premonition.

But she didn't dial it. Something was missing in her mental structure, had been missing all this time. A gap that had kept her silent all this time, about both her own culpability and Jack's.

Guilt.

She knew that covering up Jack's murders—and her

own—violated the laws she had by association sworn
to uphold. She felt the guilt of the reflexively obedient.
She felt guilty for leaving unsolved murders on her
colleagues' books when she could clear them. She felt
guilty for lying by omission to every single person in
her life—other than Jack—Denny, Carol, Alex, Riley.
But did she feel guilty that these people, the child pornog-
rapher, the elder abuser, the rapist, Gerry Graham, were
dead?

No.

Not at all.

Where did that leave her?

She patted the cat while the phone rang in her hand.

Ned and his crew had been busily fund-raising for
Kurt Resnick's defense. Jack didn't tell him that they
would be releasing their cause célèbre as soon as they
returned to the station. But they took a moment out to
study the photo of Patrick Jason Caldwell, cluck to
themselves, and insist that they had never seen him before. The beard made it difficult to be sure, of course,
but each protester and Ned himself seemed certain
they had never encountered the man, on either side of
the picket line. They also denied knowing who took a
shot at Anna and/or Maggie. Most seemed genuinely
horrified at the idea.

"You think he killed Anna Hernandez?" Ned Swift
asked them.

"We'd like to talk to him," Riley hedged.

"I have over a hundred affidavits telling the story of
Sterling Financial, and that's right here in Cuyahoga
County. Multiply that by the rest of the country, and

the question isn't which of Sterling's ex-clients would want to murder their staff. It's which ones *wouldn't*."

"But Anna Hernandez didn't work for Sterling. In a sense, she worked *against* them."

"That's what I've been saying all along! The Federal Reserve pretends it's a gatekeeper, but all it's done is hold the gate open for the Wall Street firms who want to keep making money hand over fist. Who talked Morgan into buying Bear Sterns? Who bailed them out back in 2009? Who's been printing money in order to keep them shored up without inflation sucking us all into a downward vortex? The Fed! And as their representative, this Hernandez woman—"

"Deserved to die?" Jack finished, his jaw set.

"I'm not exactly saying that—" Ned looked up at Jack, and something he saw there made him pale slightly and backpedal. "I'm not saying that, of course. I'm saying an unbalanced personality might see it that way."

"Someone overly biased, in other words," Jack said. He didn't truly suspect Ned Swift, more interested in camera angles than in actually getting his hands dirty. But he wanted to yank the guy's chain a little. He wanted to yank it until it ripped his head from his body.

Ned opened his mouth, shut it, opened it again. "I want to do anything we can possibly do to help you find this murderer, Detective. But I have never seen that man or heard his name before in my life."

Maggie, curled on her couch, cat in her lap, had the phone pressed to her ear, glad her brother had happened to call. He was the only person she wanted to talk to after such a day. His bandmates had already told him twice that he needed to mosey himself and his guitar toward the stage, their set time approached, but he kept asking her questions. "How are you doing with all this?"

"It's not like we were friends." Although they had been shot at together. Which, of course, she did *not* tell Alex now.

"You were on your way to becoming them. You connected; that's the important thing."

Musicians loved connections. "I know. I feel so sorry for her, that's all. I'm not . . . I'm not used to being personally acquainted with murder victims. And bewilderment doesn't help—the cops don't have a clue who this guy is or what he has against Sterling."

"Turn your mind off." He frequently gave her this, for her, impossible advice. Alex believed in meditation. Also in all-organic foods and P90X, but those came up in different conversations.

"For once I think I can. I'm so exhausted I'll barely be able to stumble to my bed." She could hear his drummer calling him a third time as a light knock sounded at her door. "Go play your music, bro."

"Go to bed, sis."

They each promised to obey and Maggie hung up, then gently removed the cat from her lap. The cat protested, but Maggie left it on the couch as she walked toward her kitchen, automatically checking to see if she had locked the door. Once again, she hadn't. And a shadow hovered through the crack at the bottom.

A stab of irrational fear pierced the back of her neck.

Nothing to worry about, she told herself. Gerry Graham was dead. His cronies would hardly bother to off the obscure fingerprint analyst who hadn't had a chance to convict him.

Still, she padded silently forward on bare feet. She reached for the dead bolt.

Someone knocked again.

Startled all out of proportion, she froze, her heart pounding. Deep breath. *An assassin wouldn't knock. Don't be stupid.* She put a cautious eye to the peephole.

In the hallway stood the nice delivery boy from Totally Fresh! He held up a white paper sack with the restaurant's logo. "New customer thank-you gift. Compliments of Totally Fresh!"

She opened the door, and suddenly everything made sense.

Chapter 32

Jack leaned back in his desk chair and stared at the portable whiteboard Riley had installed in the aisle. Photos of their three victims stared back at him, their photographed faces relaxed and happy—or in Joanna's case, as happy as she could emulate. They would be right to look more accusing, he thought. He had failed them completely. He still had no idea why Patrick Jason Caldwell had killed them or where the man might be right now.

"Let's sum up," Riley began.

"Let's not," Jack groaned.

"We've released Kurt Resnick, who's still pretending he killed Joanna Moorehouse, has no idea about Tyra, and, obviously, couldn't have done anything to Anna. Ned and his protesters say they don't know anything about a Patrick Caldwell. Let's say they're lying and this is some elaborate charade to call attention to Sterling's misdeeds, they hire Caldwell and then use Resnick as a spokesman, knowing that they can always pull Caldwell out of a hat for a last-minute not-guilty—"

"They couldn't know we'd find the print. Or the semen. And if they did, how'd they talk Caldwell into leaving clues to his own identity at two murders?"

Riley paced silently, back and forth in front of the whiteboard. "I said it was a theory. I didn't say it was a good one."

"Duly noted."

"Most likely Kurt is a whack job and Ned and his gang are opportunists. Then we have the esteemed Mr. Bowman, who will be picked up by the feds for bribery as soon as he steps out of his extra-roomy, drinks-included first-class seat from New York. Of all our players I can most easily see him having the balls and the resources to hire a guy like Caldwell. Maybe he balked on the merger and Joanna let spill that she had him on video. Maybe Tyra wasn't as squeaky clean as everybody thought, or maybe she figured she'd help Joanna this one last time, put the squeeze on Bowman, get the company sold, and then she—Tyra, I mean—could wash her hands of the whole sordid mess. Bowman *should* have been afraid of Anna, who would have been digging into this for all she was worth. White collar has gone over her briefcase. It seems she had her suspicions about some missing funds—no doubt part of Joanna's six hundred million—and had reams of information implicating Carter & Poe in the price fixing. But her boss at the Fed says she would e-mail weekly updates. They already had half her investigation on file and killing her would have been pointless. On the other hand, Bowman wouldn't have known that."

Jack said, "Why not Mearan? Bowman could have guessed that Tyra and Anna knew about the payoff, but he had to assume Mearan knew whatever Joanna did."

Now Riley slumped into his desk chair. "We keep coming back to little Jeremy, don't we? If our killer, or whoever hired Caldwell, considered Joanna a threat, then they had to include Mearan. He belonged in her pocket, career-wise and in every other respect. Why kill her and yet he's still walking around? Unless he's the one who did it? He hired Caldwell. How do we know he *isn't* Caldwell? Young man, dark hair—"

"Fingerprints," Jack said. "He gave his to us, and his DNA. Maggie already checked and they don't match."

"Okay, back to Caldwell as gun hired by Mearan. He gets rid of Joanna, figures he'll move right into her spot and go to New York where big money is made and big parties are had."

"Sterling isn't a monarchy. He can't inherit the CEO spot, and besides, what about Lauren? She's in his way."

Riley said, "She's got the husband and kids. He can't attack her in her living room, and apparently Caldwell doesn't know any other way to do it. He's only comfortable working in the home. Like a midwife. This is why when my girls start talking about getting a place of their own . . ."

Jack raised one eyebrow at the midwife analogy. "Maybe he's got an arrangement with Lauren. They cooked this up between them, and her outward contempt for him is just a show. They both want to make the move to Wall Street."

"That would fit. They kill Tyra because her conscience can't be trusted and string Anna along until she wants some real evidence. He promises her the Holy Grail to get her to open the door."

Riley got up to walk around some more. "All we

need to do is prove a conspiracy between Lauren—and our only evidence for same is that she isn't dead—and Mearan, and Caldwell."

"Yeah."

"Yeah," Jack said. "Except."

"Except I hate it," Riley said miserably. "I don't see it. Mearan couldn't conspire to sell a used car without screwing it up and I could see Lauren simply killing him instead of allying."

"It's more likely that Lauren is behind the whole thing—the only evidence being that she's still breathing—and she let Mearan live *because* she knows he'd be as useless to us as he is to her."

Jack rubbed his face. "If we could only find Caldwell, we could reverse engineer the whole structure."

"Except we can't find Caldwell. So, moving on . . ." Riley continued to pace, making a lazy circle around the whiteboard, brushing past coworkers' desks as they tried to finish their own paperwork amid his steady stream of words. "The handsome Mr. Fourtner at Carter & Poe. A venerable firm that could suffer mightily if it came to light that one of their own had been taking bribes—monetary and personal—to give Sterling's crap a triple-A rating. I can totally see him slicing Joanna open without mussing his perfect hair and walking away with naught a bloody footprint. But Tyra and Anna? That would be overkill."

"No pun intended," Jack added for him. "Unless he found he had a taste for it. Killing."

"Beautiful-people poster boy turned serial killer," Riley said. "I like it. Got no evidence for it, but I like it. But he knew Joanna, so he knew she'd never let Tyra in on the secret. And Anna had no proof."

"Even if Tyra stumbled on it, that still leaves out Anna," Jack said. "These three women are like trying to draw a triangle. If you can get two points to connect, the third one won't."

"No one had a motive against all three," Riley agreed. "Maybe Lauren. She wants Joanna's job, doesn't know Joanna is planning to bail anyway. Knows Tyra is a liability."

"But Anna. To her Anna is a gnat, annoying but harmless." This case had been bothering Jack from the moment he'd arrived at Joanna's mansion and seen the carnage. They had gotten onto the wrong track, he thought, and still hadn't found the right one. They had conducted the investigation just as they should have, following up all the leads, going where the evidence took them. But pulling on all those strings led only to loose, stray strings. No prizes.

"And the third falls out," Riley said. "Still no triangle."

"Can you guys shut up?" A portly detective up the aisle loosened his tie. "I can't get anything done with all your yammering."

"No," Riley said. "Or someone else will be dead by bedtime. The ladies of Greater Cleveland are depending upon our detective skills."

The other detective now rubbed his shiny black cheek. "Then they're doomed."

Jack said, "That seems to be the only thing they *do* have in common. That office is ninety-five percent male, but the victims are all women."

Riley went with it. "Okay. Women. Because they're in a position to damage him or because they're smaller, weaker? Unarmed?"

"Slender. Thirtyish. Dark hair." Jack stood up, a sudden realization pounding at his skull.

"So is Lauren."

"Lauren doesn't live alone."

"That other woman, Deb Fischer. Thirtyish."

"Short hair. Doesn't live alone."

"Oh yeah, husband and big dog. See what I mean about dogs? I floated the Rottweiler idea to Natalie but she balked. The neighbor's Pomeranian nipped her when she was a baby and she's never forgiven the species. Hannah was all for it, though, been nagging her mother for a dog since preschool. What are you thinking, partner?"

Jack stood up again, returned to the case board as if that would help him see more clearly; of course it wouldn't. The problem had always been, from the start, a case of not seeing the forest for the trees. "The money distracted us. Money always distracts. We saw millions of dollars and figured that had to be the motive, somehow, in some conformation."

"Yeah?"

"What if it's not? What if he killed these women because he freakin' likes killing women? Caldwell likes raping them and he likes knives. It's not a stretch. It's not even a step."

Riley played devil's advocate. "And he just coincidentally picks three women from the same workplace?"

"No, it's not coincidental at all. He saw them there, knew them there."

"But *doesn't* work there and still got their home addresses?"

"That can't be that hard. Even without phone books,

no one guards their home address like they do a Social Security number. He could have followed them from the office building, observed them at home, got the lay of the land. That's how he knows they live alone."

"Which leaves us back to the beginning," Riley sighed. "Where is he now?"

"Picking out his next victim. Who may be connected to Sterling and will look like these three." He studied the photos intently, willing the dead women to give him some sort of clue as to how to stop Patrick Caldwell. "They look similar in so many ways. . . . They look . . . they look like . . ."

"Like what?"

"Like Maggie." Jack pulled out his cell phone.

Chapter 33

The nice young delivery man from Totally Fresh! held up a white paper bag. "We bring thank-yous to all our new customers," he said. "May I come in?"

"No," Maggie responded instantly. Because as so often happened, her subconscious had summed up the situation much more quickly than her conscious mind could ever hope to. The clean-shaven man with black hair wore a full-length Tyvek jumpsuit that covered his shoes. He had used colored markers to create a passable imitation of the Totally Fresh! logo on the upper right chest so that through the apartment door's peephole he appeared to be wearing one of their uniformly snow-white smocks.

In his right hand, the one not holding the bag, he carried a short, thick baton like the kind used by some police forces. As the last "o" sound of her answer came from her mouth he raised it and slammed its length against her throat. She raised both hands to ward off the blow but far too late in this split-second contest;

she succeeded only in getting one or two of her fingers broken, to judge from the sharp pain that pierced her mind just as he struck her throat with enough force to throw her backward.

She heard that crackling sound, the one that always reminded her of crushing a bag of potato chips.

The back of her head hit the floor, cushioned slightly by the carpeting.

The cat howled. She could barely hear it over the blood rushing in her ears. He kicked her legs with a sweeping motion and she pulled her knees up, reacting into the automatic fetal position response to attack. Unfortunately, this cleared the way for him to shut the door, closing out her neighbors along the hall.

She opened her mouth to scream but he straddled her stomach, forcing the air out of her lungs. While she gasped for air he zipped up the jumpsuit to his neck, then removed a knife from the white bag. He pulled off the leather sheath, and its thick but razor-sharp length glinted in the flash of lightning through her windows.

She rocked her hips trying to buck him off and clasped both hands over her agonized throat, not because of the pain but because she knew what he would do next—stab her in the neck, severing her vocal cords and possibly killing her. Again she tried to suck in a breath, but the full weight of him kept her diaphragm trapped and her lungs compressed.

He raised the knife.

The nameless cat leapt from the back of her sofa and sank its claws into Patrick Caldwell's forearm. Through this blur of activity Maggie saw it bite down on the back of his hand, but she couldn't be sure. In any case, the man waved the knife hand from side to side in sharp motions and shook the animal off like a drop of rain. The cat landed somewhere with a thump and howled again.

But in the meantime Maggie had removed her right hand, leaving only the left to protect her neck, and stretched it to her side. Her hand grabbed frantically at the empty floor until it found the cat's food—the dry Purina mix nestled in the hand-carved bowl her brother had sent her.

The bowl carved from a single chunk of basalt. The bowl that cost thirty-eight dollars to ship.

The bowl so heavy she could barely lift it with only one arm and no breath.

Panic gave her strength enough to bring the bowl up, even with Caldwell holding down her right shoulder and again raising the knife above her neck. She swung it through the air the best she could, knowing it wouldn't be enough. It wouldn't be nearly enough. But if she could just distract him long enough to ease the weight, get a breath before she passed out. Her vision had already clouded with stars. She didn't have much time.

Small pieces of the cat's favorite food rained onto her face as the bowl made contact with his left temple. Caldwell's hot breath exploded in her face and the blow forced him to the side, enough to lift most of his weight from her diaphragm. The bowl slipped from her fingers and landed against the back of her sofa.

She should be able to breathe now, with her lungs

temporarily able to expand and draw air into the clusters of alveoli, to then let oxygen flow into her starved arteries and muscles. But somehow that didn't work. Her lungs expanded, but her throat bottlenecked.

Caldwell took longer to recover than she expected, but still righted himself back onto her torso, before she could draw more than a tiny stream of air into herself. He raised the knife but his right hand shook, and his left tried to staunch the blood where she had broken the skin on his left temple.

Maggie tried to think what to do next. She wasn't sure if she still had her left hand protecting her throat. Her right seemed to be lying uselessly on the floor. His weight pinned her above her hips, so she could bring her legs up and wrap them around his neck, pulling him backward—she had seen that in a movie. But simply to get her knees to bend seemed to take a long time and she needed air to get them any higher, to get her muscles to respond. There didn't seem to be any in the room. At least Caldwell, wobbling slightly, could not move very quickly either. Her vision darkened to a hazy gray.

She heard a far-off bang and some white light pierced the gray as her apartment door banged open, striking her foot hard enough for her to feel it while the rest of her body was going numb. A large figure loomed. Caldwell gave a startled jerk, shifting on top of her again, but again, this did not help her to breathe. Her lungs wanted to expand but the air wouldn't flow to them.

Jack stood in her doorway.

Caldwell leapt to his feet, unfortunately planting

one of them on her stomach. More air went out without any to replace it. Not even the hallway lights could keep her atmosphere from turning gray again. Caldwell jumped or was pulled across her, and she heard, or rather felt, a series of thumps and exhalations of breath and the rush of air that comes when two bodies are locked in a frantic struggle, but she didn't pay much attention. Her lungs burned as if the tissue had melted, and she managed only to turn to one side, her body still trying to go fetal, when she heard a distinct *snap!* break the air. Then, what seemed to be a long time later, a sliding, falling *thump* shook the wooden planks underneath her. The cells of her brain knew this to be somehow significant but her body didn't care. She was dying. She might already be dead.

Then it seemed that, without much effort, her limp form was scooped up and moving. A vague impression of moving lights—the ceiling illumination of her apartment building's hallway—and of floating weightlessly along. A pause outside a dark door.

Of course, she wasn't really weightless, to judge from the small pants of effort Jack gave out now and then. She could hear his heart beating to keep up, her ear pressed to his chest, though she couldn't be sure it wasn't her own she heard, her arteries screaming for help as her body shut down for good.

She knew she should try to hang on, put her arms around his neck to distribute her weight to help him out, but moving even her unbroken fingers had become impossible. One arm slipped off to dangle by her side, and she couldn't even do anything about that. All sensation began to leave her. Before her body shut down completely she looked up at him, a vague gray figure against the shiny square ceiling, and wondered when it was that buildings stopped playing music in elevators.

Chapter 34

She had fought them, long and hard, but they called in reinforcements in the way of orderlies, and the cowards had strapped her arms down with nylon and Velcro so they could continue stabbing her in the throat. Then she couldn't breathe at all and the world went gray again.

When her vision cleared they had removed the straps and she had a tube in her throat, gagging her. She reached up to pull it out but a nurse caught her hand and pressed a small plastic box into it.

"I know it's uncomfortable," she began.

Uncomfortable? They had cut her throat open.

"But we have to leave it in until the swelling goes down. This is your morphine drip controller. You can control it your—"

Maggie pressed the button that the nurse had thoughtfully positioned under her left thumb. Awkward with two of those fingers in a cast, but still workable.

"—self. It will help you relax and sleep."

Maggie pressed the button again, held it down.

"But it only dispenses once every ten minutes."

Bastards.

"So don't worry about pressing it too much or accidentally. The tube should come out tomorrow. In the meantime it will allow you to breathe, which I think you will agree is pretty important."

A comic.

Huh, Maggie then realized. She *could* breathe. Air in, air out. Her lungs could expand at will.

That *was* pretty great. It almost made up for the sewer pipe in her throat.

Almost.

Now that Maggie's panicked pulse had calmed, the nurse tried to amputate her arm with the blood pressure cuff. She clucked at the result. Maggie didn't know whether that was good or bad and didn't much care. A little hypertension seemed a small worry at that point.

"Are you up to visitors? There are two gentlemen in the waiting room who want to see you."

Maggie wondered who the two were. Denny and Rick? Jack and Riley? Jeremy Mearan and Anna's boyfriend? It didn't matter. She made a writing motion in the air.

The nurse had been prepared for this and gave her a half-used-up student's spiral notebook and a pen. Maggie brought up one knee and propped the paper on her thigh to write. So her legs still worked, too. Cool.

Outside rain dashed against the windows. The heavens had finally opened, releasing the pent-up volumes. Maggie handed the notebook and pen to the nurse and hit the morphine drip button again. But the first ten minutes hadn't yet expired, and the cycler didn't give the telltale churning sound that meant it was actually dispensing something.

Maggie cursed it to the electronic scrap yard as her eyes began to close.

Jack rested his head against the wall behind the thinly cushioned chairs and stared at the fluorescent lights in the ceiling. All that money floating around and it had come down to a guy who simply liked killing good-looking women. Riley was already checking to see if the stabbing victims from prior months had frequented Totally Fresh! But three at one firm—perhaps the shark tank atmosphere at Sterling *had* gotten his blood going in some way. He must have seen their home addresses when they opened their wallets to get a credit card, or, perhaps like Joanna, they ordered home delivery. Or he simply could have followed them there at the end of the day.

Rick Gardiner had entered the waiting area without a word. Now, after several minutes of watching TV news with no sound on the flat-screen in the corner, he asked why Jack was there.

"I found her. And the guy. What are you doing here?" Maggie was the guy's *ex*-wife. He also wondered why Gardiner annoyed him so.

"I tried to get a hold of her to tell her our trip is off. Your partner answered her phone, told me what happened."

"Trip?" Maggie was going to take a trip with him?

"To see a witness. Little girl who might have seen our guy. But the kid couldn't ID the sketch, said it wasn't even close, so the captain won't approve the travel."

"Oh." Jack had no idea what all that meant and didn't much care. He leaned his head back again, closed his eyes.

"So that's the end of that lead. Now I gotta come up with something else to keep the captain off my back about that damn case. I always wind up with the unsolvables."

Jack didn't respond to the whining, and the waiting room grew quiet for half a minute.

"There might be brain damage," Rick said, apropos of nothing. "If she couldn't breathe for a while."

That was why.

"If she's going to need help I'll have to call her brother. I can't do anything. We're divorced, for chrissakes."

Definitely why.

"This guy got into her apartment building without anyone seeing him?"

Jack raised his eyelids without moving a single other muscle. He felt as if he could sleep for a week, maybe two. "Don't know. He wouldn't have pulled on the jumpsuit at least until her floor, in the elevator or the stairwell. The lobby door and back door both lock, Riley said. But you know how apartments are. All he had to do was wait until someone went in or out and then catch the door before it shut." Jack had broken one of those locks to gain entry, would be turning over part of his paycheck to 740 West Superior.

"Anyone admit to that?"

"Nah. Once they found out Maggie was all right, her neighbors scattered like coues."

"I guess it doesn't matter. We've got the guy now." Something seemed to occur to Rick and he turned to look directly at Jack. He opened his mouth to say something, but a white-clad woman approached them.

"She's settling in just fine and needs to rest now. I asked her about visitors and she wrote this."

The notebook page read, in Maggie's clear block letters: "TUBE IN THROAT. TUBE IN ARM. NO VISITORS."

She had added several exclamation points after the last phrase, and underlined it twice. Jack felt oddly comforted. It sounded like pure Maggie to him. No brain damage there.

"Huh," Rick said. "But I need to talk to her about something."

Jack made his escape, leaving Gardiner to argue with the nurse. He had no doubts about who would win.

Chapter 35

The tube didn't come out the next day but it did get removed the following morning, and in another day after, the doctors released Maggie to the ministrations of Carol and the luxury of her own apartment. So when Jack stopped by the ex-patient sat in an armchair by the window, the sunlight turning her eyes to aqua, Anna's cat on her lap. She looked wan to him, bundled in an ivory blanket, the only color present in the bright red cast that held her two broken fingers steady and the deep swirling purples across the front of her neck. Wan and tiny and vulnerable as hell, which gave him a surge of very uncomfortable feelings, and he felt his fingers curl into fists. He didn't want her wan or tiny and especially not vulnerable.

Because, of course, vulnerable people talk too much. If she felt alone or that a near-death experience provided the perfect reason to reexamine one's conscience or PTSD surfaced and put her in a therapy group . . . then secrets might come to light. Hers. And his.

Bizarre, he thought. *Each of us is nervous around the other. But even more nervous when* not *around— because who might she be talking to, when out of my sight?*

He didn't have a particular purpose for the visit. Riley had insisted, then begged off for a daughter's soccer match. He itched to get a look at the unlucky eighth grader who had dared to make eyes at his Natalie. But Jack had come anyway.

Maggie was right, Jack thought, though she hadn't said a recent word about it. He needed to leave town. Pack up and move on, pick a new hunting ground where no one would be looking for a vigilante killer. Let her get on with her life. Let them both be able to breathe a little easier.

She watched him hover uncomfortably, and the corners of her mouth turned up slightly, which made her look significantly less vulnerable. In fact, she looked, for the most part, annoyed, especially when he asked how she felt.

"Like someone crushed my windpipe." Her voice came out as a hoarse croak, which he hoped would not be permanent. "Worst sore throat ever. Like it's my whole body being stabbed when I swallow." She gestured with her hands, even the one with the broken fingers, to illustrate the waves of pain that traveled up and out of herself.

"You *look* better," he said politely, lowering himself to the other end of the sofa. He always kept a physical distance between them, but with her voice so damaged he had to stay close in order to hear her. "I see your new friend is sticking."

She stroked the tabby. "The boyfriend's apartment won't take pets and it turns out mine will. He said his name is Keynes. After the economist."

"Of course."

"He's dead," Maggie said. She didn't have to specify. "Denny told me."

"Yes."

Another death at his hands, but no reason for concern over this one. He couldn't fire his gun for fear of hitting Maggie, so he'd tackled the guy and broke his neck with one quick twist. That might look a bit odd to the inevitable review board. Nothing to reprimand, but they'd start watching him.

Definitely time to move on. Forget waiting the six months he'd arbitrarily assigned himself.

Maggie said, "Carol's running his DNA against those other two stabbings from earlier this year. Rick is checking to see if they were customers at Totally Fresh!"

"They might have been a warm-up act for Caldwell, but maybe not. The Patricia Caldwell Sterling screwed over in Nebraska did indeed turn out to be his mother, so he had a reason to pick his victims from that particular office. Whether he came to Cleveland to get to Joanna or just found himself here as a karmic coincidence, we'll never know, but it turned out the same."

"What goes around . . ." Maggie said, her voice barely audible.

Silence descended for several minutes.

Jack had warned her not to admit things but as usual couldn't take his own advice. "I'm sorry. About Graham."

Maggie and the cat looked at him.

"You're right. I didn't need to interfere and I did anyway. I shouldn't have put you in that position." He didn't tell her that he had been prompted largely by concern for her. Anna had not been targeted by a bunch of disgruntled home owners, and Caldwell had not been interested in death from a distance. He believed the CIs who said Maggie had been shot at by one of Graham's protégés. He didn't tell her that because he didn't think she'd believe him. He also didn't tell her that he would eventually take care of this man because he didn't think she needed to know.

She spoke. He had to lean in to hear her words: "Meaning you shouldn't have killed him or you shouldn't have told me you did?"

"Both." Mostly the latter, but he wouldn't say so. Enough full disclosure for one day. Maggie believed in right and wrong as completely as he did, but her interpretations varied slightly. Putting her in turmoil only worked against him. "It won't happen again."

She eyed him, apparently aware of what he was, and was not, promising. But all she said was, "Thanks for the help." She didn't have to add that if he hadn't arrived when he did her neighbors would have found her dead on her apartment floor. Maybe that had made her willing to give him a pass on Graham, but Jack didn't think so. Maggie didn't work that way. She would make her decisions independent of personal reasons.

Then she abruptly croaked, "Jack."

"What?"

"Who *did* play in the Super Bowl this year?"

"I have no earthly idea."

She gave a strangled cough that startled him, and he grabbed for his phone to call an ambulance.

But she was laughing, cheekbones popping as the edges of her mouth turned up. "I suspected as much."

Acknowledgments

For most of my life I was the type of person whose eyes would instantly glaze over when someone said "business." Yet somehow I listened to the advice of critics and read *Barbarians at the Gate,* and that opened those same eyes to how fascinating nonfiction can be, even when no one gets murdered.

Though we were lucky enough to be spared by the financial meltdown, I lived in ground zero of the housing crisis, in a town that routinely appeared on lists of "highest foreclosure rates in the country," so it could be said that I had a vested interest.

I always try to do plenty of research and, thus, it would be remiss not to mention the fine books that helped me understand why the whole world shook in 2008: *Busted: Life Inside the Great Mortgage Meltdown*, by Edmund L. Andrews; *The Courage to Act: A Memoir of a Crisis and Its Aftermath*, by Ben S. Bernanke; *House of Cards: A Tale of Hubris and Wretched Excess on Wall Street*, by William D. Cohan; *Stress Test: Reflections on the Financial Crisis*, by

Timothy F. Geithner; *Dumb Money: How Our Greatest Financial Minds Bankrupted the Nation*, by Daniel Gross; *The Monster: How a Gang of Predatory Lenders and Wall Street Bankers Fleeced America—And Spawned a Global Crisis*, by Michael W. Hudson; *The End of Wall Street*, by Roger Lowenstein; *All the Devils Are Here: The Hidden History of the Financial Crisis*, by Bethany McLean and Joe Nocera; *On the Brink: Inside the Race to Stop the Collapse of the Global Financial System*, by Henry M. Paulson Jr.; *Too Big to Fail: The Inside Story of How Wall Street and Washington Fought to Save the Financial System—And Themselves*, by Andrew Ross Sorkin; *The Housing Boom and Bust*, by Thomas Sowell; *Confidence Men: Wall Street, Washington and the Education of a President*, by Ron Suskind.

As usual, I had the help of several family members to round out parts of the story: my nurse sister, Mary; my husband, Russ; and countless other people who I'm sure I'm failing to mention.

I could not have accomplished much of anything without the help and support of my editor, Michaela Hamilton; the staff at Kensington; as well as my fabulous agent, Vicky Bijur, and everyone in her office.

Don't miss the next Gardiner and Renner thriller by
New York Times bestselling author Lisa Black

SUFFER THE CHILDREN

Coming soon from Kensington Publishing Corp.

Keep reading to enjoy a sample excerpt . . .

Prologue

Rachael hated kitchen duty. Bad enough to be locked up in this hellhole but then to be put to work like some sort of slave—ridiculous. They said it was all about learning responsibility but she knew it was about the damn free labor, that's what it was about. She already knew everything she needed to about responsibility. She knew who had been responsible for her being shut up in here, and why, and how. Washing dishes until her fingers got pruney would not deliver any further insights about that.

She let the door slam behind her and moved across to lean her arms on the railing. The stairs looped down and down into a vortex of emptiness, which seemed to be the perfect picture of her life at the moment. Everything had been stripped away, piece by piece. First her mother, then her father, then her own body, taken and ripped and seared by this shithole of a universe.

No, wait. That last one wasn't due to the universe. That could be wholly set at *his* feet, and when she got out of here she would see to it that he paid in blood, lots of blood, more than he had ever broken out of her.

The universe, well, its debt had mounted—time for it to start paying. Emptiness had gotten boring.

She didn't feel the movement behind her until just before it struck.

Chapter 1

It was an old-fashioned stairwell, with wide steps, painted iron pipes for railings, and a rectangle of wasted space down the center. Plenty of room for the body to fall, perhaps the entire three stories. The final impact left a spray of blood from the girl's head across the worn terrazzo tile.

Maggie Gardiner stood with a camera in one hand and a crime scene kit in the other, surveying the lifeless body and the hallway around it. Simple, as crime scenes went. No furniture, no wet grass or old clothes, no useless debris to be sorted from vital clues. Empty steps and what remained of a child who had suffered the misfortune to land on her head instead of her feet.

Around this very ordinary stairwell sat the Firebird Center for Children and Adolescents, otherwise known as the city's juvenile detention facility—only six or seven blocks from Maggie's lab in Cleveland's Justice Center complex. She had never been there before. It smelled of disinfectant and Pine-Sol and years of mass-produced food, and the fluorescent fixtures kept it thoroughly bathed with a yellowish light. Maggie had been there for ten minutes and hadn't seen a child yet, but the air hummed with ambient noise. The various floors bulged with classrooms and restrooms and dormitories for juveniles ranging from under ten years of age up to seventeen.

The staggered bedtimes for the various dorms had not yet arrived and, freed from classes, the young people had a precious hour or two to amuse themselves at high decibels. With the doors closed it sounded as if she were in the center of a beehive. Maggie hated bees.

She also hated prisons. She'd been in plenty, processing the occasional death in custody or more often collecting hair and saliva swabs from arrested suspects, but had never reconciled herself to getting locked in with a teeming mass of dangerous and angry people. And now—even worse—a teeming mass of teenagers.

"Her name is Rachael Donahue," the director said, Mark Palmer, PhD. He stood to Maggie's left, not rushing her. He looked about sixty, was gray haired and a few inches shorter than herself, and seemed genuinely saddened over the death of a child who had been put in his care.

The Firebird Center, he had told her upon her arrival, was a care facility for children in crisis. Every resident (not inmate, he made clear) had been the victim of physical or sexual abuse at worst or extreme neglect at best. Some had not committed a crime, only run away from the abuse, though most had. The center strove to counsel both the resident child and their families until the child could return home, or until the child could be matched with a foster family in cases where their home situation could not be rehabilitated. At the same time their educational requirements were maintained, since schoolwork usually became the first fatality of crisis. Getting back on the track toward college or vocational training would get more difficult with every day lost.

Maggie steered him back to the physical layout of the building. They would need to know how Rachael came to be in the stairwell in the first place.

Along with the dorms and classrooms the center had meeting areas for legal representatives and family members, areas for intake, as well as areas for the staff to write reports and eat lunch and for the live-in dorm "mothers" and "fathers" to sleep.

Doors were locked. Some residents *could* leave, but only for certain reasons, and the times were strictly monitored. The children weren't prisoners . . . and yet they were.

And so, temporarily at least, was she.

Maggie hefted the camera with the large lens and heavy detachable flash and began to document the scene. She would photograph and measure and collect and the detectives, when they arrived, would ask the questions—yet she inquired, "How long has she been here?" of director Palmer, simply to keep him from getting bored and wandering away. After all, he had the keys to those locked doors.

She had actually meant to ask how long Rachael Donahue had been at the facility, but he said, "It couldn't have been more than ten minutes. The kitchen had brought dessert to the under-ten group and returned with the empty trays, through this door here. They had loaded up dinners for the next group into the dumb-waiter and one of the staff came out to go up and un-load, and found her."

Maggie began close-ups of the still form. The in-mates—residents, she corrected herself—apparently didn't wear uniforms. Rachael was dressed in tight jeans, black hi-tops, a pink tee, and an oversized red and purple flannel shirt. She had three rings on each hand and three earrings in each ear, with dark purple polish on her bitten nails. Dark chestnut hair—the same color as Maggie's—appeared to be shoulder length and layered into unruly waves, now soaked with blood. It had begun to thicken and clot. Her clean face was turned toward the ceiling, forty feet overhead, with eyes closed, long lashes against creamy skin.

"She was fifteen," the director said, answering a question Maggie hadn't wanted to ask.

In another world, a more just world, the girl would have been the apple of some parent's eye, instead of dying alone behind locked doors in a government fa-cility.

Maggie looked up through the spiraling steps. "Where would she have come from?"

"Fourteen to fifteen girls are on third-floor north. She should have been in the common room or her bed-room. Erica—Ms. Washington—released her to report for kitchen duty. She must have fallen right after that. We have outdoor rec on the roof but I've already asked Justin and he said he didn't see her, and she wouldn't have been able to get into the other units, the other age groups."

"Released her?"

A pained look crossed the director's face. "The doors

to the units are locked, of course, from both inside and outside."

But it's not a prison, Maggie thought.

"Else we'd have chaos. They're children, after all, made to go through doors they're not supposed to go through. All our dorm mothers and fathers have a clunky set of keys at the moment, but eventually we'll go to key cards. Then the doors will open automatically if a fire alarm goes off, lock automatically if there's an active shooter situation or something like that, but the system is under construction. The whole *building* is under construction. I'm sure you noticed all the scaffolding and new drywall on your way in."

"Yes."

"We're a work in progress, in more ways than one. But only for a few more months. Then we'll be the most secure juvenile facility in the country as well as the most therapeutic." He rubbed one rheumy blue eye. Then as if avoiding the sin of hubris, added, "Not taking anything away from my colleagues in other states, of course."

"Of course," Maggie said.

"I'm pushing hard. We're having an open house next week for the state budget committee. The federal system is finally throwing money at the mental health care crisis and we have to grab every dollar we can before their attention fades. You know how that goes."

His fellow government employee said, "Sure. Can we take a look at the video?"

Director Palmer followed her gaze to the dark half-bubbles embedded in the ceilings at each landing and winced.

Maggie did too. "They're not recording?"

"They don't even have cameras in them. Those are supposed to be installed next week, and the control panel the week after that. The manufacturer tells me that in these increasingly paranoid times, surveillance systems are selling like a cure for baldness—that's their excuse for taking so long to get all the components on-site."

Maggie couldn't imagine any kind of detention facility operating for five minutes without comprehensive surveillance, but then juvenile justice programs seemed to exist in a permanent state of experimentation.

She took close-up photos of the girl's hands, as best she could without touching them—Maggie could not move or "molest" the body in any way until the Medical Examiner's office investigator arrived. But the backs of the girl's fingers gave no signs of defensive wounds, blood, or hair. If Rachael Donahue had struggled with anyone before plunging over the railing she had done it without chipping the purple polish on her nails. She might have jumped. Three flights of steps seemed an iffy method of suicide, but would that calculation have occurred to a teen? Surely fifteen was young enough to play, perhaps try to walk on the railing or jump from one landing to another. And, of course, perhaps she had been under the influence of drugs and thought she could fly.

"Why was she here? At the facility, I mean," Maggie asked.

The director fumbled with a lifetime of protecting the civil rights of his underage charges. "Rachael? I don't think I can . . . I mean, I know you'll have to . . . I've never had an accident like this in our history."

This realization brought him up short. "Never. I've lost a great many clients *outside* our walls, of course—the world is a dangerous place for a child—but under our care, no."

Rachael had ruined his perfect record, and he seemed to allow himself one fleeting moment of self-pity before admitting, "Rachael had anger issues."

"Oh." Maggie didn't ask anything more. She had already done more of the detective's job than she should, and if Rachael had been fighting with someone, that would be their job to discover. Detectives, as a group, could get pretty persnickety when someone ducked past the crime scene tape into their territory.

Instead Maggie began to walk the stairwell, photographing as she went. At first she used a flashlight to examine each riser for shoeprints and disturbances in the dust, but quickly surmised that a great many people used the stairwell every day with marks on top of other marks from one end of the tread to the other. Maggie gave up, telling herself that any particular set of prints wouldn't prove much.

So she took pictures of the steps. She took pictures of each door she encountered, without attempting to open them. Some had a great deal of noise and movement behind them, some—such as the one labeled MAINT.—dead silent. She closed her fingers around the handle to 12–13 BOYS but it didn't budge. What she guessed to be the twelve- to thirteen-year-old males' dorm could not be entered from the hallway, only by pressing the button to the left of the door and having someone inside allow admittance. She didn't push the button.

Maggie took pictures of a long, dark hair caught where the pipe that formed the upper rail on the second landing screwed into its stanchion, the threads still rough after decades of repainting. She tucked the hair into an envelope, but the resolutely bare tile and solid barrier of the railing refused to give her any clue as to whether the girl had fallen over here, had hit her head on the railing during a fall from the third floor, or the hair had been clinging there for months.

Maggie continued upward. The third-floor landing proved equally unhelpful.

She leaned over the railing to take a photo of Rachael's body at the bottom, lying perfectly centered in the rectangle of open space. It could have been the promo shot for a horror movie, the teen star flush with the beauty of youth cut short to be resurrected in the sequel. But this was all too real, and there would be no resurrection for Rachael Donahue.

The final door felt cool to the touch and the voices beyond it seemed distant enough. The plaque read REC. 12–15. This latch turned with a light application of gloved fingers and Maggie peeked out. Cool September air brushed over a group of six boys playing basketball, their forms visible against the lit windows of the office buildings across the street. A trim young man with a sweatshirt and goatee watched them, shouting a word of either advice or encouragement. Three boys lounged around a table, also watching. It would have been a peaceful picture of youth at play if not for the razor wire atop the chain-link fence, which in turn topped the knee-high brick wall ringing the roof. If Rachael Donahue had wanted to commit suicide, Maggie now saw why she chose the interior stairwell over the outside roof. She wouldn't have been able to get over that.

"That's the younger kids' roof," Dr. Palmer said. He stood at her elbow when she had thought he had stayed at the bottom of the stairwell. When her heart receded from her throat she told him she could see that.

"Sixteen to seventeen have a separate court and roof area behind the classrooms. Under twelve have our little patch of grass below this." He added, "Children need to be outdoors—it's a very basic desire and it's good for them. Burns off extra energy and they learn to appreciate fresh air. But it's so hard to find outdoor spaces in the middle of a city, and even harder to make them truly secure—so we converted the roof. No trees, but after the reno we're going to ring the patio area, where those boys are sitting, with potted shrubs. Same thing on the other roof." He looked at her expectantly.

"That will be nice," Maggie said. She let the door shut with a heavy *clang* that echoed down the stairwell and seemed to reverberate in her ears.

"It's not much, but . . . And in a city where it's cold six months out of the year the weather creates a problem. Residents have to have warm clothing, bulkier stuff, boots, rain gear and we don't have storage space for all that. It would be easier to keep them inside all the time, but . . ." His voice trailed off as they crossed the second-floor landing.

"Are the boys and girls always separate?"

"Not in classes. Co-ed classes are normal, and it's important to keep the surroundings as normal as possible. Otherwise we keep them segregated even during recreation, except for the under-twelve group. We have to be practical."

And unexpected pregnancies would be anything but.

He went on: "It's difficult to make a facility this large homelike, so we went the other route and made it school-like. Kids are *used* to school, and keeping them in that sort of mind-set will make reentry easier."

"Reentry?"

"When they go back to their actual home, their regular school. Their 'normal' life. Unfortunately, for so many of them, their lives have never been what we'd call normal. That's why we always work from the basis of 'what happened to you?' rather than 'what did you do?' Frankly, America locks up far too many juveniles, especially considering that the majority of them have committed nonviolent infractions, like truancy and running away. Violating probation and such."

Maggie said, "And the children here?"

He blinked at her. "Here?"

"Nonviolent offenses?"

"Well, no."

She glanced at him as they reached the ground floor.

"This facility specializes in high-risk clients. The kids who have resisted more community-based interventions."

She tried to sort out that verbiage. "So—"

The doctor sighed. "Some of their crimes have been violent, yes. But it has been shown over and over that with an intensive yet secure program their lives can still be turned around. I can personally attest to amazing strides with a number of our charges."

They stood in front of the girl's body at the bottom of the steps, frozen into her final and hopeless position. "And Rachael? Her crime was—?"

"Murder."

Maggie blinked. "She killed somebody?"

He nodded, shaggy graying hair falling around his downturned face. "Two people, actually."

Loud footsteps abruptly sounded behind them, causing Maggie's heart to pound again. She really hated prisons.

But a middle-aged black woman led in two detectives she knew, and well. The red-headed Riley and his partner, Jack Renner. Maggie knew more about Jack Renner than she would have ever wanted to, and her life had been turned inside out because of it. In the span of a few months they had accumulated a number of experiences together, all of them bad.

Well, nearly all.

But for once she didn't cringe at the memories he brought into the space with him. For once she felt just a little glad to see him.

Jack might have a lot of issues, but should they be suddenly set upon by a teeming band of wilding teenagers she felt fairly sure he would do his job and at least attempt to protect her. Even though her death would remove a serious complication from his life.

Still.

Fairly sure.

Connect with

Us

Visit us online at
KensingtonBooks.com
to read more from your favorite authors, see books
by series, view reading group guides, and more.

Join us on social media

for sneak peeks, chances to win books and prize packs,
and to share your thoughts with other readers.

facebook.com/kensingtonpublishing
twitter.com/kensingtonbooks

Tell us what you think!

To share your thoughts, submit a review,
or sign up for our eNewsletters, please visit:
KensingtonBooks.com/TellUs.